IN THE HEAT OF THE NIGHT

Putting down his beer, the man on the street crosses a few feet to the car, stopping when he is in front of the door. He kneels between his friend's legs, one large booted foot on either side of him. Trying not to look his friend in the face, he puts a hand on each knee, his hands gripping them lightly.

"Yeah, that's it," the man in the car growls. "Help me out a little bit like a good buddy."

A hand moves up to touch one bare thigh, hesitating momentarily as the fingers move from the rough blue jeans to the smooth feeling of flesh on flesh.

With this new turn of events, I want to get a closer look. Climbing onto the windowsill, I crawl out onto my fire escape, making as little noise as possible. The night air surrounds my naked, sweating body as I sit on the stairs going up to the next floor and position myself so that I can see what is going on below me. The two men have not heard or seen me and I have a perfect view of the car and what is happening in it.

The man in the car is gripping the other one's neck firmly with both hands, pushing him down and then releasing him. He stands up and steps away from the car. For the first time, I see his face. He is very handsome. Not pretty like the men I see in the bars, but rugged and somehow more real.

Bending down, he unties his boots and pulls them off, following with his pants. He stands barefoot and naked on the sidewalk beside the car.

"Now you," he says to the other man, who is leaning against the car, watching him. "Strip."

It is a command, not a request . . .

—from *Wednesday, 2:00 A.M.*

Books by Michael Thomas Ford

LAST SUMMER

LOOKING FOR IT

TANGLED SHEETS

Published by Kensington Publishing Corporation

tales of erotica

tangled
sheets

MICHAEL THOMAS FORD

KENSINGTON BOOKS
www.kensingtonbooks.com

KENSINGTON BOOKS are published by

Kensington Publishing Corp.
850 Third Avenue
New York, NY 10022

ISBN 0-7582-0831-6

First Kensington Trade Paperback Printing: January 2005
10 9 8 7 6 5 4 3 2 1

Printed in the United States of America

CONTENTS

Contents

Foreplay: My Life in Porn

In the fall of 1993 I became a pornographer.

I don't remember what prompted me to write that first stroke story—probably I was avoiding some other, less appealing, deadline—but I do remember receiving a letter a week or so after I mailed it off to the editor of *Blueboy*. He couldn't, he apologized, pay me anything for the story, but he'd be happy to print it. Thrilled that someone actually liked my writing enough to publish it, I agreed (it would be the first and only time I worked for free).

After that, writing porn became a regular part of my routine. Every week I'd crank out something and send it off to one of the many men's magazines that published such things. Before long, copies of *Honcho, Torso, Mandate, Indulge, Advocate Classifieds, Men,* and *Freshmen* began appearing in my mailbox, each one featuring one of my stories amidst the pictorials of men with hard cocks and spread ass cheeks.

The name I used on those early stories was Tom Caffrey. The Tom part is easy enough to figure out. Caffrey I stole from actor Stephen Caffrey, best known for his roles in the television show *Tour of Duty* and the film *Longtime Companion*, where he played the role of Fuzzy. Stephen, with his hairy body and rugged good looks, was a favorite fantasy of mine. I decided to model Tom after him, thus making it easier to describe Tom when he was one of the characters in a story.

Why the pseudonym, or nom de porn as I called it? At the time, I was primarily writing books for young readers. I'd recently published a book on AIDS for teenagers and was becoming well

known in the world of children's literature. I was already feeling
some heat for being a writer who wrote about gay topics and who
wrote for young readers, and I thought adding to that by putting
my name on sex stories wouldn't be the wisest career move. I suppose I could have used Mike Ford (which many people have said
sounds like a porn star name anyway) but there was something intriguing about hiding behind a totally new identity.

To my surprise, Tom quickly became a favorite with readers of
erotica. He was helped, in part, by having his stories included in
John Preston's enormously successful Flesh and the Word series
of anthologies and in one of Susie Bright's Best American Erotica
collections. He also became a regular in the pages of *Advocate
Men* and *Freshmen*, thanks to then-editors Fred Goss and Gerry
Kroll.

Eventually I had enough stories to make a collection of my
own, and in 1994 *Hitting Home & Other Stories* was released by
BadBoy Books. A second collection, *Tales from the Men's Room*,
followed in 1996. In addition to writing my own stories, I also
began editing various anthologies under my real name. I approached Cleis Press about launching a series of Best Gay Erotica
titles, the first of which I edited with my friend Scott Heim (the
usual "artistic differences" between myself and the publisher led
me to leave the series after that initial collection, and it is now
edited by the wonderful and skilled Richard Labonte). I also
edited two collections of erotic fairy tales, one for women (*Once
Upon A Time*) and one for men (*Happily Ever After*), which were
published by erotica champion and unforgettable character
Richard Kasak of Richard Kasak Books. These collections fea-
tured work by some of the most innovative voices in queer literature, including Dorothy Allison, Francesca Lia Block, Carol Queen,
Pat Califia, Jennifer Levin, Heather Lewis, Linda Smukler, Cecilia
Tan, Laura Antoniou, Bruce Benderson, Michael Lassell, Poppy Z.
Brite, Thomas Roche, Lev Raphael, M. Christian, Larry Townsend,
William J. Mann, and D. Travers Scott. To date they remain two of
my favorite books, and I wish they were still available.

Eventually I got a little bit bored with the Tom stories and
began to branch out, trying my hand at stories featuring women.
For these I used a variety of pseudonyms, the most frequent of
which was Lily August. Like Tom before her, Lily also developed
a large following, and like Tom she appeared in the pages of the

Best American Erotica series. Sadly, the market for lesbian erotica is not nearly as large as that for men, so Lily's output remained relatively small. But the experience of writing from that vantage point was a lot of fun, and the Lily stories are some of my favorites.

Like all good things, my pornography career finally came to an end, mainly because I became more involved in writing the books that became the Trials of My Queer Life series. I put Tom, Lily, and my other alter egos behind me and moved on. But to my surprise, they continued to live full and happy lives all on their own. When I started touring to promote my first essay collection, *Alec Baldwin Doesn't Love Me*, I found one or two people at every reading who wanted me to sign copies of *Hitting Home* or *Tales from the Men's Room* (word had gotten out about me and Tom being one and the same). When BadBoy ceased operations and the books went out of print, I received hundreds of e-mails to my website asking where copies could be purchased.

So here, for the first time, I've collected my erotic stories. This book contains the material from those first two collections, as well as stories I wrote for other anthologies, stories written for magazines under the Tom Caffrey name and other pseudonyms, and pieces that haven't been published anywhere at all.

Ten years ago, when these first stories were written, the gay erotica field was just beginning to explode. Writers and editors such as M. Christian, Laura Antoniou, Thomas Roche, Michael Rowe, and Pat Califia were releasing wonderful, groundbreaking work. We all grew up together and saw the world of sex writing change, moving from magazines to books to websites and then back again. We saw the market become glutted with badly conceived, badly written, and badly edited material. Most of us went into hibernation for a time, waiting for it to get better. Some of us are still in hibernation. But none of us will ever forget the fun we had.

I once received a fan letter, written to Tom Caffrey, that said, "I love your writing because it's so much more literary than the other erotica out there. But when are you going to write a real novel?" Well, I have written real novels. And in most of them there's sex. Why? Because writing is about capturing life on paper, and sex is a part of life. I started writing porn for fun and money. I kept writing porn because these stories gave me an opportunity to explore different types of writing, to play with creating scenes and moods and situations. I saw them as exercises of sorts, much as a pianist might practice scales or a pitcher might throw balls through an old tire hung from a tree branch. Some began with a single image I wanted to capture, while others were about confronting the characters with challenges and forcing them to make decisions. Yes, some of these stories are "just" about sex. But others are about much more.

One final note: Everyone always wants to know how much of a pornographer's work comes from real-life experiences. The answer is, not much, at least in my case. The majority of these stories are complete works of fiction, and even the ones that *are* based on real events or real people have been changed in some way. Tom is not Mike. Nor is he always the same Tom. (Although the fictional Mr. Caffrey, like his inspiration, tends to be dark-haired and hairy-chested, he has occasionally gone blond and shaved himself smooth when the plot has required it.) And the Mikes in the stories aren't me, either. The fact is, there are only a handful of good porn names—Mike, Jack, Scott, Jake—and they all get used here, much as they get circulated among every new generation of porn stars. So please, don't read too much into these. Just enjoy them.

Wednesday, 2:00 A.M.

My first apartment in New York was loud, hot, and situated on a street that saw a lot of action. Frequently I would wake up in the middle of a summer night, unable to sleep. Sometimes it would be because of the heat, and sometimes because people outside were talking. One night, when it was clear there was no way I was getting back to bed, I turned on the computer and came up with this.

It's the heat that wakes me up, sticky wet ribbons that flutter at my face and trouble my dreams until I rise up out of them into semiconsciousness. The night is uncommonly hot, simmering with the kind of heat that arrives only in the last days of summer when the fading season closes in and holds the city close in its grasp, refusing to let go. My hair is wet against my neck and my throat burns with thirst as I fumble for the glass of water on my bedside table. The rattling electric fan next to my bed provides only the slightest of breezes, and it has been barely three hours since I fell into a fitful sleep. Outside it is oddly silent, the usual summertime noises of sirens and sidewalk chatter absent.

The sheets are soaked with sweat and wrap around me like the thin walls of a cocoon. I feel like a dead man trapped in a shroud and kick them off anxiously so that they fall onto the floor and I am lying naked on my bed. The room is only half-dark, the strange pale shine that always seems to rise from the city at night pouring in my curtainless window and filling it with a gloom that settles over everything like mist. I can see the outline of my body clearly, while the details are dim, the feet and hands disappearing in shadow. I have a hard-on, and it presses painfully against my belly as if it is too full of blood and my nuts are sore with the ache of holding too much cum. For some unknown reason I want terribly to jerk off, to feel the thick length of my cock slip beneath my fingers and then the shudder in my hand as my cum spatters across my belly.

My hands move in and out of the pools of light as I run them over my chest lightly from my hips to my throat, shivering at the touch of my own fingers on my flushed skin, my breath drawing in sharply when I twist my tender nipples. Lifting my arm behind my head, I turn my face and press my nose into the wet patch of hair there. The smell is familiar and arousing, and my tongue slides lazily along the skin, soaking up the bitter taste and feeling the heavy muscle of my bicep rise and fall against my cheek.

My hand wanders down my stomach to trace the curve of my balls and thighs while I think about the many rooms in the city around me where men are making love to one another, their bodies slick with sweat as they wrap each other in their arms and their mouths meet, tongues slipping between soft lips and hard teeth. The heat moves around me as my fingers caress my nuts like a lover's lips, gently tugging and releasing. Drawing my feet up I spread my knees and my hand slips into the crack of my ass, the hair there damp with sweat as I finger my hole roughly, my wrist pressed tightly against my cock and ballsac as I imagine some unknown man sliding his prick deep inside me as my legs press against his sides.

Before I can begin to stroke my prick, I hear a car turn down my street. Not an unusual occurrence by any means, but this one stops outside my building and the motor turns off. I hear a car door open, but do not hear it close. I close my eyes and try to jerk myself off, but my mind races from one image to another too quickly and I am not able to concentrate on any one long enough to bring myself off. Several times I feel the familiar rumbling in my groin begin to well up, only to have it recede back into stillness. Frustrated, I give up and lie back against the pillows. My prick lies against my skin, hard and unsatisfied.

Rising from my bed, I go to the window and look out past the iron boundaries of my fourth-floor fire escape. At this hour the street is deserted, empty even of the usual inhabitants who come out after the rest of the world has gone to sleep to resume whatever business they are forced to end with the first shimmers of sunrise. A quiet babble of muted voices floats over the rooftops, and I think that probably they too have been driven by the heat into the cooler shadows of the park in the next block, where they can sit with their feet in the fountain while they reinvent their pasts for one another and anyone who will listen. Other than the rustle of their conversations, the city is dead.

The car is parked directly under my window, its front half submerged in the pool of light created by the streetlight, the rear swallowed up in darkness. It is a big beast of a car, the kind driven by boys who learned at an early age how to service its engine themselves. The drivers of these cars are very often found in small towns where life is played out in factories and local pool halls, the supporting roles being assumed by girls with teased hair and red-lipsticked mouths who willingly give in to the men whose rough, grease-stained hands caress them in backseats on Saturday nights.

My sister's first boyfriend had a car very much like this one. He would roar up to the house after his shift on the construction crew ended and she would run out, laughing as she bent in the window to kiss him. On warm nights he would bring the hose from around back and spend an hour or two washing his prize, Led Zeppelin blaring from the 8-track tape deck as he lovingly went over the shiny metal skin from top to bottom while my sister sat in the grass painting her nails. I would stand behind the curtains and watch him, mesmerized by the way the thick muscles of his shirtless chest and arms moved as he worked the sponge over the black paint. Once, when it was very hot and he was wearing only his boxer shorts, my sister turned the hose on him, soaking him so that the material clung to him and I could see the shadow of his bush and the outline of his cock as he chased after her. That night I jerked off into my hand, thinking about what I'd seen while I listened to the sound of his voice coming through the screen door from where they sat on the steps talking.

The car door on the driver's side is open, and a young man is sitting with his feet resting on the sidewalk while the rest of him remains inside the car. Another man is sitting on the sidewalk itself, his knees drawn up in front of him. He is holding a bottle of beer and smoking a cigarette that sends threads of smoke into the air. While the face of the man in the car is hidden in shadow, I see that he is wearing a T-shirt, jeans, and heavy work boots. The man seated on the sidewalk is dressed similarly in jeans and a white T-shirt, although he is wearing black motorcycle boots. He is dark haired, and his arms are well developed. I imagine him working in a warehouse, his hands encased in thick gloves as he carries boxes from one place to another, never thinking about what might be in them as his mind looks ahead to the time when he can fuck his girlfriend again.

"I can't believe we drove all over looking for those stupid bitches," he says, his voice low. "Wasted all damn night and they're probably sitting somewhere wondering why we never showed."

"Don't really matter," says the man inside the car. His accent is heavy with the flatness of someone who has spent a lot of time in southern New Jersey. It is a sound I hear often on the streets of my neighborhood on the weekends, when carloads of young men like this one come in to spend their paychecks in the local bars. "We got beer. We got the night to ourselves. Might as well enjoy it."

They drink in silence for a quarter of an hour, the sidewalk sitter's cigarette glowing hotly as he inhales and blows clouds of smoke like an offering skyward. I feel strangely guilty watching them, as if I am some intruding spirit spying on them from the heavens. But the scene is oddly entrancing, both because it is unexpected and because it is out of place here on my empty street so late at night, and I stay where I am. I am surprised to find that my cock is still hard, and I stroke it idly while I watch the two men sit in the stillness. Then the man inside the car speaks.

"It's too fucking hot," he says. "I'm sweating like a bitch here." He pulls his shirt over his head in one quick movement and tosses it into the backseat of the car. Framed by the doorway, his chest is broad and powerfully muscled, his nipples large and his torso tapered at the waist. It is the body of a man who has spent many hours at the gym. His pecs are two fleshy mountains, and his abdomen is striped with lines of muscle. There is no hair anywhere on him, and his smooth flesh shines warmly.

"That's better," he says, stretching back on the seat so that all I can see is his flat stomach and what is below it, the large soft bulge in his jeans. He runs his beer bottle over his skin, leaving a wet trail, and lets it rest between his legs.

"It's too bad we didn't meet up with those two," he says, grabbing teasingly at his crotch. "My cock could use a little action right about now."

His friend takes a long swallow of beer, emptying his second bottle. "Use your hand when you get home," he says, standing up and unzipping his pants. "It'll do the job just fine and you don't have to buy it a drink or pretend you like its perfume." He moves away into the shadows and I hear the gentle pounding of piss hitting the ground.

"Can't wait that long," the man says. He sits up and fumbles at the fly of his pants, his fingers awkwardly pulling the buttons apart. When they are undone, he pushes his pants down until they are just above his knees. His half-hard cock, long and fat, lies across his thigh. I can see the clipped bush around its base and the heavy sac that rests on the seat between his legs.

"What the hell are you doing, man?" his friend says when he turns and sees what is happening. "Someone's gonna see you."

The man laughs. "They're all asleep. Besides, what do you care?"

He grips his prick lightly in his fist and begins to stroke it slowly. After a minute it stiffens in his fingers and stretches out to its full length, the wide head resting on his stomach somewhere an inch or two above his navel. He pushes his pants down farther so that he can spread his legs wider and starts to jerk off in earnest, his hand sliding along the shaft in easy rhythm.

The man on the street, perhaps made more bold by the alcohol he has been drinking steadily, laughs nervously as he watches. "You are one crazy fucker," he says.

The man in the car continues to play with his cock, stroking it harder now and holding it in his fist so that it stands straight up from his groin. "Why don't you give me a hand here," he says. "Feels pretty hot."

"Fuck you," comes the answer. "I ain't playing with no guy's dick."

"Why not?" the man taunts. "Bet you'd be pretty good at it seeing all the practice you get with your own."

The man on the street starts to protest, then stops suddenly. Putting down his beer, he crosses the few feet to the car, stopping when he is in front of the door. He kneels between his friend's legs, one large booted foot on either side of him. Trying not to look his friend in the face, he puts a hand on each knee, his hands gripping them lightly.

"Yeah, that's it," the man growls. "Help me out a little bit like a good buddy."

A hand moves up to touch one bare thigh, hesitating momentarily as the fingers move from the rough blue jeans to the smooth feeling of flesh on flesh. He continues on until he reaches the base of the cock, his fingers closing around the thick shaft. As he does, the man stops playing with himself and lets his friend take over, putting his hands behind his head as the other man begins to stroke him in hesitant movements, fisting the unfamiliar prick.

"Just like playing with yourself," the man in the car says. "Do it just like you was doing your own dick."

With this new turn of events, I want to get a closer look. Climbing onto the windowsill, I crawl out onto my fire escape, making as little noise as possible. The night air surrounds my naked, sweating body as I sit on the stairs going up to the next floor and position myself so that I can see what is going on below me. The metal of the stairs is warm and presses roughly against my ass and the bottoms of my feet. The two men have not heard or seen me, and I have a perfect view of the car and what is happening in it. I look into the black face of the windows across the street and pray that no one turns on a light.

The man on the ground is stroking the big cock in his hand more smoothly now, running from the base to the heavy crown and wrapping his fingers around the head. His other hand is exploring the man's stomach and chest, feeling the hardness of the muscles. When the man puts a hand on his head and pushes him down, he stops his hand motions and begins to lick the fat balls that sit in front of his face. I see the back of his head move in slow circles as he runs his tongue over the warm folds of skin that hold the ripe fruit. I imagine what it must be like for him, tasting his friend's balls for the first time, so solid against his tongue, so warm in his mouth. I rub my own nuts as I watch him, stretching them out in my fingers and letting them fall back and swing below me.

The man inside the car jerks on the head of his tool as his nuts are sucked, every so often gripping his cock tightly and slapping it against his belly, the soft thuds barely audible four stories above. Louder are his groans, which roll from his throat like raw silk and fill my ears with their sound. After a few minutes he puts one huge hand on the other man's neck, his wide fingers pale against the dark hair, and draws him up. Pressing his lips against the solid shaft he says, "Suck my big cock."

The kneeling man's head rises up momentarily as he takes the other's dick between his lips. He slides down the fat tool slowly; it is obviously his first time with another man's prick in his mouth. His movements are awkward at first as he learns quickly how to breathe with so much flesh in his throat. But soon he is sucking on the big crank, his back and shoulders moving in rhythmic waves as he moves up and down, his hand following behind his lips as he works more and more of the thick shaft into his mouth.

Watching him blow his hunky friend, I stroke my own cock in much the same way, my fingers miming the motions of his mouth. Now I am even hornier than when I woke up, and every touch of my fingers on my dick brings aching tendrils shooting up from deep inside me. My skin is rivered with sweat from the heat, and I can feel it rolling down my sides in tiny drops, dried by the occasional breath of wind on my body. I feel myself getting closer and closer, but I don't want to come yet, not before I see what the studs below me are going to do, how it will all end. I have a feeling it isn't over yet and hold off my own need as I wait to see what comes next in their after-hours scenario.

The man in the car is gripping the other one's neck firmly with both hands, pushing him down and then releasing him. I can tell he is going to come by the way his hips rise off of the seat as he drives his cock into the teasing lips. When the man on the ground tries to pull away, I know that he is shooting deep in his throat. He holds the man's head in place until he is spent, only letting him go when his climax has ended. The man on the ground turns his head to the side. He has not been able to swallow all of the man's load, and a string of cum slides from his mouth to the street. It hangs from his lips in a thick thread, swaying slightly before falling away. He wipes the back of his hand across his mouth.

He stands up and steps away from the car, reaching for a bottle of beer to wash away the taste in his mouth. The man inside slides out, following him, and for the first time I see his face. He is very handsome. Not pretty like the men I see in the bars or in the fashionable parts of town, but rugged and somehow more real, more alive. His neck is thick, his jaw wide, and his whole body moves with masculine strength. His nose is slightly crooked, as though it has been broken in a long-ago game of football or during a brawl with another man over a lost bet in some dark bar. His hair is shaved so close to the skin that it forms a halo around his head under the streetlight.

Bending down, he unties his boots and pulls them off, following them with his pants. He stands barefoot and naked on the sidewalk beside the car. His body is bathed in light, and his still-erect cock stands out as he raises his hands and stretches them over his head. He reminds me of an animal, confident in both his power and in his complete control over his surroundings. I freeze, afraid that he will look up and see me watching him. But although he pauses for a moment, he does not turn around.

"Now you," he says to the other man, who is leaning against the car watching him. "Strip." It is a command, not a request.

When the other man does not move quickly enough, he steps in to help, tugging his shirt from his pants and pulling it over his head. Not as muscular as that of his friend, the dark-haired man's body is still remarkable. As his T-shirt slips over his head, I see two patches of hair beneath his arms, the only dark spots on his otherwise smooth body. His jeans are the next to go, dropping to the ground to reveal a short, fat cock already hard. His crotch looks as though it has been shaved clean, as do his balls.

The bigger man grabs the prick before him and begins to jerk on it roughly. "Nice piece you got here," he says, fingering the hairless balls.

Dropping to his knees, he starts to suck the other man's dick while playing with his own cock, which throws a long shadow over the pale surface of the sidewalk. He works expertly, moving his mouth from the shaft to the balls beneath, his face buried between the spread legs. After a minute, the standing man places his hands on the wide shoulders below him, his fingers kneading the thick muscles, his prick slipping in and out of the man's mouth smoothly and evenly as he gets serviced.

I no longer care if anyone is watching me or not. My hand glides rapidly along my dick, squeezing thin strands of precum from the head as I take in the scene below. My arm aches from the repeated motions, and I can feel the skin on my cock turning raw, but I don't stop. I spit into my hand and use this to grease my shaft, cooling the searing heat somewhat. My back is pressed so tightly against the stairs that the metal has started to bite into the skin.

The big man stands up and takes his buddy by the arm, maneuvering him so that he is standing in the ring of light. He pushes the other man against the front of the car so that he is lying with his arms splayed out over the hood, his legs spread behind him. He pushes the waiting ass cheeks apart with his big hands and plunges one long finger straight into the hole at their center. The man on the car bucks slightly as the finger tears into him, pushing back against his invader, who shoves him roughly down until he is still. Sliding his finger in and out, he loosens the tight ring of muscle until the man beneath him is rocking back and forth on his hand easily.

Pulling his finger out, he positions the head of his cock between the man's cheeks and pushes forward, driving into him in one swift thrust. I can see the man's face grimace in pain as his chute is filled with his buddy's prick. Then the lines of his mouth slide slowly into relaxation as pleasure wraps its shining arms about him. As the man behind him starts to fuck him in slow strokes, he rubs his hands over the smooth metal of the car's hood as though it were the skin of his lover's back.

The man pumps the ass beneath him in ever-increasing movements, the shadows cast on his naked skin from the surrounding buildings trembling like leaves in the wind as they stretch and tense with his motions. I can see clearly his long cock as it pistons rapidly in and out of the smooth mounds as he enters and retreats. His hands grip his friend's waist tightly and the muscles of his ass dimple and fill in again as he thrusts harder and harder.

My hand moves over my prick swiftly as I watch them fuck. Spreading my legs, I slide my finger into my hole as far as it will go, massaging the opening as I imagine the man's cock pounding my chute. Bringing it to my lips, I smell the musky scent of my ass and pretend that it is his. I slip the finger into my mouth and suck slowly and hungrily as I continue to pound my tool in time with the men who have made me so excited. I am getting very close and hope I can hold out until the end.

The man getting fucked is running his face over the car's surface, his tongue licking at the metal. He puts his hands under him and tries to push away, to reach his own dick and give it some relief, but he can't. His hands reach up and grasp at the glass of the windshield as he writhes against the hood, pinned there by the weight of the larger man and the force of his hammering cock. Finally the man pulls back, allowing his captive to stand while still driving his prong into the tight ass. The dark-haired man's cock bobs free as his body is rocked by the motion. He grabs hold of it and fists it wildly, his balls slapping madly beneath his hand as he rushes to bring the action to its conclusion.

Leaning back, he rests his head on the other man's shoulder as he comes. A long arc of white blasts from his prick and scatters over the hood. His arm continues its pumping motions as wave after wave spurts into the air. Then he is pushed forward and collapses on top of the car as the other man pulls out and jerks himself the rest of the way. Standing with his legs spread, he thrusts his hips forward and cranks his meat in short, quick strokes until he too sends a gush of jism into the night. The thick spray flashes momentarily in the lights before raining down on the prostrate form of the man on the hood.

Having lasted to the end, I finally allow myself the release I have craved since waking. My balls tighten as I finish the last few strokes and blow my load. As my body shakes with the crash of my coming I have to bite my lips to keep from crying out. The cum shoots from my prick in four long volleys, and I watch glassy eyed and exhausted as it falls through the air to the street below, landing only feet away from the car but unnoticed by the two men. A final shot coats the steel bars of the fire escape with a sticky stain as I fall back against the stairs. When I open my eyes, I see that the two men have picked up their clothes and gotten back into the car. As I sit above them wrapped in the heat and darkness, the cum drying on my skin and my cock hanging spent between my thighs, I watch as the headlights shine on and the car moves slowly down the street away from me, leaving me alone with the quiet.

Becoming Al

I like stories about transformation. I also enjoy the way sexual desire can bring about incredible changes in people. That's what this story is about. I like to think of it as an X-rated Flannery O'Connor story.

Albert Grant sat in the balcony of the Showtime All-Male Theater wondering if he was expected to jerk off. Just in case, he had stuffed several tissues into the pocket of his jacket as he left the house, and they made a small lump against his side that rustled lightly when he moved his arm. Also in his pocket was a crumpled advertisement that he had found three days earlier while walking from the grocer's back to his apartment. The ad, printed on a small square of blue paper, was twisted around one of the iron rail posts of his steps, and he had nearly stepped on it as he was ascending to his door. He'd picked it up not because he was interested in what it said, but because it annoyed him to have his freshly swept stoop dirtied.

He hadn't actually read it until he'd unpacked the groceries and put them away, the cans marshaled in neat rows behind the glass of the cabinet doors, the milk tucked neatly into the refrigerator. Then he'd taken the piece of paper from the counter where he'd dropped it and started to throw it away, stopping when he noticed that there was a picture of a nude man on it. The man had an unusually large penis, and Albert found himself staring at it helplessly, amazed at the way it hung between the man's legs demanding to be noticed. The ad had been very well printed, and Albert could see every curve of the man's big cock clearly, his eyes following it down from the man's neatly clipped bush to the point at which it flared into a fat, inviting head.

He'd looked at the prick for several minutes before moving his eyes up to scan the rest of the man's body. He appeared to be Italian, with a muscular body that had not been overworked and a chest covered in short, dark hair. Too rugged to be considered pretty, the man's face was what Albert thought of as handsome.

His dark eyes looked out from under sleepy lids, the brows over them thick and arched. The shadow drifting over his cheeks suggested that his beard would be heavy.

He looked like any one of the construction workers Albert often saw standing around roadwork sites, their hands resting confidently on their waists and their deeply tanned torsos filmed with sweat as they gazed down manholes or off into the distance at something he himself could never quite see. He was both attracted to and afraid of them, and if one of them chanced to look in his direction it took him several hours to forget his face.

Apart from his big cock, what interested Albert most about the man was the easy way in which he stood in the picture, as if he'd just stepped out of his dusty work clothes and was headed for the shower or on his way to bed after a long day. There was nothing self-conscious about either his stance or his expression, and Albert wondered if the man was thinking at all about the many men who would see his picture and want to make love with him. He could not imagine exposing himself like that before a camera, and the idea that someone might look at his picture the way he was looking at the man's made him distinctly uneasy.

According to the ad, the man's name was Tony Gioconda, and he was going to be appearing live on stage at the Showtime three times a day for one week starting the next Tuesday. Albert had no intention of going anywhere near the Showtime. It was in a section of town frequented more by drunks and prostitutes who crawled out of the city's smaller cracks when dusk settled in than by architects who lived in brownstones. But he kept the ad anyway, folding it carefully and tucking it into his wallet behind his American Express gold card.

Over the next few days Albert found himself thinking often of the man. His face would drop into Albert's mind suddenly and without warning while he was doing something completely unrelated, like washing the dishes or drawing up the floor plans for a new restaurant. Once, when he was in the middle of giving a presentation to a client, the image of Tony Gioconda's prick rose up before him, eclipsing the face of the corporate president sitting across the table, and he'd had to excuse himself for a few minutes to go into the bathroom and jerk off thinking about the big cock sliding into his throat.

These interruptions of his usually ordered routine had a surprising effect on him, similar to what would occur if he turned a corner on a familiar road and suddenly found himself in a new place. At first they annoyed him, the way they rippled the smooth surface of his life in unexpected patterns. But then he began to welcome, even invite, them. Every so often he would take the ad out of his wallet and look at it. It pleased him to have the man's picture folded and resting in his back pocket, as if somehow they knew one another and shared some kind of a history. After repeated foldings, the paper was crossed by pale, thin lines that neatly sectioned Tony Gioconda's body into squares. Albert liked the way the different parts of Tony's body were framed by these windows, especially the way his cock hung in the center square like a fine cut of meat in a butcher's display, something for hungry men to gaze at longingly.

Once he had stood naked before a mirror and compared his body to Tony's. He would examine one part of himself and then look at the corresponding area of the picture, noting the differences between them. At thirty-seven, he was in very good shape. His stomach, while not as ridged and tight as Tony's, was flat. His chest was smooth and fairly hard, if not sculpted into the twin rises of the Italian's, and his arms were evenly muscled. His face was strong, his blue eyes intent beneath light brown hair.

Assuming the same pose as Tony held in the ad, he noted the way his cock and balls hung. In school he had often sneaked glances at the penises of other boys as they stood awkwardly in the showers trying to focus their eyes anywhere but where they really wanted to look. He had been especially intrigued by one boy, the son of a local politician, whose cock seemed always to be half-hard, rising slightly up and away from his balls in a thickening arc. The boy seemed either not to notice or not to care that anyone saw his erection, soaping himself as if he were in his own shower at home. Albert had stood next to him several times, and once the boy's dick had brushed his leg when he turned to rinse himself. He had made no apology, and Albert had been forced to cut his own shower short to avoid being caught with the hard-on that was beginning to rush up from between his legs. That night in bed he had masturbated furiously, his hand rubbing over the burning spot on his thigh.

He looked at his cock as it was reflected in the mirror's face. The head, rounded to a blunt point, hung a little ways beyond his balls. He was always amazed when he became hard how much larger his cock became. Soft, it always appeared slightly small, like it belonged to a teenage boy instead of a grown man. But hard, it grew to a surprising length, sticking straight out from his body in a thick line. He knew from his limited experience that men enjoyed it, but he had never been able to ask any of his partners how it compared to others they had had.

After inspecting the rest of himself, he had gone to bed, where he dreamed that he was once again in the school shower room. Someone was standing very close to him, and because it was very steamy, he couldn't tell who it was. Then the steam opened up and Tony had stood before him. Albert had looked on in surprise as Tony reached out and took his cock in his soapy hand, jerking it slowly until it was hard. Then he had dropped to his knees and begun to suck on it while Albert put his hands in Tony's shiny wet hair. The dream had been very realistic, and when he woke up he saw that he had come all over his stomach and decided that he would go to the Showtime that evening.

Having made his decision, he was able to work the whole day without thinking about it. Then, he had come home, changed his clothes, and taken the bus to a stop near the theater. The driver had not even looked twice at him, and Albert, who imagined that the man must know exactly what it was he was about to do, told himself that it was because the driver saw this kind of thing all the time. After walking several blocks past stores that sold liquor, cheap clothing, and videos catering to every fetish imaginable, he'd found the Showtime. The panes of glass on the doors were blackened, and there was a poster outside of Tony Gioconda, on which he was crouched so that the head of his penis nearly swept the floor.

He gave his money to a tired-looking Asian woman who sat behind a thick screen of Plexiglas, wondering if she knew that she was collecting the fare for men's most secret dreams, and went through the door into a stale, smoky hallway carpeted in red. There were several other men leaning against the walls, and they looked up hopefully when he came in. He glanced briefly at their faces. One, a silver-haired middle-aged man still wearing his suit from work, attracted him briefly, but he moved on. He quickly found the stairway to his left and went up into the balcony. It was empty except for three or four men scattered among the seats like grains of rice after a wedding.

Choosing a seat in the middle of the row directly behind the railing, he'd settled into the sagging blue velvet cushion, checking carefully first to make sure there was nothing still wet on it. As he waited for the minutes to pass until the show was scheduled to start, he looked around at the men he could see from his vantage point above the main floor. He had expected the population of the theater to be composed of the old and the unattractive, and was surprised that most of them looked very much like himself.

Behind the small stage at the front of the theater was a large white screen, on which was flickering a picture of two men, one white and one black, fucking on a bed. The bed appeared to be in a hotel room, and Albert was amused to see that the filmmaker had put a small Bible on the bedside table. The black man was fucking the white one, who was on his hands and knees with his head on a pillow. The black man was thrusting savagely at his asshole, and Albert wondered why it was that men in porn movies always slapped the asses of the men they were fucking. The image made his dick stiffen slightly in his pants, and he shifted his position to lessen the pressure at his crotch.

Just as the black man started to shoot his load onto his partner's back, the film was cut abruptly. The lights dimmed to inky blackness, and the house was swallowed by shadows. A white light swept over the stage, and the sound of music spat out of the mouths of tinny speakers set throughout the house. A curtain behind the screen parted, and Tony Gioconda walked onto the stage wearing a policeman's uniform and carrying a billy club.

Albert found himself very attracted to the uniform, and his attention was riveted to Tony, imagining the way the material would feel under his hands. As the music thumped and growled, Tony moved around the stage, grinding his body along with the beat. He was shorter than Albert had imagined and wore dark glasses that hid his eyes. Still, as he watched Tony come to the edge of the stage and run the billy club between his legs, he felt his balls tighten.

The first thing Tony took off was his shirt, slowly unbuttoning it and then turning to let it fall down his back to the floor like a great blue leaf. When he turned back to the audience, he was rubbing his hands over his chest, pinching his nipples and then pushing his hand into the front of his pants. After a few more minutes, he undid those as well, pulling them down and off in one surprisingly fluid movement.

Wearing only a pair of small dark blue briefs and black leather motorcycle boots, he began to tease the audience, pulling the underwear down until the top of his bush was exposed, then cruelly pulling them back up. He turned around and let them see the firm globes of his ass, bending over as though waiting for one of them to run on stage and begin to fuck him. Finally, he yanked the briefs off, revealing his cock.

From the balcony, Albert could not see in great detail, but he could tell that Tony's prick was beautiful. Long and thick, it swung heavily as he continued to move around the stage. Like the boy's in Albert's high-school gym class, it swung half-hard over his balls. Then he began to jerk off, stroking his cock slowly as he stood on the stage. His eyes were fixed on a point somewhere in the audience, and Albert wondered if he was looking at someone in particular. His hand made long pulls on the big dick, his fingers squeezing the head and holding it out toward the men sitting in the seats before him.

Making sure that no one was watching him, Albert unzipped his pants and pulled his cock out, leaving his balls inside. He was filled with a peculiar excitement as he sat back and started to play with his prick, all the while keeping his eyes on Tony. He heard the quiet sounds of men moving in the darkness around him, and this made him even more aroused, knowing that if they looked closely they would see him taking part in this most personal pleasure. He kept his hand moving in time with Tony's, enjoying the feeling of his hot flesh beneath his fingers.

He brought himself to the edge several times, feeling a swelling in his groin and slowing his hand just enough to prevent his load from escaping. His balls were starting to ache, but he was determined to wait. Finally, when he saw Tony's eyes close, he knew it was almost time, and he began to pump himself quickly. As Tony grabbed his balls tightly and thick bursts of white streamed from his cockhead, tumbling onto the stage, Albert came in a rush of pleasure, squirting his cum onto the floor between his legs with a soft, wet sound.

Then it was over, almost as abruptly as it had started. The music ended, and Tony disappeared behind the curtains. The lights rose slightly and the men on the screen started in right where they had left off. The black man's face twisted into a grimace of pleasure as he finally released his load in a great white arc that covered the other man in a sticky sheet. Albert tucked his cock back into his pants and zipped up quickly. Standing up, he left the balcony and, pushing past two men kissing in the stairwell, exited the theater and rushed into the dark mouth of the evening.

The next night he found himself once again boarding the bus that would take him to the theater. When he got off at his stop, he walked briskly down the street, this time knowing exactly what it was he was looking for. As he handed his money to the old woman behind the window, he started to blush, thinking that perhaps she remembered him from the night before. But if she did, she made no indication, and he forgot about her as soon as he pushed through the doors and found himself once more in the red-carpeted hallway and felt a tightening in his stomach.

He paused at the stairs that led to the balcony and then moved on into the lower area of the theater. This was more crowded than the balcony had been, with each row occupied by at least two, and sometimes three, men. As Albert walked down the aisle sticky with layers of dried and fresh cum, he noticed the silver-haired man he'd seen the night before having his dick sucked by a young man in shorts and a Mickey Mouse T-shirt, his prick sticking up from the zipper of his suit pants as the other man moved up and down it soundlessly. The man looked at Albert and smiled in recognition, then pushed his partner's face farther down onto his cock.

Albert took a seat in one of the few empty rows, on the aisle several rows away from the stage. He looked at his watch, saw that he had a twenty-minute wait, and began to watch the movie that was playing itself out on the screen. In this one, a thin man with bad skin and a prick as long and skinny as the rest of him was sticking it into the ass of a short, dark-haired man, who was in turn being blown by another man, who had a crude tattoo of a woman with enormous breasts on his arm. Over the course of twenty minutes, the trio changed positions several times before the man with the big dick and the man with the tattoo came on the dark-haired man's face.

Then the lights dimmed again and the familiar music blurted into the room. It was louder, because he was nearer the speakers than he had been before, but he was able to tune it out as Tony emerged from behind the screen. This time he was dressed as a construction worker, wearing a tight white T-shirt tucked into jeans.

Albert watched him go through his routine, holding his breath as each article of clothing came off and more of Tony's body was revealed to him. Sitting so close, he was able to see the delicate swirls made by his chest hair and the sweat that gleamed on his skin as he danced under the lights. When Tony had stripped down to his briefs, which were white this time, Albert was able to see the outline of his delicious prick where it curved along his groin, the head threatening to burst from the waistband.

Despite his close proximity to the stage and the presence of a man across the aisle, Albert was preparing to jerk off along with Tony when Tony came to the edge of the stage, paused, and then, much to Albert's surprise, moved forward into the aisle. Albert turned and watched as he walked past him, the smell of his sweat hanging on the breeze he caused, and sat on the lap of a fat man six rows back. The fat man put a heavy paw on Tony's crotch and squeezed, a wet grin crossing his fleshy face. Albert wanted to run back and slap him, but Tony got up and moved farther up the aisle.

After stopping at a few more seats and letting the men in them touch him briefly, Tony turned and moved back toward the stage. Albert sat very still, not wanting the man to see he had been watching or, God forbid, sit on his lap. When he felt a hand on his shoulder, he jumped. Looking up, he saw that Tony had stopped at his seat. But instead of sitting on his lap, he took Albert's hand and pulled him to his feet.

Albert allowed himself to be pulled forward, unable to say or do anything. When Tony urged him up the stairs to the stage, he followed, thinking that perhaps he was still at home in his own bed and dreaming what was happening. Standing under the hot lights, he looked into the eyes of the man whose picture he had in his pocket and listened to him say, "How about helping me out here?" Tony was smiling, and Albert nodded at him.

Tony took Albert's coat and tossed it aside, then began to unbutton his shirt. When it was hanging open, he started to rub Albert's chest, his fingers massaging the skin. He pressed forward, and suddenly the hair of his chest was against Albert's skin, soft and inviting. Instinctively, he put his hands on Tony's back and pulled him closer until he could feel Tony's cock pressed against his own.

Tony pulled Albert's shirt off and then fumbled with the buckle of his belt. Albert helped him, oblivious now to the fact that he was undressing on a stage in front of a room filled with other men. He knew only that he wanted nothing more than to be naked with Tony, to feel his flesh against his. In a few seconds he was standing in only his briefs, and Tony was kissing him. Albert kissed him back, his tongue forcing itself into Tony's mouth, his hands finding Tony's nipples and rubbing them roughly. When they broke apart, he looked into his dark eyes and knew that he would go along with whatever Tony wanted.

Tony took Albert's hands and slid them down to his waist. Albert felt soft material under his fingers and pulled at it. Tony's cock fell into his hands, and he held it tightly. Then he dropped to his knees and put the head in his mouth. It was leaking precum, salty and thick, and Albert was soon working up and down the shaft as it stretched to its full length. As he sucked, he worked Tony's balls with his hand, stretching them out and letting them fall back.

When Tony was completely hard, he began fucking Albert's mouth in long, slow strokes. Albert watched the inches of flesh pass his lips, felt the head as it pressed against him. His own prick was hanging from his shorts, and he jerked off while he sucked Tony's tool. The lights on his back were hot, and he could feel rivers of sweat beginning to run down his skin.

Tony put a hand on his chin and urged him to his feet, then turned so that Albert's cock was pressed against the crack of his ass. He started to grind against him, so that Albert could feel the heat from his skin as it moved along the length of his prick. When Tony bent over, exposing his fresh pink hole in a forest of dark hair, Albert knew what to do. Spitting into his palm, he slicked his cock and pressed the head against the tight opening.

Pushing roughly, he plowed into a warmth as sweet and welcoming as a hot bath. Tony pushed back against him and slid onto his crank until Albert's balls were slapping his ass cheeks. Closing his eyes, Albert began to fuck him, putting his hands on his waist to steady himself. Tony groaned as the walls of his ass stretched to accommodate Albert's thickness, but he never slowed the speed of his thrusts.

Before long, Albert was slamming his cock into Tony's willing ass, the sweat on his belly making wet slapping sounds whenever it came together with the other man's reddening ass cheeks. He was aware that none of it should have been happening, and that made him fuck Tony even harder, as though if he slowed down Tony and the whole theater would dissolve in a pile of dust. He opened his eyes and saw that Tony was jerking his big prick as he was getting plowed, and he was vaguely aware that in the front row another man was busily beating his cock as his neighbor sucked on his balls.

When he finally came, after what seemed like hours of moving in slow motion, he pulled out of Tony's ass and turned him around, letting his load stream over Tony's hairy stomach in four long spurts that drained his heavy nuts and left his breathing ragged and his legs weak. Tony was still stroking his cock and waited until Albert was able to stand behind him and pinch his tits before coming himself, his flood gushing over Albert's hand where it held his balls and falling onto the stage in thick threads. When he was finished, he took Albert's hand and led him behind the screen into a dark room.

"Thanks a lot, man," he said, putting his hand on Albert's back. "I don't always know if that's going to work. Sometimes you get guys up there and they freeze up—can't get it up and all. But you looked like you'd be into it, so I risked it."

Albert couldn't think of anything to say, so he said simply, "Thanks."

Tony handed him a towel, and he wiped himself off. "So, what's your name?"

Albert paused momentarily, then heard himself say, "Al." Then, more confidently, "My name's Al." He liked the way it sounded, short and barked from the throat like a declaration.

"Good to meet you, Al," Tony said. "I have to go get showered before the next show. But if you want to stick around, we could get together after I'm done."

Albert looked at Tony's expectant face and started to put his pants back on. "I'd like to," he said. "But I have to go home."

Tony smiled. "Too bad. Well, come by whenever you feel like it, then. I'll be here."

Albert nodded and started toward a door that looked like it led to the outside. He found himself in the lobby again. As he walked out the door and onto the street, he fumbled in his pocket. The ad was still there, and as he walked to the bus stop he unfolded it and looked at Tony's picture. As he did, a feeling of deep satisfaction rose up in him, blooming into a warmth that filled every pore, and he decided that it might be nice to walk home for a change.

Diving the Pit

Every so often I like to just start with a particular image and see what grows out of it. This story started that way. I liked the idea of a punk kid dancing wildly. I also think my ongoing crush on Henry Rollins had something to do with it, although these days Eminem makes a nice substitute as well.

Shortly after midnight the club is teeming with people. While there are a few women scattered around the room, it is mainly young men I see as I make my way up the stairs to the main floor. Most seem barely over the legal age for being there, a reflection probably of the type of music this bar caters to—what we used to call punk but which now goes by the less threatening and vaguer title of "alternative." They stand alone or in small groups, their bodies covered in tattoos, their noses and lips pierced by knots of metal. They hold cigarettes in their fingers like knives and seem filled with the promise of sex in all its many forms. While they maintain the strict appearance of having no interest in one another's bodies, I sense that the subtlest shift in time or place would find all of them naked with one another, fucking strangers in dark corners or on their knees sucking cock while someone beat off in their faces.

The band they have all come to see is an hour late already, and the crowd is growing restless. They have been drinking steadily all night, and this has only fueled their impatience. They stamp their feet and chant the name of the band in an eerie chorus, entreating them to come out like a band of children calling to their playmates to join a game. Their cries drown out the grungy strains of the Ramones tape blasting over the speakers, the power chords and familiar growl drowned out by calls for this band they have paved the way for. A few unseen hands throw bottles at the equipment sitting on the stage, sending fragments of glass scattering over the floor.

I stake out a position toward the back of the room, where I can have a good view of everything going on. The air there is thick with the smell of beer, smoke, and sweat, and it heightens my senses. I lean against the bar and take a long draft on my drink. The alcohol burns in my throat and settles hotly in my stomach. I feel its warm breath working up my insides and relax.

After another few minutes the lights go down and the band takes the stage to a roar of approval. As they launch into their first number, the crowd begins to move in time with the pounding beat. This is rock and roll at its hardest, angry and raw, and the dancing is the same. As guitars grind and the singer spits his words into a buzzing microphone, arms and legs flail in a twisting knot of bodies. Heads bob up and down in time with the driving bassline. The room quickly fills with the heat of moving bodies and the smell of sweat grows stronger, mixing with the acrid stench of the dry-ice machines pumping out clouds of filmy smoke that roll across the floor and surround everything with their gauzy touch.

The area in front of the stage is the most frenzied and the most dangerous. It is the mosh pit, where die-hard concertgoers throw themselves against each other in violent celebration of nothing at all. The center of the surrounding maelstrom, it is populated by young men whose rage finds an outlet in the battering of the body, both their own and those of others. In this arena noses are frequently bloodied and bodies bruised by the force of flying hands and the sting of heavy boots as moshers collide with each other and spin away again to connect with someone else.

Tonight the pit is filled with nearly naked men slamming against one another. When they are eclipsed by a cloud of smoke, their shadows jump and leap against the scrim of dry ice like puppets in a sadistic pantomime. Watching those who have adventured into its madness, I am filled with a strong desire to join them. Normally I avoid moshing, preferring to stay to the sides and listen to the music, sometimes venturing to the fringes of the fray but never going into its heart. But tonight I am searching for something different. I am on edge, and I need a release. I have neither fucked nor been fucked in several days, and my craving to be near other men is strong.

One young man in particular draws my attention. He is shirtless and wearing cutoff shorts worn thin in many places from hours of rubbing against his skin during nights like this one.

Shorter than I am by several inches, he has the powerful build of a bulldog, his arms and legs roped with thick muscle. His chest is broad and hard, covered in short dark hair that swirls around his nipples, which are pierced through by small circles of steel. Like many of the men in the crowd, his head is shaved, a light shadow of stubble just beginning to dust the pale skin of his scalp. He has a Vandyke beard and there is a tattoo of barbed wire curled around his bulging left bicep.

He is dancing wildly, his body thrashing from side to side as he slips into the music and rides it like a leaf over water. His fists beat at the empty space around him as he loses himself in the droning rumble of the drums, hammering the song's underpinnings out of thin air. His eyes are closed, and the smile on his face is one of complete contentment. He is beautiful, and I want him terribly. Without thinking, I push through the crowd so that I can be nearer to him, parting the wall of spinning bodies roughly and shoving past dancers until I am separated from him only by two or three other people. I can see the sweat on his skin clearly as he moves, claiming his space with sudden jabs of his elbows when someone gets too close.

I let myself fold into the music until my heart is tangled up in the beating of the bassline and my head swims. My feet move on their own and soon I am one of the many faceless revelers in the pit. As bodies swarm around and past me, I keep one eye on the dancing man nearby, wondering what it would be like to touch him, to fuck him. My prick begins to stiffen as I imagine running my tongue over his back, plunging it into his armpit or beneath his balls. I rub myself through my jeans as I feel my body being pummeled on all sides by other moshers.

As the music plays on, people climb onto the stage and throw themselves off into the crowd to be caught in a safety net of welcoming hands. Diving the pit it is called, a ritual of the underground music scene. There are no bodyguards positioned to stop them; it is both expected and encouraged. The wounds gathered as results of failed dive attempts are worn proudly, the chipped teeth and bruised faces symbols of bravery. I watch as a tall young man with long hair clambers up and then leaps out over the mosh pit, his hair twisting around his head as he flies, landing on his back on the outstretched hands of his friends. They lower him to the floor and wait for the next diver.

Finding myself in front of the stage, I pull myself up onto it. I have never dived before, just as I have never braved the mosh pit. But I see this as a chance to enter the world of the man whose body tempts me, to prove myself to him. Standing to one side of the wailing singer, I look out into the sea of sweating, masculine faces, all looking up at me expectantly. I find his face, look into his eyes. He sees me and stares back. "Dive," he mouths, and others around him take up the chorus. "Dive. Dive. Dive," they chant, skinhead mermaids luring me into their depths.

Bending my knees, I jump headlong into space, flying for a moment above the raised arms before falling downward. My body is caught by dozens of hands, held aloft by the contact of unknown fingers on my bare skin. As I pass along from person to person I feel hands grab my erect prick, squeeze my balls. I search for the face of the one I am looking for, but because of the flashing lights and the ever-shifting bodies I can't distinguish one from another. When I am finally lowered to my feet and stand once more on the floor, I find that I am next to him. He turns and grins. "Nice dive," he shouts over the music.

I nod my thanks and begin dancing again. He does not move away from me, and I can see every line of his body as he moves. I feel his sweat spray across my face as he shakes his head and I lick the salty drops from my lips. His hairy chest brushes my arm, and I feel a sudden stirring in my nuts when I realize he is pressed against me. Then he turns again, and all I see is his back. I stare at the muscles flexing beneath his skin and reach out to touch him. I run my hand across his shoulder momentarily just to feel the heat of him, hoping that in the fury of bodies he will not notice.

I am surprised when he backs up closer to me, his body touching mine. When enough time has gone by that I know it is not simply an accident or the force of other bodies pushing him against me, I put my hand on his waist, leaving it there to see what he will do. He leans back until his shoulders are against my chest, my growing hard-on pressed into his ass. He is still rocking to the music, and the motion of his skin against mine is electric. We have moved out of the center of the mosh pit and are in a less active but more crowded area. Because of the number of people and the billows of chemical smoke, no one notices that I am holding him.

I run my hands around him to the front, feeling the hair on his stomach and the firm ridges of his abdomen. One hand travels up his chest, stroking the soft hair and fingering the coldness of a nipple ring. The other slips into the waistband of his shorts, where I find that his cock is hard against his belly. It is amazingly thick, and the bulletlike head fills my palm easily. The movement of his body forces his shaft to slide against my hand, and I stroke him as much as I can within the confines of his pants.

I jerk him off surrounded by dozens of unknowing witnesses while the band hammers out song after song. Several times people bump into us, but none notices what is happening. His cock becomes harder as I play with it and my fingers slide along the smooth sides, pumping him to the edge. When he comes, he fills my hand with a heavy, wet load, spurting several times. Pulling my hand out, I bring it to my lips and lick his cum from my fingers. It is still warm, and the stickiness of it coats my tongue and throat deliciously as I swallow. I run my fingers over his face and slip one into his mouth, letting him suck himself from my hand. His beard is rough under my palm and his lips sweet and wet. I want more.

"Come on," I whisper in his ear.

He follows me through the crowd until we come to a doorway that leads into the club's bowels. No one stops us, so I go through. Walking down a short corridor, I push open the first door I come to. I pull on a string hanging by the door and a single bare lightbulb burns with weak light. We are in what appears to be a storage room. Crates of empty beer bottles line one wall and the room is filled with wooden boxes. I usher him inside and push the door shut behind me, making sure it locks. Through the walls the music is nothing more than a dull thumping, like the heart of a giant beast pushing blood through its veins. I turn to look at him.

"What's your name?" I ask him, drawing my finger from his crotch to his neck. I don't need to know, but I am curious.

"Jesse," he answers. His voice is low, guttural, and it is hard to hear him.

"How old are you?"

He looks away from me. "Twenty-three."

I know he is lying, but I pretend to believe him. Probably he has added two or three years to his age. It doesn't matter. Away from the crowd he is even more attractive than I first noticed. I see now that his eyes are blue, his lips full and soft. I look at the bulge in his pants and remember how he felt in my hand, the way his body shook when he came. Thinking about jerking him off has made me hungry for him, and I am anxious to begin.

"I'm going to fuck you," I tell him. "Show me your ass."

He drops his shorts and takes them off, managing to pull them over his heavy black combat boots. His balls and crotch have been shaved and his cock, already stiff again, looks even larger against the naked skin. It stands out from his body in a heavy arc, the fat tip dipping down over his sac, remnants of dried cum still streaking the pale skin. I quickly slip my own shirt off and pull my pants over my boots. Folding them neatly and placing them on a crate, I give him time to look at me before I move toward him. His eyes travel down my muscular body to my hard prick and I see that he is more than willing to take what I have to offer. This is what I have waited for, what I need, and my body is filled with tremors of expectation as I think of what is to come.

I walk around behind him and study his ass. It's so perfect that it's breathtaking. His rounded globes are smooth and clean, his legs hairy. The bare moons of flesh look as though they have never been touched. I smack a cheek and feel the firmness of his skin and muscle beneath my hand. Gripping one mound tightly I leave a handprint when I let go, the red skin fading to pink after a few seconds. I am going to enjoy fucking this ass later, but there are other things to come first. I move back around to stand in front of him.

"On your knees," I order, and he drops to the ground in front of me. His legs are spread and his hands rest on his thighs as he waits. Holding my cock in my fist, I let him look at it for a minute as I stroke it to full hardness. I see the change in his eyes as he gazes at the thick shaft and realizes he will be taking it up his butt. He licks his lips as he anticipates the way it will spread his hole and slip into his chute. Gripping my piece loosely, I slap his cheeks with it several times. I love the way it feels when my prick hits the heavy bones of his jaw, the way his beard scrapes the sensitive skin. He opens his mouth and I let him lick just the head of my big tool. When he starts to close his lips around it I pull away.

Positioning the tip above his face, I release a thick stream of piss that splashes down over his nose and mouth. It is unexpected, but he does not make any attempt to move out of the way. As the bitter water runs over his lips he opens them and drinks it in, his throat rippling as he swallows what he can catch. The sight of it rushing over his beautiful face and dripping from his chin to trickle down his chest pleases me, and I move my still-spurting dick down so that the pale yellow torrent washes his torso and soaks his cock and balls with my juice. When I am drained, I shake the last drops onto his face. The smell of it rises from the floor, where it has puddled around his knees.

"There's some on my boot," I tell him. "Lick it off."

Bending forward, he slides his tongue obediently along the piss-spattered surface of my boot. His ass cheeks part as he stretches his legs wider and bows below me, supported on his hands. His cockhead trails through the pool of urine as his face moves over my foot and he washes every drop from the leather. When he is finished, he moves on to my leg, licking shining beads of piss from the hair on my thighs as he travels up toward my crotch.

When he reaches my cock, he looks up expectantly. My prick is bobbing before him only inches from his waiting lips. I stroke it until a drop of precum glistens at the tip. He sticks his tongue out and I slide my hand up my cock. The droplet hangs for a long moment and then falls in a thin string into his mouth, where he slurps it up like sweetest honey. Filled with lust for him, I put the head of my prick against his mouth and he takes it in greedily. I force the entire length into his throat quickly, putting my hand on his neck and pushing him forward onto it. To my surprise, he takes it without too much trouble, and soon my balls are banging against his chin as my head pounds deep in his throat.

I let him suck me at his own pace for several minutes, enjoying the way his lips slide over my shaft and pull hungrily at my engorged knob. He knows what he is doing and brings me close to the edge several times. His hands pull roughly on my balls while he blows me, stretching them out until they are sore and aching. I like that he is in control for the moment, and enjoy watching him milk me until I am slick with his spit and the precum that is oozing steadily from my dick.

When I feel myself nearing a climax again I take control and start to fuck his face harder. Holding him still, I slam my cock again and again into his hot mouth, his face pressing into my belly with each new thrust until I wonder how he can breathe. My balls begin to pound as my pent-up load claws its way through my insides. Pulling out of his mouth I come all over him. Fat globs of jism pepper his handsome face, covering his eyes and nose as I shoot repeatedly. Long strings of it streak his beard. He opens his mouth and I release another blast onto his outstretched tongue, where it drips from his lips.

When I have finished shooting, he is covered in my jism. It paints his face and chest and smears his mouth and hands where he has tried to wipe it away. His fat dick is hard as a rock, standing up between his legs as he plays with it. I push my slimy cock back into his mouth and he sucks on me until I am hard again. Then I pull out and tell him to stand up. I push him onto his back on top of a dusty box and he pulls his legs up. His ass cheeks are spread wide and I can see straight into the center of his clean-shaven pucker. The skin is pink and tender, darker and rosier as it nears his hole. As he breathes, the tiny slit flutters open and closed.

When I kneel, my face is positioned right in front of his hole. As he holds his legs back with his hands, I lean forward and lightly run my tongue along the clean lines of his cheeks and up to his balls. I can feel the stubble of his recently shaved skin beneath my tongue as I lick the ridge from his asshole to his ballsac and take one of his fat nuts into my mouth. His body tenses as I suck forcefully, my tongue pressing first one sensitive globe and then the other against the roof of my mouth.

Moving back down, I lick his asshole with long strokes of my tongue, letting the tip tickle his pucker until he begins to groan. I know that this is torture for him, and I take my time. When his mancunt is good and wet, I slide into it, my lips pressing against his skin as I burrow deeply in his chute. His thighs close around my face as I push in, stretching him wider and wider. The harder I fuck his ass with my tongue the more he groans, until he is whimpering for me to stick my cock in him.

Instead I stand up and push two fingers into his shitter. He squirms as I spread them and loosen his hole, fisting his prick as I work my hand further into him. His face is contorted with pain and ecstasy, and by the time I have four fingers slipping in and out he is almost crying. I slap his ass sharply while I plow him, the sound mixing with his heavy moans as he writhes around.

"I'm going to shoot all over the fucking place," he says.

Pushing his legs back, I ram my tool straight into his asshole until I slap forcefully against him and my balls are pressed tightly to his cheeks. His head is thrown back as he takes the pain, and his cock is standing stiffly up from his belly. I grip his dick tightly at the base to prevent him from shooting and feel it swell in my fingers as he almost comes. I twitch my prick inside him and watch him gasp, his lips parting slightly. His ass ring tightens around my shaft as spasms wrack his body.

I start to pump him, grinding in and out of his hole in long thrusts. Before long I am slamming into him again and again, my hips bucking furiously as I satisfy both of our needs. He is jerking his big crank with one hand, the tattoo around his arm twisting with each stroke while he pulls on one of his nipple rings with the other. I can smell the rich scent of his boots as they rub against my shoulders, and turn my head to lick the smooth leather. The metal rings of the eyes scrape my tongue as I run it along the length of his boot, his calf gripped tightly in my fingers.

As I increase my movements he stops playing with his tits and begins rubbing his balls, kneading them in his fingers as he pounds his cock. I can feel his touch on my shaft as it passes back and forth over his ass lips, and it's too much. Yanking my prick out of him, I pull him to his feet and turn him around. I push him so that he is leaning against the wall and shove my dick back up his ass. Because he is shorter than I am, he has to rise up on his toes to take all of me as I ram my tool deep inside him.

Putting my arms around him, I twist his tits roughly, pulling on the metal rings and stretching his throbbing buds out. My mouth moves to his neck and I lick the vein at his throat, following it to the sensitive spot beneath his ear and biting his skin as I fuck him from behind. My belly rubs against his ass cheeks and back as I nail him mercilessly and I feel his hard-on jump with each slap of my body.

I clamp my hand around his cock and beat him off. After only a few dozen strokes he starts to breathe in long gasps. Cum explodes from his reddened dickhead and covers the wall in a pearly smear. The sight sends me, and I give one final wicked push into his ass before emptying my balls. I fall against him and press him to the wall as the jism rushes out of me and fills his depths. I feel like I did flying out over the mosh pit, completely alive. I stay there until the rush fades, my body pressed to his, my heart beating against his skin.

Sliding out of him, I wipe my cock on his thigh, leaving a wet streak on his skin. His chest hair is matted with his own cum from where he has been slammed against the wall, and his ass is red from all of my pounding. He smells wonderfully of piss and sweat and sex. Pulling him to me I kiss his mouth for the first time, tasting my cum and urine on his tongue. His skin is sticky in my hands as he wraps his arms around me. I lick his face clean while I hold him, my fingers probing his ravaged asshole. The sound of music leaks through the walls, and when I feel his cock rising between us I know I will be diving the pit again soon.

Memories of War

I was listening to the Andrews Sisters singing "Boogie Woogie Bugle Boy" one afternoon and the image of two soldiers meeting in a USO came to me. I'm sure Patty, LaVerne, and Maxene would be horrified to know what they inspired, but there you are.

Under the best of conditions, the small town of Asherville, North Carolina, wouldn't have much to offer a young man looking for excitement. This was especially true in 1943. With the war raging a continent away, most of the town had been put to military use, largely because of the airfield located there. In happier times it had been the sight of daredevil air shows, where reckless pilots dipped to only feet above the sea as the people on the beach enjoyed picnic lunches and pretty girls walked the wings of biplanes to the shrieks and delight of children with cotton candy–sticky faces. Now it was home to a small air base, where flyboys still wet behind the ears were trained to defend their country and then shipped off to do battle with the German Luftwaffe. My job was to teach them as much as I could and then hope they remembered it.

In the dog days of August, the heat that descended every evening at dusk made the sleepy town pull tighter into itself as people shut themselves inside, trying to cool off with rattling window fans and mason jars of iced tea thick with sugar and mint. For a lonely GI looking for some way to pass the time, the best answer was to head on down to the USO, where you could at least hear the latest songs by the Andrews Sisters or listen to a radio broadcast of DiMaggio slamming one home for the Yanks.

One Friday night after a day spent teaching the finer points of night navigation, I was feeling restless and decided to head down to the canteen for a drink. When I got there the place was packed, the floor crowded with men in their familiar light brown uniforms drinking and laughing. A number of the local girls were there as well, their high-pitched giggles bursting from the rumble of male conversation like tiny colored lights.

I pushed my way through the crowd to the bar, waving at several of my buddies sitting at a table with their arms around their girlfriends for the evening. By the smiles on their faces I knew that Monday I'd be hearing all about their exploits and how well the girls had done their patriotic duty. The bartender, a young man who'd been kept out of the army because of a bum leg, was busy getting drinks for the dozen or so soldiers already waiting. I leaned against the bar and waited my turn, watching the crowd. Someone had put another record on, and the dancing was going fast and furious.

"This guy takes much longer and we'll be toasting the end of the war."

I turned to see who was speaking. Leaning against the bar next to me was a man about my height. Solidly built, he had wide shoulders and a broad chest. His hair, cut military short, was light brown, and his eyes were a startling shade of blue. He held out his hand and I took it, his fingers closing around mine tightly as he pumped my arm in a single gesture of introduction. "James Henry," he said, a touch of Southern accent in his drawl, "but my friends all call me Hank." His teeth when he smiled were even and very white.

"Name's Tom," I said. His sudden appearance had taken me by surprise, and I found myself uneased by his good looks.

"I was just getting a suds. Can I get you one?"

"Sure, thanks."

Hank turned and waved the bartender over. "Hey, guy, how about a couple of beers for my buddy and me."

The bartender fished two brews from out of the cooler behind him and set them on the bar. Hank took one of the bottles and placed the edge of the cap against the counter. Hitting the top with his fist, he sent the bottle cap sailing. A burst of foam poured out of the bottle, and Hank lifted it quickly to his lips, downing the escaping beer.

He handed me the bottle and repeated the procedure with the remaining one. Clinking his beer against mine, he said, "Here's to the war," and took a deep swallow.

We resumed our conversation, and I found out Hank was with

the army infantry. I told him about my job at the airfield, and soon we were chatting like old friends. Hank was from Mississippi, the son of a Baptist preacher. He'd enlisted rather than take his chances with the draft, and he was in North Carolina finishing up his training. His easy way of talking and frequent jokes were very appealing, and I found myself talking to him more than I'd talked with anyone since being stationed in North Carolina.

As Hank was telling me a story about the time his father had found him drunk on homemade moonshine, a girl came up and tapped him on the shoulder. She was a small thing with blond hair done up in a wave and she had bright red lips. "Hey there, soldier," she said, smacking her gum and smiling at the same time. "How'd you and your friend like to take a turn on the dance floor with my girlfriend and me?"

Hank looked over at me and winked. Then, giving her a wide smile, he said, "Sure thing, hon. You lead."

The girl took his hand and led him onto the dance floor. Her friend, a carbon copy of the first girl with dark hair instead of light, pulled me along behind them. The song was fast, and we were twirling the girls around quickly. Hank seemed to be enjoying himself, swinging the blond girl between his legs and lifting her up in the air like a paper doll, and I was feeling a little depressed at the thought that it would probably be her lips and not mine against his later in the evening. I tried to feign enthusiasm for my impromptu date, and she didn't seem to notice that I wasn't thrilled with having her in my arms.

Finally the song ended, and the dance floor emptied. As the two girls disappeared into the powder room, Hank grabbed my hand and pulled me toward the door. "Let's get out of here while we have the chance," he said.

Outside the air was sticky with heat. Hank took out a handkerchief and wiped his neck. "Christ, that was a close one. What do you say we take a walk and cool off some."

It sounded like a good idea to me. I was enjoying spending time with Hank and wasn't anxious for the night to be over just yet. Even if I couldn't have him, at least I could put off the inevitable moment when he'd head back to his room and leave me alone with my fantasies of what could have happened.

"We could head on over to my rooming house," I suggested. "I think there's some iced tea in the fridge."

Hank agreed readily, and we set off up the street to the house where I'd found a small room to rent. I could have stayed at the base, but I liked the peace and quiet of being by myself. As we walked, Hank was quiet, saying only a word or two about how hot it was. He was acting very differently from the lively man I'd met in the bar, and I wondered if he was thinking about the girl he'd left behind.

We reached my rooming house and opened the front door. No one was around, and we walked up the stairs to my third-floor room in silence. Once we were in my room and the door was shut, Hank turned and kissed me on the mouth. When we parted, he stood and looked at me anxiously, as if waiting for my reaction. "I've wanted to do that all night," he said. "But I wasn't sure if you went in for guys or not. If you don't, just tell me and I'll get out of here."

I answered him by kissing him back, my lips meeting his in an anxious embrace. Looking into his eyes, I saw the fear become joy as he realized that I wanted him as much as he wanted me. After a few seconds, Hank's arms went around me and he began to kiss me passionately, his tongue exploring my mouth like wildfire. His hands on my back pulled me close, holding on fiercely as our mouths worked against each other.

Still kissing me, Hank unbuttoned his shirt and removed it, laying it on the arm of the chair by the radio. He had on an undershirt, and a spray of hair tumbled over the neck. His chest and arms were muscular, the ridges and curves outlined by the cotton of his T-shirt, which clung to him slightly from the heat. The sweat on his chest formed a damp shadow beneath the whiteness, and his nipples swelled against the material.

Hank switched on the radio and the sounds of Glenn Miller's "Moonlight Serenade" spilled out into the dusky room. He came over and put his arms around my waist, holding me so that our bodies rubbed together and I could feel the rise and fall of his chest as he breathed. I rested my head on his shoulder and breathed in his scent as we made slow circles in the river of moonlight that slipped over the windowsill. He smelled of Burma-Shave lotion and soap, and the cotton of his undershirt was soft against my cheek.

As we danced, Hank hummed along with the song, his voice low in my ear. Having him in my arms filled me with a happiness I hadn't felt in a long time, and I ran my hands over the muscles of his back, just enjoying the feeling of another man's body, so hard and solid and familiar. When I raised my head, I saw that Hank was looking back at me, his eyes studying my face.

He kissed me again, his mouth warm and wet, my tongue slipping softly between his lips. He drew me in farther, his cheeks sucking gently as I kissed him. Breaking away, he began to unbutton my shirt, taking it off and laying it next to his on the chair. Then he grabbed the edge of my T-shirt and pulled it over my head, dropping it to the floor.

For a moment he simply stared at me. Then he smiled. "You look beautiful," he whispered. "Like some kind of angel come out of the shadows."

His hands ran over my naked torso, his fingers making me tremble as they danced over my skin. He touched the soft gold hair that rained down my chest and fell in a line to my crotch, tracing it with his finger. He brushed his fingertips over my nipples, making me catch my breath as he paused over them for a moment before moving on.

I helped him off with his undershirt as well, and we stood before each other. His chest was patterned with more of the hair I'd seen at his collar. It scattered out over his pecs and trickled down his belly in a thick, soft swatch. I embraced him and felt his chest rub against mine, the hair rough, the heat from our bodies forming a common skin between us where we touched.

Hank kissed my neck, running his tongue from my ear to my throat. My hands were in his hair as he moved over my chest, his lips surrounding my nipple and sucking. He slid to his knees slowly, letting his mouth linger on my tit before descending down my stomach to my navel, leaving behind a trail of desire.

Fumbling with my belt, Hank managed to undo the buckle and slide my pants down. His hands grasped my ass firmly as he buried his face in the crotch of my boxers. My cock, hard from his touch, was sticking out and he mouthed it through my shorts. His tongue licked at my shaft, wetting the cotton with spit as he worked from my tip to my balls, pushing his face between my thighs.

Tugging at the waistband, he yanked my boxers down to my feet, where they puddled with my pants. My prick swung free, sticking straight out from my body toward Hank's face. He ran his hands over my legs and under my balls, squeezing them gently. Leaning forward, he ran his tongue in a line from just above my nuts up my shaft until he reached the head. Opening his mouth, he slipped the entire length of my prick into his throat in one slow, teasing stroke. I groaned as his lips passed over inch after inch until they met my sac, his nose pressed against my light bush.

Hank was an expert cocksucker, bringing me to the point of coming several times but slowing down just as I was about to spill my load in his hungry mouth. Every so often he would give me a rest by taking one of my nuts into his mouth and sucking it before resuming his work on my prick.

I wasn't in a hurry to have it end, but I wanted to taste his body. I pulled out of his throat and brought him to his feet, dropping to my knees before him. Looking up at him, I unbuckled his pants and shoved them down his legs. My heart beat wildly as I waited to see what he'd been hiding beneath his uniform.

His boxers were stained with thick streaks of juice in the front, the head of his prick swelling tightly against them so that I could see its outline clearly. I pulled them down, too, and finally got a look at what was between his legs. His cock, longer and much thicker than mine, sprouted from an explosion of bush, the fat head pulling down over his low-hanging balls. A string of precum dripped from the tip, and I slurped it up, tasting the heady man scent that belonged to him, my tongue sliding against the smooth surface of his cockhead like hands over silk.

Hank's cock barely fit in my mouth, and my lips stretched uncomfortably to accommodate his width. But I loved the feeling of his meat filling my throat and got most of it down fueled by the sheer excitement of sucking his prick. Hank, seeing his big tool buried in me, pressed forward until the last few inches disappeared past my lips and his fat balls were swinging against my chin.

"Christ, Tom," he said. "No one's managed to get it all the way down before. Feels like slipping into a warm bath."

He began to rock his hips, pulling his cock out and sliding it back in gently as I sucked on the delicious shaft. As his length became slick from my sucking, it was easier to take all of him in. Massaging his balls with my hand, I ran my mouth up the underside of his prick to the head, milking precum from the slit. Hank's juice was musky and thick, and the taste of it intensified the need I had to have him in me.

After sucking on him for a few minutes, I stopped and pushed him into the big armchair. Hank leaned back in the soft cushions, putting his hands under his knees and pulling his legs back so that his feet were resting on the arms of the chair. His beautiful ass was spread before me, the thick globes of his cheeks inches from my face, his balls hanging deliciously down between his hairy thighs. Unlike his legs, his ass cheeks were smooth, the skin between them pink and bare.

I licked the crack of his ass, darting my tongue across his tight hole, running it in long strokes beginning behind his balls and moving down until it slipped into the wet pucker of his chute. Hank pushed against me, thrusting my tongue into his moist hole. I licked eagerly, kissing his hole and slicking it with my spit. Before long, I was exploring deep inside him, my tongue licking the walls of his tunnel as he writhed against my face.

While I ate out Hank's ass, I fisted his big cock, pressing his balls against my face as I ran my hand over his thick piece. He was leaking steadily from the rimming he was getting, and I was determined to give him more. I slurped up some of his quicksilver and used it to grease his hole, working my tongue as deeply into his ass as I could. Every time I sucked at his tender hole more lube dripped onto my fist, and I used it to jerk him off.

I felt his hands on my head, stopping me. "I want to make love with you," he said breathlessly.

I stopped working on his ass and he stood up. Taking my hand, he pulled me to my feet and led me to the bed, our cocks bobbing as we walked. I lay down and Hank lay on top of me, covering me with his body. The sheets of the bed were cool on my hot skin, and the combination of their touch, the warmth of the night, and the smell of Hank made me horny as hell. As we kissed, our hands traveled all over our bodies, caressing and exploring.

We were a tangle of sheets and bodies as we rolled over one another. Hank licked me all over, his mouth exploring my armpits, his tongue sinking into the valley of my ass as I sucked on his balls. He made love to me like no one else had ever done, allowing himself to do whatever brought pleasure to both of us. Every touch of his hands drew moans from my lips, every kiss drew pangs of desire from my balls until I was so worked up I thought that if he even touched me I'd spill my load.

I wanted Hank inside me, and when he was lying on top of me I brought my legs up around him, pushing his cock against my belly. There was a small bottle of hand lotion on my bedside table, and I handed it to him. Squeezing some into his hand, he rubbed it over his dick and onto my hole, pushing his finger past the tight ring of muscle and thrusting back and forth until I was loose enough. Kneeling between my thighs, he brought my legs up over his shoulders and slid his prick into my exposed butt.

His cock felt wonderful in my ass—thick and rock hard. His thrusts were easy and gentle, filling me and retreating in steady rhythm. As he made love to me, he ran his hands over my thighs and across my stomach. His chest fur brushed the undersides of my legs as he rocked in and out, my balls slapping against his stomach.

Hank began to move faster and faster as I loosened up. At the same time, I jerked on my cock, humping my fist in time with his thrusts. Hank put his hands under my knees and pushed my legs back. Pulling almost all the way out, he fucked just the first few inches of my chute, massaging my sensitive prostate with his big head.

A ripple began to fan out from my ass and cascade through my body as he deliberately brought me to the brink. I started to moan and Hank slammed into me, fucking me furiously. His balls pounded my ass, and he pulled my legs tight against him so that he could penetrate me as deeply as possible, his hands locked around my ankles.

That was all I needed. Hank pushed me over the edge and I started to fall. My cock twitched and a thick spray of spunk slathered my chest in sticky drops. I cried out, and my ass ring tensed around Hank's piece as I emptied my load again and again into the air, his still-thrusting prick urging the last drops from my aching balls. Hank also came, great waves of sticky heat filling my chute as he shot, his mouth open in a silent roar, his breath ragged.

Hank collapsed on top of me, my cum spreading out and sticking us together. He lay there for a few minutes, his softening cock still in me, his heart thumping against my chest. Then he kissed me gently and pulled out, rolling onto his back, his prick falling over his thigh. After a quick shower together, we slid between the sheets and slept until dawn, Hank with his arm around me and his soft cock pressing against my ass.

Hank and I spent every night of the next two months together, making love in my little room. Once we even did it in the darkened balcony of the town's one theater during a late showing of *Mrs. Miniver*, Hank sucking my cock while the wartime trials of Greer Garson and Walter Pidgeon flickered on the screen above us.

We were separated when the war called us to duty overseas— Hank to France and I to Germany. We managed to meet once in Paris, where we made love on a snowy winter night in a drafty apartment borrowed from a friend on leave. But it was hard to keep track of each other as the war moved from front to front and we were carried with it, and eventually the letters stopped coming.

Over the years I've thought several times about trying to find Hank again. But those were different times, and we're now both different people. My memories are mine and his belong to him, and I hope his are as sweet as mine. I still have a picture of Hank taken in Paris on our last day together, his laughing face captured in black and white. The edges are cracked from traveling in my rucksack from place to place as I moved across Europe, and it's a little faded now. But when I want to remember that first night I just look at it and everything comes back to me.

Home-Court Advantage

I hate basketball. I find it totally unwatchable. But I thought try-ing to make it sexy would be fun. Besides, there was always a group of Latino guys playing hoops on the court near my apart-ment in New York, and I found them really sexy.

As I watch Ray move around the court, I am transfixed by the way the muscles flow beneath his skin. There is something painfully beautiful about a man using his body so freely, and Ray is a very beautiful young man. Tall and muscular, he has retained the body of the swimmer he once was, and is still close enough to his youth that he is unconscious of the small ways his body will begin to fail him as he grows older. His brown hair has reddened from a summer of being outdoors, and his back still has the fading remnants of a burn from a day spent too long in the sun.

He is playing smoothly, maneuvering the ball between the other men as though their lunging bodies form the walls of a maze he must get through in order to win his freedom. The ball seems connected to his hands by invisible threads, passing from one to the other seamlessly as he weaves his way between his oppo-nents. His feet attack the asphalt in short, staccato bursts as he looks for an opening and takes it, darting past a big black man, who swears loudly when Ray lifts the ball skyward and follows it up toward the waiting net.

The ball slips from his fingertips, is on the verge of being swal-lowed by the steel mouth of the basket, when another hand shoots out of nowhere and crashes into it, sending it spinning away. The smile waiting to be born on Ray's face dies just as suddenly, twist-ing into a frown that scars his handsome face. He looks around to see who has done this to him, ruined his perfect shot.

It is a Latino boy. He appears to be about eighteen, uneasily straddling the line between adolescence and manhood. I have not seen him here before, but now that he has caught my interest, I am surprised that I did not notice him earlier. Short and dark, he is solidly built, the thick muscles of his bare chest pumped from hours of working out. He is wearing thin white gym shorts that set off his burnished skin and cradle his cock and balls in a heavy bulge. A St. Christopher medal hangs from his neck, a spark of brilliance in the afternoon light.

He glances over at Ray briefly and grins, a reef of white teeth rising between his full lips. He is not mocking, only acknowledging their shared moment, but Ray becomes angry. I can tell by the way his hands rest on his waist, the way he lets his head hang slightly as he kicks at the asphalt with his foot. When a teammate slaps him on the back in a gesture of support, he moves away.

The ball is back in play, passing from man to man like a sun falling through the sky. Ray is on the outside, determined to make up for his loss. He tries to put his mind back on the game, to focus only on getting the ball into his hands and taking it with him into the air. But the young man is with him at every step, watching for the smallest crack in Ray's game. The rivalry between Ray and this boy arouses something in me, the way they are simultaneously attracted to and distanced from each other, each needing the threat of the other to test his own strengths.

When Ray turns, the ball neatly pivoting with him, he comes face to face with his opponent, who grabs the ball easily, for the moment claiming it as his own. He is angry, and his anger is his downfall, his single-mindedness overtaking his every move. His normally confident steps falter as the need to win clouds his judgment and he misses several easy opportunities. When the Latino boy gets by him, neatly tucking the ball into the basket, Ray storms off the court.

He comes over to me, his eyes downcast, and stands silently as the other men continue to play. I don't look at him; don't say anything. But when I catch the Latino boy's eye, I wave to him. He trots over and stands in front of me.

"That's some really good playing you're doing out there, uh . . ."

"Luis," he says, and shakes his head as if to brush off my praise. "Thanks." He motions to Ray. "This guy doesn't make it very easy for me, though."

Ray mutters a response, wanting to get away from the boy as quickly as possible. He senses what is about to come and thinks that maybe he can pull me away before it happens. Luis doesn't seem to notice his agitation, his eyes back on the men as they continue to play.

"You look like you're working up quite a sweat," I say, and Luis nods. "Hot as hell out there today. Gonna get myself somewhere cool when I'm finished here."

I let a suitable pause fall, waiting for the natural rhythm of the seduction to swing back. I think this is the one, and I enjoy the game. "Why don't you come over to our place to cool off?" I ask. "We're just around the corner here. We can have a drink."

"Maybe," he says quickly, and I know that he will, that something in him understands what is being offered. He returns to the game, and after a few minutes during which Ray and I say nothing to one another, he comes back over.

As we walk home, Ray is silent, and I know that he is hurt that I have asked this boy to come home with us. When we get to the apartment, Ray drops into a chair and stares sullenly at Luis as I get glasses of iced tea from the kitchen. Luis downs his drink in one long swallow, then wipes his mouth on his arm. "That was good," he says. "I'm feeling better already."

I smile at him. "Why don't you take your shorts off," I say.

It is abrupt and evokes the response that I want. Luis looks at me for a moment, surprise turning his face into a frozen mask. He does not know if I am serious, nor what to do if he decides that I am. "I'm not really into that," he says unconvincingly. "I mean, I've never—"

"But you want to," I interrupt. "Don't you." It is a statement, not a question, and I know it is true. It's something behind the eyes that tells me, the same thing that told me Ray was ready when I'd seen him three years before pulling himself from the waters of a pool at the gym. The eyes are different, but the need is the same.

For a moment, anger roils behind his dark brown eyes and he looks as though he might try to leave. But I know that he won't, that he wants what's going to happen more than he's ever wanted anything before. When too much time has gone by, and he realizes that the space during which he could safely leave has slipped away and he has by his inaction committed himself, he begins to take off his clothes.

Looking first at Ray and then at me, he removes his sneakers and pulls his shorts down, pausing briefly before finally dropping them to the floor and revealing his cock. His body is hairless but for the swatch of closely cropped hair surrounding his prick, which is uncut and very thick. It hangs between his legs proudly, out of proportion to the rest of him. Despite his hesitation, his nakedness has made him easy, and he rubs his balls carelessly with one hand as he waits for me to tell him what to do. I don't look, but I know Ray is watching intently from his position behind me.

"Turn around," I tell Luis.

He turns, and I am rewarded by the sight of the firm globes of his beautiful ass. The flesh is lighter than the surrounding skin, the color of leaves in the fall against the coppery background of his body. The muscles of his back ripple down toward the flawless twin hills, forming a clean line leading into the dark crack that halves the smooth curve of his mounds. He stands with his legs planted apart, and I can see below his sac the foreskin-shrouded head of his cock hanging like a bat wrapped in its wrinkled wings asleep.

"Bend over," I order, the sight of his almost perfect ass pleasing me immensely.

Luis spreads his legs wider and lowers his torso so that his head is almost even with his knees. His hands are on his thighs supporting him, and his St. Christopher medal swings from his neck. As he moves his head lower, his ass spreads open and a dark pink flower blooms between the cheeks. The lips of his hole are smooth and soft, opened slightly by the stretching demanded of his muscles by the awkward pose.

I stand behind him, holding an ice cube that I have taken from my glass. Bringing it close to his skin, I move it over his back, the cold whispering above but not touching his flesh. I can sense him tensing with the anticipation of feeling the ice's touch and tease him by bringing it close, only to pull away again. When I finally press it into a spot between his shoulder blades, I feel him flinch as the cold penetrates his flushed skin.

I slide the ice over his back and descend toward his buttocks. Melting water follows behind my hand, slipping along the hollow of his spine in a thin silver line. When I reach the cleft of his ass cheeks, I lift the sliver of dying ice and watch as the cold water trickles in a narrow thread between his mounds and rinses over his asshole, making it twitch sharply. Drops roll down the smooth flesh below his pucker and hang deliciously from his wrinkled sac before falling wetly onto the floor between his feet.

Kneeling behind him, I lick the muscular curves of his cheeks, tasting the water where it clings to his warm skin. The space between his balls and his ass is smooth, and my tongue sweeps cleanly along it until I sink into the warm fold of his hole, wet with drops of ice water. He is very tight, and I suspect from the way he resists when I press against him that he has never had anything in his ass before. But I push insistently, and my tongue slides slowly into his warm opening, creating an ever-widening passageway as I add my spit to the water. I can feel the muscles loosening as I move further inside, welcoming the pleasure I am bringing to him, and finally he relaxes.

His ass is clean and hot, and eating his virgin hole makes me want even more of him. I look out of the corner of my eye and see that Ray has taken off his clothes and has his hand wrapped around his cock, jerking off slowly. He is still wearing the leather ring he put on before going to the park, and his balls are circled tightly by its grip, pushed slightly up and away from his body. Taking my mouth away from Luis, I stand up. He is still bent over, and I reach between his legs, grasping his balls tightly. His prick is hard as a rock, and I feel it slapping against my fingers as I tug on his nuts.

Pulling his balls down, I watch his asshole stretch, lengthening into a thin line, and I want to fuck him. But that's not what will happen, not yet anyway, and I push the thought to the back of my mind. Instead, I lick my middle finger and slide the tip into his ripe cherry. He bucks forward at my entrance, but I am still holding on to his nuts with the other hand, and he stops when he feels my fingers pull him back.

"Don't tell me you've never had anything up your ass before, Luis," I say, feigning surprise. "You never lie in bed at night fingering this tight hole of yours while you think about some man fucking you? Maybe one of your basketball buddies?" I lean down and let him feel my breath on his neck. "Bet you shoot a thick load all over your belly thinking about it. Am I right?"

Luis says nothing until I push further into him, the warmth of his chute around my hand making my balls wince impatiently. Then he moans, "Yeah. Yeah, sometimes."

I thrust into him until my palm is flat against his ass. He has loosened a little, and I am able to glide in and out of him, rotating my finger slightly so that he opens even more. The pink skin of his hole is deepening to a darker red as I finger him.

"Tell me about it," I prod him. "Tell me what you think about while you finger this hole."

He is groaning now and has to catch his breath before he answers. When he does, he speaks softly, pausing often as a low grunt interrupts his speech. "There's this guy works in a grocery store on my street. Real big guy. Hairy chest. Sometimes I think about doing stuff to him. Him doing stuff to me."

I am fucking him steadily now, adding another finger to the one already deep inside him. "Doing what?" I ask. "What do you want to do to him?"

"Christ," he grunts as I stretch his hole by spreading my fingers. "I think about sucking his dick, licking his fat hairy balls. I think about him sticking it up my ass in the back room."

I picture this in my mind, this boy being fucked from behind by another man, and the thought causes my prick to swell. "That's very good," I tell him, removing my finger and motioning for him to stand up straight. His cock is sticking up at an angle, and the thin skin is stretched tightly over a darkened head. While it hasn't become much longer, it is incredibly thick.

"Into the bedroom," I say, and Ray gets up, his prick bouncing in front of him. Luis follows him into the bedroom, and Ray lies on the big bed, his back against the pillows.

"Go over and kneel in front of Ray," I tell Luis.

He does as I've told him, positioning himself between Ray's spread thighs. Ray's cock rises straight up at Luis's face, and there is a skin of sticky precum slicking the head and the upper part of his shaft where he has been using it as lubricant. I slowly remove my shirt and shorts, letting Luis have a good long look at Ray's cock, and settle into a chair positioned across from them for just this purpose. Ray is looking at Luis hungrily. I can tell that he is looking forward to this, but he doesn't know that I have a surprise in store for him.

"Suck his cock," I tell Ray.

Ray looks at me, bewildered. This is not usually how it works, and he is caught off guard. Still, he does as I tell him, moving so that he is on his hands and knees in front of Luis, who is also con-

fused. He had been expecting to suck Ray's prick, and I know that
he is disappointed. It is all part of the play, making him wait.

I watch Ray as he reaches out and takes the big prick in his
hand, sliding the foreskin back slowly, his tongue slurping up the
thick ooze that comes from beneath it. I know that he loves this,
and that it both infuriates and arouses him to have me see so.
When I fuck him later this evening, after Luis is gone, I will make
him tell me what it tasted like, what it felt like in his throat.

When Luis's head is exposed, Ray slips it into his mouth, his
cheeks bulging with its width. Working slowly, he slides down the
thick shaft, forcing Luis's cock into his throat. Luis is still kneeling, his hands on Ray's shoulders for balance. Now he pushes his
hips forward, sinking the last inches into Ray's mouth. He moans
softly as Ray begins to move back up his dick, and I know that
Ray is using his tongue to tickle the young man's prick and urge
more juice from it. I feel ghostly echoes of this familiar trick on
my own shaft and think about the many times I've been in Luis's
position, the many times I've fucked Ray's mouth just like this.

Ray no longer cares that I am watching him and begins to suck
Luis's fat prick in earnest, his hand jerking the length of the tool
as his mouth caresses the tip. He is bent over Luis's crotch so that
his ass is sticking into the air. As he feasts on the hot flesh in his
throat, I get up and take a dildo from its place in a chest beside the
chair. Quickly lubing it, I come up behind Ray and slide it into his
exposed hole.

It is not overly large and goes in easily, but still Ray is taken by
surprise. I see him pause, Luis's cock half in and half out of his
throat, as he adjusts to the thickness in his chute. The dildo is settled firmly in Ray's ass, and I snap a leather lead attached to its
base to the ring around his balls to keep it in place. I give Ray's
cock a quick jerk and feel a spray of sticky wetness drip from his
piss hole onto my hand. When I bring my fingers to my lips, I
taste his familiar saltiness on them.

I return to my chair and watch Ray resume his work on Luis's
prick. He is sucking in long strokes that start at the base and
travel fluidly up to the tip. Luis is breathing heavily, and his fingers are starting to dig into Ray's shoulder. I tell Ray to stop, and
have him lie on his back. The dildo in his ass makes this uncomfortable, and he is forced to keep his legs spread.

"Work on his tits, Luis," I say. I know that Ray's nipples are still sensitive from a workout I gave them the night before, and I wait to see what he will do when Luis's mouth is on them. Luis moves his mouth across Ray's chest and finds one of his tender buds. As his lips close over it, he bites softly, and Ray cries out. Luis pulls away, but I order him back. "Keep sucking."

Obediently, he renews his work, his tongue licking at Ray's chest. Ray writhes beneath him as Luis's mouth beats at his sore tit, and Luis responds by sucking harder, working the other nipple with his fingers until Ray is almost crying. As he grows more confident, he strays from the nipple, moving his mouth into the hollow at Ray's throat and then, as Ray lifts his arm, into the patch of dark hair he finds hidden there. Ray has momentarily forgotten their rivalry and runs his hand along Luis's back, gripping the firm flesh of his ass tightly. After a few minutes, he puts his hands on Luis's shoulders and urges him down to his cock.

Luis is kneeling between Ray's legs, looking down at his dick. He leans forward and awkwardly takes the head of Ray's prick into his mouth. Not knowing what to do with his hands, he puts them on Ray's knees. He looks like he is drinking at a fountain.

"Lick the shaft," I encourage him.

He runs his tongue down the length of Ray's long cock, stopping at the balls and then moving back up, holding Ray's dick in his hand as he tastes it. Ray takes over and pushes Luis's head down onto his crank, sinking several inches into the young man's throat. Luis gasps and tries to pull away, but Ray holds him by the neck until he discovers that if he stops struggling he will be able to breathe even with the flesh in his mouth. He begins to move up and down Ray's cock, sucking hungrily at it as he discovers his rhythm.

I can tell by the look on Ray's face that Luis is doing well. He has his eyes closed, and as Luis works his mouth over the stiff prick, Ray's mouth twists in lines of pleasure. He puts his hands in Luis's black hair and urges him to move faster. Before long, the entire length of Ray's cock is disappearing between the eager lips.

I watch Luis's back as he sucks Ray's prick, the way the muscles bunch and relax, the way his ass rests on his heels as he rocks slightly back and forth. His cock is still hard. It slaps against the bed as he moves, and I imagine that the rasping of the sheets against his foreskin must be agonizing. It is probably his first time sucking another man's cock, and watching him discover the power of it arouses me. I think once more about sticking my dick into his hole and squeeze my balls tightly. My cock is hard, but I don't touch it. I like to feel the pressure building inside, wrapping its strong fingers around my prick and gripping it tighter and tighter.

Luis is fumbling with the leather strap that encircles Ray's balls. Although I have not told him to do this, I am pleased by his initiative, and don't stop him. When it is off, he stops sucking Ray's cock and looks at it. "Put it on," I tell him.

He wraps the strap around his fat balls and snaps it in place. Immediately, his prick fills with blood and swells even larger. He strokes his dick and shudders at the increased sensation of his fingers on his skin.

"Use the dildo," I command. He puts his hand on the base protruding from Ray's hole and pulls on it, sliding it a few inches out. Then he pushes it back in, fucking Ray's ass slowly. He positions himself so that his knees are on either side of Ray's neck, his head between Ray's legs and his engorged tool sliding over Ray's face. As he moves the dildo in and out, Ray sucks on his cockhead, until they are moving in time with one another, the dildo entering Ray's hole as Luis's cock pulls out of his throat.

As I watch them, I am amazed at how naturally the inclination toward pleasure comes. Luis seems to instinctively know what will please him, where to place his cock so that Ray can best service it. In time, he will become an expert at lovemaking, and I envy him the experiences he has yet to have. As he fucks Ray, Luis mouths his nuts as well, his lips picking up the heavy balls and exploring them. I know that Ray will not be able to hold off much longer, so I tell Luis, "Fuck him."

The word is harsh and strikes Luis like a hand across his face. I know that he has never done this, taken another man, and that he is not sure how it is done. But something buried deeply inside him calls out, and his body responds. He pulls the dildo completely out of Ray's chute, then positions himself between his legs. Ray makes no move to stop him, and I know he wants this as much as I do, wants to be this man's first.

Luis puts Ray's legs over his shoulders and points his cock at his asshole. He does not know to go slowly, and plunges fiercely into Ray's depths. Even though his ass has been loosened by the dildo, Luis's width is hard to take, and Ray's breath escapes from him in a sharp gasp. But Luis has begun, and he can't stop. He pulls out and slams himself again into Ray's hole, their skins colliding with a smacking sound. St. Christopher is dashed repeatedly against his chest as he thrusts quickly and savagely, his big tool plowing into Ray repeatedly, his hands gripped tightly around Ray's ankles.

I know he will come quickly and begin to stroke my aching cock. I watch his ass dimple and release as he pumps Ray's hole and think how beautiful the two of them are. Ray's head is thrown back on the pillows, his mouth open as his breath comes ragged and short. I have fucked him like this many times, and I know the sweet warmth of his ass well. But seeing him from the outside, as a spectator, I can take in the whole of him as he responds to the dick inside him, watch as he succumbs to the cock in his ass.

As Luis continues his thrusts, Ray shoots his load, splatters of white scattering across the bed like stars. His skin is streaked with his jism, long splashes of it crisscrossing his chest, speckles of it clinging to his hair and dotting his face. Luis sees it, too, and comes. Although his shot erupts deep inside Ray's ass, it is no less spectacular, waves of pleasure rippling across his face and seeming to roll through his whole body as he experiences his first time with another man and finds that it is what he has been waiting his whole life for.

I come thinking about his joy, a torrent spouting up onto my belly as I lean back and release the pressure in my overloaded nuts. As the drops of cum hit my chest and begin to slip down toward my crotch, I see Luis pull out of Ray. He rolls onto his back, a smile pulling at his mouth and his still-hard cock flat against his belly, and I know that the game has just begun.

The Blue Dragon

I was sitting at my favorite sushi bar one night, watching the chef form the rice, and the opening of this story came to me. I find food very sensual, and I wanted to play with that theme a little. By the way, there really is a type of fish that can cause the eater to have hallucinations, although I've never tried it myself.

The first thing I noticed about him was his hands. The fingers were long and thin, the nails rounded and cut short. He was rolling a rice ball, scooping the sticky white grains from the big heated pot at his side and then shaping it in his palm until it was a perfect oblong. When he had it completed, he took a sliver of fish—pale pink with an edge of yellow fatty skin—and laid it over the waiting bed. He leaned over the counter and placed the fish on the small wooden board in front of me.

"Tuna," he said simply. "You will like."

I nodded my thanks and picked the rice up with my chopsticks, lifting it carefully to my lips. The fish was fresh, with a hint of sea still on its skin, and melted into the smooth taste of the rice. It was delicious, and I smiled.

"It's very good," I said to him. "Tastes wonderful."

He nodded his satisfaction and went back to his work. I enjoy sushi, especially when it's made correctly by an experienced chef who knows his work. Many people shudder at the idea of eating raw fish, but sushi is one of the most pleasing of the Japanese art forms, requiring as much skill as a delicate water-and-ink painting or the three perfectly worded lines of a haiku. It takes years of practice to learn just how to roll the rice into a shape that is not too small or too large and how to slice the fish correctly so that it fills the mouth with a subtle taste, hinting at more but not overwhelming.

Because of my work as a journalist with an international investment magazine, I travel frequently to Japan. My favorite city is Osaka, on the southern side of Honshu, the largest of the Japanese islands. Situated on a beautiful bay surrounded by green mountains, Osaka has one of the largest outdoor fish markets in the world. The tuna, mackerel, sea trout, and octopus are lifted in great dripping nets from the holds of the boats that crowd the piers and dropped, shining and flopping, onto the decks, where fishermen and merchants buy and trade until the catch is gone. Minutes after the buyers disperse, the fish are seen in the countless stalls that line the water's edge, laid out on beds of crushed ice for buyers to inspect.

The best fish end up in the sushi bars, the traditional meeting places of the Japanese. There the sushi chefs slice and arrange the day's catch into simple, beautiful shapes eaten by the customers that crowd the rooms heady with thick smoke from the hand-rolled cigarettes popular in the city. Over steaming cups of green tea, diners point with their chopsticks to what they want, watching as it is prepared in front of them, nodding their approval when something pleases them, frowning when it does not.

Whenever I am in Osaka I make a point of going to the sushi bars, trying the specialties of the different chefs. I had never been to this particular bar before, but the concierge at my hotel recommended it, saying that the service was the best in Osaka and that it had some special offerings available nowhere else in the city. It had taken me some time to find it, wandering through the crowded streets and asking directions several times before finding the doorway, unmarked, between a discount electronics store and a brothel offering to fulfill my wildest dreams for only four thousand yen.

The concierge had been correct; this was the best sushi I'd ever had. The fish was hours old, the rice grains sticky and sweet. And the chef was a true artist. He handled the knives flawlessly, deftly peeling slices from the pieces of salmon and tuna and chopping the cucumbers and seaweed into ribbons translucent as the thinnest paper. He moved quickly and fluidly, finding his way around the table without hesitating. He made a roll of eel, wrapping everything up in a slip of crisp seaweed paper and slicing it into six pieces. He brushed the pieces with the thick, sweet sauce used to bring out the subtle flavors of the eel and then laid them in front of me.

He watched my face as I ate, waiting to see if I liked his creation. When I nodded my satisfaction, he broke into a smile. Waving the bartender over, I asked him to bring a bottle of the chef's favorite beer, a traditional way of thanking him. When it arrived, I toasted him with my own glass.

It was quiet in the bar, so we began to talk as he worked. His English was very good, he told me, because he had once spent a year at the university. His name was Kamo, and he had been studying the art of sushi for over ten years. Like many Japanese, Kamo was slight of build, with delicate features and a fine-boned face. His black hair had been cut short on the sides but left long in front so that it hung down over his forehead and nearly covered one eye. His dark blue robe was tied in front with a sash of white.

As the evening progressed, Kamo prepared many different things for me—treasures dipped from the seas, like soft folds of urchin rich with the taste of salt, and the firmer pieces of conch, the flesh pinkish gold and sweet on my tongue. Most of the things I had had before, but he also presented me with several things I had never seen and for which he knew only the Japanese words. Each time he gave me something new he watched expectantly until I nodded my delight, then his face broke open in a happy smile.

As I watched Kamo work, I began to wonder what it would be like to make love with him. His movements were very sensual, controlled and fluid yet at the same time expressing great pleasure from doing his job well. I imagined him moving his hands over my body in that same attentive way and felt a stirring in my groin. The more I thought about Kamo, the more worked up I got. I envisioned sliding against his smooth, naked skin, feeling the hardness of his cock pressing against my leg as I kissed his soft mouth. I could almost feel his thick dark hair beneath my fingers as I pictured his head moving up and down my prick, his lips warm and welcoming, his tongue teasing.

The Japanese are generally very reserved, and I knew that asking Kamo straight out to come back to my hotel with me was out of the question. Besides, I didn't even know if he was at all interested. He had been friendly all evening, but for all I knew he had a wife and three little kids somewhere. I decided the best thing to do was just enjoy the great food he was placing in front of me and be grateful for an evening of the best sushi I'd ever had. But the more my growing hard-on pressed insistently against my pants, the more I thought about rubbing my hands over his smooth ass, and the more I wanted him.

It was almost midnight, and the bar had pretty much emptied out. I was drinking a cup of tea and wondering if I was going to end up shooting my load into my hand in my hotel room when Kamo asked me if there was anything else he could get me. I was just about to say no when I decided to go for broke. "Well," I said, hoping he wouldn't see how nervous I was, "I understand there are some very special things to see in this part of town. I'd sure like to see them, and I was hoping that maybe you could show them to me."

Kamo looked at me, a strange light rising in his eyes. He smiled slightly and nodded his head. "I thought that perhaps you would be interested in something special. I see by the way that you enjoy what I make for you that you appreciate the unusual."

I grinned back at him. "Yes, I do," I said. "The more unusual the better."

Kamo wiped his hands on a wet cloth. "You wait here," he said. "We will go where I will show you something I think you will like very much."

Kamo went into the back of the bar. As I waited for him, I started imagining all of the things that I could do to him. My cock was rock hard, and I couldn't wait to free it from its prison in my pants and let Kamo go to work on it. I felt Kamo's hand on my shoulder and turned around. He had put on a dark robe over his clothes. "We will go now," he said.

When we exited the bar it was raining, a strong downpour typical of the coastal towns. Because it had been clear when I left my hotel, I had foolishly not brought an umbrella. Luckily, Kamo had one, and I held it over us as we scurried through the narrow streets. While I could hardly tell where one street melted into another, Kamo moved us swiftly through the maze of buildings that make up the area near the wharf. Despite the umbrella, we were both soaking wet by the time he led me up a narrow stone stairway and stopped in front of a big red door.

Producing a key from the pocket of his robe, Kamo fitted it into the hole and turned it sharply, pushing at the same time. The door swung inward, and we entered. Inside, I shook the rain off as best I could and looked around. We were standing in a small entryway with a stone floor and bare white walls. Directly across from the one we had entered was another door.

"Is this your house?" I asked Kamo.

He nodded. "It is a very old place, once used by Shinto monks. Now it is home."

Kamo led me to the other door, stopping first to remove his shoes. When I bent to remove my own shoes, he stopped me. "I will do it for you," he said as he knelt in front of me. "You are my guest."

He quickly untied my laces and pulled my shoes off, holding my foot in his hand. His fingers grasped my sole gently, rubbing slow circles over the skin for a moment before releasing me. Placing the shoes on a small mat next to the door, he rose and opened the door. Stepping through, I found myself in a large room filled with soft light that came from several oil lamps that burned with golden tongues of flame. There was no furniture but for a low wooden table surrounded by many large pillows thrown over thick carpets that covered the floor.

The only other thing of interest was a large fish tank that stood in one corner. About four feet long and three feet high, it was filled with green plants and a single piece of white coral. The water shone with pale light, and bubbles rose from one corner. I could see shadows darting amongst the waving leaves, but they never stayed in one place long enough for me to see what they were.

"You are wet," Kamo said. "Come with me and you can dry yourself."

He led me behind a large screen at one end of the room and into another, smaller space. From the futon on the floor, I guessed it was his bedroom. Kamo opened a small chest and removed a white robe. He handed it to me. "You may change in there," he said, pointing to the bathroom.

I went into the bathroom and shut the door. Removing my wet clothes, I hung them on a hook behind the door. The rain had temporarily sent my boner into submission, and my dick hung limply between my legs. But once I started thinking about Kamo's body, it jerked back to life. I tied the belt of the robe loosely around my waist and went out to see what Kamo was doing.

He wasn't in the bedroom, so I checked the living room. Kamo was arranging pillows around the table. While I had been in the bathroom he had himself changed into a white robe. When he saw me, he waved for me to come sit down. Confused, I walked over and sat where he pointed. I wondered now if we'd both had the same thing on our minds when we left the bar. While I was aching to sink my prick into his ass, he had laid out plates like we were having a dinner party.

Kamo went over to the fish tank and scooped something up with a net. Returning to the table, he placed in front of me a small bowl. Inside it was a fish. About three inches long, it was a strange blue color, with two yellow stripes on either side of its head. Kamo disappeared again and returned with a round bowl, about a foot across, and a bottle. Putting both on the table, he sat across from me. "You are going to see something very special," he said.

Still puzzled, I watched as he poured a clear liquid from the bottle and filled the bowl almost to the top. Then he reached into the smaller bowl, lifted out the fish, and dropped it splashing into the other one. For a minute the fish sat at the bottom of the bowl, not moving. Then it began to swim in circles, its mouth opening and closing rapidly. It moved faster and faster, as if running from something. As it did, its blue color began to brighten, as if it were being lit up from the inside.

Finally, after circling the bowl madly for several minutes, the fish stopped completely, its mouth open wide. Kamo waited to make sure it would not begin swimming again, then reached into the bowl and lifted the fish out. Picking up a long, sharp knife, he sliced the fish quickly, peeling away the electric blue skin to reveal the bright pink flesh beneath. After cutting two strips, he placed them on a small white plate.

"What is it?" I asked.

"Very rare," Kamo said. "Fish is very poisonous. If cut wrong, it can paralyze you instantly. But done correctly, it can bring great pleasure."

I looked at the thin strips on the plate. "What was it swimming in?"

"Sake and herbs," Kamo answered, lifting one of the slices in his fingers and raising it to my lips. "Eat quickly before its power fades."

Reluctantly, I opened my mouth. Kamo placed the fish on my tongue, his fingers momentarily brushing my lips. I waited to feel my body becoming motionless. But when nothing happened, I concentrated on the taste that was filling my mouth. A sensation both hot and sweet was soaking into my tongue and traveling into my throat. I swallowed the fish and felt the warmth move with it into my belly. It was like nothing I had ever tasted before. As I tried to pinpoint exactly what it was like, I felt my head begin to swim. My mind began to cloud over, and I shook my head to regain my focus.

"No," Kamo said through the veil that was falling over my mind. "Do not fight it. Let the pleasure come."

Relaxing, I felt my head clear again, leaving behind a sense of heightened awareness. At the same time, my arms and legs began to feel heavy, as if a great weight were pressing on them, and everything around me seemed brighter and warmer. I looked at Kamo and saw him pick the other piece of fish from the plate and eat it. He closed his eyes, and when he opened them a few moments later, I saw again the brightness I had first noticed in the bar.

He rose from his seat and came around to my side of the table. "Come," he said, holding out his hand. "We are ready now."

My body refused to move on its own, and Kamo had to help me rise. With slow steps, I followed him to an area of the room where the floor was thick with pillows the dark blue of midnight. Kamo pulled at the belt at my waist and let my robe fall open. He slid his hands underneath it and pushed it off my shoulders, letting it fall to the floor so that I was standing in front of him naked. Because I was held in the grip of the strange fish's drug, I could only stand while he looked at me, feeling like a statue being perused by a museum visitor.

Kamo reached out and ran a hand lightly over the dark fur of my chest, my skin tingling where his fingers crossed it. "You are very beautiful," he said. "I like your hair very much."

I laughed, knowing that the fact that he did *not* have hair was exactly what I liked. My voice sounded low and far away, like someone calling through a rainstorm. As if pushing my way through water, I reached out to remove his robe, but he stopped me by taking my hand and pulling me down onto the soft pillows. I sank easily into their softness and lay back, letting myself fall into them so that I was reclining with Kamo positioned between my spread legs.

He ran his fingers down my belly and to my waiting cock,

which was hanging half-hard across my thigh. His long fingers circled the thickness of my stiffening shaft and squeezed lightly, stroking it to life. "It's beautiful," he whispered appreciatively, as my prick filled to its full length.

I closed my eyes, the feeling caused by eating the fish filling my head, and waited to feel my cockhead slip in between his lips. But Kamo seemed content just to keep jerking me off. While his one hand kept up a steady rhythm on my dick, his other hand went under my balls, cupping my big nuts in his hands. "They are like the fruits of the lemon tree," he said, smiling up at me. "Round and firm."

Right then I didn't care what he thought they looked like. Although I found it hard to move, the rest of my senses seemed to have intensified. His fingers brushing my balls were sending bursts of excitement through my belly, and I just wanted to have his tongue on them. "Suck them," I whispered as best I could, putting my hand on his head and using what was left of my strength to grab a fistful of his black-blue hair in my fingers. Wrapped in my grip, his hair was soft and thick. I spread my legs wider and pushed his face between them until I felt his nose at the base of my cock. His tongue snaked out and tickled my aching nuts, licking in slow circles around first one and then the other.

Kamo worked his way under my sac and lifted my legs so that he could get at the sensitive area above my asshole. His mouth moved over my skin slowly and deliberately, covering every inch of my flesh with kisses that burned like cold fire. His delicate movements were making me crazy, and I couldn't wait to see what he had in store for my cock.

All of a sudden I felt him put one of his fingers, wet with spit, at the opening of my hole. I opened my mouth to ask him what he was doing, but nothing came out. After pressing gently but insistently for a moment, his finger slid inside, my ass muscles closing around its thin length. Kamo fingered me for a minute while his mouth worked on my balls, then he pulled out. Reaching into the pocket of his robe, he removed a string of silver beads. Each one was about half an inch in diameter, and the string was about six inches long.

I thought he was going to tie it around my balls like a cock ring, but instead he took the first bead and placed it against my hole, pushing it inside easily. He did this with each of the other beads, until the whole string of them was inside my ass and all that was left was a short length of string hanging from my pucker. I didn't know what the hell he was doing, but it sure felt good. I could feel the balls inside me, moving back and forth as I rocked against the pillows.

This whole time Kamo was still wearing his robe. Now he knelt with his back to me and let it fall off of his shoulders. My eyes went wide as I saw what he had kept hidden from me. The pure white skin of his back was covered with a tattoo of a dragon. Its head was centered between his shoulders, and its body stretched down toward his buttocks and then disappeared, its tail sweeping around to his stomach. The dragon was covered in thousands of tiny scales, each one shaded in perfectly in blue. The fine lines were etched on his body like veins running just below the skin. The detail was amazing and looked as though it had taken months to complete.

Kamo turned to me, his eyes oddly bright. "You wished to see something special," he said. "It is special enough for you?" he asked.

I stared back at him, unable to move my lips. The dragon's tail curved around his waist and down his groin, the end disappearing under his balls and circling back up the other side so that the base of his prick was encircled by it. His entire body appeared to be shaved completely smooth, not even a single hair marring his pubic area.

Kamo stretched himself on top of me, his mouth finding mine, and I pushed my tongue roughly between his lips. Kamo kissed me back, his mouth drawing me in. As he sucked at my tongue, I felt him grind his stomach against my cock, his hairless skin sliding along the pulsing shaft. Reaching down, Kamo moved my hands so that they were cupping his ass, the fingers closed around the curves of his buttocks so that I felt their roundness against my palms. Kamo pressed back against me and ran his mouth over my neck in a rush of hot kisses. His white skin shone out against the sea of blue pillows we were floating in like a strange, delicate fish.

As I lay under him, the strange paralysis holding me tightly, Kamo moved over my chest, biting softly on my nipples and rubbing his cheek against the hair that covered my pecs. The fact that I could not move my hands to touch him through the fog that had enveloped me increased the longing in my balls, and I wanted to cry out for him to satisfy me.

Finally, he moved down my belly toward my anxious cock. Without touching it, he placed his lips on the tip, sucking only the head and caressing it with his tongue as he lapped up the stream of sticky fluid that had begun to flow from my slit. Slowly he moved down the length of the shaft. I was amazed that he could get such a thick piece of meat into his small mouth, but he had no trouble. Soon his lips were pushed into my bush, and I was throbbing deep inside him. He moved back up my cock, his throat pulsing around it like a warm hand.

Kamo began to move quickly up and down my dick, his lips sliding easily over it. Every motion of his mouth felt like a thousand tongues caressing my cock. I felt my balls starting to tighten and knew that if he kept it up I was going to lose my load down his throat before I had a chance to fuck his beautiful ass. Kamo seemed to sense it, too, because he stopped sucking me. Moving up, he straddled my chest, his smooth legs holding me tightly between them.

His cock was hard now, jutting up and away from his body. It was perfectly formed, the sculpted head round and tapered atop the straight shaft. His balls hung neatly in a sac of smooth skin, and the dragon's tail curled perfectly around them both. Kamo moved forward so that I could suck his exquisite prick. It slipped in easily until not only the shaft, but the balls as well, were filling my mouth. I sucked hungrily, eating up the delicious flesh that slid in and out of my throat with each movement of Kamo's thrusts. I let Kamo's balls slip out of my mouth so that I could feel them against my chin as I blew him.

As I sucked his cock, Kamo fingered the tight slit of his asshole. He moaned as he slipped one finger in, pushing roughly to get through the small opening. Pulling himself from my mouth, he moved back until his ass was resting against the head of my prick. Feeling the smooth flesh of his buttocks against my aching piece, I almost washed his back with a wave of cum, but I was able to hold back. I didn't think my big tool would ever get into his tight hole, but he pressed against me until the head of my prick pushed between his ass lips. Slowly I entered him, my head parting the walls of his chute like a boat moving through the sea. I groaned loudly as he surrounded me with his warmth, his tight ass swallowing my meat greedily.

I looked at Kamo's face and saw that his eyes were shut tight, a smile crossing his face. He had his hands on my chest, and his fingers tugged gently at my tits while I slid into him. When I was fully inside him, he began to slide back and forth slowly, fucking himself with my dick. I lay beneath him, unable to lift my hands to touch his skin but filled with intense desire as I watched him pleasure himself with my tool.

As Kamo pumped my cock, something caught my eye, and I noticed for the first time that there was a mirror behind and to the left of where we were lying. A big antique frame sat on the floor, and in the large glass I could see the shadowy form of Kamo riding my prick. It moved up and down with him, my cock disappearing into his tight hole and reappearing as he devoured inch after inch of me. Above me his face was a mask of delight, his eyes and mouth reflecting the pleasure he was feeling deep inside him.

Looking again in the mirror, I caught my breath. While the outlines of our bodies were barely visible in the shadows, the dragon tattoo on Kamo's back was sharply defined. Just like the skin of the fish we had eaten, the dragon radiated with a luminous blue light. Each line and curve shone as though coursing with strange blood, seemed in fact to almost move across Kamo's back. I watched as it pulsed and flowed on his back, the claws scratching at his shoulders, the mouth opening in a silent roar. Kamo seemed to take no notice of what was happening beneath his skin, rising and falling along my prick in heated strokes, his cock slapping against my stomach as he moved.

I wanted to run my hands over his back, to see if I could feel some of the movement I saw reflected in the glass. But I was still bound to the floor by the mysterious weight. Whatever was happening to Kamo didn't appear to cause him any pain, so I watched silently as the dragon twisted and turned over his flesh. The harder he thrust against me, the harder the dragon writhed in the mirror.

As fascinated as I was with the strange events, the rising heat in my groin was a stronger attraction. Kamo began to push my cock deeply into his tight ass. As he did, he reached behind me and grasped the string that was hanging from my hole. Still riding me, he pulled on the string, and the beads slipped one at a time from my chute. The feeling was unbelievable and sent me into a shuddering, out-of-control rush of pleasure like nothing I'd ever felt before. This seemed to break the invisible chains that wrapped around my body, and I cried out, my voice echoing through the room as all of the passion that had been building up in my throat spilled out at once.

Now that I was able to move again, I plunged one last time into Kamo's depths, my load crashing into him in a shuddering wave as I squeezed his ass in my hands. I could feel the cum gushing from my prick as I pumped more and more cream into him. Kamo continued to work my prick with his ass muscles as he came, too, long ropes of ivory squirting from his bobbing cock, falling on my chest and splashing my neck. At the same time, his eyes flew open. They glowed with the same mysterious blue light as the dragon and appeared to see nothing. His mouth was stretched wide, mouthing but not voicing his ecstasy.

Then he shut his eyes, and when he opened them again they were the same black color they had always been. He collapsed against my chest, my cock still inside him, and lay still. I ran my hand over his back, tracing the muscles from his shoulders down to where I could feel my cock enter his asshole. I half expected to feel the dragon's scales under my fingertips but touched only warm skin. Inside the mirror, the glass was dark, the only reflection that of Kamo's body on mine.

Turning the Tables

They say that the biggest homophobes are the ones who want to find out what it's all about. . . .

Being a fairly quiet guy, I usually don't go in for political things like marches or demonstrations, preferring to lend a hand by writing letters and checks. But after weeks of hearing gay-bashing politicians on the news trying to win right-wing votes in upcoming elections and reading their hateful editorials in the press about how people like me are after the children of America, I figured that after thirty-three years it couldn't hurt me to support my community a little bit by showing up in person for something. So when some of my friends asked me to go with them to a rally supporting a local gay candidate for state human rights commissioner, I said I would.

When I got to the park where the rally was being held, there were several hundred people there. Many of them were wearing pink triangle pins and carrying signs voicing their particular concerns, from antidiscrimination legislation to domestic partnership rights. A large number wore the familiar red ribbons of the AIDS crisis and passed out safer-sex information and condoms. I pocketed a rubber handed to me by a shirtless muscular man with a shaved head and a tattoo on his rippled abdomen that said HIV+. Then I spotted my friends and went over to join them.

The rally started a few minutes after I arrived, and it was really amazing. The candidate, a woman who had spent many years in public service and had recently come out, spoke about the importance of rights for lesbians and gay men. Each time she said something the crowd agreed with there were whistles and clapping. When she brought her lover on stage with her, the place went wild with cheering. Everything was going really well when I heard some commotion behind me. "Hey, fag boys," a deep, mocking voice yelled out. "I've got a nine-inch dick that hasn't shot off in a couple of days. How would one of you like to drain it for me?"

I turned around and saw a group of college-aged men standing several feet away. One of them, a big jockish guy wearing a Yankees sweatshirt, was pointing at us and grinning. "See," he said. "I told you that would get the fairies' attention."

I started to just turn away from the jerk and ignore him when something inside stopped me. Maybe it was the rally, maybe it was just a lot of pent-up frustration; I'm not really sure. Whatever it was, before I knew it I was walking over to the guy. Stopping right in front of him, I looked him in the eyes as I said, "Nine inches, huh? Who's it belong to, your mother or your girl-friend?"

The man's face reddened with rage as his buddies started laughing at him. "Fuck you, faggot," he screamed. "No pansy talks to me that way."

Not feeling like getting into a fight with the guy, I walked back to my friends, leaving the fuming man yelling insults at my back. As I did, a large group of men and women closed in around me and blocked the enraged asshole, who was trying to get away from his friends. A small woman wearing a Lesbian Avengers hat walked up to him and said, her voice filled with quiet rage, "Unless you want a whole bunch of really angry dykes to show you out, I suggest you leave. Now."

The man looked at her and spat on the ground. "Fucking lezzie," he snarled. "You need a man to show you how it's done." The woman didn't move, silently standing her ground until the guy and his friends finally backed off and walked away. They left quickly, the crowd chanting "shame, shame, shame" until they had disappeared from sight. The whole experience made me feel very alive, as though I had stood up to the class bully and won. While I didn't even know the woman who had supported me, I felt like we had fought the battle together. When the rally was over, I walked back to my apartment feeling very proud of myself.

I live in a warehouse district, made up largely of meat-packing and storage facilities that are crowded with workmen during the day but empty at night. I like it that my neighborhood is nearly always deserted after six o'clock; it's kind of like living in some sort of ancient ruins. After the noise and excitement of the rally, it was nice to be surrounded by peace and quiet. The sky was dusky with oncoming night as I made my way through the empty streets, and I was enjoying the descending evening shade.

I was taking my usual shortcut through the alley running between two old deserted ironworks near my building, and wasn't really paying much attention to what was going on, when suddenly someone came rushing up behind me and pushed me against a wall. The breath was knocked out of me as my body slammed into the bricks, and I felt the weight of a large man pressing against me. I've been mugged twice since moving to the city, so my first thought was that the guy would just grab the wallet out of my back pocket and leave.

"Thought you were really cute back there, didn't you, queer boy?" a voice hissed in my ear. My heart froze as I recognized it as the voice of the guy who had harassed me at the rally. He must have followed me all the way home. "You and that dyke bitch making me look dumb in front of everyone," he continued, pushing me more forcefully against the wall so that my face was scraping against the rough brick. "Well, now you're the one who's going to look bad, soon as I finish roughing your pretty face up a little."

I thought about screaming for help, but I knew the chances of anyone being around to hear me at that hour were small. Besides, it would just make the guy crazier than he obviously already was. I was on my own. The guy had bent my arm behind me when he shoved me, and one hand was still on my wrist. His other one was on my collar, pushing against my neck. There wasn't much I could do.

"Let's just take a little trip inside here," he said, pushing me through an open doorway and into a cavernous room filled with old bits of industrial equipment and other trash, the remnants of the foundry that had thrived during the days when the city was an active shipping port. "We don't want to draw any attention to ourselves, now, do we?" he said mockingly as he pushed me roughly in front of him. He continued to hold my arm behind my back as he looked around. "There's got to be something around here I can use to teach you a lesson," he said.

While he was searching, I tried to think back to what my friend Anne had taught me about self-defense after the last time I'd gotten mugged. I'd thought it was all a waste of time until Anne, who weighs about 90 pounds, had me on the floor with her knee at my throat in less than three seconds flat. She had taught me a couple of things, but it had been a long time ago, and I wasn't sure I remembered what to do. But then, just as at the rally, I felt myself overcome by rage at the man whose hands were digging into my arm.

Taking a deep breath, I pushed back against my attacker, throwing him off balance just enough so that I was able to bring one foot up and stomp down on top of his as hard as I could. At the same time, I broke free from his grip and, bringing my arm up, slammed my elbow in the direction of his face. I felt it connect with his flesh and heard the sound of bone smacking against bone as I drove him backward with the blow.

Wheeling around, I saw the man standing behind me holding his hands to his nose. Blood was dripping from his fingers, and the front of his sweatshirt was stained with drops of red. An expression of surprise was on his face as he looked down at the blood and saw what I had done, and his eyes were dark with pain. Before he could come at me again, I ran toward him and tackled him, my arms going around his waist as we both tumbled to the floor.

I landed on top of him, hearing the sharp intake of air as his back smacked against the concrete. My knee was between his legs, and I held his wrists over his head, my body pinning him to the floor. While he was a big man, he was only a couple inches taller than I, and my anger was making me even stronger than usual. I looked down at his bloodstained face. "Looks like things didn't exactly turn out the way you wanted," I said.

"I'm going to kill you, you bastard," he yelled, trying unsuccessfully to throw me off.

Putting my knee on his stomach so that he couldn't move, I pulled the belt from around my waist. Holding his wrists together, I wound the thin strip of leather around them and pulled it tight, sliding the end through the center several times to secure his hands. When I was sure that he couldn't get loose, I eased up on him and put my hand on his stomach. Fumbling with his buckle, I pulled it open and yanked his belt off, then threaded it through the bonds around his wrists so that it acted as a kind of leash.

Standing up, I pulled on the belt, bringing him to his knees. He tried briefly to scramble to his feet and run, but a quick kick in the chest pushed him back to his knees. "Don't bother," I told him. "I

can't have you following me home, and I want to put you someplace where you can sit for a while and think things over before
the cops come get you. And don't bother screaming, because you
know as well as I do that nobody's going to hear you."

Making him walk on his knees, I led him into a corner of the
warehouse where steel catwalks crossed overhead. Several sky-
lights above us let in the moonlight that had crept in as night fell,
and we stood surrounded by the pale light. Moving behind him, I
threw one end of the belt over the crossbars of the walkway
above. Then I pulled it down so that his arms stretched up and he
had to get to his feet. When he was standing, his knees buckled
slightly so that he couldn't quite get his balance, I secured the belt
around the metal bar. There was no way he could break out of it,
and he stood glaring at me as I smiled triumphantly. "What a
pretty sight," I said. "A fag basher all tied up nice and pretty like
a punching bag for me to work out some of my aggression on."

"Fuck you," he said. "You wouldn't even know what the hell to
do with a real man, you fucking pansy. It was just a lucky shot you
got the first time around."

"I don't know," I said, walking over and running my hand over
his bloodied face. "Looks like pretty good work to me." He tried to
pull his face away, but I held it tightly in my grip and looked into
his eyes. Some of the anger I'd seen earlier had been replaced by
fear, but I still saw a lot of rage roiling behind the darkness.

"What is it you're afraid of, anyway?" I said. "You afraid that
maybe we're just as good as you are; that in fact we're just like
you?" I ran my hand over his sweatshirt. "You afraid we're just as
good at sports? That maybe one of your precious Yankees is a full-
blown cocksucker and you don't know it?"

"There's no way I'm anything like you," he said. "No fucking
way."

Running my fingers to the bottom of his sweatshirt, I slipped
my hand underneath and onto his bare skin. I could feel thick hair
on his stomach, spreading out over his torso as I moved slowly up
to his chest, pushing the sweatshirt up as I went along. "Get your
fucking hands off me," he said.

I took my hand away, letting him think he had won. Then,
grabbing the collar of it, I pulled. The material ripped, and I kept
pulling until the front of the sweatshirt hung open in tatters, his
whole chest bare. His pecs were rounded and well developed,

shaded in the soft dark hair I'd felt earlier, and the hair went right up to his neck, where it had been clipped into a neat curve. While I hated the guy, I had to admit he had one damn fine body.

"You touch me again and I'll scream my goddamned head off," he said. "Cops will have your ass in jail for sure."

I laughed, watching his face fill with confusion. "You're the one that likes going around beating up queers," I said. "What are you going to tell the cops, that some little faggot went and beat you up?" I walked over and ran my finger up his belly to his chin, pushing it up so I could look into his face. "Or maybe you'll tell them that you're the queer one."

He spat at me, a spray of wetness hitting my face. Picking up an old rag from among the trash scattered on the floor, I wiped my face off. Then I balled up the dirty cloth and pushed it into his mouth, silencing him. He tried to spit it out, but couldn't. "You know," I said, putting my hands on his chest again, "they say the guys who make the most noise about hating gay men are the ones who have something to hide. Maybe we should find out just what kind of secrets you've got hidden away."

Ripping more of his shirt, I pulled it off of him so that he was standing bare chested. The moonlight washed over the ripples of his body, which were evident even through the hair that covered his chest. His raised arms were thick and solid, and the ridges of his abdomen were clearly defined. Moving behind him, I saw that his back was just as beautiful, the shoulder muscles bunched tightly where his arms were pulled overhead.

I put my hands on his back and started to trace the curves of his bone and muscle slowly, feeling the heat of his skin beneath my hands. I ran my fingers up to where his closely cropped hair had been shaved on his neck, brushing my fingertips along the line where skin met hair. I could feel him shiver as I did this, and I knew he was enjoying it in spite of himself. "Feels good, doesn't it?" I said in his ear.

I moved back in front of him and saw that his eyes were closed, as if he was hoping it was all a bad dream and he could wake up somewhere else. Reaching out, I pinched one of his large, firm nipples between my fingers and watched as his eyes flew open. I continued to rub it as his face was creased by winces of pain and then pleasure as his body began to respond involuntarily to my touch. I gripped the second one and twisted that as well, feeling them both swell as I worked them over. He was writhing against the restraints as I played with his tits, and I felt a perverse burst of pleasure as I watched him.

Leaning down, I took one between my lips, fluttering my tongue over it lightly and cooling it by blowing on it. I licked the overheated bud and the skin around it gently. Then, moving my mouth over his mound, I slipped my tongue into the dark cavern of his armpit, licking and sucking at the damp hair. When I drew away, I saw that he was still looking at me, only now the rage had turned to a look of confusion, as though he was ashamed at feeling pleasure from what I was doing to him.

"Bet none of your girlfriends ever did that to you," I said as I slipped my hand down to his waist. Quickly unbuttoning his jeans, I slid them down his legs, where they settled between his feet. He was wearing white Jockey shorts, and there was a considerable bulge in the front. Rubbing my hand over it, I could feel a fat cock and set of big balls nestled between his thick, muscled legs. I could feel my own prick start to stiffen as I played with his package, and wondered what he would look like erect.

Grabbing the waistband, I ripped his shorts down the front and pulled them away, throwing them onto the dirty floor. His dick was as big as it had felt and hung nicely between his legs, the clipped head hanging along his thigh. I was surprised to see that his bush had been neatly trimmed and that his balls, unlike the rest of him, were shaved smooth and bare. Hefting his sac in my hand, I rubbed the soft skin. "Not many straight boys I know shave their equipment," I teased, watching him turn his eyes away. "You must like it this way."

Letting go of his cock, I went behind him to survey his ass. His cheeks were thick and meaty, the curving mounds smooth at the top and then shaded with dark hair closer to his legs. I hit his butt with my open hand and felt him tense under my touch. Kneeling, I parted his cheeks and looked into his wrinkled pucker. Like his balls, it too was clean shaven, the skin pale and white. Leaning in, I licked the tight opening, tasting the sweat and musk of his skin. The hair on his ass brushed against my cheeks as I pushed my tongue between the tight lips of his chute, pulling them farther apart with my fingers. Inside he was warm and clean, and my tongue swept along the lines of his walls easily, pushing deeper and deeper into him.

I licked at his rosy hole for several minutes, pulling my tongue out of him and then sliding back in, massaging his ass cheeks roughly. When I pulled away, I reached between his legs and found that his cock had hardened. Thick and pulsing, it stood up at an angle above his dangling nuts. Standing, I wrapped my hand around the throbbing tool from behind, giving it a couple of long pulls. "Just as I suspected," I said. "If this is nine inches then mine should be starring in porn films."

Stroking his prick some more, I felt him moving his hips so that his cock slid along my fist. "Looks like someone's a little horny," I said. Wetting my finger in my mouth, I slipped it back down to tickle his asshole. "Looks like that hole of yours is just waiting for something," I said as I probed his opening. "Maybe it's time for someone to give you what you need." I pushed harder, and my finger slipped in up to the second joint. I felt his ass ring clamp around it as I invaded him, and I wiggled it to loosen him. "Just relax," I said. "You know you want me in there."

With a little more pushing, I was able to get a whole finger inside him. Then I pulled out and, without warning, pushed two back in. His whole body spasmed as I stretched his shitter open, and he stumbled against the belts as he leaned forward to escape the pain. I relaxed, letting him get used to my presence, and then started to slowly fuck him with my hand. After a few minutes of continuous stroking, his ass was loose enough for me to put another finger in, and soon I was gliding in and out on the juices that started to leak from his virgin hole.

Reaching around him, I felt his prick again. A heavy load of cock slime was dripping from his engorged head. Pumping him a few times, I pushed out another stream and watched over his shoulder as it dropped to the floor in a long, sparkling thread. "Couldn't be you actually like this, do you?" I said. He didn't respond, so I pulled my hand out of his ass and grabbed his balls tightly. "Maybe I should just leave you like this," I threatened. "Let you hang here with your big cock all stiff and your balls aching for the cops to find tomorrow morning. How would you like that?"

After a moment he shook his head, and I could hear him trying to speak. I pulled the gag from his mouth. He breathed in several long breaths and then said, quietly, "Don't stop. Please don't."

I fingered his ass some more and he started to whimper. "How badly do you want it?" I demanded. "How badly do you want another guy in your ass?"

"I want it," he whispered. "I want you inside."

"Tell me how you want it," I said, adding another finger to his ass so that he groaned. "I won't do it unless you ask nicely. After all, you weren't so nice a while ago, were you?"

"Please," he whined. "I'm really sorry. You have to fuck me. You have to fuck my ass. I can't stand it anymore."

I hurriedly undid my own pants and pulled out my raging poker, which had long ago stretched out to its full size, not as long as his but quite a bit thicker. I rubbed the big head against his asshole, letting him feel my meat just a little bit. "Tell me how you've always wanted it," I ordered.

"Okay," he said, practically begging. "I've wanted it for a long time. Now do it. Fuck me. My balls are about to burst."

I still had the condom I'd picked up at the rally in my pocket. Fishing it out, I rolled it down my prick, then pressed the tip against his slimy hole. I slid just the head of my cock inside him, just enough to drive him crazy. "Oh shit," he cried out as I penetrated his crack. "Stick it all in. Stick your big dick right up me."

Gripping him around the waist, I slammed into his ass so hard that the belts tying his hands together creaked under the weight. He grunted loudly as I plowed into his tender shitter and forced him onto his toes as my cock drove upward. I could feel his ass cheeks against my groin as I buried myself inside his butt, my balls pressed tightly against him as I drove every inch of my crank into him. "Feels good having a dick up your ass, doesn't it?" I growled as I started to pump him.

He began to moan almost immediately, and as I fucked his ass harder and harder he let out groan after groan, his voice rolling through the big, empty room. He took every beat of my prick with another whimper of pleasure, and when I pulled out and fucked just the first couple inches of his ass tunnel he started to beg again. "It feels so fucking hot," he said. "Put the whole thing back in. I'm going to shoot all over the place."

I plunged in again and started to screw him really hard, slamming into his ass repeatedly. It was strange to think that only a couple of hours ago he had been calling me a faggot and wanted to beat the shit out of me and now he had my cock deep in his ass and was begging for more. As I fucked him, the idea that I had turned the tables on the guy and taught him a lesson made me even more excited. I knew we were both going to come shortly, and I wanted to make it good. My head was swimming from the heat of it all, and after several more pumps of my cock I started to blast away inside him, filling the rubber up with a big load.

As soon as the guy felt me coming in his ass, he came too. His ass tightened around my still-spewing cock as he came, and I felt his body convulse over and over as he blew his load. Thick ropes of jism flew from his untouched prick and fell to the floor as his prick released blast after blast. When he was finished, I slipped out of him and pulled the rubber off, carefully keeping my load trapped in the tip.

Standing in front of him, I looked into his face. The blood had dried under his nose, and his eyes were half-open. He was breathing heavily, and his spent cock was still hard. Reaching up, I undid the belt that held him prisoner and he collapsed to his knees in front of me. He looked up, his wrists still bound in front of him. Holding the rubber to his mouth, I tipped the sticky contents toward him. He opened his lips as my cum splashed out and over his chin, drinking in as much as he could. My load dripped from his chin onto his chest, where it stuck to the hair in thick drops.

When I had drained the rubber, I tossed it aside and brought my sticky prick to the man's lips. "Wash it off," I told him. He opened his mouth and began to lick me clean, his tongue warm on my skin as he tasted his first cock. Watching him suck me, I began to get hard again as my dick swelled with new heat. "Oh, yes," I said as I put my hands on his head and guided my prick into his eager throat. "There's still a lot you have to learn."

A Winter's Tale

I lived in New York for almost a decade. Every year, usually in the middle of one of the city's slushy winters, I said I was going to move. Then we would have one of those glorious snowstorms that turned the place into a wonderland, and for the day or so that it lasted I would be in love with the city again.

It had begun to snow in the late hours of the afternoon, a few tentative flurries that surprised and delighted schoolchildren on their way home for dinner and annoyed rush-hour commuters caught unprepared for the sudden change in the weather. On the streets, shoppers and travelers pulled their collars tighter against the wind's tickling fingers and remarked casually that it would end soon. But instead of sweeping in and out in a hurry, the snow remained, and within a few hours what had at first been nothing more than a mid-December novelty became a steady fall that wrapped around the shoulders of the city's skyscrapers in a thin but persistent embrace that took even the weathermen, long ago accustomed to looking foolish, by surprise.

By eleven, when my night began, everything in the city was blanketed with a good six inches of soft, powdery whiteness. It wasn't a lot, really, but in New York terms it was the snowfall of the year, and certainly enough to keep most people inside with cups of steaming coffee. I felt as though I were driving through my own little world as I navigated the limo through the darkened streets, my headlights cutting through the steadily falling snow while the few people who were out walking scuttled in and out of the thin yellow streams like shadows behind a stage's fluttering scrim.

Because of the unexpected storm, most of the usual clients had canceled for the evening, leaving me free to take on last-minute calls. Shortly after picking up my car, I got a call from the dispatcher to make a pickup at a restaurant in the Village. A businessman needed a limo to take him back to his uptown hotel. It was an easy run, and I had time before I had to be there, so I enjoyed the silence of the frozen city, taking in the way the colors of the traffic lights played over the swirling snow as I moved down Seventh Avenue.

I found the restaurant and waited, sitting on the silent Village street amazed by how quiet it was. Usually the neighborhood would have been filled with people going to dinner or returning home from the movie theater on the corner. But no other cars drove by, and the only people I saw were a couple wading through the growing drifts behind two large black Labradors, who plunged noses first through the snow, tails wagging as they explored their new world, their big paws leaving deep prints as they passed by.

The restaurant door opened and light spilled onto the sidewalk like water thrown from a bucket as two figures emerged wrapped in coats and scarves. Crossing the street quickly, they walked toward me. I got out of the limo, feeling the cold kiss of the snow greet my cheek as I opened the back door and held it for them. With a nod of thanks, the two men got into the backseat, and I closed the door behind them. Returning to my own seat, I waited for instructions.

Looking in the rearview mirror, I studied my passengers. One of the men appeared to be in his early forties. He was wearing a dark suit beneath his long coat, and his short silver hair was slicked back. He wore small, round, gold-framed glasses and was busily brushing stray snowflakes from his coat sleeve. The other man seemed to be Middle Eastern, his brown skin and black hair a sharp contrast to the other man's pale coloring. He looked to be about thirty and was dressed in a rich golden brown suit with a flowered silk tie closed with a neat knot at his throat. A scarf hung around the shoulders of his blue greatcoat.

The silver-haired man leaned forward. "We aren't in any real hurry," he said, his voice low and pleasant. "Why don't you just drive around for a while. When we want to stop, I'll let you know."

With that, he leaned back in his seat and pressed the button on the control panel that raised the narrow window separating the back of the car from the front. As the glass slid upward and the last few inches of space between us closed, I saw him lean forward and take the other man's face in his hands.

Starting the car, I turned on the wipers and cleared the snow from my windshield. Gliding down the street and onto the avenue, I began to drive through the city. So close to midnight, it was almost entirely deserted and I drove slowly, watching the snow tumble out of the sky and scatter across the streets. The car was warm, and it was nice and quiet inside while the snowstorm raged all around. With nowhere to go, I had all the time in the world. I turned the radio to a classical channel, and the sound of a string symphony surrounded me with its soothing voice.

As I drove, my thoughts turned to my two passengers. I knew nothing about them except that the silver-haired man's name was Aronson and that he was staying at the Park Plaza Hotel. Other than that, they were complete mysteries to me. I wondered who they were and what they were doing together on this blustery winter's night. Most of all, I wondered what was going on in the backseat at that very moment as I drove through the sleeping city. The little I'd seen before the window closed intrigued me, the sliver of passion growing into visions that filled my head with thoughts of skin against skin and mouth on mouth.

I glanced at the small television monitor set into the dashboard. It's attached to a small camera mounted in the back of the car, and the passengers don't even know it's there. Drivers use it to keep an eye on riders who might be drunk or who need to be woken up before getting to their stops. Otherwise, it's usually turned off. Although I knew that spying on passengers wasn't by any stretch of the imagination the right thing to do, I was curious to know what they were up to.

Reaching over, I turned it on. The screen flickered to life, and soon I had a perfect view of the action taking place in the rear of the car. Although it was black and white, and the picture wasn't always the clearest, I could certainly tell what was going on. Both men had removed their overcoats and suit jackets, pushing them aside. The dark-haired man was settled back against the seat, and Aronson was kissing him passionately. His mouth moved over the other man's face and neck slowly as he explored with his tongue, tracing the lines of his throat. The dark man's hands were on Aronson's back, their brownness shadowy against the whiteness of his shirt as he pulled him in closer.

Aronson continued to kiss the other man as his hands moved around to undo Aronson's tie and unbutton his shirt. When it was unbuttoned, he slipped the shirt over Aronson's shoulders and pulled it off. Aronson had a nice body, solid without really being muscular, the lines and curves of his back showing his years and experience. His chest was covered in short hair the same soft silver color as that on his head. The other man's hands ran over the broad expanse of his back and down around his waist, taking in the feel of him as he rose up to push his groin against Aronson's belly.

Aronson, obviously aroused, pulled roughly at the man's shirt, slipping the buttons open hurriedly in his haste to undress him. As it fell away, I saw that the man's chest was covered in thick swirls of coal-black hair that ran from his neck down to his groin. Aronson's face moved over the man's torso eagerly, licking in slow circles at the hair visible between the white folds of his shirt. He took his time, sucking on the exposed nipples and letting the man's hair brush his cheeks as he worked his way down his belly.

When he reached the man's stomach, he began to fumble with his belt, his hands clumsy with desire. When he had it open and had pulled the man's zipper down, he worked his pants down and off. Then he pulled his own off as well, pushing both pairs out of the way and kneeling on the floor of the limo, which was now scattered with discarded clothes.

The two of them were wearing only their underwear now, Aronson in boxers that clung to the mounds of his ass tightly as he bent forward and sucked at the dark-haired man's cock through the soft cotton of his briefs. He mouthed the bulge between the man's legs hungrily, his lips sliding along it roughly while the man's hands rested lightly on either side of his head. Several times Aronson moved down and shoved his face deep between the other man's legs, his mouth filling with white cotton as he sucked and tugged on the balls hidden behind the soft material.

Grabbing the waistband, he yanked the briefs off to free the man's dick. It sprang up from a tangle of dark hair, long and thick and straight, and lay against his belly. The head, round and dark, was oozing a stream of precum that silvered the black hair on the man's groin with sticky drops. A set of heavy balls rested between his spread legs, their weight spreading over the soft leather of the seat.

The sight on the monitor of the man sitting in the back naked with his beautiful prick hard against his stomach really turned me on, especially since I knew that in actuality he was only a few feet away from me. I could feel my own cock straining inside my uniform pants, and rubbed it with one black-gloved hand while the other rested on the steering wheel. I kept one eye on the road and one on the monitor as I waited anxiously to see what Aronson would do.

Sliding his own underwear off, Aronson freed what was also a good-sized prick. Long and very thick, it nicely matched the rest of him, sticking straight out from between his legs. He positioned himself next to his companion on the seat, and the two men sat side by side as they jerked themselves off and played with one another's balls. Running their hands over each other's chests, they kissed deeply, enjoying one another's bodies.

They were delicious contrasts to one another—dark and light— and it was wonderful to watch them stroke their cocks while we moved unnoticed through the streets. Aronson held his dick tightly in his fist, pulling up on the head sharply with each stroke of his hand. The other man was more relaxed, slowly rubbing his shaft with two fingers while his thumb swirled around the crown, sweeping up drops of precum to use as lube. I laughed to myself as I imagined the few people out in the storm watching the car go by and wondering what was going on inside it.

After a few minutes of watching the other man play with his dick, Aronson sank to his knees on the car floor and once again positioned himself between the dark-haired man's legs. Luckily, the camera was mounted so that it looked down right over his shoulder. I could see every move as he leaned forward, took the man's prick into his mouth, and slowly worked every inch into his throat. I was amazed that he could get the whole thing down so easily, and felt a tugging in my balls as I saw his nose buried in the other man's bush.

The dark-haired man's hands went onto the back of Aronson's neck and began to guide him up and down the heavy shaft in his mouth. Aronson obliged willingly, silently sucking at the thick tool as it pushed past his lips. When just the head was inside his mouth, he paused, running his tongue around the edge and darting into the piss slit before pressing downward and once again burying the cock to the root in his throat.

Watching him give such excellent head was too much. Reaching down, I unbuckled my pants and managed to slide them off enough to free my aching prick. Gripping it in one hand, I stroked myself in time with Aronson's movements, the leather glove slipping sensuously along my shaft just as Aronson's tongue lovingly washed the dark man's massive dick. I squeezed the head gently and watched some drops of precum roll onto the soft leather that encased my fist. Bringing it to my lips, I licked my juice off, the smooth taste of the leather mingling with the sweet stickiness on my tongue.

The dark-haired man had pulled his knees up so that he was half lying on the seat with his legs spread. While Aronson continued to work on his cock, the man slipped one hand down under his balls and slid a finger into his asshole. He moved it in and out slowly, fucking himself while he got serviced. His eyes were closed, and his face was a mask of pure pleasure as his fingers slid in and out of his ass, the thick hair around his opening brushing his hand with every stroke.

Aronson began to suck faster, and I saw the dark-haired man's body tense as he neared the edge. A few more strokes of Aronson's expert mouth was all he needed. He came, his mouth opening in a silent roar of ecstasy. Aronson's throat muscles moved furiously as he gulped down his lover's load, and when he finally raised his head, a thick strand of cum stretched from his lips to the head of the other man's dick. I had to clamp my hand tightly around my own shaft to keep from coming at the sight.

After licking the man's cock clean, Aronson got up and knelt on the seat once more, his knees on either side of the dark man's body. The man pushed himself lower, so that Aronson's cock was pointed straight at his mouth. Resting his hands on the back of the seat, Aronson leaned forward and drove his dick deep into the dark-haired man's throat. I saw the muscles in his ass tighten as the man took the length of his fat piece in completely, closing his lips around it. His hands moved over Aronson's back and ass while he sucked him.

Reaching the edge of the city limits, I was now driving along the water, the thin black ribbon of the frosted river rolling along beside me. It was so beautiful that I decided to head onto one of the bridges linking Manhattan with the outside world. Momentarily taking my eyes off of the monitor, I pulled onto the approach ramp and up the snow-covered climb to the upper level of the bridge. My dick was still hard and insistent in my palm, and I pulled on it steadily as I drove, keeping myself constantly on the agonizing border between intense need and the pleasure of release.

When I looked back to the monitor, I saw that the dark-haired man had slipped two fingers into Aronson's ass. Still sucking his cock he pumped his hand steadily in and out of the dark space between the man's round, firm ass cheeks. Aronson pushed himself back against the invading fingers, fucking himself shamelessly. He was rocking on the man's fingers while his dick slammed repeatedly into the lips that welcomed him in eagerly.

Driving slowly along the upper deck of the bridge, I looked out at the lights of the city blinking lazily through the screen of snow. The music in the car surrounded me with gentle ripples of sound, and the road before me was clean and empty. The action on the monitor continued uninterrupted, and I felt all alone in the world with just the images of the men making love behind me and the hardness of the cock in my hand as I floated over the black water below.

On the monitor, the dark-haired man was holding his prick in his fist while Aronson lowered himself slowly onto it. Several inches were already buried in Aronson's willing ass, and he soon pushed the remaining length of thick shaft inside himself until he was impaled on the big dick, his asshole stretching around it greedily. Once inside, the dark man began to rock his hips slowly, driving himself up and into Aronson's butthole. His hands gripped Aronson's ass tightly, the long brown fingers pressing into the flesh as they began their lovemaking.

As the fucking sped up, I began to jerk myself in rhythm with their movement. The dark man was pumping himself quickly into Aronson's hole, the head of his dick slamming in and out rapidly, and my hand flew along my shaft along with him, the leather surrounding my skin tightly. Aronson was playing with his cock while he got fucked, and his hand was moving quickly along his tool as he worked himself over.

We had reached the highest point of the bridge's rise, the pale winter moon hanging what seemed like only inches above the limo's roof, when the dark-haired man rose forward, pushing Aronson backward. Never taking his dick from Aronson's ass, he laid him down on his back on the opposite seat. Pulling Aronson's legs over his shoulders, he began to pound his ass furiously in long, hard strokes. The camera looked directly into his face as he fucked, and I had a perfect view of his dick slamming in and out of Aronson's ass. Aronson gripped his cock tightly as he continued to jerk off. I could feel my own load starting to rise and hoped I could wait for them.

I didn't have to wait long. After only a few more thrusts, the dark-haired man gave one final shove deep into Aronson's butt and came. He remained still while his load tore into Aronson's insides, his fingers gripping Aronson's legs. Aronson came then as well, holding his spouting dick straight up and throwing his head back as a torrent of cum roared from his overworked prick and splashed all over his chest and that of the man still buried deep inside him. Thick drops clung to the dark man's torso and slid down his belly as blast after blast coated him in Aronson's hot jism.

Seeing them both come sent me over the edge. I groaned loudly as my load flew from my cockhead and covered my gloved hand in sticky streamers. Some of it fell to the floor as I shot repeatedly, and several long spurts stained the front of my shirt in wet streaks. Somehow I managed to keep the car steady as my body rocked with an intense orgasm from my boots to the top of my cap. It was all I could do just to stay on the snowy bridge as I gasped and shuddered from the intensity of the release.

When I was finally able to breathe again, I looked at the monitor. In the back, my two passengers were putting themselves back together, fumbling with shirts and pants and ties. When they had restored themselves to some semblance of order, Aronson kissed the other man deeply and then lowered the window. As it opened, I hurriedly tucked my sticky cock back into my pants and zipped up. I snapped off the monitor and pretended that nothing was out of the ordinary.

"This was a lovely ride," Aronson said evenly when the window had fully descended, his voice betraying nothing of the passion I had just witnessed in him. "But we've finished our business and I think we can go back to the hotel now."

Without another word, he rolled the window back up. We had reached the other side of the river, and after handing my return token to the sleepy tollkeeper, who seemed more than a little surprised to see someone traveling in the snow, I turned the limo around and headed back into Manhattan. As I drove across the bridge through the snow and fell out of the night sky and back into the glowing hands of the city, I fingered the sticky glove now resting in my pocket and lost myself in the music pouring from the radio, replaying my winter's tale in my mind.

Going Down Under

Australian man. Airplane. Forbidden sex. Did I need a reason?

I have to confess, I don't particularly like to travel. Or rather, I like the excitement of going to new places; I just don't like the process of getting there and coming back. Sitting for hours in hard plastic chairs waiting for connecting flights, trying to read incomprehensible train and bus schedules, and navigating through foreign cities without knowing the language are not things that make me look forward to leaving home, no matter how enticing the destination. Once I get there, I'm fine. It's the coming and going that make me wish my wanderlust didn't kick in quite so strongly every few months like a bitch going into heat.

So when my editor called me in and said she was sending me to Sydney to cover the Australian rugby finals for the magazine, I took the news with mixed emotions. On the one hand, spending a week down under looking at a bunch of sweaty ballplayers was certainly no hardship assignment. On the other, it meant a twenty-four-hour plane ride to get there. I wondered if I could just get something to knock me out for the trip so I wouldn't even know what was going on until the plane landed and someone woke me up.

But as usual my desire to see someplace new won out, and a few days later I found myself boarding a Qantas jet with a crowd of other folks taking the late flight to the world's end. As I passed from the heat of the New York evening into the artificial coolness of the airplane, I breathed in the sweet smell of the jet's piped-in air and felt it fill my head with its reassuring etherlike touch. I waded through the tangle of people milling in the aisles and trying to push their bags into the overhead compartments and found my seat. I had requested a window seat over the wing because there's more leg room in that row, and if I was going to have to sit for a day and a night, I wanted it to be somewhere I could at least stretch out. The layout of the plane was such that there was one seat next to mine, and I prayed no one would be in it.

After stowing my one bag, I settled in. There was nothing else to do, so I watched the other passengers getting on. My eyes were on the alert for any talkative old ladies or small children, both of whom make any kind of enclosed travel a misery with their tendencies to tell rambling, uninteresting stories and to kick the backs of the seats. I also wanted to see if anyone was heading my way to take my preciously guarded companion seat.

The plane filled up quickly, primarily with business types and couples, none of them toting children or the elderly. As more and more poured into the cabin, the seat next to me remained wonderfully unoccupied, and I started allowing myself to believe that it might just stay that way. I opened the in-flight magazine thoughtfully provided in the seat pocket that also held my airsick bag and emergency evacuation procedure card, and thumbed through looking for pictures of rugby types to pass the time. Unfortunately, there weren't any to be found, so I started to read an article about the quaint eating habits of koalas.

I was halfway through the article when someone dropped a large book onto the seat next to me. Startled, I glanced sideways, my eyes coming to rest on a buckle holding closed a brown leather belt that cinched a pair of chinos. Moving my gaze up, I traveled over the planes of a blue cotton work shirt until I came to a man's face. He was busily cramming his carry-on bag into the overhead and wasn't looking at me, so I had time to look him over.

About thirty, he had auburn hair that was cut short but was slightly tousled, a lock of it falling over his forehead as if he'd been running. He was a large man, standing an inch or two over my own six-two frame, and his face was wide and rugged, his jaw and neck flecked with a dark shadow even though he was clean shaven. His shirt was open at the neck, and there was a splash of the same auburn hair visible in the exposed hollow of his throat. His sleeves were rolled up his thick forearms, and his hands were wide and strong with thick fingers, one of which was encircled by a thin gold wedding band.

He finished storing his bag and sat down. When he looked over at me, I saw that his eyes were a light gray. He smiled slightly and held out his hand. "Hi," he said in a rich, low voice heavy with an Aussie accent that made me take notice instantly. "I'm Aiden. Looks like we're stuck together for a while."

I took his hand and his fingers closed around mine warmly as his flesh pressed heat against my palm, his wedding band a cool accent on my skin as he held my grip for a few moments. "Nice to meet you," I lied, bitterly disappointed that I wouldn't be sitting alone. "I'm Tom." *Great,* I thought, *not only do I have to sit next to someone, but he's the one attractive man on the whole flight and he's married.* It was going to be one long trip.

Aiden shifted around in his seat, getting more comfortable. His chest was wide, and he filled up the space easily. I felt the pressure of his shoulder against mine as he settled back and stretched his long legs, trying out the space, and it left an unexpected warm feeling when he sat up again. "Not so bad," he said. "Usually I can barely move."

"I know what you mean," I said, putting my magazine away as the takeoff light went on and the stewardesses started their canned spiel about what to do in the event of the plane tumbling into the sea. The plane was taxiing into position, and I turned my attention to the view outside my window. I could still feel where Aiden had rubbed against me and tried not to think about it as the runway fled away beneath me in a dirty river. The plane shook lightly as it gained speed, and soon I felt the wheels leave the ground as it leapt into the air. I watched the familiar sight of the runway dropping off abruptly into the water of the bay, and looked down as the plane rose higher and higher and the visible landscape closed in on itself like a kaleidoscope coming into focus.

When we passed up into the arms of the clouds and the plane was surrounded by nets of white, I sat back again. Aiden was leaning back, his fingers gripping the armrests tightly and his eyes closed. He was breathing shallowly, and the muscles of his neck were tight. "Are you okay?" I asked.

"Oh, yeah," he replied. "I just don't like takeoffs. Once we're actually up, it's okay."

"Well, we're pretty much there," I said. "I think you can open your eyes now."

Aiden blinked a few times, looking past me at the view outside the window. His hands released their hold on the armrests, and he wiped them on his pants. "That's better," he said, obviously embarrassed. "I know it sounds weird, but once I see the clouds, I kind of feel like the plane can't fall through them. Like if something happened, the plane would just sort of sink into them and float around until it could be fixed." He looked at me quickly and then looked away. "Pretty strange, eh?"

I laughed a little. "No, not really," I said. "I think it's kind of nice. Beats the hell out of the alternative."

It was his turn to laugh. I noticed he was turning the ring on his finger absentmindedly. "Bet your wife will be glad to have you back," I said.

He stopped fingering his ring and leaned back, the smile on his face fading into a harder line. "So what takes you to our great island?" he asked, ignoring my question. His voice was polite, but it had lost a bit of the friendly tone it had had a moment before.

I told him about the sports magazine that I work for, and about the story I was working on. He seemed mildly impressed but didn't ask any questions. He seemed to have gotten very shy all of a sudden. When I asked him about himself, he said something vague about having been in New York on business and that now he was going home. Then he opened his book and started to read. Since he seemed not to want to talk any further, I went back to my magazine. Before long, I was deep into an exposé on the pleasures of rock climbing in the Australian outback and had almost forgotten that Aiden was even there.

When I finished reading everything I could in the magazine, I looked at my watch. We'd only been in the air for forty-five minutes, and already I was bored. I looked out the window into the swirling vortex of clouds moving past the plane and thought about what Aiden had said. I wondered why the mention of his wife had made him fall silent and looked over at him. He was still reading, his eyes scanning the page slowly, and he took no notice of me. *Oh well*, I thought, *at least he isn't bothering me with endless chatter*.

Reaching down, I pulled a paperback out of the small bag I'd pushed under my seat. It was a thick one, something I'd picked up at the airport book shop thinking it would last me through most of the long trip. I leaned back in my seat and opened it to the first page. It was an occult thriller, something about a man being haunted by the ghost of a girl who'd been killed in the house he bought and who was now causing no end of trouble. Despite my disdain for the writer and his megaselling books, I found myself deeply engrossed in a matter of minutes, grudgingly turning the pages to see what would happen.

After about eighty pages, I suddenly realized that something was pressing against my arm. Turning my head slightly, I saw that Aiden had shifted again so that he was leaning against me slightly, his arm lightly pushing against mine. He was still reading and didn't look up at me, but the pressure didn't let up. I went back to my book, not moving my own arm and wondering if he was aware of what he was doing. I tried to get back into the story, but my concentration wandered as I felt the heat of his body through my shirt, never moving. To my surprise, my cock started to swell.

I tensed my arm slightly, to see if Aiden would move away. When he did, I felt disappointed and chastised myself for pushing him away. I tried to lean more in his direction, to resume our contact, but he had shifted his weight to his other side, and I would have had to practically fall over to touch him. Deciding that it was all an accident, I resumed reading. Unfortunately, my prick was half-hard from the unexpected contact with Aiden's body, and all I could think about was how his arm felt against mine.

Before long, I had created a whole fantasy scenario in my head. I imagined finding Aiden naked, lying on his back in the white sand of a beach. His skin was damp with sweat, and I was rubbing my hands over his muscular back, feeling him tense and release beneath my touch. I imagined stroking the strong mounds of his ass, the way it would feel to rub the hair on his thighs. I pictured him rolling over, his cock stretched out along his belly waiting for me to take it in my mouth. After a few minutes, I could almost feel him fucking me, my back in the warm sand while his strong hands parted my thighs and his dick slipped inside my asshole.

My cock was fully hard now, making an obvious bulge in my pants. I held my book over it, hoping Aiden couldn't see, and tried to forget the image I'd just conjured up. If he did notice, he wasn't looking at it and went on turning the pages of his book every few minutes. I put my hand on my crotch and pretended to look out the window while I tried to will my hard-on away. The sky was quickly moving from a dark purple to the blackness of night like a bruise forming beneath the skin, and the cabin was growing dimmer with every passing minute as the plane dived headlong into the darkness. Throughout the plane small spots of light were bursting into life as people turned on their reading lamps.

I sat for over an hour just staring out the window and watching the night fold in around the plane. The images of Aiden faded away slowly as I watched the stars come out, and I had almost managed to get things back to normal when I felt something move along my leg. Aiden's knee was pressing against mine, and his touch was like fire, instantly making my dick fill with blood until it was hard again. *Oh shit*, I thought, *this guy is going to drive me crazy, and he doesn't even know what he's doing.*

I left my leg pressed against Aiden's while I continued to look out the window. The pressure remained constant, never increasing or decreasing, for a good fifteen minutes while the picture of his naked body flooded my mind once more and I imagined slurping on his big cock. Finally, I couldn't stand it any longer. I moved my knee closer to his, pressing more firmly. Much to my surprise, he didn't move at all. After a few minutes, I stole a quick glance at him to see what he was doing. He was sitting in the half dark, his book on his lap and his head back. His eyes were closed and he was breathing slowly. His hands were clasped over his book, the fingers loosely entwined in one another. He was asleep.

Leaning back in my seat, I felt my arm press against his once again. This time, he didn't move away from me. The feeling of being forced against him in the confined space of our seats was very arousing, and I closed my eyes as I once more thought about making love to him. My hand worked playfully at my hard cock as I imagined sucking Aiden's dick and pictured his hands moving over my body. I tried to envision the hair on his chest, how it would look tumbling down his belly, how it would feel beneath my tongue as I worked my way over his nipples to his stiff tool. I ran my tongue over my lips as I thought about taking his fat balls into my mouth, sucking the sweat from them while he moaned above me.

The fact that I couldn't actually take my cock out and jerk on it made me even hornier. I knew I was probably leaking like crazy inside my boxers. The more I thought about making love with Aiden, the harder I got. I rubbed myself as much as I could in such an open place and wished to God I'd had the sense to grab a blanket from the overhead compartment when I got on. I even thought about going into the bathroom and jerking off, but that meant moving past Aiden. It also meant giving up the torturous feeling of his body pressed against mine. Even if he was asleep, I was still getting off on having him so close but so untouchable.

Putting my hand on my knee, I let my fingers hang down and brush lightly against Aiden's leg. The rough material of his pants met my fingers as I traced a small circle on his leg, waiting for him to abruptly pull away. But he stayed where he was. Emboldened, I made a larger circle with my fingers, pressing a little more firmly. When he still didn't move, I felt my heart beating faster. *This is nuts*, I told myself. *The man's asleep and you're getting all hot over him.* I moved my leg a little closer to him, until our calves were tight against each other.

I took my hand away and continued to press my knee against him. A few minutes went by that seemed like hours as I thought about what to do next. Aiden's eyes were still shut, and his hands hadn't moved. Then I felt his leg rise up slightly along mine, as though he were rubbing against me. It was a small movement and could have been made in sleep, but it was enough for me to take a chance. I put my hand full on his thigh, my fingers pressing into hard muscle. His leg was broad, and my hand stretched across it heavily as I rubbed him, waiting for him to leap out of his seat and start yelling.

Instead, he pushed his leg up against my hand, moving his hips forward. His eyes stayed closed, but one hand moved down to rest on top of mine, the big fingers closing around mine. I almost shot a load at his unexpected touch, the way he held me making my balls ache. I looked at his face and saw that the muscles of his jaw were fluttering, as if he was very nervous. Still, he left his hand on mine, rubbing me gently where I was touching his leg. I looked around to see if anyone had noticed what we were doing, but the cabin was shrouded in darkness, and the passengers across from us were sleeping soundly.

Drawing a deep breath, I brought my hand up Aiden's thigh to his crotch, where I rested it right on his cock. He was hard, and his prick made a thick line under his pants. I rested my hand there for a few moments, while the realization that he'd been as hard as I was dawned on me. He moved his book so that it covered his crotch, my hand hidden beneath it. He held the book open so that anyone coming by would see only the dust jacket lying flat across his stomach.

He still made no move to open his eyes, but his hand continued to rest on mine, pressing it down on his prick. He was large, and I felt along the length of him while my own cock sent shivers of anticipation throughout my body. Feeling his dick while surrounded by so many people was getting me really worked up, and I wanted more. I reached under the flap of his fly and found the tiny metal head of his zipper just beneath the buckle of his belt. Gripping it tightly, I tugged down slowly, the small teeth gnashing silently as I opened him up.

When I had his zipper open, I slid my fingers inside and into the warmth of soft cotton Jockeys. After some fumbling, I slipped past the waistband, pushing his underwear down slightly as I grabbed his cock. His dick was hot in my hand, long and thick with a rounded head that pressed against my palm like a stone warm from hours in the sun. I gripped it tightly in my fingers, feeling the heat pulse beneath the thin skin, the vein on the underside swelling and ebbing. My hand rested in his pubic hair, and I felt the muscles of his belly tensing as he breathed slowly.

"You have a nice cock," I said, leaning over to talk into his ear.

I saw his throat move as he swallowed nervously, but he said nothing. I pumped his shaft a few times, slowly moving my fist up and down the couple of inches of dick I could play with in the tight confines of his pants. I ran my thumb over the engorged head and swept up a few drops of sticky precum that oozed from his slit. His juice was thick and clung to my skin as I massaged it into his shaft. I milked out some more and brought my hand to my lips. Slipping my fingers inside my mouth, I licked off his cock honey, savoring the rich, heady scent of his jism.

"Nice," I whispered to him, returning my hand to his pants and squeezing his tool. "I'd like to taste some of that pouring down my throat when I make you come."

Aiden groaned involuntarily as I tugged at his cock, filling my hand with the length of him. My fingers entwined in his public hair, and I pressed them down into the space between his legs. Taking my cue, he spread his thighs slightly, shifting in his seat so that I could play with his balls. The pouch of his underwear was soaked with his sweat and precum, and his balls were damp with the same delicious wetness as I held them in my hand. Large and round, they were nestled in a smooth pouch.

"Oh, yes," I growled in his ear, breathing hotly on his neck. "I'd love to have your balls in my mouth. I'd suck each one so gently, pulling it inside with my lips and letting my tongue trace the roundness of its curves. I'd suck them until you blow your load right up your belly."

"Oh, Christ," Aiden said in a hoarse whisper, finally breaking his silence. "I'm gonna shoot off if you keep that up. You'd better be careful."

I gave him a few more teasing strokes, then sat with my hand gripping his prick. I could feel his dick jumping at the base, tensing as he tried to hold off his orgasm. I was tempted to finish him off, to watch his load fly up from his crotch and splash over his shirt and the seat in front of him. But I had more plans for him, and they included leaving him hard for a while longer.

"Your wife ever make you this hard?" I asked him, leaning in so that my breath crossed his flushed skin.

"No," he said, choking back another moan as I pinched the tip of his dick. "Not even bloody close."

He was leaking so much that my hand was soaked with pre-cum, the thick streams that poured from him running into his bush and making a sticky mess. While I rubbed some of it into his skin, I continued to talk to him in a voice so low and controlled that anyone trying to listen would think we were talking about stock prices or football scores.

"Feels like you enjoy having another guy play with your cock," I said. "You ever do it before?"

"No," he said in his low, thick voice. "I mean, once with a buddy in school when we were both drunk. We jerked off together."

"What was it like?" I asked, stroking him slowly.

Aiden leaned back in his seat, sliding my hand along his shaft. "We were in his car," he said. "After a soccer game. We'd had some pints and were sitting in the dorm parking lot. Jack said he was horny, and I told him to go wank off. He said he would if I did too."

"And what did you do then?" I said, rubbing his thigh with some of his cream and kneading the muscles.

"He unbuttoned his jeans and pulled out his cock," Aiden said after a long pause. "He had a hard-on."

"Tell me about it," I demanded.

"It was big," Aiden said breathlessly. "Really long and fat. It stuck straight up. He was stroking it." His words were clipped and came out raggedly, as though remembering what had happened was going to make him shoot his load.

"What did you do?" I prodded.

Aiden's eyes were still closed, and I could feel his cock stiffening even more in my grasp as he thought about his experience. "I took mine out, too," he said. "Played with it."

"What did your buddy do?"

"He watched me," Aiden said softly. "Watched me jerk my dick. We must have tossed off for at least half an hour."

"Did he say anything?" I asked.

Aiden's brow furrowed as he thought. "No," he said finally. "He just kept stroking his prick and watching me play with mine."

"Did you touch him?"

"I wanted to," Aiden said. "But I didn't. It looked so big. I wanted to feel it in my hand. But I was afraid."

I rubbed the head of Aiden's dick in my fingers. "How did it end?" I urged.

"He came first. Shot his load all over the floor of the car. I remember it came out in three long spurts, and he pulled on his balls when he came."

"Did you come, too?"

Aiden smiled. "Yeah," he said. "I came, too. All over my letterman jacket. Couldn't push my cock down in time, and gushed all over the front. I never did get it out."

I stroked him a little faster, making him breathe harder. "And you never did anything with him again?"

"No, we never even mentioned it. I jerked off a lot thinking about it, but we never did anything again. I never did anything like that with another guy."

"But I bet you still have that jacket, don't you?" I asked, pushing my hand deeper into his pants and rubbing the spot behind his balls.

Aiden's hand slipped into my lap and started to play with my cock, tentatively moving along the length of my hard-on. I shuddered as he fingered my swollen head and ran one thick finger down my shaft. "I still have it," he said. "Sometimes I put it on and jack off thinking about what I would have done with Jack."

Having him work on my cock, however nervously, was bringing me dangerously close to coming. The thick hair on his forearms brushed against my hand as our crossed arms moved along each other, and I was overcome with the need to be close to his body and the agony of not being able to. I willed the pounding in my balls to go down as I kept my steady pumping on Aiden's tool. "What do you think about?" I asked him.

He cleared his throat. "I think about sucking his dick," he said slowly. "About how it would feel to lick his cock and balls."

I pulled harder on his nuts, wrapping my fingers around the shaft of his dick. His crotch was hot, and his skin was beginning to get very sticky from all of the lube dripping from his lips. "What else?" I prompted, sliding a finger down behind his ballsac and into his hairy ass crack.

His fingers were steadily working along my trapped dick, massaging me roughly. He gripped me tightly when he answered, as though he was imagining Jack's dick in his hand instead of mine. "I think about him fucking me," he said quietly.

He'd said exactly what I wanted to hear. Urging some more hot fluid from his cock, I pulled my hand from his pants. My fingers shone with his wetness, and there was a fine hair trapped between them. Pulling the hair from my hand, I put it in my mouth, my tongue running along its rough length as I tasted his precum and the scent of his musky crotch for the second time. At the same time, I pressed my fingers against his lips. When they parted, I slipped two fingers inside, resting the tips along the ridge of his teeth. His tongue licked at them gently, surrounding my fingertips in warmth as he cleaned me.

"Tastes wonderful, doesn't it?" I said, fucking his lips slowly with my fingers. "Like a man should." He began to suck harder, and I pulled my fingers out of his mouth, letting them slip slowly along his neck and along his open shirt, just brushing against the exposed hair.

He opened his eyes and looked at me then, his expression telling me he wanted more. I wanted him just as badly. "Go into the bathroom," I told him, zipping him back up. "I'll follow after you."

Aiden didn't wait to be told twice. Making sure he looked presentable in case he ran into anyone on the way to the rear of the plane, he stood up and walked slowly down the aisle. I went right behind him, watching his ass as he moved and thinking about what I was going to do to him. When he got to the bathroom, he reached for the handle and pulled. The door didn't move, even after he gave it another tug, and it was then that I noticed that the occupied light was on.

"Oh, Christ," I moaned as he looked at me helplessly. "We'll just have to wait a minute." I leaned against the wall, my impatient cock beating in my pants. Aiden leaned back, too, and because of the narrow hallway he was forced back against me. My dick pressed against his ass, and I couldn't resist putting my arms around him and pulling him close, relishing the sheer size of him in my arms. He was still hard, and feeling his meat in my hands made me want him desperately. I kissed the back of his neck and ran my tongue into his ear, savoring the taste of his skin. "I want to fuck you right here in the aisle," I whispered, and his prick surged against my fingers.

Just then, the door opened, and a woman came out holding the hand of a little girl. I released Aiden just before she turned and smiled at us apologetically. For all she knew, we didn't even know each other. "Sorry," she said sweetly. "I hope you haven't been waiting long."

"That's okay," Aiden said, smiling back at her as he darted into the bathroom. I went right behind him, seeing her puzzled expression as she realized that two grown men were going in together. "He needs help," I said as I moved past her and patted the little girl on the head. "You know how it is."

As soon as the door was shut, I put my arms around Aiden and kissed him hard. The smallness of the bathroom made it hard for two big men to move around, but that made it all the more exciting as I pulled him to me and drove my tongue into his mouth. His broad back stretched under my hands as I moved over it, feeling his muscles and grinding against him while our tongues played against one another. He moved forward, pinning me against the door, and I felt his cock pushing against me. "I want this so much," he said hoarsely.

We were both so anxious that it all seemed like a blur of tongues and hands and mouths as we explored each other's bodies. Fumbling with the buttons on his shirt, I opened it to reveal his beautiful, hairy chest. My mouth quickly found one of his large, firm nipples and began sucking while my hands ran through the thick fur that fell from his throat to his groin in a heavy swatch. The feel of it against my face, combined with the smell of him, made me crazy for him. I licked a trail down his belly, darting my tongue into the depression of his navel. I ran my hands behind him, pulling him into my face. His back was smooth and hairless, the heavy muscles dipping into a smooth arc just above his ass crack. I knelt in the cramped space, barely fitting, with my face pressed right into his bulging crotch.

I worked his belt buckle open quickly, pulling at it with trembling fingers and unzipping him. I tugged both pants and underwear down his legs and freed the cock I had been teasing earlier. It fell out and hung between his legs heavily, the head drooping down over the set of full balls I'd had only a small taste of. He was cut and very thick. His bush was heavy but short, and the first few inches of his shaft were sprinkled with the same beautiful auburn fur. His skin was slick with the precum I had milked from him, and more of it drizzled from the slit on his dickhead.

I took him all in one quick slurp, burying his prick in my throat and pushing my nose into his crotch. He cried out as I swallowed him, and I felt his dick fill with heat as he almost came from the sensation, but I clamped my lips around the base and waited until he had calmed down enough for me to begin working up and down the length of him. His cock was perfect, straight and full, and I slurped up every last drop of his musky juice as I washed him, sucking it down like water. He groaned as I worked his shaft with my lips and tongue, and pumped his hips slowly in and out of me.

I worked open the buttons of my own pants, managing to free my desperate piece. I stroked it while I sucked Aiden's prick, matching the strokes of my hand with the movements of my mouth along his tool until I was ready to blow my load all over the floor. When I was just about to come, I let Aiden's cock fall from my lips. "Now suck me," I said, looking up at him. "Do what you've always wanted to."

I stood up and Aiden dropped to his knees, pausing first to give me another deep kiss. He held my aching cock in his hand and started to lick the head slowly, in teasing circles. I grabbed his hair and shoved my prick down his throat until he started to gag. "Like that," I said, moving him up and down my prick by holding his head. "Suck it like you know you want to."

Aiden relaxed, letting me slide in and out of his mouth at will while I fucked his handsome face. I could tell he'd never done it before, but he was giving it his best shot, and he was going to be one fine cocksucker with some practice. But right now I was horny as hell and didn't have time to show him how to do it right. I wanted something else from him. After a few minutes of working on his hot mouth, I pulled away. "Stand up," I told him.

He stood up facing me, and I turned him around so that he was facing the small mirror over the even smaller sink. Moving behind him, I pressed myself against his ass and ran my hands around him, feeling once more the beautiful hair on his chest. I pulled back and unbuttoned my shirt so that I could feel him against my bare skin. When I held him again, my own hairy chest slipping over the skin of his back and shoulders, I saw his smile in the mirror.

"You like this, huh?" I said, slipping my cock into his ass crack while I grabbed his dick from behind.

Aiden humped my cock sensuously. "Oh, I like it all right," he said. "It's even better than I thought it would be."

I continued to stroke his cock while I slid a finger in between his butt cheeks. Finding his asshole, I fingered it slowly while I jerked him off. In the mirror, his reflected face was a vision of ecstasy. He gripped the edge of the sink and pushed back onto my hand, impaling himself on my finger. For a moment, all I heard was the soft humming of the airplane engines while he rocked on my hand, his balls filling my palm as they swayed with the motion of the plane.

I pulled my finger out and spat into my hand. It wasn't the best lube to use, especially for his first time, but it would have to do. Besides, we were both so horny I probably could have dry fucked him and he would have taken it with no problem. Spitting some more, I rubbed it into his hairy hole, stretching him a little more. Then I positioned the head of my dick against his opening and pushed in. He stiffened as I slid deep into him, but the only sound from his throat was a soft moan.

When I was pressed tightly against his ass, I started to pump his dick with my hand as I fucked him in short thrusts. My other hand played with his tits, moving from one to the other while I slid in and out of him. He was stiff and full in my hand, and every thrust from my dick made his jump, spilling out a fresh load of precum that I used to slick his shaft. I increased my movements until I was pulling nearly all the way out of him and plunging back in.

Just then, the airplane hit a spot of turbulence and dropped slightly. The sudden movement forced me up into Aiden, and I felt his ass tighten around me like a fist. I began to fuck him harder and harder as the plane was jostled by the winds. He took every beat of my cock with another moan, and I could tell by the way his dick was throbbing in my hand that he was close. I started to pump him faster, and soon he was groaning loudly. "I'm going to come," he said, his head falling back against my shoulder. "I'm going to fucking come from your dick inside me." His hands reached back to grip my waist, as if he was trying to push me even further inside him.

"Do it," I ordered, giving his prick several more strokes. "Shoot your load all over my hand."

Aiden began to gasp as his balls released, sending a thick arc of jism spurting across my hand and the sink basin. It smacked into the metal wall in front of him with a wet retort and slid toward the floor. This was followed by several more long streaks of white that blew from his cock and splattered his belly and the sink with more spunk until my hand was making a sloppy lather along the length of his overworked tool.

"Oh, shit," I said, starting to come. "That looks so damn hot." My own dick exploded in Aiden's virgin ass as I held his still-hard meat in my fist and released my load. Over and over again I emptied rounds of cum into his welcoming shitter, pulling him onto me and holding him tightly in my arms until I was spent.

When I had finished coming, I looked in the mirror. Aiden's front was covered in small drops of his own cum. The sink and the wall were streaked with his load, and he was grinning like an idiot. I'd never seen anything so beautiful. I kissed his neck while my cock slid out of him, and his hand closed around mine. I could feel his wedding band on his finger as he held me.

"You look really great," I said, the realization that once the plane landed he'd be back in a woman's arms dampening my enthusiasm. "But somehow I'm not sure your wife would approve."

He nodded. "Doubtful," he said seriously. Then he turned to me, his eyes shining as he pulled my hand to his greasy, hardening prick once more. "Especially when I tell her why it is I'll be holed up with a Yank sports writer in Sydney for a while."

Back-Alley Ball

I love looking at pictures of working-class men from the 1920s and 1930s. There's a toughness about them that's incredibly sexy. I've often imagined what it might have been like to be a gay man then, especially one who was attracted to the roughs who made places like New York the town it was.

"Watch his left, Tom," someone shouted from behind me. McCauley was sidling forward, his meaty fists held up in front of his red face. My last punch had landed neatly in his stomach, and for a minute he looked like he might go down. But he had rebounded, and now he meant business.

Seeing that the Irishman was back in the fight, the men crowded around to watch began betting furiously. Crumpled bills were pulled out of pants pockets and changed hands like leaves in the wind. Anxious voices yelled out encouragement to the man their money, in some cases a week's pay, was riding on. For many of them, whether they would be able to buy dinner for their families that night depended on who was left lying on the ground and who was left standing.

McCauley and I circled one another slowly, each waiting for an opportunity to land the punch that would bring the fight to an end. McCauley was a nasty son of a bitch who worked on the docks moving freight, and he had both the muscles and the bad temper that went with the territory. He had been known to down a dozen pints and take on three men at one time when his mood went sour or he thought he had been slighted, and more than one street fighter had his career ended after going a round with the man.

I usually tried to avoid fights that drew a lot of attention, preferring smaller rounds with guys who'd had a few too many and wanted to prove something to themselves or their buddies by taking on a bigger man. At six-four and 253 pounds, I gave them something to dream about. I let them get in a few good shots until the crowd that inevitably gathered to watch was in a betting mood. Then, once the pot got big enough, I'd go into action. One good sock to the jaw and the other guy was usually out like a light. When he woke up, he didn't know what hit him, and I'd be a couple of bucks richer.

But in the years after the stock market crashed, Hoover sent the American economy into the biggest downward spiral in history, and he left office with the dubious distinction of having midwifed the Depression. I'd made it through the first few years after the crash relatively easily, picking up some action here and there around the city's drinking areas. But by 1932, money was difficult to come by, and I'd had to raise the stakes.

That's why I was sweating it out trying to hold off the big dockworker. So far I'd managed to stay away from McCauley's strong left by keeping one step ahead of him. But that also prevented me from getting in any good punches myself. If something didn't happen soon, we ran the risk of the cops hearing the cheering and coming by to break up the action.

The bettors were anxious to have the fight over with as well, each one calling out encouragement to the man his hopes were pinned on. McCauley, probably because he was better known and this was his turf, had the most supporters. But when I landed the hit to his gut, the chorus of voices calling my name had swelled a little, renewing my quickly fading confidence.

I waited for the opening I needed, my fists balled in front of my face as I danced around. Suddenly McCauley faltered, dropping his fists momentarily. Sensing the opportunity, I stepped forward. As I did, McCauley recovered from his bluff and landed a solid left to my nose. My head flew back under the impact and blood scattered in a dark splash. The Irishman's trick was a common one among back-alley scrappers, and I should have known it. But I was anxious to get the fight over with, and now I was paying for it.

The crowd went into a frenzy as those who had bet on McCauley began to collect their winnings. They stopped when they saw that I was still standing. Even McCauley was staring at me in awe, as if waiting for me to crash like a tree that has been cut through and is holding on by one last filament. My white shirt was speckled with red, and I looked down at it as if it were the first time I had seen my own blood. I touched the side of my nose and felt pain bloom in my head.

McCauley, furious to see me still standing, rushed at me with a howl. I caught him in midstride with a jab to the chest, knocking him back. As he staggered under the unexpected blow, I landed a right hook to his jaw, sending him to the ground for good. The crowd, at least those who had bet on me, cheered, and the winners collected their rewards.

A couple of men came over to pat me on the back and say congratulations, but I was more interested in the money I'd won. I found the guy I'd delegated to be my holder and he handed me some bills. "About fifteen bucks there, I'd guess," he said. "Most of it you won in the last three minutes of the fight."

I thanked him and pocketed the cash. It wasn't the most I'd ever made, but it would hold me over for a few rounds of drinking and pay for a couple of nights at the flophouse I was crashing in. And as soon as the word got around that I'd decked McCauley, every two-bit tough in town would want to try and get a piece of the new boy who'd downed their king. It wouldn't be hard to keep a string of fights going.

My nose was still hurting, so I stepped into a bar for a shot of whiskey to dull the pain a little. Although Prohibition had knocked most of the gin joints out of business, you could still find a watering hole if you knew where to look, especially in this part of town. The do-gooders with their signs and Bible verses were too scared to come down there and drive out demon alcohol.

The bar—actually a small room you got to by going behind the beef carcasses in a slaughterhouse—was filled with smoke and the smell of home-brewed liquor. I waited while the bartender pulled a couple of drafts for some customers and then ordered my drink. Although the flophouse I was staying in was no palace, I wanted to get back and get some sleep.

The bartender brought me my beer, as well as some ice for my nose. I put a couple of coins on the counter and pushed them toward him. As he was putting his hand on them, an arm reached out and stopped him. "Hold it, Pete. This one's on me."

I turned to see who the voice belonged to and found myself looking at a man in a dark jacket. A few inches shorter than I, he had a dark complexion and eyes. His short black hair was neatly combed and slicked back over his head, and he was clean shaven.

He smiled warmly and shook my hand, his grip firm and sure. A thick gold ring encircled a finger on his right hand, and the watch on his wrist was expensive looking. He wasn't the type to be hanging around this part of town, and I wondered what he was looking for.

"That was a great fight out there," he said, the accent in his voice heavy with the masculine cadence bred on New York's rougher streets and out of character with his expensive clothes. "You won me seventy-five bucks. Figure I owe you one."

I nodded. "Thanks."

The man took a long sip on his whiskey and wiped the foam from his lip. "You always been a fighter?"

I laughed, wincing at the pain shooting through my head from my sore nose. "Used to be a steamfitter. But I kept coming home from the bars with a split lip or a black eye. Finally figured if I was going to get roughed up I might as well get paid for it. Been doing it ever since."

The man chuckled. "Funny how we get ourselves pushed into things, isn't it?" He took a cigarette out of a pack in his shirt pocket and lit it. The smoke swirled from the end and hung thickly in the air around his head. "By the way, my name's Haber."

"Tom. So, you really won seventy-five bucks off me, huh? That's quite a bit of dough to have to throw around these days."

Haber laughed. "Guess it is if you don't have it."

He downed the rest of his whiskey and looked at me. "How'd you like to make another hundred?"

I stared at him in amazement. A hundred bucks was more than I'd ever make from two weeks of fighting. I tried to look cool as I asked him, "How?"

Haber leaned toward me. His hand brushed against my leg. "I'd like to get my own taste of that body of yours. Come out back with me and the money's yours."

This guy was gambling big. If he'd asked the wrong guy what he'd just asked me, he might have ended up with his head bashed in. Now I knew what he was doing at the bar, and I knew I'd be able to give him just what he was looking for.

I finished my drink, giving him a minute to worry about whether I was going to deck him or not. When I saw him start to get fidgety, as if he were about to run out, I nodded. "Sure. Let's go."

I walked ahead of Haber, leading him out the bar and across the sloppy floor of the slaughterhouse to the back door. The alley behind the bar was dark except for a dim light coming from a sign that buzzed outside the entrance at the end where it emptied onto a side street. Once it had said MEAT, but somewhere along the line the *A* had died out, leaving a gap in the word like a missing tooth. The alley was largely empty except for a few scattered bottles and the stink of piss from the men who sometimes used it to empty themselves before going home.

Haber walked carefully through the alley to the rear, where some crates of empty Coca-Cola bottles were stacked. I stood in front of him, letting him look at me in the dim light. He reached out a hand and ran it lightly over my shirt, fingering the suspenders that ran down my chest and connected with the buttons on my waistband.

"You're a tough guy, Tom," he said softly. "I want you to show me just how tough you can be."

I pushed him back, feeling his back meet the wall with a dull thud. Leaning forward, I pressed my mouth against his. His lips were full and smooth, and I could taste the remnants of the cigarette and whiskey on them like a thin skin. The feeling of my two-day beard growth against his face excited me, and I kissed him harder, forcing my tongue between his teeth and flicking it against his.

As we kissed, Haber's hands ran over my sides and around my back, pressing me against him. I could feel the hardness of his cock through his pants, pressing against my leg. It was surprisingly big.

"I want it rough," he whispered. "I want you to do it to me hard."

I pulled away from him and stood looking at him, my hand rubbing my own prick as it stiffened inside my pants. Haber looked at it stretching along my thigh and began to moan softly. I massaged my balls roughly, enjoying the lust I saw building behind his eyes.

"Would you like to touch me, Haber?" I asked him.

He nodded, licking his lips nervously.

"Good. Then I want you to strip for me. Get rid of those clothes."

Haber undressed quickly, throwing his jacket on the ground, then stepping out of his highly polished shoes and kicking them aside. His shirt went next, revealing a chest covered in dark hair that ran down his stomach and ended in a thick patch at his waist. When he unzipped his pants, he pulled them off hurriedly. He was not wearing underwear, and his cock swung freely when he stood back up. It was even bigger than it had felt through his pants. The heavy shaft ended in a wide head, and the balls beneath it were plump and round.

Haber stood in front of me completely nude, seemingly oblivious to the fact that someone could walk out and catch us at any time. I stepped forward and took his hand, placing it on my chest. Haber began to fumble with the buttons of my shirt, his hands shaking as he tried to loose the buttons from their holes until finally I had to help him. When my shirt was open to the waist, he reached in and stroked the muscles of my chest, letting his fingers glide over my smooth skin. My nipples were stiff, and he tugged at them gently, pinching them between his thumb and forefinger.

Putting my hands on his shoulders, I pushed him to the ground. When he was on his knees in front of me, I leaned back against the wall. Sliding my hand into my pants, I slowly unbuttoned my fly, watching the hunger in Haber's face grow as he waited to see what I had in store for him. Leaving my suspenders on, I spread the material open and reached in. Pulling my cock out, I let it hang in front of Haber. He stared at the shaft, thick as his wrist, and at the fat head that swayed before his lips. Because I still had my suspenders over my shoulders, my pants pulled up and under my hefty balls, pressing them close to my prick and making it stand out even further.

"Now," I said, "I want to see that dick in your mouth, and I better not feel any teeth on it. Is that clear, Haber?"

Haber nodded, then leaned forward, brushing his lips against my dickhead. He opened his mouth and began to slide the head into his throat. Grabbing him by the hair, I pushed forward, slamming the full length of my cock into his tight throat. He let out a yell that was muffled by the thick meat stretching his mouth, then sucked hungrily.

"You like sucking my big cock, don't you, Haber?" I growled, doing my best to sound like the street rough he wanted me to be. "You like sitting naked in this slimy alley servicing my prick."

Haber answered by squeezing the length of my prong tightly with his lips and throat. His spit was slicking my skin, and I slid in and out easily, my hand guiding his head so that he maintained the speed that gave me the most pleasure. I got off on watching my cock disappear between his appreciative lips, then emerge again until the head appeared and he waited, lips slightly apart, until I buried it home again.

After a few minutes of deep-throating him, I pushed Haber away. Pulling him up, I looked him in the face. "That's one hungry mouth you have, cocksucker. I hope your asshole is just as hungry."

I pushed Haber over the stack of Coca-Cola bottles next to me. His upper body lay across the top crate, his butt spread out in front of me. The mounds of his ass were round and firm, covered with the same hair that dusted the rest of him. I slapped one of them sharply, enjoying the feel of my hand on his tensed muscles.

I stood behind Haber and let my cock fall on his back, just above the valley formed by the globes of his butt. Spitting into my hand, I rubbed it along the length of my prick. Then I spit again and rubbed my fingers into the crack of Haber's ass. His hole was eager, opening to my finger and surrounding it in a kiss. I pushed in deeply, feeling him press back against me until I was buried up to the knuckle in his sweet warmth.

"You're a horny bastard, aren't you, Haber? You can't wait to have me plowing your butt."

Haber was loosening up, but I knew he wasn't loose enough to take what I had for him without at least some pain. He knew it too, and it excited him. He squirmed against my hand invitingly, begging me to enter him. Pulling my finger out, I positioned the head of my prick against the opening of his chute and pushed. Because I was really getting off on fucking Haber in the alley, I was even thicker than usual, and the walls of his ass screamed around the shaft of my cock as it invaded his hole.

Once I was in, I didn't give him any time to adjust to my size. Pulling out, I rammed back in immediately. Haber was whimpering, his hand clutching the edges of the crate tightly, but he never once asked me to stop. He was enjoying my overpowering him, absorbing every thrust of my hefty tool.

I fucked Haber's ass steadily, pulling out just enough to tease his ass ring before plunging back in. My balls slapped his hairy ass wetly as the mixture of spit and his ass juice slipped from his hole and slid over my sac. The more I pumped him, the more excited I got, until soon I was bucking in and out of his ass fiercely. With each thrust the bottles in the crate rattled, the glass tinkling together like the voices of an onlooking chorus.

Grabbing Haber under his arms, I pulled him up roughly and pushed him flat against the wall face first. This new position forced his ass to hug my cock tightly. And because I was taller than he was, I had to crouch somewhat, creating a wonderful ache in my thigh muscles. Pushing upward, I could ram my crank straight up into him until his ass cheeks rested against my legs.

Leaning forward, I rubbed my belly against Haber's back as I fucked him. He hugged the wall tightly, his lips pressed against the brick as he groaned from the reaming I was giving him. I could feel his cock rubbing against the rough stone with each thrust.

Then I couldn't hold back any longer. Pulling out of Haber, I turned him around and pushed him to his knees once more. I fisted my cock three or four times and the spunk rocketed from my overworked balls, gushing across his face and onto the wall behind him. I shoved Haber away from me, staying within my role as rough. Looking down I saw that the fur of his stomach was sticky with ropes of silvery cum. He must have shot his load at the same time I did.

Putting my prick back into my pants, I buttoned up quickly, tucking my shirt into the waistband. Walking over to Haber's jacket, I picked it up and took his wallet out of the pocket. Counting out five twenty-dollar bills, I folded them roughly and jammed them into my pocket, then tossed the wallet on the ground.

As I walked toward the end of the alley and the street beyond, I heard Haber behind me putting on his clothes. Fingering the crisp bills in my pocket, I thought maybe the Depression wasn't going to be so bad after all.

The Checkup

I used to go to an incredibly sexy dentist. One day, while having extensive surgery for an impacted wisdom tooth, I distracted myself by thinking up this story.

"You're going to have to relax some more if I'm going to get my whole hand in," he said. "Right now I can barely get four fingers in there because you're all tensed up."

He was wrong; I wasn't tense. It was just the opposite. He'd been working on me for almost an hour already, and I was becoming very sore from the insistent prodding of his thick fingers. But I loved having his hand inside me, loved the way it filled me so well. And even though he was fully clothed, I was becoming increasingly aroused by my close proximity to him. I even welcomed the pain, knowing that it came from him. As his hands, encased tightly in blue latex gloves, rubbed invitingly against my skin and patiently massaged my aching muscles, I tried to calm myself so that he could get as far in as he wanted to be.

"That's better," he said as I forced myself to stretch just a little bit farther, small fingers of pain scratching at my nerves, and he was able to slide his fingers deep inside. "You're getting much better at this."

I tried to smile, wondering if he would notice. His fingers moving back and forth over my insides felt like a cock burrowing deep within my ass, and he was really getting me worked up. I'd gotten hard almost the moment he'd laid his hands on me, and now my prick was aching from being stiff so long without being touched. I closed my eyes and tried to imagine him fucking me, picturing the look on his face as he rammed his prick into my hole. Just as I was getting to where I could almost smell the sweat and lube on our bodies, he pulled out, shattering my daydream.

"There," he said. "Looks good. All I have to do is polish up the surface and your filling is finished. You'll feel like you have a brand-new set of teeth. I can't believe you did the whole thing without novocaine, though. You must like the pain."

I laughed. "Just don't like the needle, Doc." Little did he know.

As he busied himself getting his instruments together, I ran my tongue over the spot he'd been working on. Now that I was able to close my mouth, the pain had faded to a dull ache in my jaw, a delicious reminder of his presence. The surface of my tooth was rough where he had replaced my filling, and my whole mouth was filled with the heavy taste of his gloves.

I know most people don't like to go to the dentist, but I really enjoy it. I love lying back in that big chair with some man's hands in my mouth, his fingers pressing against my tongue, especially now that latex gloves are standard equipment. I like giving in to him, being in his complete control. I even like the instruments, the way the metal scrapes along my teeth and slides cold and sharp along my gums, ready to prick me if he should falter. I especially like the way my mouth is sore for a few days after a good cleaning, a reminder that someone's hands have been in there.

I especially look forward to seeing Dr. Wolf. The man looks like he should be skating around an ice rink playing forward for the Canucks instead of holding up dental X-rays and looking for cavities. A big man, he has the beautiful black hair and dark eyes characteristic of French Canadian men, and he draws his words out in a heavy accent that makes me hard whenever he opens his mouth, even if all he's doing is telling me to floss more. Every time I have an appointment with him, I end up going home and jerking off for hours thinking about him fucking me. On this particular day he had been a little rough on my mouth, and I was already creating the fantasy I would get off on as soon as I was alone with my cock.

Finished with whatever he was doing, he came back and leaned over me. The lower half of his face was covered by a surgical mask, and all I could see was his nose and eyes over the top of the white square. I opened obediently as he brought his hands to my mouth and began to look around inside with a small mirror. I tried not to stare as I memorized the way his thick hair fell casually over his forehead. I took in all the details of his face, from the fine, strong lines of his nose to the dark beard growth that covered his cheeks, storing them in my mind for later use.

Standing next to me, he was pressed against my side as he worked, and I was acutely aware of the pressure of his body against mine. Putting the mirror aside, he took my jaw in his hand and held it firmly as he probed the area of the filling with his fingers. I concentrated on looking at the space where his shirt hung open at the top, trying not to get too worked up. In the hollow of his throat I could see dark fur where his chest hair began in a thick spray.

I pictured him shirtless, and my cock grew another two inches inside my pants, scraping against my zipper painfully. Averting my eyes in an attempt to hold off my hard-on, I tried looking anywhere but at him, carefully scrutinizing a wall chart about partial plates. But I couldn't help it and ended up staring at his forearms, at the line where the blue latex of his gloves gave way to more hair, which swirled in soft, thick ripples over his skin up to his elbows. I imagined him jerking himself off, how beautiful he would look with his hand holding his prick, his arm moving up and down as he brought himself off. I pictured the hair of his forearm dotted with the white of his cum as he shot all over himself, torturing my cock with the vision.

Inside my mouth, his finger was rubbing steadily along my gumline, moving in small circles around the tooth he'd been working on. My tongue was brushing against his hand as he worked, and through the latex of the glove I could feel the muscles moving beneath his flesh. I started to think about sucking his cock, about the way it would slide in and out of my mouth. I wanted him to wear a rubber when I sucked him so that I could feel his prick beating through the thin skin. I imagined the tip swelling in my throat, growing warm as his cum shot into it and was caught.

It was all too much for me to take. Without thinking, I began to suck gently on the finger that was rubbing my gums, closing my lips around it and letting my tongue trace its way along the length of it. I felt his hand jerk, as though he thought I was going to bite him. I played my tongue over his hand to let him know I wasn't going to hurt him, and he relaxed a little. A tremor of excitement ran through my body as my fantasies began to move from the hazy world of my mind and became flesh and bone. My lips moved over the surface of his gloved hand slowly as I took in the smell of the rubber, making love to it with my mouth, all thoughts of my circumstances lost in the heat of raw lust.

During all this, I kept my eyes away from Dr. Wolf's face, afraid that looking at him would force me to lose my nerve. I concentrated on his hand, on his fingers and how good they felt. When he didn't pull away from me, I let myself move my gaze up his chest to his face. He was looking right at me, his dark brown eyes intent. Beneath the white gauze of the mask, a smile played across his lips. Never taking his eyes off of me and still holding my chin in his hand, he started to thrust his fingers in and out between my lips, letting the tips glide over my teeth and rest just inside my mouth so that I had to lean forward to suck them back in.

Reaching out, I let my fingers fall onto the forearm of the hand I was sucking, stroking the soft hair. The muscles of his arm were thick, stretching sinuously as he moved his hand back and forth over my face, covering my lips with the taste of his gloves. I gripped him tightly, enjoying the feeling of cool latex melting into warm skin several inches above the wrist. As he slid his hand back and forth over my lips, his grip on my chin tightened, holding my head firmly in place as he worked me into a frenzy.

I ran my hand over his chest, feeling the solidness of his body beneath the thin fabric of his blue shirt. His tits were hard, and when I ran my fingers over them he pressed forward against my hand. Taking this as encouragement, I unbuttoned his shirt and pulled it from his waistband. Undone, it hung open, exposing a torso washed with black fur. Running my hand over his belly, I was surprised to find that his body was remarkably well developed, ridged and furrowed like a well-plowed field. His nipples, pink and tender looking, peeked from the forest of hair like two small buds bursting from the earth.

Bringing my hand to his neck, I traced a line down his chest to his waistband, lightly drawing my fingers across his skin and making him shiver. Then, moving back to his chest, I took one of his nipples between my fingers, pinching it. He flinched at the touch, but did not pull away. Still holding it tightly, I tugged on it, forcing him to lean down toward me and letting his hand fall from my lips. When his face was inches away from mine, I reached up and undid the white mask, dropping it to the floor. He gazed down at me, his eyes filled with lust, and I kissed his mouth gently, my tongue teasing his lips with small flutters.

Then I kissed him harder, putting my hand on his neck and pushing deep into his mouth. He sucked in his cheeks, drawing me farther into him and running his tongue against mine hungrily. I felt the scratchiness of his skin against my face as I ground myself against him, the taste of him sinking into my mouth, the smell of his skin surrounding me. As we kissed, he put one hand on my crotch and rubbed my prick slowly, sliding up the length of it and squeezing the head through my pants.

He was still pressed against my side, and I could feel his growing hard-on through his pants. Pushing him away from me, I undid the buttons of his pants and let them fall away. He shrugged his shirt off and stepped out of his pants, standing next to me in white workout briefs that came halfway down his hairy thighs. The fly was held closed by two small buttons, and his balls made a hefty sac that hung at the crotch invitingly. His thick cock was pushed up toward his waist, and the head was pushing out against the skintight material in sharp relief.

I ran my hands over the back of his shorts, feeling the curves of his ass and the muscles of his legs. He was pulling at my shirt, ripping it open quickly and nodding appreciatively when he got a look at my smooth, gym-hardened body. Unbuckling my belt, he put his hand under me and lifted me up in the chair a little, sliding my pants down and off. Because I was not wearing any underwear, my prick sprang up the moment my pants slid over it. It rose up from my stomach, a smear of cock drool dripping from the head.

Dr. Wolf got onto the chair and straddled me at the waist, his knees fitting comfortably into the side pockets meant for the patient's elbows. The touch of his underwear on my cock as he sat on me was almost enough to make me come, but I held myself in check waiting to see what he had in mind. Putting his still-gloved hands on my chest, he worked his fingers over my nipples and then down my sides, tickling my skin. As he thrust slowly along my dick, my prick slid between his legs and under him, the head pressing against his balls.

He put his hands on the top of the chair and laid his body along mine. By turning my head, I was able to push my face into the thick, damp hair of his armpit, my tongue licking eagerly at the sweaty skin. As his furry belly rubbed along mine, I explored his body with my mouth, moving along his throat and down his chest, lapping at the hair that covered his skin. When I felt one of his nipples beneath my tongue, I sucked on it firmly, biting down. He responded by thrusting his prick tightly against my stomach, where I felt the entire length of it burning into me.

Unable to wait any longer, I put my hands on his waistband and pulled his underwear down until the head of his cock was exposed. Fat and uncut, it slipped in and out of the sheath of his foreskin as he rubbed against me, the thin skin gliding over the ridge where his head joined the shaft. It was much larger than I had imagined, and the sight of the fat knob surrounded by its translucent wrapper made my ass tingle with anticipation. The shaft itself was immensely thick, and a line of hair ran up the underside for several inches.

Reaching inside, I pulled his balls from their nesting spot, letting them hang over the edge of his bunched-up underwear. The wrinkled sac was oddly smooth compared to the rest of his body, and his nuts sat in my hand like perfectly round stones that had been sitting in a fire and still retained the heat. Behind them, I could feel the hair in the space just below his ass crack. Putting my fingers around the base of his cock and balls, I was unable to touch my fingers together. As I squeezed, his prick swelled with blood, the head turning a dark red color.

Pressing my cock against Dr. Wolf's, I held them both together tightly, feeling the vein on the underside of his beautiful piece beating all along the length of my tool. His huge balls splayed out over mine, rubbing against them as I played with our dicks, pumping them slowly. He was really leaking juice, and it trickled from his piss hole in a thick stream, running over his head and streaking my hand and cock in sticky strings. I loved the way his foreskin rode over his head, like the skin of a fruit peeling away to reveal the delicious flesh underneath, and I wanted to taste him in my mouth.

"Let me suck it," I pleaded. "Put a rubber on it and fuck my mouth. There's one in my wallet."

He got down off the table and shucked his underwear all the way off. Then he fished in my pants pocket and pulled out my wallet. I know you're not supposed to keep rubbers in a wallet because they can dry out and all, but I kept one there just in case of emergencies. Dr. Wolf found it and pulled it out. Because he was still wearing the latex gloves, he was having trouble getting the package open.

"Let me do it," I offered.

I love putting condoms on guys' pricks, and the idea of dressing up his massive tool was getting me hot and bothered all over again. Pulling out the rubber, I held it up. Like his gloves, it was blue, like a piece of summer sky in my fingers. I sniffed it, letting the scent fill my head. Dr. Wolf pushed a button on the arm of the chair and the back went down slowly until I was almost flat on my back with my head elevated slightly. Then he mounted me once more and inched his way slowly up my stomach, letting his ass slide along my skin. When his cock was bobbing just inches away from my mouth, he stopped and waited.

Placing the condom at the tip of his cock, I carefully rolled it down his shaft, watching as his thickness filled the thin skin and stretched it until it looked like a layer of clear water running down his prick. Leaning forward, I licked his rubber-encased head, tasting the sweet lube that coated it and letting my tongue linger on the sticky smooth surface for a moment. Then, quickly, I slipped him into my throat, surprising him with the speed of my movements. He groaned as my throat swallowed several inches of him, straining against his girth.

I could feel the loose tip of the condom tickling my throat as I savored his cock in my mouth. I sucked at the rubber that surrounded his prick, my tongue massaging his crank and tracing every line of his piece where it creased the smooth surface. Slowly I inched more and more of him into me, pushing forward a little at a time. Finally, I felt the ring of the condom break my passage and tasted hot skin beneath my lips as I buried my face in his bush and the last of him was inside me.

Dr. Wolf put his hands on my face, guiding my movements along his cock. He slid in and out steadily, each time pausing for a moment when the tip reached my lips and letting me suck hard on his foreskinned crown. The feel of his gloves on my skin and the rubber in my throat were intoxicating. I ran my hands over his back and ass, pushing him deeper and deeper into me, urging him to blow his load.

He didn't need much encouragement. After a few minutes of

pumping my mouth, he began to moan, and his hands gripped my
head tightly. I sucked harder, really stroking his meat as he
thrust, and I could feel him growing even thicker as he reached
his climax. I waited breathlessly, anticipating the swell of the rubber. When it came, it was spectacular. The base of his prick
twitched, and I felt the rubber ripple as his load raced up his shaft
and exploded into the tip. It filled quickly as he came, the empty
rubber expanding under the force of his jism until it became a hot
bubble in my throat. Churning with his blast, it hung in my throat
like a drop of delicious water waiting to fall before some of the
cum found its way up the sides of his shaft and the tip decreased
in size.

Dr. Wolf slipped his cock out of my mouth and pulled the rubber off quickly. It hung from his hand, the tip fat with cum. He de-
posited it on the instrument tray attached to the chair, where it
lay just out of my reach but right where I could see it, all wrinkled
and filled with his essence. Just looking at it made my balls
tighten. I wanted to hold it and feel the cum sliding around inside
the empty skin. But he had other ideas.

Moving down my body, Dr. Wolf took my cock in his lips, the
warm heat of his mouth surrounding me as he quickly began to
suck me. At the same time, I felt his gloved hand rub my ass, urging me to spread my legs. I pulled my legs up on either side of me,
and he stretched out between them along the length of the examining chair, his feet hanging off the end. With my asshole exposed
to him, he began to stroke it. The latex rasped over my hole roughly
as he fingered it, probing for entry while he deep-throated me.

Pressing harder, he slipped one finger into my ass, the slippery
surface of the glove sliding in smoothly. As he fingered me, he
kept up his movement on my cock, matching the thrusts evenly.
He really knew how to work my tool, moving from my balls to the
tip in long, smooth strokes. As I watched my cock disappearing
down his throat, I could hardly believe that he was the same man
who had drilled my tooth not so long before.

Soon two fingers were pumping away at my ass, stretching it
even wider. The latex slid over my sphincter wetly and easily now
that I had loosened up a little, and Dr. Wolf was gliding in and out
quickly. When he was able to get three in, he stopped sucking my
dick. Kneeling between my legs, he continued to fuck me with his
hand, twisting and turning his fingers as he kneaded my insides.

His other hand roamed over my body, rubbing my tits and squeezing my balls until I was ready to shoot all over myself. When he grabbed my dick and started pumping it, I thought I was going to pass out.

Dr. Wolf's prick had become hard again as he fingered me, and now it stood up between his thighs. Pulling his hand away from my ass, he aimed the still-sticky head at my hole and pressed in. His dick pounded into me, pushing me back against the chair as his weight was thrown against my legs, which slid over his shoulders as his gloved hands went around my thighs and held me tightly. He wasted no time, pumping my ass in hard bursts that slammed his balls against my ass cheeks and made the entire chair shake. With each thrust, he seemed to move deeper and deeper into my chute, stretching me and filling me with new stores of pleasure. My ass was burning from the heat of his strokes, yet I never wanted him to stop.

Still ramming his pole into me, he snatched the used condom from the table and held it against my face. I could feel the warmth of his spunk through the rubber as he pressed it to my lips, and I sucked it into my mouth, letting the heavy weight rest on my tongue. He drew it away from me, running the end over my lips and my cheek, holding it just out of reach of my tongue. I strained my head to reach it, but the weight of him pinned me back.

He was battering my ass mercilessly at this point, and I knew he was going to blow another load, this time deep in my ass. Milking his shaft with my butt muscles, I rocked against him, my sweaty skin sticking to the surface of the chair with wet smacking sounds. He leaned into me, pushing every last inch of him inside me as he came to the edge.

At the same time, he put the open end of the rubber against my lips, urging me to take it into my mouth. I did so eagerly, my tongue slipping into the opening and discovering there the tastes of rubber and cum all mixed up together. Dr. Wolf tipped the condom up, and I saw his load slide down toward my waiting mouth at the same time as he was getting ready to blow in my butt. As he began to spurt deep within me, the delicious cream flowed out of the rubber and filled my mouth with the thick taste of his cock, coating my teeth and tongue in rich waves that streamed into my throat as I sucked every drop from the condom.

Dr. Wolf was still emptying his balls into me when I let the empty rubber fall from my lips onto my chest. One latex-clad hand was now clamped around my cock, pumping it as he continued to fuck me. It didn't take long for my overloaded balls to respond, and I spattered his hand with a skyrocket of white that roared from my prick straight up onto his stomach, where it clung in shining droplets to his thick fur. He pressed my dick against his belly, smearing it in the cum-soaked hair, holding it tightly as we both finished shooting.

As the last drops slid from my burning slit, I felt his load begin to slip out of my hole as he pulled out. Laying himself on top of me, our sticky skin pressing together wetly, he covered my mouth with his and kissed me deeply.

"You really should remember to brush after eating," he said, pulling back and licking his lips. "And I think maybe we need to put you on an every-three-month schedule."

Varsity Meat

Once, while house-sitting in college for a very respectable couple, I discovered an enormous studded dildo beneath their bed (I was vacuuming, in case you're wondering). Years later, the memory came to me and this story somehow emerged from it.

Jeff and I had been sharing a suite since the fall term had started in September. It was an odd pairing, I in pre-law and he a phys ed major. I would have loved to have seen the secretary in the dean's office grinning as she picked through the applications, found the two students the least similar, and assigned us the same room. We were, in fact, different in almost every way. Jeff was from a small steel town in Illinois and a real outdoor boy. He'd played baseball and field hockey in high school and had escaped the stranglehold of his hometown by leading his team to the state finals three years in a row and winning an athletic scholarship to Bradley.

I, on the other hand, had spent most of my life among the cultured streets of New York's Upper East Side. The closest I'd come to playing team sports was navigating the subway at rush hour or making the rounds of the parties my banker father threw for his clients and fending off their daughters who, drunk on champagne, cornered me in the coatroom and attempted to find out what was inside my tuxedo pants. I was at Bradley mainly because my father and two brothers had gone there.

Physically Jeff and I were like night and day. Although my body was tight from gym workouts, I was only five-eight and small boned. With my blue eyes and blond hair, I could have been a poster child for Midwestern wholesomeness. Jeff was just the opposite—a big man with black hair and dark, brooding eyes. His body was hard from physical work, and he wore his strength like a suit of invisible clothes. He stood six-three and well over 230 pounds, and I always used to joke that no one ever told him while he was growing up that taking up that much space was a sin.

Despite our differences, we got along well. Our schedules rarely put us in the suite at the same time, and when it did we had separate bedrooms and didn't get in each other's way. Because of our different academic regimens, we had no classes together, and when Jeff went off to his various team practices, I'd be going off to the library. On rare occasions we hung out together in the living room that we shared, but most of the time we kept to ourselves.

The problem was that I had become very attracted to Jeff. Ever since I'd first seen him—carrying his big steamer trunk up the stairs single-handedly, his muscular legs and firm ass straining in his hiking shorts—I'd fantasized about making love with him. When he'd taken his sweat-soaked shirt off and I saw the short carpet of hair that covered his chest, I was in heaven. It was all I could do not to drop to my knees and blow him right there as he was introducing himself to me, his massive fingers gripping mine in a solid handshake.

I sometimes lay in bed in the morning listening to him take a shower, my cock in my hand. In my mind I'd picture him slowly removing his clothes, revealing inch after inch of his hairy legs and the thick cock I imagined hung between them. I'd think of him soaping up his round, firm ass and shoot my load all over my belly.

It got so that whenever I saw Jeff I'd get a raging hard-on. I'd spy him on campus walking with any one of the many girls who followed him around and feel my cock start tugging in my pants. More than once I'd run to the nearest bathroom and jerked off, spewing my spunk as I thought about sucking his sweet prick. Once I even saw him in the library and pumped a load all over my hand in the back stacks of the periodical section moments before the librarian came around the corner looking for a back issue of *Time* for a student.

One day, when I knew Jeff was at soccer practice and wouldn't be getting back for at least another hour, I snuck into his room. I'd gotten especially horny when I saw him leave in his sweats with the big mound of his cock jiggling in front, and I wanted to jerk off in his room. I looked around to see if there was anything of his lying around that I could use to help get me off and noticed that his closet door was open a crack.

Opening it, I saw that there was a pile of dirty laundry on the floor. I picked through the jumble of shirts, socks, and pants until I found a pair of his underwear. The elastic was slightly stretched around the leg openings, and there were faint, yellow stains around the pouch. I pushed my face into the crotch, breathing in the rich smell that had been left by Jeff's cock and balls. The cotton was soft and worn, and I rubbed it over my lips, sucking on the stained material.

Licking the big jock's underwear had made my prick stiffen, and I unbuttoned my pants, releasing it from the confines of the denim. It was throbbing with heat, and I stroked it slowly as I fantasized about sucking Jeff's cock in the locker room after a practice, his balls heavy with sweat, his dick hard and needy. I dreamed of licking his furry armpits and tasting his skin as he pulled on my balls.

Just as I was getting to the part where Jeff bent me over the changing bench and stuck his fat prick into my asshole, I heard the front door open and slam shut. Jeff had come home early. I couldn't get out of his room without him seeing me, so the only thing to do was pull the closet door shut and hope he didn't open it. All I needed was for him to catch me with his underwear in my mouth.

I had just gotten the door pulled as shut as possible when Jeff walked in. There were so many unwashed clothes on the floor that I couldn't get it all the way closed, and a small crack remained. Through it I watched as Jeff put down his gym bag, praying he wouldn't want to add anything else to his laundry pile. He sat on his bed and removed his sneakers, tossing them into the corner. Then he peeled off his sweatshirt, revealing the hairy chest I loved so much. Finally, he pulled his sweatpants off in one smooth motion, leaving him naked.

His cock was just as beautiful as I imagined it would be. Even soft, it hung far down over a set of heavy balls covered in hair. Jeff must have worked up quite a sweat at practice, because the fur on his stomach was swirled in wet circles, and his hair was tousled as if he'd just left the shower without drying it.

I thought Jeff would head right for the showers, but instead he lay down on his bed and spread his legs. His hand went between his thighs and he started to slowly tease his cock and balls, rubbing them lazily. He traced his fingers lightly through the bush at the base of his sac. Then he ran them up his groin to his chest, stopping at one of his big pink nipples and pinching it.

By now his cock was growing hard at a rapid rate. I watched it swell, getting thicker and thicker, stretching across his thigh and rising until it lay flat against his stomach. It was incredibly fat, with a round head that extended out from the shaft like a helmet and ended in a smooth point. The hair on his nuts continued up the shaft a few inches, then gave way to smooth, tight skin a shade lighter than the rest of him.

Jeff continued to knead his balls with his big hand. His sac was soft and loaded with two of the biggest nuts I'd ever seen, like two eggs in a velvet pouch. As he rubbed his nipple, Jeff put his fingers around his ballsac, stretching it out so that his cock, still untouched, rose up a few inches and then slapped down against his belly with a soft thud. From my hiding spot in the closet I had a perfect view of the action on Jeff's bed. Watching him play with himself was turning me on, and I was slowly stroking my dick in time with his ball play.

Jeff opened the drawer of his bedside table and pulled out a bottle of lube. Holding the bottle upside down, he squeezed a thick stream onto his palm. Reaching down, he wrapped his hand around his cock and began to work it up and down, coating his tool with silvery liquid. He stroked his prick slowly, dragging his hand upward until it reached the head, then rolling it over the tip and squeezing it before moving back down the shaft. He did this for several delicious minutes, and I watched entranced as he explored every inch of himself. Seeing his fingers wrapped around his cock, the tip protruding from his fist as he jerked off, made my own nuts ache as I thought about what it would feel like to have him in my ass.

Jeff stopped playing with his meat and squirted some more lube onto his fingers. I thought he was going to resume jacking off, but what he did next took me by surprise. Sliding his hand between his thighs, he brought his feet up to his waist, spreading his meaty ass slightly and giving me a look right into his hole. The tight pucker was pink and clean shaven, a smooth circle in his otherwise furry ass. Jeff rubbed the area with his hand, slicking it with lube. Then he began to rub his ass ring with his fingers, sliding the tip of his index finger in and turning it slightly.

When he was loose enough, he slid the whole finger in, groaning as he did so. When his palm was flat against his balls and his ass lips were snug around his finger, he began to thrust slowly.

I was so shocked at seeing Jeff fingering his hole that for a moment I stopped what I was doing and just watched. He was twisting his nipple with his free hand and moving his hips to get his finger as deep inside himself as possible. After a minute, he slid a second finger in beside the first one, stretching himself wider.

Pulling his fingers out, Jeff reached once more into his drawer. This time he pulled out a dildo that was at least a foot long. Just looking at it made my asshole hurt. Using more lube, Jeff covered the dong in a sticky film, stroking it as if it were his own cock. He positioned its enormous head at the opening of his chute and eased it in. His face was set in a grimace of pleasure and pain as he steadily pushed the massive toy into his bowels, his asshole stretching around its thick pink sides in an obscene grin.

Jeff didn't stop until all twelve inches were inside his gut and the end of the dildo was flat against his ass cheeks. I could see that some precum had begun to ooze from his piss hole, trickling down his furry belly. Using one hand, Jeff began to work the dildo in and out of his ass slowly, letting his muscles get used to the invader. He pulled his knees up toward his chest to give himself more room, the cock spearing him right through the center of his ass. As he fucked himself Jeff also took time to beat the real meat between his legs.

Soon he was moving the dildo in and out quickly, sliding along on a sea of sweat, lube, and the ass juice that was running down his cheeks. He would pull it out until the tip of the head was just inside his hole, lingering for a moment before shoving it all the way back in, moaning as his chute was stretched out by its girth. His big balls hung down on either side of the dildo as it traveled in and out of his hole, moving in time with his hand.

By now Jeff was lying with his legs in the air, his ass spread as wide as possible. His cock stuck straight up as he pounded it, his balls slopping against the thrusting dildo. Finally, with a loud grunt he slammed the dildo home as a geyser of cum erupted from his dick, exploding into the air and falling back onto his chest in big, hot drops.

The sight of my jock roommate with a fat cock up his ass and cum on his face was enough to send me over the edge, and I shot

into Jeff's underwear. The force of my own orgasm was so intense
that my muscles went weak, and suddenly I found myself falling
forward. Because my legs were entwined in my pants, I couldn't
keep my balance. The closet door opened and I tumbled out, hitting the floor with an unceremonious thud, Jeff's shorts still
wrapped around my cock.

I waited for Jeff to jump off the bed and start beating the life
out of me. Instead, I heard him laughing in great deep bursts.
"Christ, Tom, that was some entrance. Good thing you didn't land
on that boner of yours."

I rolled over and looked at him, the aforementioned boner
rapidly sinking into oblivion. "You mean you aren't mad at me?"

Jeff grinned. "Hell, no. I knew you were in there the whole
time. Why'd you think I put on such a show?"

I had managed to untangle myself from my pants and was sitting up. Thinking about what I must have looked like falling out of
the closet made me start laughing. "Yeah, well, it was a great
show."

"And it's just beginning," Jeff said. "I've been thinking about
sticking my cock up that tight ass of yours for a long time. Now's
a good time to do it."

He was still lying down, and his prick was hard again. As he
talked, he was jerking off slowly. The dildo was still lodged in his
asshole, and the end rested between his thighs, held in place by
the pressure of his weight against the bed. I stood up and was surprised to see that my cock had also filled out once more. My cum
had dried on the skin, and small spots of flaky spunk dotted my
shaft and head.

Jeff moved over on the bed and I lay down next to him on my
side so that I could see him stretched out alongside me. I still
couldn't believe that I was finally going to touch the body I'd se-
cretly lusted after for the last two months. Like a kid in a candy
store, I reached out and grasped his prick, feeling it fill my hand
with heat, the vein throbbing fiercely against my palm. It was still
slick with lube and cum, and I slid my fingers up it until I was
holding the tip, my fingers closing around it as if it were a ripe
fruit.

Reluctantly, I let go and stroked the hair on Jeff's stomach,
moving up his chest, tickling his tits and rubbing the muscles beneath his skin. Leaning over him, I took one of his nipples be-

tween my teeth, biting gently on the firm round bud of flesh. Jeff put his hand on the back of my head, pushing my face tightly against his chest. I sucked harder, licking in broad strokes the thick hair around his nipple.

Running my hand between Jeff's thighs, I tugged on the dildo, pulling it out an inch or two and twisting it slightly. Jeff responded by pulling me on top of him so that I was straddling his chest, my balls and cock spread out between the hills of his pecs like a fallen tree lying on a forest floor.

Jeff put his hands on my ass and pushed me forward until my cock was inches from his face. Leaning forward, he took the sticky tip into his mouth, his lips closing around my head in a firm kiss. I put my hands on either side of his head, stroking his short hair and feeling the muscles of his neck move as he sucked me in deeper, washing off the dried cum with his tongue.

Jeff took in all of me with no hesitation. When my balls were scraping against the stubble of his chin, he ground his face against my groin before pulling back until the tip of my dick was just inside his mouth. He ran his tongue lightly around the head, tracing the edge and then sucking it back down his throat. His mouth felt wonderful, and I loved the touch of his lips and tongue on my sensitive skin.

While Jeff was sucking my cock, his hands were exploring my ass. He held my cheeks tightly, squeezing them and occasionally slapping my butt with his palm as he pushed me into his throat, his strong fingers rubbing deeply into my muscles. He slid his hand between my cheeks, pushing at the ring of my ass. I relaxed, letting him push inside, feeling small jolts of pleasure shoot through my belly as his thick knuckle plowed past my sphincter.

Jeff's finger was so big it felt like I was getting serviced on two ends—my cock fucking his beautiful, rugged face while my hole was being filled from behind by his big hand. I rocked back and forth as he fingered me roughly with two and then three fingers, stretching the walls of my shitter and massaging my hole into a frenzy.

Removing his fingers, Jeff inserted his thumb into my ass, his fingers tugging at my nuts. As I'd pull out of his mouth he would push in with his thumb, keeping a steady stream of pleasure running through my body. Nearing the brink, I started moaning above him, excited by the thought of pouring my load down his throat. Instead, Jeff let my cock fall from his mouth and pushed me back.

When I felt the tip of his prick against my ass, all of my jerk-off fantasies ran through my mind. Many times I'd imagined how thick the shaft would be, how the head would feel sliding into my chute. Now it was lying beneath my cheeks, hard, insistent, and very real. I leaned forward a little and slid against its length, feeling the head push against my balls and exit between my thighs, watching as our pricks rubbed against each other.

Jeff was worked up from the fingering he'd been giving my hole, and I could tell that he wanted to have his meat buried in my ass. I was just as steamed, especially when I recalled the load he'd shot fucking himself, the remnants of which now made sticky smears on my ass cheeks from sitting on his chest. I reached behind me and lifted Jeff's dick until it was positioned tightly against my hungry butthole. Easing back, I sat on the fat head, wincing as it tore into my tender ass. Even the fingering he'd given me couldn't prepare me for the ramrod that was hammering at my door.

Despite the pain at his thickness, I wanted Jeff deep inside me. I held my breath and pushed back, sliding him into me quickly, groaning as the walls of my shitter expanded to accommodate him. I'd never had anything that big up my butt before, and it was an amazing sensation. I could feel the head plowing deep into me, pushing its way through my insides.

I was amazed when I felt my ass touch Jeff's bush. I had probably ten inches of thick man meat inside me. The fact that it was Jeff's made me even more excited, and I had to stop myself from coming on the spot. Jeff's eyes were closed, and he was smiling slightly. His knees were pulled up, and I rested against them. Pulling myself forward, I began to ride Jeff's horse cock, letting the inches slip in and out as I twisted his tits.

As Jeff's head slid over my prostate, my cock jumped and oozed precum until I was drooling with the stuff. Jeff took my cock in his hand and began to beat it in time with my motions. I squeezed my ass muscles tight, bringing groans from his throat. Then, remembering that the dildo was still buried deep in his butt, I reached behind me and found the end. His hole was still slimy with lube and juice, and it was easy to pull the dildo out a little, especially since his legs were already raised to support me. As

I fucked Jeff's ass, he began to thrust harder, his hips moving in time with mine, burrowing into me deeply.

The force of his thrusting, combined with the pleasure of fucking his ass with the dildo as he plowed me, brought me to a boil. My whole body shook as my load shot from my prick and slopped over Jeff's neck and lips, the final spurts falling onto his hairy forearm as he continued to jerk me off. Feeling my cum on his mouth, Jeff licked it off. I felt his thrusts become harder and more heated, and he started to moan. Pulling the dildo almost all of the way out, I pushed it back in until the end was smack against his beefy ass. As the cock buried into him, Jeff's prick swelled inside me as he poured his jism into my belly in great heaves.

After he came, I remained on Jeff's chest as his cock grew soft within me. I rubbed my cum from his chest and fed it to him on my fingers, then bent to kiss him, tasting my scent on his tongue and lips. As we kissed, I felt him slide the dildo out of his butt and drop it to the floor.

"You looked like you really enjoy that dildo in your ass," I said, rolling onto my back next to him.

Jeff laughed and reached for my prick. "Yeah, I do," he said. "But now I think it's time for the real thing."

Bacchanal

I don't remember where this story came from, really. I'd actually forgotten about it until I was looking through material for this collection and my friend Katherine said, "You have to use that Zeus one. I love it." I think I just wanted to write something very dreamlike and magical. Then again, who needs an excuse to fantasize about Greek gods?

If I had been at home, I would have chalked up the emptiness of the bar to the fact that it was only a little past six. But in Greece, the locals started congregating as soon as the shops had closed for the day. I had been in Cernunos for three months working on my latest book, and each night after work I'd walk down to the bar and soak up the local flavor. Usually the tables were crowded with groups of laughing people downing glasses of ouzo by the time I got there, so the eerie silence that greeted me as I came through the doorway was out of place.

Basil, the bartender, was standing behind the bar washing glasses. I walked over and took a seat at one of the stools. "Where'd everybody get to?" I asked.

Basil turned and set a glass in front of me. As he filled it with the thin local wine I had come to love so much, he smiled quietly. "You don't know what tonight is?" he asked, looking at me with his liquid brown eyes shining.

"Yeah, it's Friday. This place should be filled with about sixty people by now. I should be trying to figure out whose interested in taking a nice American man home for the night and you should be yelling at Nico to hurry up with another case of ouzo. So what gives?"

Basil laughed softly. "Tonight is not like other Fridays," he said mysteriously. "Tonight is special. Tonight everyone is home, where I will be as soon as I finish washing up these glasses."

"I don't get it," I said. "Is there a curfew or something I don't know about? Did someone come in and turn the whole village into a convent?"

Basil started to dry a glass with the white towel around his waist. "Do you know about Greek mythology?" he asked.

"Greek myths? You mean gods and goddesses and all that shit?"

Basil nodded.

"Sure. I mean, I read it all in school. Jason and the Argonauts. The Trojan Horse. What about it?"

"Do you know of Bacchanal?"

I shook my head. "No, sounds like some kind of cure for jock itch."

Basil didn't laugh. "Bacchanal," he said, "is the feast of the gods. One night a year the barrier between the worlds is thin enough for them to cross over, and they come to celebrate their power. It is dangerous for mortals to see them."

"Wait a minute. You're telling me that tonight the gods are going to appear in the village and live it up while you all stay inside? That's nuts."

"Maybe so," he said. "I'm just telling you what the stories say."

I finished my drink in one gulp and put the empty glass on the bar. "Well, I hope the gods have a good time," I said. "I'm going to go back to my room and work on my book some more. I've got a deadline to meet."

I waved to Basil and left the bar. Stepping into the cool evening, I looked up. The sky was just beginning to blush pink as the warm Grecian sun slipped into the arms of the clouds, and the air was cool with a breeze carrying the salty taste of the ocean. The streets were as empty as the bar had been, and I walked alone through the winding, narrow lanes of houses and shops. No dogs ran up begging for food, no one hawked fish from the stalls. The windows, normally filled with women chattering to neighbors across the street, were shuttered and silent.

I reached the house I was renting for the summer and walked up the stairs to my bedroom. I opened the shutters and looked out toward the hill that rose up just outside of town. At the top perched an ancient temple overlooking the sea below. It was this view that had made me decide to take the rooms. Since they had been largely ignored by archaeologists, the ruins were still mostly

untouched. The only people who ever really went there were the
kids who played hide-and-seek in between the crumbling pillars. I
had set my desk up underneath the window and tried to break my
frequent writer's block by wondering what had happened there in
years gone by.

I wrote for a while, but the story line kept slipping away from
me. The wine Basil had given me had gone to my head with un-
characteristic strength, and I decided that the best thing for me
was a good night's sleep. Since everyone was apparently shut in
for the night, there wasn't much else to do. I shed my clothes and
lay down on the cool, white sheets of the bed. The wind in the window swept over my skin, and I quickly fell asleep.

Some time later, a noise disturbed my dreams, and I turned
over on the bed. The sky outside was now blue-black, and stars
blazed against the backdrop in sharp relief. A full moon hung
framed in my window, as round and pale as the abandoned shell of
a sea creature. The noise came again, a low murmur like heavy
waves falling on the shore. I got up and went to the window, looking for its source. Below me the town was still and empty, the
houses showered in gold from the moon. The sound seemed to be
coming from out near the temple. Looking in that direction, I saw
a faint glow shining between the pillars of the ruins, as if someone
had started a bonfire inside. *It's probably a bunch of kids having a
little Bacchanal of their own,* I thought, and tried to go back to
sleep.

But the sound was infectious. When I tried to close my eyes, it
became louder, filling my head and echoing through my mind. I
tried putting the pillow over my head, but it didn't help. No matter how hard I tried, I just couldn't go back to sleep. And for some
reason, my cock had started to stiffen. It was stretching half-hard
across my belly, begging me to take it in my hand. Deciding that I
was never going to go to sleep now, I got up and pulled on my
jeans and a T-shirt.

Without knowing quite why I was doing it, I left the house and
headed out of town on the path that wound up the hill to the old
temple. The air around me was cool, and I shivered as I walked
barefoot along the sandy path, realizing that I had forgotten to
put on my shoes. Reaching the crest of the hill, I found myself in
front of the ruins. The crumbling columns reached up from moss-

covered rocks into the night sky like the legs of a giant whose head swam somewhere in the stars. Light spilled out from between the pillars and poured down the long steps that led up to the doorway, the stones worn smooth from the feet of the ancient faithful.

Climbing the steps, I peered in cautiously through the doorway, not wanting to interrupt whoever might be there. Inside, the temple was filled with flickering light from torches placed on the columns. Just as I thought, there was a huge bonfire burning in the center of the floor. Groups of people were standing around the fire and sitting on the various pieces of stone scattered throughout the ruins, and I relaxed. It was just a bunch of kids after all.

But as my eyes adjusted to the firelight, a very different picture came into view. All around the temple were naked men. Some were leaning against the pillars, others were sitting near the fire drinking from large cups. But most were fucking. Large carpets had been spread over the stone floor, and on them men, some in couples and some in groups, were making love. The moans that came from the writhing bodies rang through the cavernous room, and I realized that it was the same noise that had invaded my sleep.

I stared transfixed, watching the roomful of men grunting and thrusting against one another. The sound of their lovemaking entered my mind, and I felt my senses escaping from me as the smells and sounds of the orgy filled my head. Then I felt a hand in mine and came back to reality. Standing in front of me was a man. His black hair fell easily over his forehead, and his dark eyes looked like stones. His well-muscled chest was smooth and brown skinned. My eyes traveled down the ridges of his abdomen, and when I got to his waist, I paused, not believing what was before me. Below the man's waist, the smooth silk of skin gave way to thick fur, and his legs were like those of a goat, ending in tapered hooves split up the middle. Between his legs hung a long, thick cock and a set of overripe balls the size of oranges. I shook my head and just stared at the creature standing in front of me.

"What's the matter," he said in a laughing voice, "you never see a satyr before? Or just not a prick that big?"

I looked back up, noticing for the first time the two small horns rising from either side of his forehead. There was a huge grin stretching across his bearded face, and his eyes were flashing.

"Um, no, I haven't seen a satyr before," I said, wondering what the hell was going on.

"Well, there's a first time for everything," he said, taking my hand and pulling me into the room.

As he picked his way between the various piles of men on the floor, the satyr kept up a steady chatter. I was trying to catch a glimpse of what was going on around us, but every time I would stop to get a closer look he'd pull me away. Finally we found our way to the middle of the room, where the bonfire was crackling. A knot of men was standing there talking. When we came up, they stopped and looked at me. The satyr turned to me. "First," he said, "we have to get rid of those clothes."

He reached over and pulled up my shirt, tossing it onto the fire, where it quickly went up in flames. There was a murmur of appreciation as the men watching looked at my workout-toned chest. Then the satyr reached for the buttons on my jeans and let them fall to the floor. My cock jutted out from my body, swaying over my balls. I could feel the heat from the bonfire soak into my skin, and the blood started to rush to my dick, swelling it to its full length.

The satyr leered at my erect cock approvingly. He was stroking his own prick, and it stretched fat and heavy in his hand, a string of silvery juice hanging from the tip of the uncut head. I knelt next to the fire and the satyr moved toward me, stopping when his cock was bobbing in front of my face. Reaching out, I grasped his fat piece in my hand, barely getting my fingers around its girth. Coarse hair ran halfway up the underside of the shaft, and the skin below it was hot to the touch. Pushing from my mind the thought that a creature like a satyr shouldn't even exist in the real world, I slipped my tongue into his foreskin, sucking up the pool of precum and thick funk waiting under the loose mantle that stretched over his swollen head.

The satyr pressed against my lips and slid into my mouth smoothly. I relaxed and let the full length of him work its way down my throat. Soon my face was pressed against the tangle of rough hair on his groin and I was breathing in his scent, a heady musk like that belonging to a woodland animal. His heavy balls dangled against my chin, and I reached up to knead them, my fingers folding around the warm pouch. I placed my other hand on his waist, tracing the line where the skin of his human torso melted into the pelt of his goat legs as he pumped my face slowly, pulling out just enough for me to take a quick breath before sliding back in.

I could feel the satyr's prick swelling as I massaged it with my mouth, stretching his long foreskin between my lips as he worked his pole in and out. I tugged on his nuts, urging them to give up their treasure, waiting for him to come. Suddenly he pushed his cock as far as he could down my throat, his spunk gushing out and into my welcoming mouth in thick splashes. I swallowed greedily, milking the last drops from his straining cock. His cum was rich and fruity, like wine that had been sleeping in a cellar for many years and had soaked up the dampness from the earth. I gulped greedily, as if I were pouring the very essence of the earth into my guts, partaking of the same force that made the trees grow straight up from the ground and moved the moon through the heavens.

The feeling slipped into my mind, and I was floating away on a slow river. At the same time, my senses took on a new clarity. The room grew to new dimensions as I gazed around with a heightened ability to see what was happening even in the darkest corners. The fire burned more intensely, and I felt its beating in my chest. I looked up at the satyr and saw he was laughing.

"Now, mortal," he said, "you will partake of things you have never imagined."

I felt myself being lifted and carried by strong arms. I was laid on my back on a soft carpet, and then hands were caressing me. Looking around, I saw that the satyr had disappeared and I was surrounded by several other men. From somewhere came the smell of flowers, and someone rubbed warm oil over my chest and down my belly, working my muscles with a steady rhythm. I felt fingers close around my cock and begin to stroke it, gliding on the film of oil, coaxing spasms from my overheated balls. At the same time, a mouth covered mine and a tongue slipped between my lips, bringing with it another taste of the heady perfume.

I was enclosed by other bodies. Although I could not make out their faces, I felt the heat from their skin, took in the scent of their crotches and armpits as I rolled between spread legs and open arms. My mouth traveled over hairy mountains and through smooth-shaved valleys, working its way into the dark caves of assholes and taking in the strength of cocks engorged with lust and blood. The satyr's potion had brought me almost to the point of madness, and I felt intensely the needs of the men around me. I sensed their mounting excitement as they slipped their pricks in and out of hungry mouths and gasping asses. Whenever someone came, his moans sang through my head and I felt his jism flood my soul.

For hours I swam in a sea of fucking bodies while the bonfire burned. Over and over I shot my load, sometimes into the hot void of an ass, other times into the throat of someone whose own prick was slammed deep into my gullet. It became impossible to distinguish one man's cock from another's fist, my own asshole from that of the man I was fucking. I would look up from taking a squirting prick between my lips and see a man riding my straining cock, his well-muscled torso rising and falling as he claimed my shaft with his ass cheeks, his face a mask of ecstasy. All around me men were jacking off, and their ropes of spunk slathered over my chest and legs, slicking my throat and mouth with salty pearls.

I was hungrily licking up the juices from between the ass cheeks of a beefy neighbor, my prick nestled deep in his willing throat, when the room was filled with a mighty rustling, as if many birds were descending at once. I felt a hand on my shoulder and looked up into the eyes of the satyr. "Come," he said. "The master wishes to see you."

I stood slowly, rising from the orgy as if stepping out of a rushing stream. A body rolled over to fill my empty space, and the flow of passion continued with barely a ripple. The satyr led me to the other end of the room, slowing as we approached a large throne I hadn't noticed before. As we came closer, I saw that a man was seated in the chair. He was looking out over the room, as if searching for something, and at first he didn't appear to see us. The satyr pushed me forward so that I was standing right in front of the throne and the man tuned his attention to me.

I looked into his face and saw that his skin was tanned the color of honey. His eyes, dark beneath a tangle of wild hair, pulled me in as if I were tumbling into pools of water. I could feel his gaze traveling over my cum-stained body, appraising what he saw like someone perusing a piece of art before buying it.

Finally, he smiled slightly, showing off white teeth behind his full lips. "You have done well, Pan," he said to the satyr. "This is one of the finest I have seen in at least a century."

"Thank you, Master," the satyr replied happily. "He is a beautiful boy. And he is rather long down below for a mortal."

The man's eyes swept down to my cock. While it had diminished somewhat in size during the inspection, it was still half-hard against my leg.

"Yes," the man said slowly. "I think he will be the perfect ending to the night's festivities."

The man rose from his chair, bringing himself up to almost seven feet tall. His massive body was draped with a piece of white material cinched around the waist by a silver cord. He strode over and stood before me. The satyr scampered over from his place by the throne and fumbled with the knot in the belt. Freeing it quickly, he slipped the belt from around the giant man's waist and pulled the cloth free.

Naked, the man was a sculptor's dream. His huge chest was chiseled to perfection, the delicately pointed nipples standing out stiffly from smoothly rounded pectorals. His long neck led down to a stomach outlined with valleys and plains like a landscape seen from above. His arms were heavily muscled, the veins running like rivers down their sides, ending in broad hands with long, thick fingers. The smooth curve of his ass cheeks melted into strong legs, and his feet were wide and solid. Clean shaven, the lines of his body were clearly defined and as smooth as marble.

But what had my attention was his magnificent cock. Between his legs hung the biggest, thickest piece of meat I had ever laid eyes on. Easily twice as long as any I'd ever seen, it was as wide around as my wrist. The enormous head stretched almost to the knee, the full, round tip grazing his thigh. The surface of the shaft was entwined with veins that climbed its length like ivy over a column, and behind it his egg-shaped balls swung heavily like twin moons orbiting an obelisk.

The man ran one big finger down my body from the hollow of my neck to my groin, leaving in its wake a searing heat that soaked into my skin. He gently pinched my nipple between his thumb and forefinger, and my tit rose into his hand as it swelled with a sweet ache, crying out for more. But he released it and, taking my hand, led me toward a platform near the fire. The satyr and a group of men followed, closing behind us like waves rolling over stones.

When he reached the platform, the man picked me up and

placed me on it, pulling himself up beside me. Stretching his long body out on some pillows, he leaned back, spreading his legs invitingly. His prick had filled with his heat and lay against his belly. He looked at me expectantly, and I crawled between his legs until I was hovering over his cock.

He put one hand behind my head and pulled me down to his waiting dick, rubbing my face roughly along his shaft and down into his balls, then back up again to the very tip. Opening my lips as wide as I could, I managed to fit the head into my mouth, amazed that I could suck it without choking. My tongue washed all over the globe of his prick, licking up the delicious syrup that slipped from between the thick lips of his cockhead. Slowly I pushed a few more inches of his delicious meat into my throat, feeling my muscles protest as they stretched to new limits. Streams of spit slipped from my mouth, and I used it to grease the length of shaft still beyond my lips, my fingers carrying it up and down the inches of flesh in slow motions that allowed me to feel every ridge of the mighty prick in my hand.

Releasing his prong from my mouth, I began to travel down his dick, tracing the throbbing vein under his shaft with the tip of my tongue. Reaching his balls, I kissed the silky folds of his sac, feeling the heavy fruit inside tumble and fall over my lips as I feasted on them hungrily. The skin of his thighs rubbing on my cheeks was like velvet, and I rubbed eagerly against him, pressing his balls into my face and stroking his beating cock. As I milked his prick, streams of sticky juice flowed over my fingers and down my arm. I licked it up, letting the sweet fluid roll down my throat like water, quenching my thirst with his honey.

Again I sensed a wave of pure pleasure enfold my body. Feeling all control flood out of me, I began to lick and suck wildly, wanting to taste every inch of his magnificent body, breathing his man scent into my lungs. I lay on top of the reclining giant, my mouth flying over his stomach and up to his nipples, taking them in between my lips and exploring their hardness. I sank my tongue into his armpits, washing them clean, and sucked at his fingers when he touched my face as if they were extensions of his cock.

Returning to his prick, I licked at his thighs, following the muscles of his legs down to his feet and back up again. My tongue explored the secret pathway beneath his balls, finding its way into the cavern of his ass. Lunging against his meaty buttocks, I buried my nose in his crack, searching for the hot, pulsing center that lay buried there. Wetting my lips, I slid easily into his hole, twisting my face slowly and slurping greedily at his tasty opening.

As I ate out his ass, I felt his hands on my neck, pushing me farther and farther into him. My own cock was beating against the stone of the platform, my balls aching from the need that pulsed in them like a heartbeat. I wanted to jerk off furiously, but couldn't take my hands away from the strong thighs that surrounded my face.

Suddenly there were fingers wrapped in my hair, and I was pulled unwillingly away from my banquet. Once again I heard the familiar roaring in my head and looked around. From the top of the platform I had a view of the entire temple. The whole floor was a knot of writhing bodies. Cocks were flying in and out of mouths and assholes as the men they belonged to delighted in one another's bodies. All around me rivers of cum flowed over sweating chests and burning lips that sucked it in, then passed it to other mouths in long, deep kisses.

I started to turn but was pushed onto my hands and knees. I felt the big man move behind me, spreading my legs with his thighs as he took up position. His cock fell onto my back and slipped down into my ass crack, slicing the halves of my butt with its thickness. Slowly he rubbed against me, his hands pressing down on my back as he moved back and forth. I wanted to have his prick inside me, even though I knew it would probably rip me to pieces. Something primeval within me called out for his manhood, begging him to fill me.

As I imagined being taken by this strange man, I felt the tip of his prick push against the opening of my chute. My ass ring tightened, resisting, then he shoved roughly and was through, his crank pounding into my insides like a lightning bolt. I opened my mouth to scream, but nothing came out as the breath was knocked from me. As inch after inch poured into my ass, I moaned in agony, the pain turning into ribbons of pure ecstasy rolling over my bones and wrapping around my heart. I couldn't believe I was taking such a big tool into my chute, but on and on it came, stretching me with its thickness until I felt his taut stomach pressed against my hungry cheeks. When he pulled out, I felt the absence of his prick and cried out for it to return until it was once more buried in my bowels and I felt whole again. The man's hands grasped my shoulders tightly, pulling me against his hips as he tore into me repeatedly, his chest pounding my back as his balls slapped my thighs.

As he fucked me the man made no sound, silently bearing down on me with his weight, driving his cock into my gasping hole. My whole body was rocked with the forceful motions of the dick in my ass, and as my head bobbed up and down I caught glimpses of the men in the temple, snatches of bodies moving in and out of focus. Excitement turned to frenzy as the moans from the floor rose up, surrounding my head with a roar like a thunderstorm. My body was a sponge, soaking in the lust that streamed from the bodies making love, turning me drunk with pleasure.

I wanted it to go on forever, to sail on the rush of pain and pleasure in and out of days. But I knew that if I rode the wave too long I might not come back from where it took me. Already I could feel my mind slipping away from me, dizzy with the exquisite pain that held my body in its grip. I pushed back on the prong burrowing in my insides, squeezing my ass muscles tightly around it, drawing it farther in. I felt the man speed up his wordless thrusting. At the same time, I felt my own balls tighten in anticipation.

Falling against me, the big man gave a final shove, driving his cock up and inside me until I thought it would pierce my heart and come out my chest. He shuddered, and his load spilled into me as if a dam had burst. Gush after gush of spunk filled my bowels as his balls gave up their juice to my sucking chute. I felt it stream deep into my belly, then run back out my choking asshole like the tide leaving the beach, coating my legs with thick waves as he continued to pump me while he came.

At the same time, the roar in my head turned into a primal howl, roaring out of my throat and filling the temple with its raw power. My own cock spurted an arc of cum through the air, hitting me in the face as I bowed my head. My load splattered against my cheeks and dripped from my lips as I tried to lap it up.

Unable to keep a hold on the emotions sweeping through me, I collapsed on the platform, and the big man's prick slipped out of my ass. I felt tongues begin to wash my body as men licked eagerly at the thick cum that dripped from my empty hole and trickled down my legs. I shut my eyes, waiting for my head to clear.

When I opened them again, the temple was empty. A thin, pale light was peeking in around the columns, and a light breeze grazed my skin with gentle fingers. I was alone on the bare platform, which was now covered in moss and crisscrossed by cracks. Getting up, I stretched, feeling strangely alive and filled with energy.

I couldn't remember how I had gotten to the temple or what had happened there, but the dull ache in my ass reminded me of at least part of what had gone on. I cursed myself for having drunk so much that I couldn't even remember who had fucked me. My jeans were lying on the floor below the platform, and I slipped them on, hoping I could get back to the village without meeting anyone.

I turned to leave the temple, and for the first time noticed a statue sitting at one end. Walking over to it, I looked into the face of the big man who had filled me so completely the night before, the warm flesh now cold, unfeeling stone. In a rush, everything of the night before came back to me, a jumble of sounds and smells, sensations and tastes. As I gazed at the beautiful marble, I searched for some clue to who the man was, but found none.

Finally, I wandered out of the temple and down the steps into the time between dawn and morning. Coming up the hill was a boy, a herd of black and white speckled goats behind him. He did not seem surprised to see me there with no shirt or shoes.

"Good morning," he said. "I see you have been a guest at the house of Zeus."

I looked at him, trying to figure out why he seemed so familiar, where I might have seen his ruddy face.

"Zeus," I said. "As in king of the gods?"

The boy smiled, his white teeth breaking out from behind his red lips. "Yes, I hear he is a very good host. Especially on Bacchanal."

He turned and headed toward the hills, his goats following. As he walked away, I caught a glimpse of the two small horns almost hidden by his curly hair. I started to call out, but he had disappeared around a bend, leaving me standing on the hilltop as the awakening sun washed away the last of the night's shadows.

The Burning of Leaves

A short meditation on the nature of desire and being desired.

Every November, just before he thought the snow was coming, my father and I would gather up the leaves scattered over the farm by the old maple trees. Very methodically, we went to each tree, scooping the fallen leaves up in gloved hands. We stuffed them into bags and carried them behind the barn, where we piled them in the old stone fireplace.

My father would make a hollow in the pile of leaves, pushing them into a bowl-like shape. Into this bowl he would put a large pinecone. Then he would take a match out of his jacket pocket and, in that way known to all farmers but kept a secret from the rest of the world, strike it against his fingernail and bring it to life.

Once the match was lit, he cupped it in his hands and knelt by the pile. Touching the match to the pinecone, he would blow softly, encouraging the small fire to take hold. When the pinecone was burning, he carefully placed leaves over it, until the hollow was once again filled in, the pinecone slowly smoldering at its center.

Because pinecones burn very slowly, it took a long time for the fire to work its magic. I could see the smoke crawling out through the spaces in between the leaves and rolling along the ground under the colder air. But the flame itself was invisible.

Still, I knew it was there, slowly burning its way through the pile from the inside, growing in intensity and fury. I waited for that moment I knew would come when, unable to remain beneath its paper-thin yellow-and-brown skin any longer, the fire would roar upward, sending a wave of heat flowing over my face, the remaining leaves collapsing at last into the fire's heart.

When this happened, I would stare into the very center of the fire, not caring that the heat was burning my skin or that the smoke was stinging my eyes. I thought that if I looked hard enough I might see what the fire had revealed, the part of the leaves that couldn't be burned away, the thing that made them alive.

Many years later, the fall has come again, and the time for the burning of leaves.

When he touches me, I sense the match being struck against my skin, feel the flame spark up and take hold of the edges. As his hands move over me they burn gently, pulling at the first layer of what I have worked so hard to build up. I am surprised at how easily he can make the years fall away, at the strength of his fingers as they strip away the time I have spent avoiding this moment. Although I don't want to, I touch him, shivering when I realize that I am going to let him do this to me.

His mouth against mine is soft, and there is power behind it. Kissing me, he breathes heat beneath the quiet, cold flame that has been sleeping within me. Awakened, it stirs uneasily in its nest, stretching lazily as it grows stronger. Along with his breath, the fire slips inside my mind and I no longer remember how to get away from him, no longer want to.

Despite the mind-numbing veil of heat I remember that I am playing with fire. Even as his arms encircle me and he pulls me in deeper, I hear my father's warnings about lighting matches, about the terrible consequences of being too careless. I wonder if this man knows what it is he is doing, or if he even cares. For a moment the fire is pushed back as I am surrounded by the fear that what is happening has not been created by the two of us, that it is, for him, nothing more than a continuation or remembrance of something he has begun in another place with another man. I hold him with my eyes closed, afraid that seeing his face will reveal that he is making love to someone else.

It takes some time to rid myself of this ghost, and it never does go away completely. Still, he is able to close my thoughts off enough to bring me back to where he is, enough to make me want what he is offering me to be the only thing that matters. I cannot see his eyes in the dark, but I listen to what his hands are saying, and I choose to believe them.

Unleashed once more, the flame reaches out, its strength increased by having been kept at bay. I can feel it gripping my heart. It throbs steadily and hungrily, filling me with heat that pushes at my skin from the inside, rolls over my bones in waves. I find myself wondering if he can feel it, too, where his body lies against mine.

I want to pull him down into my body, down through skin and bone and muscle, so that he can know what he has done, so that he can taste the burning ache that he has put there. I want to take his fire into me, feel it rage wildly through me and roar out through my skin, tearing away everything I have buried inside me in a blinding wave of heat and light. His breathing sounds in my head like wind howling through bare branches, blocking out whatever I am thinking. I try to match the rhythm of his heartbeat, try to feel the blood moving through his veins and become part of it.

As he enters me, the fire stirs restlessly. It has waited patiently for too long. The carefully constructed walls that I have used to keep him out begin to tremble as their supports are burned away. For a moment I am terribly afraid, afraid that he will burn away everything I am and leave me with nothing, afraid that I have played a deadly game and lost.

Then the walls begin to collapse. They crash madly through one another, falling away and disappearing into the white-hot center where the fire has been waiting patiently all this time to consume them. The last barrier gone, the flame rushes through what remains of my defenses, and I no longer care what it leaves in its wake because I know that it has cleansed me. It rises up through my skin in a final storm of heat, pouring out and washing the face of the little boy watching the leaves burn.

Through the flames I see him looking down into me, searching for what the burning has revealed.

Riding the Rails

I used to live outside of New York and commute into the city by train every day. The ride home always provided time for idle thought, and the presence of a particularly hunky conductor one afternoon was the seed for this story.

The 5:17 train was about to leave when I reached my gate, the buzzer that sounded departure echoing loudly through the empty station. Cursing my client for calling the last-minute meeting that made me late, I put on a burst of speed. I just managed to slip into the last car by putting my briefcase in between the closing doors. There was going to be a nice scuff mark on the leather, but at least I wouldn't have to wait another hour for the next train out.

Since I'd started working for a law firm in the city six months ago, the train had become a regular part of my life. I still wasn't used to getting up half an hour earlier in the morning to catch the incoming to the city, and more than once I'd had to leave some hot number standing in a bar to catch the last express home. But despite the dent it was putting in my social life, the long ride was good for getting work done, and I did enjoy leaving the city behind me after a long day.

The train was packed, stuffed to overflowing with business types anxious to get back to the suburbs and forget the day's aggravations. Some had stacks of paperwork or laptop computers spread out, trying to finish up whatever they'd left undone before leaving the office for the day. Others were trying to relax, reading newspapers or paperback thrillers. I counted at least seven people reading the latest John Grisham novel as I looked for a seat.

There was only one empty seat, in one of the sections where two rows faced one another to form a square. Usually these were taken up by groups of guys playing cards on the way home, but not today. An older man was sitting in the aisle seat, and two young women sat across from him. Mumbling my apologies, I squeezed past them into the window seat.

As usual, the air-conditioning was on the blink, and the train was hot as hell. Luckily, the windows opened, letting in some air. I leaned back and loosened the collar of my shirt. My station was the last stop on the train, and it was going to be at least an hour and a half until the train got there. If I was lucky, I might be able to get some sleep.

The train was creeping along the elevated tracks that stretch out of the city, and the steady humming of the engine was putting me to sleep when a booming voice startled me awake. "Tickets, please. Have your tickets ready." The conductor had entered the car, making his rounds to check the commuting passes. I fished in my shirt pocket for the blue monthly ticket I'd just gotten in the mail. I knew from experience what pricks the conductors could be if you weren't ready the minute they came by.

The conductor was making his way through the car, repeating the familiar "tickets, please" every few feet like clockwork. A couple of times I heard him giving instructions to people who needed to transfer, punching their tickets and barking out answers to their questions like a drill sergeant. Since my seat was almost all the way in back, it took a while for him to reach me. When I heard him say "ticket, please" I looked up, directly into a pair of beautiful blue eyes and a ruggedly handsome face. What I could see of his hair under his uniform hat was dark blond and cut short, and he had a mustache.

"Thank you," he said, looking quickly at my ticket and handing it back in one huge hand. His fingers were long and thick, and his arms were covered with the same burnished golden hair as on his head. After checking the rest of the tickets, he moved on to the next row.

"I love taking Jon's train," the woman across from me said to her friend. "He really makes sitting here a lot easier to take." I completely agreed with her but didn't say anything. Instead, I closed my eyes and tried to fall asleep again. But all I could see was Jon's face and those blue eyes. I wondered if his chest under his white shirt was as hairy as his arms and felt my cock start stirring in my pants.

Quickly, I shifted the briefcase on my lap, hoping no one would notice my unruly dick acting up. I tried to get Jon's face out of my head, but as the train rolled on beside the river I continued to think about him. My rock-hard cock was pressing against my groin, and my balls felt trapped inside my boxers. I desperately wanted to jerk off and couldn't wait to get home, where I could lie on my bed and shoot a load off thinking about the hunky ticket puncher.

Finally, the train started to make its stops. Beechwood, Irvington, Briarcliff Manor. As each stop neared, Jon's voice came over the loudspeaker, waking those who were dozing and reminding passengers to take all of their belongings with them when leaving the train. Every time his deep baritone rang through the car I felt a tug in my nuts.

The train emptied a little more at each stop, and finally I was alone in the car. I stretched out, putting my feet up on the seat across from mine. Now that there was no one to see me, I put my hand between my legs, lazily massaging my aching balls through my pants and daydreaming about Jon.

The train bounced over a bump in the tracks, and I opened my eyes. Jon was sitting in the seat across from me, watching me intently. One hand was resting on his obviously hard cock, the fingers rubbing the head where it lay halfway down his thigh. He had a big grin on his face. "You know you're not supposed to put your feet up on the seats, don't you?" he said slowly. "I'm afraid I'm going to have to fine you for that."

He leaned over and pulled the tie from around my neck, letting it slide around my throat. Then, taking my hands in his powerful grip, he wrapped the silk around my wrists, tying my hands together. Pulling them over my head, he wrapped the other end of the tie around the lower bar of the steel frame that rose out of the back of the seat to hold cardboard advertising posters. While it didn't hurt me, I knew that I wouldn't be able to break the knot he had tied. All I could do was sit there looking up at him.

I was afraid someone would come in and see us, but Jon seemed unconcerned. Outside, I could see the summer landscape flashing by in a blur of green, but inside all there was was the deep blue of Jon's eyes as they stared into mine. Slowly, he undid the buttons on my shirt and pulled it open. He ran his hands over my chest, pinching my nipples slightly as his fingers moved over them. Then he untied my shoes and pulled them off along with my socks. Finally, he unbuttoned my pants, removing them and my shorts in one quick motion and tossing them on the floor of the train.

Freed from its prison, my cock stuck straight up toward my chest, my balls slipping down between my spread legs to rest on the cool vinyl of the seat. As a result of all my fantasizing, a string of precum was dripping from the tip of my dick, forming a silvery spiderweb between my cockhead and my stomach. I wanted badly to stroke my throbbing meat, but all I could do was wait and see what happened next.

Jon sat down and looked me up and down. He unbuckled the black leather belt at his waist and pulled the zipper of his blue uniform pants down slowly. Then, shifting his hips forward, he slid the pants off, pushing them down his thighs. He wasn't wearing underwear, and as his pants moved down his legs more and more of his cock was revealed. It was as thick as my wrist, with a head the size of a lemon. His stomach was covered with thick dark brown hair, but his balls were smooth and bare, hanging heavily beneath his stiff prick.

Once his pants were off, Jon shed his shirt, exposing a well-built chest with nipples that stood out against his tanned skin. As I'd hoped, it was also covered with thick swirls of fur. Still wearing his hat, he leaned back in his seat, placing one foot on either side of me so that I had a good view of his prick. Wrapping his fingers around his thick piece, he began to jerk off slowly, letting his hand slide gently up the shaft and then squeezing the head before traveling back toward his balls. As he milked his cock, precum began to drip from the lips of his swollen dickhead. He wiped some away with his fingers and worked it into the skin of his prick. Soon the length of his dick glistened wetly with his juice.

Watching this hunk stroke his cock was making me horny as hell, and the fact that I couldn't touch him made me even hotter. I couldn't keep my eyes off his hand as it moved up and down his hard-on, thinking about what it would be like to have him inside me. My own prick was begging to be stroked, too, but the knot that held the tie around my wrists only got tighter the more I pulled against it. The fucker must have been one hell of a Boy Scout.

Jon was really enjoying watching how worked up I was getting. As he pumped his meat with one hand, the other worked his tits, rubbing his nipples between his fingers and tugging at them until they were as hard as rocks. Then, smiling wickedly, he spread his legs even more, putting a foot on the armrests on either side of me. Hefting his bull balls in one hand, he pulled them up, holding them against his cock like a bunch of flowers. His meaty ass cheeks were spread, giving me a look at the rosy hole at their center.

Squeezing some more cock juice from his shaft, Jon wet one long finger and ran it under his nuts and down toward his asshole. Still pumping his prick, he slipped his finger in between the lips of his tight cherry, slowly turning it as he penetrated his ass. As I watched Jon fuck himself, my nuts almost blew, despite the fact that no one was touching them. Jon's finger slid slowly in and out, matching the rhythm of the train as it traveled over the tracks, pushing his hips up until his whole finger was buried inside his hole. The shadows coming in the window ran over his body like a film on a wall, bathing him in flickering light as if I were watching him under water.

As he fingered himself faster, pushing his finger deeper and deeper between his legs, I could feel the heat from his skin where he lay close to my body. But every time I would move so that he was touching me, Jon would pull away, keeping himself just out of my reach. He was stretching his ballsac, rolling his nuts around in his hand and slapping his hard prick against his stomach while he worked on his ass. The sight of this big stud fucking his own asshole was almost more than I could take.

Finally, when I thought I couldn't stand it anymore and was about to beg him to untie me, he stood up and turned around. Placing his hands on either side of the seat, he leaned over, pushing his hairy ass right at my face. I watched it come toward me, waiting to bury my face between his hot mounds. But Jon stopped just before the smooth curve of his delicious butt reached my mouth.

Pulling against the tie, I leaned forward and ran the tip of my tongue over the warm skin of Jon's ass, feeling the rough hair, tasting his sweat. I traced the line of his muscular cheeks and licked as far as I could down his leg, wanting more than anything to stick my tongue into his man crack and taste what was waiting in there.

Jon pushed back a little more, just enough for me to get my nose in between his ass cheeks. I was rewarded with the rich scent of his musk, so strong it clung to my face where I pressed against him. Eagerly, I snaked my tongue into him, working it in as far as I could go. The sides of his ass closed against my tongue as I slid it up and down the sides of his crack, licking him clean. Then he pushed back roughly, and I tasted the sweet center of his butthole. My hungry tongue dived into the wrinkled opening to his chute, and I tasted the precum he had fingered into it just minutes earlier.

As my mouth worked on his asshole, I could see Jon's shadow against the wall. He was jerking off, pushing his fist against his balls on the way down and pulling at the head as his hand swept up again. The more I tongued him, the harder he pounded his meat, the motion of his hand throwing long shadows across the floor. His balls swung steadily under him, every so often slapping against my chin as I nuzzled deep in his butt.

Soon he began to moan audibly and rammed himself against me, forcing my tongue into the depth of his spit-slicked ass chute. I heard him let out a low groan and felt his body stiffen. Pulling my face away from his ass, I saw thick ropes of cum flying from his cock, spattering the blue vinyl of the seat in front of him with wave after wave of cream. Jon gripped his prick tightly, coaxing still more cum up his shaft and out the tip. It hung heavily from his engorged dickhead for a few seconds, then rolled off and fell slowly onto the seat like honey from a spoon.

Jon turned around and faced me. Amazingly, his cock was still as hard as it was before he came. The vein in his dick throbbed once more, and another pearl of cum appeared. Jon wiped it away with his finger and brought it to my lips. He slipped his finger into my mouth, working it between my lips like it was his asshole. I sucked the jism from his finger, surprised at how warm and sweet it was.

Jon stood over me, his cock pointing at my chest, his balls hanging like overripe fruit about to fall from a tree. I could smell the rich scent of his crotch as his hand continued to move steadily up and down his still-stiff dick. Kneeling over me on the seat, he leaned forward, and the head of his prick pushed against my lips, warm and still wet from the load he'd just shot. I let my mouth close over it, stretching my lips to fit the whole thing in, hoping I'd still be able to breathe. I could feel the vein that ran under his cock and down to his balls pulse against my tongue as inch after inch of rock-hard flesh sank into my throat, coating it with a mixture of sweat and cum.

Jon hovered over me like a dark angel, his hands grasping the sides of the steel frame, his hat casting a shadow over his eyes. Sweat ran slowly down the valleys of his chest, and his mouth was set in a grim line as he fucked my face. His upper body rested against my arms where they extended over my head, and as he slid in and out of my mouth I felt the muscles of his chest tense and relax beneath their blanket of soft fur. His breathing was soft, and he moaned low in his throat as he ground his crotch against my face.

After a few minutes of letting me taste his delicious prick, Jon pulled out. He let his balls hang in front of me long enough for me to suck on each one, then pulled away. I thought he was going to shoot another load over my face, but he had other ideas. He stood up and reached down, pulling my legs up so that I was pushed back against the train seat with my feet resting on his chest. He grasped my ankles in his hands, closing his fingers around them tightly. It was the first time he had really touched me, and I felt a quick stab in my groin as my dick responded eagerly.

Still not touching my cock, Jon ran one hand over his chest, wiping up some sweat. Then he reached for my ass and slid his fingers up and down my crack, spreading my cheeks and stroking the sides. He quickly found my waiting hole and pressed his fingertip against it. It opened easily, and I felt his thick finger enter me. He investigated my chute, moving his finger in and out slowly, teasing me.

Putting his hands under my ass, he lifted me so that I was even with his waist. My legs slipped over his shoulders, and his strong arms locked around my thighs, pinning me against his sides. Still tied to the steel frame, I hung a few inches above the seat, supported by Jon's hands.

Jon's cock was still slick from the tongue washing I had given it, and it slipped smoothly into my ass. He lingered a moment as the tip penetrated my hole, letting me adjust to his size, then slid the rest of his prick in in one quick motion, not stopping until his balls came to rest against my ass. He stayed there not moving, letting me feel the heat in his cock as it pumped steadily inside my ass like another heart.

Then he began to fuck me. At first he moved slowly, pulling all the way out until just the end of his dickhead was inside my asshole and then sliding smoothly back in. As he pumped me, his blue eyes looked steadily into mine, never moving away. I stared transfixed as he filled and emptied me with his cock, gasping as he entered me, waiting for him to return when he pulled out. Then he began to speed up, thrusting in and out quickly, pulling my ass against his belly with each thrust. My wrists were aching where the tie pressed into them, but still I wanted more of him. Behind Jon, I could see the liquid gold he'd shot running down the back of the seat. The pressure in my balls was rapidly growing, and I knew that I was going to come any second.

Jon sensed that I was close. As the train flew over the tracks, he pumped me harder and harder, jackhammering his swollen prick into me. My asshole sucked eagerly at his dick, swallowing every inch he fed me. I felt the boiling in my nuts come to a head, rising up my shaft, and watched as a stream of spunk shot from my cock and covered my chest. Jon continued to pound me, and my ass muscles clamped down on his dick as I shuddered and another load of cum erupted from me, this time hitting me in the face and neck.

As I licked my own cum from my lips, I felt Jon swell inside me, stretching the walls of my chute until I was sure they'd burst. With one final grunt, he fell against me and came, his cock filling me again and again with waves of heat as his balls emptied their juice deep in my ass. Jon pulled out of me and lowered me back onto the seat. I was covered with cum, and my ass was still burning from the fucking he'd given me. He untied the knot that held my hands behind my head. There was a dull pain in my arms, and I rubbed my wrists to get the blood flowing again.

Jon was getting dressed, pulling on the familiar uniform as if he'd just stepped out of the shower and was getting ready for work. His hat had stayed on during the entire ride. Looking at his watch, he picked my clothes off the floor and handed them to me.

"We're almost at your station," he said. "Don't forget to check the surrounding seats for your belongings before leaving the train."

The Boys of Summer

When this story first appeared in the Hitting Home *collection, I was shocked to discover that the entire section featuring the characters at summer camp had been edited out without my knowledge. Citing fears of it being mistaken for pedophilia, the editor had removed it. In doing so, she removed the heart of the story. This piece isn't about boys having sex; it's about the powerful effect of first discovery and how that can return years later in a different form.*

I hadn't seen Brian in almost twenty years, so when he walked into my sporting-goods store it took me a minute to recognize the man in front of me as the boy I had known. But as soon as the feeling of having met him somewhere before blossomed into full remembrance, it all came rushing back at once.

The summer I was twelve, I was sent for two long weeks to a camp in the forests of upstate New York. I've forgotten the name now, but it was something vaguely Indian, the kind of place with lots of unfinished wood and legions of blue-shirted counselors scurrying around trying to combat adolescent angst with classes in beaded belt work and organized swimming relays. I have always been something of a loner, and the idea of having to spend fourteen days with dozens of other boys who enthusiastically enjoyed the prospects of archery and sing-alongs was not something that appealed to me. As I watched my parents disappear down the dirt road in their station wagon to a summer of freedom, I breathed in the overwhelming scent of pine and felt the doors of the prison close on me in a wash of sickeningly fresh air.

When I arrived at my cabin, my worst fears were confirmed. The place was filled with a group of loud, hyperactive adolescents busily engaged in trying to drag a small, screaming boy clad only in undershorts out of his bed. The boy was holding on to the sheets desperately and looked like he was trying very hard not to cry. The other boys had taken a hold of his legs and were tugging on them, taunting him in mimicking voices as he begged for them to leave him alone. "Come on, Morris," one of the boys said. "Give us a good show." The speaker, a fat redhead whose new white tennis shorts cut deeply into his pudgy legs, was grinning stupidly as he yanked on the younger boy's hands, trying to break his grip. Morris let loose with a howl and vainly tried to kick the redhead in the stomach.

Just before the boys pulled Morris away from his bed, the door at the other end of the cabin opened and another boy entered. He was shorter than the redhead, but his body was sinewy with muscle. Unlike my pale, freckled Irish complexion, his skin was tanned a dark honey color, as if he had spent most of his life outdoors, and his blond hair was tousled in an offhand way, falling carelessly over his blue eyes. He was carrying a fishing pole, and his legs were speckled with mud.

When he saw what the redheaded boy was doing, he dropped his pole and rushed forward. His left hand knotted into a tight fist and swung up as he moved. When it connected with the redhead's face, there was a satisfying smacking sound followed by a thud as the bully hit the floor of the cabin heavily. A spatter of red burst from his nose, and he began to wail, his fat hands covering his face.

The other boys were immediately silent, staring first at the boy on the floor and then at the boy standing above him, his hands clenched at his sides. Morris, who had scrambled back into his bunk, was smiling happily down at his tormentor. "Thanks," he said to his rescuer.

The boy nodded and went to retrieve his fishing pole. Without a word, he placed it under his bunk and then left the cabin as quietly as he had entered it, leaving the other boys staring after him. Because I had gotten to camp late in the day, there was only one bunk left, the one directly above the blond boy's. I hastily threw my stuff onto it and then went out to go after him.

I found him by the lake, sitting on a rock and tossing stones into the water. "Hi," I said. "I'm Tom."

He nodded. "Brian," he said, his voice soft and low, unlike mine, which was starting to break with alarming frequency.

"That was great what you did in there," I said. "I mean really great."

Brian grinned. "It was kind of cool, seeing Hayes fall on his ass," he laughed. "He had it coming."

I sat down next to him, and we started to talk. Brian was thirteen and lived on a small dairy farm. He had won a trip to camp from the local 4-H club. He missed his dog, a big bear of a mutt named Sam, and hated almost everything about camp except the lake. I in turn told him about my running battle with my older sister, my father's job at the steel mill, and my secret wish to someday pitch for the Yankees.

For the next week and a half, Brian and I did everything together. We were like two sides of the same coin—he light and I dark. For both of us, the horrors of camp were lessened by each other's company. After that first run-in with Hayes, the other boys kept Brian at a safe distance, and by association with him I was viewed as an equally dangerous animal. Because we didn't cause any trouble, the counselors were content to leave us to our own amusements as long as we were back at the cabin before lights out, and we spent the days exploring the forests or paddling around the lake in a stolen canoe we hid in the weeds.

On the Thursday before camp was to end, everyone went on an overnight camping trip to an island about an hour from the camp. By hiding under the cabin, we managed to elude our counselor, who was so busy trying to keep thirty boys under control that he didn't notice our absence. Once they were gone, we came out and looked around the empty cabin happily. We had it all to ourselves for one night.

"What shall we do?" I asked Brian.

He grinned at me. "Skinny-dipping. Last one to the lake is a rotten egg!"

Brian grabbed a towel and was out the door and down the path to the water before I could even start. As I followed him, a trail of scattered clothes marked his progress—shirt, shorts, and shoes discarded as he ran. By the time I got to the shore I was just in time to see the pale moon of his backside as he jumped with a whoop into the lake. His body slipped into the water, sending up a splash as he disappeared below the surface.

I quickly shed my own clothes and followed him. The water was cold, but the feeling of swimming without clothes was wonderfully exciting, the water slipping freely around my dick and balls. I dived under and swam toward Brian, catching a glimpse of his skin through the murky darkness. But before I could reach him, he disappeared. I came up for air and looked around but couldn't find him. Suddenly he burst up next to me. "Gotcha," he yelled, and put his hands on my shoulders, pushing me down.

As I swept past his body on my way down, I felt his cock brush against my ass and back, my hands scraping his legs. This contact made my own dick stir, and as I swam back to the surface I wondered if he had felt the same thing. In the way that boys do, I had sometimes questioned what his dick looked like, if it was bigger or smaller than mine. But now that I had felt its physical presence between his legs and the feelings it stirred in me, I wanted another look.

Brian was paddling in place when I broke through the water's skin. "It's getting cold in here," he said. "What do you say we go in?"

I nodded, and we swam to the shore. As we emerged from the water, we avoided looking at each other, and I wondered if Brian was thinking about the same thing I was. Wrapping our towels around us, we ran back to the cabin. Once we were inside, we dried off roughly. Brian dropped the towel and sat on the edge of his bunk, hugging himself with his arms. "Christ, that water was freezing," he said.

Now that he was sitting still, I got to look at his dick for the first time. Between his legs, his balls had shrunk and pulled up close to his body, the wrinkled skin prickled like gooseflesh and slightly bluish. His cock was shriveled into itself, the pink head sitting in a nest of soft skin. His pubic hair shaded his crotch with a fine golden spray so different from the dark shadow that was just beginning to come in around my own dick.

Looking at Brian's cock, I remembered how it felt rubbing against my back in the lake. I wanted to touch it, but I didn't know what he would do if I did. I dropped my own towel and sat down next to him, not saying anything. When I looked over, I saw that he was staring at my dick, too.

Nervously I reached out and gently cupped his balls in my hand. They felt strangely small, like acorns in their tight sac of flesh. His skin was still damp with lake water, and the skin beneath his ballsac was cool and slightly gritty with sand from where he had dried himself with his towel. Brian spread his legs wider and pushed his cock up into my palm. Without looking over, he placed his hand on my stomach and moved it down my groin. He stopped when he reached my dick, as if he didn't know what to do next. Finally, he wrapped his fingers around the head, rolling it around in his palm.

I lay there with Brian's dick in my hand, feeling for the first time a cock other than my own. I had played with myself enough times to know what it was like, but touching another boy's dick filled me with a new kind of excitement, a feeling of warmth that crept along my skin as I felt Brian's blood beat under my hand.

Brian's eyes were closed, as if he was holding his breath. I looked down at his cock in my hand. It was beginning to stiffen as I caressed it, stretching up from his hairless balls. The tip was flushed a deep pink, and a drop of precum glistened against the lips. Brian reached over to his shelf and picked a bottle of hand cream. "It's for mosquito bites," he said. "But it should work."

He squeezed some of the pale green liquid into my hand, and I smeared it up and down his cock. The lotion was smooth and cool, and my hand slid easily up and down the length of Brian's dick, jerking him off. After a few minutes, I felt his dick swelling inside my fist, and suddenly he gasped. A spray of sticky cum shot over my hand, and I felt the warmth of his jism on my skin.

I released Brian's softening prick and sucked on my finger, tasting the salty slickness of his spunk on my tongue. Brian was lying back, his mouth in a half smile. My own cock was standing straight out, rock hard from the excitement of giving my first hand job. I started to jerk off, but Brian stopped me. Pushing me back against the bed, he wiped a mixture of cum and hand cream off his belly and used it to stroke my dick until I came, my body shuddering so intensely I thought I might crumble into dust.

Afterward, we lay holding each other, feeling the afternoon sunlight soaking into our skins. That night we stayed out late, searching the skies for bats before falling into Brian's bunk exhausted and happy. We spent the night together, our arms around each other as we slept alone in the cabin. When the rest of the camp returned the next morning we got holy hell for skipping the overnighter, but it was worth it.

Neither one of us ever discussed what had happened, taking it I suppose as a natural part of growing up. Camp was over in two days, and we never got the chance to repeat our lovemaking. And despite promises to write afterward, we never did.

* * *

But now Brian was standing in front of me, just as if he'd never left. His face was wider, and he sported a closely trimmed beard, but his eyes were still bright blue and his hair, while cut short, was still the color of late-summer corn. He had grown into a big man, standing well over six feet with broad shoulders and a chest that filled out his blue work shirt well and muscular legs that looked great in the faded jeans he was wearing.

He looked up from the piece of paper he was holding and started to ask me something. Then he stopped and stared intently for a few seconds until recognition flashed across his face and he broke into a smile. "I'll be goddamned," he said. "Tom Caffrey."

I reached over and shook his hand, his fingers closing around mine in a firm grip. "You've grown up a little bit since the last time I saw you," I said.

Brian laughed. "You've done some filling out of your own. Looks like you've turned into a regular woodsman."

"Hey, if you're going to sell this stuff you have to know how to use it."

"This is your store?" he asked.

"Well, mine and the bank's. What brings you in here?"

"A little business of my own. I run wilderness tours for executive types. Heard about the mountains up here and thought they might make a good spot for my next trip. Thought I'd check it out myself first. I just got in and need to pick up a few things before I head up."

"Sounds just like the sort of thing you'd get into. What do you need?"

Brian smoothed out the list he had crumpled when he shook my hand. "Just some small stuff I forgot to bring. Lantern wick, bug spray, that kind of crap."

I looked at Brian's hand. There was no wedding band on his finger, and I hadn't seen anyone come in with him, but that didn't mean he was alone. I wasn't sure if he still went in for what we did in the cabin twenty years before, but I sure did and I wanted badly to find out just how much he'd grown up.

"You going up there alone?" I asked cautiously.

He nodded. "Yeah, all by myself. You remember how it was—the great loner. Besides, not too many people want to sleep in a tent with a guy who snores." He made loud sawing sounds and laughed.

"Well," I said. "It just so happens I know those mountains pretty well, and I wouldn't mind getting out of this place for a night. Besides, I can get you a good deal on the stuff you need. I know the owner. What do you say?"

Brian grinned. "I'd say that would be just fine. What time do you want to head out?"

"Meet me back here at three. It should only take an hour or so to get up where we want to be, and then we'll have the whole night to catch up."

Brian said good-bye and left the store, promising to be back in a few hours. Right at three, I heard his truck pull up and he came in. After checking with my assistant to make sure she knew where everything was, I grabbed the equipment I'd gathered together and headed out.

Riding in Brian's truck up through the mountain roads, I found out more about his life since we'd parted. After high school he'd joined the army. Given his dislike of anything approaching being told what to do, this surprised me. But the army had trained him to be a ranger, and once his tour was over he'd started his business, which by all accounts was doing very well. He made no mention of any romantic attachments and never asked me about mine.

The spot I wanted to show him was up a crude dirt path the locals called a road but anyone else would call a washout. Brian's truck clawed its way patiently upward, though, and it wasn't long before we pulled into a level area hidden behind a stand of towering spruce trees. The trees formed a windbreak for a grassy clearing, and there was a small mountain lake filled by a narrow waterfall that crashed down from a break in the rocks.

Brian was more than impressed by my secret find and walked around nodding his head and smiling. "Tom, my boy, I think you have found paradise," he said solemnly, patting me on the back.

"I thought you might like it," I said. "No one around for miles, and your very own swimming hole."

Brian had a small tent that, once it was framed together and sitting up, looked like a green uprising in the grass that surrounded it. Once we had spread our sleeping bags out and put the rest of our gear safely inside, we lay in the grass staring up at the sky.

"It makes me feel thirteen again," Brian said, a blade of grass between his teeth.

"I know what you mean," I said. "You do feel small out here."

Brian sat up and looked over at me. "Let's go swimming in the lake, like we used to do at camp."

He stood up and started taking off his shoes. When he had them off, he started running for the water. "Last one in's a rotten egg," he bellowed.

As I chased after him, I became twelve again. His clothes, bigger now but thrown aside with the same childish abandon, were strewn over the grass where he had run by. I saw him pause at the edge of the water, his ass pale as it was when he was a boy, and dive in. Once more I followed him, the water closing over my head and taking me back twenty years.

When I came up, Brian was floating a few feet away. "Colder than it looks, isn't it?" he said. "Hard to believe we didn't turn into ice cubes swimming in this stuff. Better move around or you'll freeze solid."

We swam around for a while, but neither of us initiated any playful games, and I resigned myself to the fact that Brian and I weren't the same boys we had been back in camp. Still, it was relaxing to be in the water, floating peacefully and knowing that Brian's cock was somewhere below the dark glass of the lake. If I couldn't have him, I could at least fantasize about it.

Then a fat drop fell squarely on my face, and more followed. Looking up, I saw angry black clouds scuttling over the sun.

"Looks like we'd better head in," I called to Brian.

We swam to shore and hurried out of the water, racing for the tent. We got inside just as the heavens opened up, zipping the flap closed and hearing the rain hit the canvas above us.

Brian was sitting on his sleeping bag, toweling off his head. I did the same, warming up as I wiped the water off my skin. When I'd finished, I looked at Brian. He was watching me intently, sitting with his legs pulled up, leaning forward and resting his hands on his knees. His thick forearms were covered in soft golden hair, as was his chest. A trail of it spilled down his rippled abdomen, splashing into a pool of bush between his thighs. His cock hung down over heavy balls, the thick shaft ending in a fat tip that was slowly growing thicker.

Brian leaned forward and without a word crawled across the few feet that separated us. Putting a hand on my chest, he pushed me back and slid on top of me. I put my hands on his back and felt the heat and muscle rippling beneath his skin. Pulling him down, I felt the hair on his chest press against my own, mingling like shadows and light. His face was over mine, and he leaned down and kissed me, his lips parting to draw my tongue in.

I wrapped one leg around Brian's body, pulling him tighter into me. He ran his mouth over my face, kissing my cheeks and biting softly at my chin before moving down my neck. My hands traveled over his body, feeling the curves of his muscular ass, slipping into his crack and then under him to feel his stiff cock. Now fully erect, it pressed against my stomach as he rubbed his body up and down.

As Brian sucked intently on my nipple, I kneaded his balls, running my finger along the area behind his nuts and sliding it gently into his asshole. He groaned as I pressed against his pucker, pushing me deeper into him until he'd taken in most of my finger and I cupped his balls in my palm. He ground his ass against me, inviting me to fuck him harder. Soon I was sliding in and out on his ass juices and a steady stream was flowing from his cock onto my belly as I milked his insides.

Brian slid off my hand and knelt between my legs, pushing them apart with his knees. Taking my aching prick in one big hand, he began to jerk slowly while sucking on the head, his lips moving in time with his hand motions, his beard tickling my shaft. As my cock slid in and out of his throat, I thought about the time we'd made love. Since then I'd had my prick buried in a lot of asses, but none of them ever felt quite like that first time with Brian had. And over the years a lot of guys had wanted to plow my butt, but I never let them. I didn't really know why; something just wasn't right. But now I understood.

"Brian," I whispered. "I want you to fuck me."

Brian looked up at me, my cock still in his hand. "Are you sure?"

I nodded. "I've been waiting for this for twenty years."

Brian turned and rummaged in a backpack next to the sleeping bag. He pulled out a familiar-looking plastic bottle. "Well," he said. "I guess it's a good thing I brought this, then."

He flipped the top on the bottle and squirted some liquid into his palm. Once I smelled it, I knew just what it was—the same hand lotion we'd used the first time.

I laughed. "Old habits die hard, huh?"

Brian smiled. "I use it to jack off with. Reminds me of old times."

He coated his prick with the lotion, then ran his hand along my ass crack. His finger found the opening to my chute and pressed in, sliding easily on the thick cream. He went slowly, turning his finger and loosening my tight muscle until I relaxed. Then he pulled out, put my legs up over his shoulders, and pressed the tip of his cock against my waiting hole. Pressing forward, he slid in in one smooth movement, his thick cock stretching me and bringing tears to my eyes. I thought he'd never get the whole thing in, but soon I felt his balls brushing my ass and he stopped.

I breathed slowly, letting myself get used to his prick in my ass. Despite the pain, it felt great having Brian buried in me. I felt his cock twitch, felt his hands on my thighs pulling me closer. Then he began to fuck me, pulling out slowly and pressing back in in steady rhythm. As he did I jerked off, my hand matching the movements of his thrusts, my balls slapping softly against my fist when Brian pushed into me all the way.

He pushed my legs back toward my chest, his hands under my knees, so that he had a full view of his cock slipping in and out of my asshole. His motions became harder and deeper, his prick filling me again and again as he reached places I never knew existed. I could feel the pressure in my balls mount as I let myself open to Brian's cock. His prick was bringing me to the boiling point, and every time he slapped against my ass I was coming closer.

Finally, he pounded into me one last time and the spunk flew from my nuts, coating my chest and neck as I gasped for breath. Brian wrapped his arms around my legs and pulled me forward, at the same time plunging into me. With a loud grunt, he came deep inside me, his prick flooding me with its cargo of hot cum.

Afterward, we lay in each other's arms as we had as boys, listening to the rain fall on the tent. As I drifted into sleep with Brian's head on my chest, I felt as if the years had melted away and I were once again the boy who had found himself at summer camp. Only this time, I knew the summer didn't have to end.

Dirty Pictures

I actually did find some nude Polaroids on a New York City street once, but they weren't nearly this interesting. That, combined with the fact that so many garbagemen are incredibly hot, fueled this story.

I work as a garbageman for the city of New York. The paper pushers who write our job descriptions like to call us "sanitary engineers," like we somehow take people's discarded newspapers, crusty cat-food tins, and broken television sets and turn them into machines for studying the motion of the stars or something. But what we really do is go around in the dead hours before dawn scavenging scraps of other people's lives and hauling them away to a big landfill out in Long Island, where they're buried in mass graves cared for by flocks of screeching gulls. It's not a real pretty job, especially during the long hot stretch of a steamy New York summer, but it's a living.

Most people never notice the men who scrape away the city's daily coat of grime while they sleep. We're the invisible ones, who come out after midnight and disappear before the noon sun reaches its high point. I've been doing this work for almost seven years now—a quarter of my life—without anything special to speak of happening to me. I've even gotten used to the daily ritual of getting up at four to make it to the truck yard by four thirty and then going to sleep when most people are coming home from work to begin their real lives.

Then, a couple of months ago, something happened that turned my usually routine workday into something much different. I was at the end of my haul, working down Seventeenth Street toward Eighth Avenue. I only had one final row of buildings to attend to, and I couldn't wait to be finished. The city was broiling in a midsummer heat wave, and even in the early morning the temperature was already hovering near eighty. I was sweating like crazy, a big stain soaking the front of my blue coverall from throat to crotch. I couldn't wait to pull my wet, stinking clothes off and stand under a hot shower for a good long time.

I was thinking about how good the water would feel on my aching muscles when I picked up a cardboard box sitting at the curb and got ready to toss it into the back of the truck. I was swinging it into the jaws of the big crusher when something fell out and fluttered to the ground. Catching the motion out of the corner of my eye, I put the box down and bent down to see what I'd dropped. It was a Polaroid picture, and when I saw what it was a picture of, I almost dropped it again.

Framed by the thin white lines of the border was a shot of a naked guy. His head was cut off where the top of the picture severed his neck like the blade of a guillotine, but the rest of him was perfectly clear. He was a big guy, with a thick chest and muscular arms and legs. His body was covered in black hair, and his fist was wrapped around a huge cock. He was squeezing it tightly, and the big head was red and swollen. His other hand was stretching out his hairy ballsac.

I just stood there staring at the picture, unable to take my eyes off the headless man. It wasn't like I'd never seen a naked guy before. It was just that I never expected to see one fall out of the trash I was hauling. I mean, sure, I come across a lot of discarded porn mags, but this was a real surprise. People are usually pretty careful about throwing out pictures of themselves, like whoever finds them will have control over their souls or something. I rarely find actual snapshots of people, especially ones where they're playing with their dicks.

I was even more surprised when I realized my cock was starting to get hard from looking at the snapshot. I could feel it stretching inside my overalls, pressing against my stomach. Fumbling nervously with the cardboard flaps, I opened the box and almost shot a load from what I saw. Inside were dozens of Polaroids, all of different nude guys jerking off. Some were standing up and some were lying on beds waving their cocks at the camera. Some were bent over, their fingers shoved up their assholes. There were even a couple with two guys in them, where one would be sucking the other's cock or sticking his dick up the other guy's butthole.

None of them had faces. There were just bodies and, in the case of guys sucking, mouths filled with thick pricks or ripe balls. There were armpits being licked by eager tongues, and at least one shot of just an asshole smeared with globs of lube, the hair swirled around the opening in wet strands. The bodies were fat and thin, black and white and brown, hairy and smooth, young and old. And their cocks were all different, too. Some had big fat monsters that swung heavily between their legs; others had small, thin pricks sticking out from their bodies. It was as if someone had crept into bedrooms all over the city and captured what he saw there on these tiny windows of film.

There were also some used rubbers in the box, scattered among the pictures like the discarded skins of strange animals. The thin blue and white sheaths were wrinkled and wet looking, the tips filled with dried cum and the outsides streaked with faded lines of lube. I reached out and touched one, feeling the softness of the rubber under my fingers. When I picked it up, the end swung down heavily, and I realized that the thick liquid that swelled out the tip was a recent load. Whoever the box belonged to must have put it out that morning and had a good time before he did it.

I riffled through the box and pulled out a handful of photos, stuffing them into the pockets of my work pants. I also put the used rubber in there, tying the end off so that none of the cum would leak out. I could feel how hard my cock was when I put my hand in my pocket, and gave it a couple of quick jerks. I tossed the box with the rest of the pictures into the truck and hit the button that brought down the big steel sweeper. I watched it crush the box, spilling out a feast of headless naked men that was quickly swallowed into the belly of the truck. My cock ached as I thought about the pictures in my pockets, and I couldn't wait to get home and look at them again.

I finished the rest of my route in record time, depositing the truck at the yard and racing home. I didn't even bother to shower once I got there, pulling off my sweaty clothes and dropping onto the bed as soon as the door was closed. Spreading the pictures out across my chest and stomach, I looked at them while I jerked slowly on my tool, the cool breath of the window fan tickling my overheated skin in thin ribbons. My dick was rock hard from all the anticipation, and it felt like steel beneath my fingers, warm steel pulsing with blood and desire.

As I moved my grimy hand up and down my shaft, I picked up

each picture and looked at it, imagining what was going on when it was taken. My favorite was a shot of a man sitting in an old red velvet armchair. His legs were spread, with his knees hooked over the arms of the chair, and in his hand was a long, straight dick. His balls were smooth, and his bush was clipped short. His stomach was wide and flat, the muscles bunched into heavy ropes. His chest and belly were covered in light blond hair, and I could see that he had his head thrown back. His free hand was between his legs, and he had two fingers shoved up his hairy hole, spreading it wide open for the camera.

I tried to picture what the guy who took the photos looked like while I cranked on my meat. I imagined him telling the man in the chair what to do. I could practically hear him saying "Stick your fingers in that hole" while he snapped the shot. Did he jerk off while he watched? Did he fuck the guys when he was done shooting them? Picking up the used rubber and untying the end, I fingered it while I brought the feeling in my balls to a fever pitch with my hand. The weight of the man's load against my palm was reassuring and arousing, and I thought about him shooting it. I could almost see the photographer stroking himself off while his models posed for him, his hand jerking furiously on his crank.

Tipping the condom upside down, I let the contents splash out onto my chest. The cum was cold and wet against my flushed skin, but it felt so hot to have another man's load on my body that I didn't care. I rubbed the unknown man's jism into the hair on my chest and belly while I finished myself off. My fingers were sticky with his juice and with my sweat as I massaged him into my balls and slipped into my hairy asshole, and I shot my own load all over my stomach. My balls tensed as volley after volley blew out of my cock and slopped over my hand and the pictures still lying on my stomach.

There was cum everywhere, from my neck to my crotch. Drops of it stuck to my thighs and ran down my sides until I couldn't tell if it was mine or the man's whose rubber I'd found. It didn't matter, it was the hottest jerk-off session I'd ever had. My prick was still throbbing long after I'd finished coming, and the feeling of being covered in spunk was enough to make me want to blow all over again.

Picking the cum-drenched pictures off my body, I wiped them

off as much as I could and stuck them in a drawer for later use.
Then I showered, lathering up and jerking off again while I thought
about the mysterious photographer and what he must be like. I
had to see him, and I decided that I'd go back to the building later
that night and see if I could find him. I knew it was crazy, but the
tugging in my balls every time I thought about him told me I had
to do it.

That night, at about eleven o'clock, I found myself standing
across the street from the brownstone where I'd found the box
that morning. The heat of the afternoon had never died down, and
the air was thick and dry as bone in my lungs as I stood looking up
at the three floors of windows, trying to figure out which ones belonged to the guy I was looking for. I was glad he didn't live in a
big building, where it would have been impossible to find him.
This way, I only had to eliminate two of the floors.

The lights in the second-floor apartment were out, so I concentrated on the other two. The windows on the first floor were covered by blinds, and those on the third were wide open. I stood for
about half an hour waiting for some kind of a clue, my dick hard
from nervousness and the excitement of doing something totally
unexpected. My mind raced with all the reasons why I shouldn't
be there, and I fought them down by waiting for the building to
open up and give me some sign that I wasn't out of my mind. But
the brick walls seemed determined to keep their secrets safe
within, and nothing happened that would help me make my next
move.

I was just about to give up and leave when I saw one of the
first-floor shades go up. An elderly woman poked her head out,
leaning on the windowsill and looking up and down the street.
With her thick glasses and rolls of fat billowing out from her
sleeveless housedress, she didn't look like she was responsible for
the box of delights I'd discovered there that morning. *Okay,* I
thought, *that means he must be on the top floor. Now how the hell
do I get up there?*

Moving around to the side of the building, I found the fire escape. By standing on a trash can, and with no small amount of dif-
ficulty, I was able to pull myself up to the first level, grunting and
straining as I hauled my body over the edge of the platform. *This*

is fucking nuts, I thought as I sat there trying to get my breath.
*You're going to get arrested for trying to spy on some guy, and
you don't even know for sure that he lives here.*

But the memory of the pictures and what they'd done to my
cock kept me going. I crept slowly up the fire escape to the second
floor, stopping to peek in the window. The room inside was completely empty, and from the faint patterns remaining in the dust
that covered the floor, it looked as though no one had lived there
for quite some time. That meant the third-floor apartment was my
only chance. I scrambled up the remaining stairs and found myself
outside the window. I sat there for a minute, making sure no one
in neighboring apartments saw me while I worked up the courage
to look in the window.

Like the front windows, the side ones were also curtainless, as
well as being pushed open halfway to let in the breeze. All that
separated me from the room inside was a thin screen. Peering
around the corner, I was able to see directly into what was obviously the bedroom. A light was on, and I could see clearly what
was inside. There was a big bed pushed up against one wall, and
an armchair opposite it. I recognized the chair as the one from the
photos, and my dick jumped sharply in my pants as I realized I'd
gotten the right place.

Now that I was actually there, I had no idea what I was doing.
I couldn't just open the window and go into the guy's bedroom.
But I also couldn't bring myself to leave; I was too curious now to
go without seeing what he was like. Before I could decide on my
next move, I heard voices from the other room, and someone came
into the bedroom so quickly that I barely had time to dip my head
below the windowsill before whoever it was saw me. I was scared
to look up, in case the occupants were looking out the window, so I
just lay there listening to what was going on, feeling my cock
through my pants and my heart pounding in my chest.

"Take them off," I heard an authoritative voice say. "I want to
see your dick."

The command was followed by the muffled sounds of someone
removing his clothes. I heard his shoes drop to the floor as he removed them, then the appreciative murmuring of the same masculine voice that had ordered him to strip. "Nice cock," he said.
"Get it hard." I heard footsteps as he walked across the floor, then

the sharp slap of a hand against skin. "Nice ass, too," he growled. "Can't wait to see my dick stuffed up it."

Hearing what was going on was too much. I couldn't just lie there listening. Lifting my head, I nervously looked over the very bottom of the screen. What I saw almost made me come in my shorts. Standing with his back to me was a tall man with short black hair. He was naked, and through his spread legs I could see the head of his dick hanging over his balls. He was holding a Polaroid camera and barking orders to a man kneeling on the bed. The man, a smooth-skinned Latino guy with a big, uncut prick, was slowly stroking his cock. His foreskin was sliding over his engorged knob while strings of precum flowed out and slid over his shaft.

"Looks fucking hot," the dark-haired man said, snapping a photo. "Now play with your asshole."

The Latino guy turned around and pulled his ass cheeks apart, showing the pink center of his pucker. He slid a finger in until it was right up to his knuckle, then began to fuck himself slowly while the other man took pictures. As he snapped one after the other, they fell like leaves from the camera, piling at his feet. From where I knelt on the fire escape I could see that none of them showed the Latino man's face.

"That's great," the black-haired man growled. "You've got me so fucking hard I can't wait." He put the camera down and moved toward the bed. His cock was stiff, and he pumped the thick shaft quickly as he moved in behind the Latino man. Then, in one quick thrust, he shoved his whole dick into the man's ass until his balls were banging against his butt.

"Oh, yeah," he moaned. "You can take the whole fucking thing, can't you, you little slut."

The Latino man squirmed against the bed as the big man impaled him on his cock, hammering away at his hole until his dick was sloppy with sweat and juice from the violated ass. The big man put his hands on the other one's cheeks and pulled them wider, forcing himself inside in long angry thrusts. He was groaning and throwing his head back with each movement.

Watching the two men fuck was getting me really worked up. Pulling my fly open, I pulled out my tool and started manhandling it, jerking off in rhythm with the dark-haired man and pretending

it was my ass he was screwing. Within a few minutes I was ready
to come, which was a good thing, because the big guy yanked his
dick from the Latino man's asshole and started jacking off. With a
few strokes of his hand, he came. Long jets of cum streaked over
the prone man's back, landing in wet stripes on his skin.

Seeing the big stud come made me shoot my load in a blazing
rush. I squeezed my cockhead as it spat out a blast that splattered
against the bricks of the wall. My balls tensed as jism flowed out
of them and dripped onto the slats of the fire escape in heavy
drops, emptying onto the street below. A low groan escaped my
lips as I gave in to the pleasure wrapping my body in its grip.

It must have been just loud enough for the man inside to hear,
because he jumped off the bed and ran to the window. Before I
could even move, he had thrown up the screen and was reaching
out for me, his big hand closing around my wrist. "What the hell
are you doing out here?" he demanded angrily. I was so scared I
couldn't answer him. I just knelt there on the fire escape, looking
up into his beautiful dark brown eyes.

When I didn't answer, his eyes moved down to my prick, and he
smiled slightly as he took in my slimy cock, still held tightly in my
hand. All I was conscious of was the way my breathing seemed to
have stopped and how his fingers felt closed around my wrist. To
my horror, I was still rock hard.

"I think you should get inside," he said, pulling me toward him.
Nervously, I scrambled over the windowsill and into the bedroom.
The Latino man was still on the bed, and he stared at me as I
stood awkwardly in the center of the room. The dark-haired man
pulled the screen closed again, then walked over to stand in front
of me. "Do you always spend your nights jerking off on fire escapes?" he asked as he gripped my chin in his hand and forced my
eyes up to his.

Again I couldn't say anything. Everything else melted away as
I concentrated on the way his fingers held my face and how his
eyes bored into mine. While I tried to get my tongue to work, my
skin burned where he touched it, filling me with a sweet pain that
gripped my balls and squeezed tightly. I felt as though I'd done
something forbidden, seen something that I never should have
seen, and gotten caught. It made me feel slightly dirty, like when
I was a kid and I'd look at the magazines in my dad's underwear

drawer and jack off, afraid the whole time that he'd walk in and catch me, half hoping that he would.

Only this time he had walked in, and I knew I was going to pay for it. When I didn't answer fast enough, the man moved his hand down and grabbed my cock by the base, pulling up on it until I cried out. "There," he said, smiling, "I finally got a noise out of you. And you seem to like it, too."

I could feel my face filling with color as he continued to tug on my balls and I gave in to the feeling. I *did* like it, and he knew it. His strong fingers encircled my cock and balls and squeezed tightly, filling my prick with blood. I tried my best not to gasp, but when he pinched the swollen tip of my dick in his other hand, I almost came. He laughed. "Take your clothes off," he ordered simply, letting go of my pounding cock.

Hurrying to obey him, I tore at the buttons on my shirt and clumsily pulled off my boots and jeans. When I was naked, I stood with my hands behind my back, waiting to see what he would say or do. He sat on the bed the whole time, his eyes on my face as the Latino man buried his head in his lap and slurped on his big dick. He didn't seem to be in any hurry and allowed the man to take his time washing every inch of his cock. Then he pushed him away and stood up.

Coming toward me, he let his fist move along the length of his dick as he walked, stroking it slowly and fiercely, as though pumping it full of life. When he was right in front of me, he stopped. Taking my hand, he moved it so that his cock was against my palm. My fingers closed around it, and I felt him tense so that the hardness swelled up against me.

"Do you like that?" he asked. I nodded, feeling the warm flesh under my fingers as I pulled on his shaft.

He pulled away suddenly, leaving my hand empty. "That's only for good boys," he said, grabbing me by the back of the neck. "It seems to me you've been a bad boy. A very bad boy. And you know what happens to bad boys, don't you?"

I swallowed hard, knowing that I had to answer. "They get punished," I whispered.

He pushed me toward the bed. "That's right," he barked. "They get punished. Now suck Jose's cock."

Jose leaned back against the pillows on the bed and spread his legs. His cock was stiff, and I remembered that he hadn't come yet. As soon as I was kneeling on the bed between his thighs, he grabbed my head and sank the entire length of his dick down my throat. It tore at the sides as it roared down my gullet, but I was so worked up I took every inch of him. He was uncut, and thick ooze poured from beneath his taut foreskin as I teased it with my tongue.

I sucked on Jose as best I could, wishing it were the dark-haired man's tool I was servicing. Behind me, I heard the whirring of a camera as he started taking pictures of me sucking Jose's dick. Thinking about all of the photos I'd found in the box, and knowing that now he had ones of me, made me even hornier. My lips slipped up and down Jose's spit-soaked shaft rapidly as I coaxed him to coming.

Suddenly I felt a stinging pain on my ass, followed by a red-hot burning sensation that seemed to roll over my skin like water. Before I could figure out what it was, the pain came again. Jose's cock jumped in my throat as I tried to pull away and see what was causing it, but I felt a strong hand push my head back down.

"You stay where you are," the dark man's voice ordered. "It's time for the punishment bad boys like you deserve."

The slapping came again on my ass, and I realized that I was being spanked with a belt. Each blow on my tender ass pushed me once again onto Jose's cock, and I swallowed him hungrily as the beautiful warm pain sank into my muscles repeatedly and I tried to absorb it by sucking harder on the cock in my throat. There were tears in my eyes, but it was the most amazing sensation I'd ever felt. It was the same way my father had punished me as a kid, bending me over and slapping my ass until I cried. When he'd finally let me go, I'd run from the room to the bathroom, where I'd jerk my dick and come, sobbing, all over my hand.

The strokes moved up my ass to my lower back, crisscrossing my skin in short, sharp lashes of pain that made my dick harder with every touch of the leather. I started to anticipate the next blow and let the force of it travel through me, drawing my lips tightly around Jose's prick at each slap on my skin. My ass cheeks were still on fire from the working-over they'd received, and soon my whole back was tingling with the remnants of the belt's sting.

While he beat me, the man continued to tell me what a bad boy I was. It felt a little strange, a man of thirty-three being called a boy, but it didn't seem to confuse my dick, which remained hard throughout my punishment. When I felt him move in behind me and spread my ass cheeks with his hands, a long pull of anticipation tugged at my balls.

As he sank one thick finger into my pucker, the man slapped me hard on the ass. "This is what happens to boys who look at things they shouldn't," he said, pulling his finger out and replacing it with the head of his cock. Then he slammed into me all at once, pushing himself deep into my ass.

Pushed forward, I felt Jose's stomach connect with my nose as his prick disappeared into my mouth. My asshole stretched wide as the man started to fuck me, and I was glad my throat was filled with Jose's cock so I couldn't cry out from the pain that seared my shitter. He hadn't even lubed his dick, and it was killing me.

Still, it felt wonderful to be used by him like that. His pictures had given me such pleasure, and now I was paying the price for daring to try and get more than that. His rough hands gripped my ass tightly as he savaged me, and the combined feeling of his thick tool pounding my insides while his fingers pinched at my skin sent me into a frenzy. I slobbered over Jose's cock as I satisfied my mouth with him, pumping his shaft mercilessly while behind me my hole was being tormented by the hottest, roughest fuck I'd ever had.

Jose came in a rush of jism that flooded my throat with warmth and sent me swallowing crazily to contain it all. Several thick gushes escaped his dickhead before the flow slowed, and I gulped down every drop of it. Behind me, the dark-haired man saw what was happening and blew his own load in my butt, pumping faster and faster as his sticky juice streamed inside me.

It was all too much, being taken at both ends, and I lost control, spewing drops of cum all over the bed as my balls gave up their heavy load. Jose's cock slipped out of my mouth, and I rubbed my cheek along his wet shaft while I moaned, sucking the last dribbles of cum from his piss slit. My ass clamped around the still-hard dick invading my hole, and the dark-haired man gave me a final slap as I emptied myself beneath him.

When I was finished, he pulled out of me and jerked me to my feet. Barely able to stand, I slumped against him while he pulled my head back and rammed his tongue into my mouth. He bit my lip hard while his tongue explored mine. Then he pulled away as suddenly as he'd come, and I dropped to my knees. Scattered on the floor were the pictures he'd taken of me. One showed his hard pole piercing my willing asshole. Taken from above right before he started to fuck me hard, the photo showed him with half of his dick penetrating my hole, as well as the red marks on my back from his beating. My face was buried in Jose's crotch. Seeing myself taking in both of their thick cocks made me ache to have them back inside me.

"Take it," the dark-haired man said. "It's what you wanted in the first place."

Not daring to look up at him, I scooped up the picture. Then I quickly found my discarded clothes and pulled them on, still not looking at Jose or the other man, who watched me silently as I dressed. Cum had matted the hair on my belly into sticky tangles, and I ran my fingers over it while I pulled my shirt on. I knew that I would not wash it off before I fell asleep that night, and the thought made me shiver as I tucked the photo into my pocket.

When I had pulled my boots back on, I turned to go. Neither man said a word to me, but both smiled as I walked to the window, slid the screen up, and climbed back onto the fire escape. It seemed the only proper way to leave. Taking a final glance at them as I started down the ladder, I saw the dark-haired man pick up his camera and begin shooting again while Jose did something to himself out of my sight.

After dropping the last few feet to the ground, I walked down the street as easily as if I was out for an evening stroll. But as I thought about how it felt shooting off on that fire escape, and being punished for it afterward, my dick stirred in my pants. It felt just like it did when I was a kid looking at those magazines in my father's drawer, and I knew that, just as I'd returned to those magazines time after time, I'd be back again for more of those dirty pictures.

Southern Comfort

Louisiana is one of my favorite places in the world. There's a magic to it that has to be experienced to be believed. The same goes for Louisiana men.

Spending the summer sweating it out in Louisiana was not something I especially wanted to do. But when the offer came to teach a course in Southern writing at a college there, I weighed the option of getting paid to lead a group of freshmen through the pages of Faulkner and O'Connor against three months of painting houses to make ends meet and said I'd do it. A month later I packed everything I owned into my battered old Toyota and set off, saying good-bye to the dull little town I was living in while doing my graduate work and promising to return in the fall.

I made the trip in two days. Interstate 55 outside Chicago winds down through Illinois, dipping briefly into Missouri and slicing off a northeastern corner of Arkansas before plunging deep into Mississippi. By the time you hit the straightaway that takes you into Louisiana, you've had a healthy spoonful of the pure South. The farther you drive, the closer the heat pulls in around you, descending in a heavy veil that clings to your skin and won't go away no matter how much water you pour down your throat. As I rolled along beside muddy rivers crowded with boats hauling everything from steel to cows and through stands of ancient trees cradling clouds of moss in their arms, I felt as though the real world were slowly slipping away behind me and I was entering a place where time meant very little. I looked uneasily at the tiny hands doggedly circling the face of my watch, wondering if perhaps they weren't slowing down just a little.

The heat refused to bow to the haggard wheezing of my failing air conditioner, and I had the windows rolled down as I passed by the lazy, dark waters of Lake Pontchartrain outside of New Orleans. Another hour brought me to Boudreaux, my home for the summer.

Boudreaux is one of many small cities that spot the Mississippi Delta like freckles on the neck of a proud woman, and while it hasn't yet reached the point where it's become self-conscious, it has expanded to accept the conveniences of a larger place. Navigating the streets lined with stately old homes, I was aware that things there had probably not changed all that much in the last hundred years, and that beneath the neon lights of Chinese takeout restaurants and the eight movie screens of the multiplex beat a heart fueled by the sea and the slow heat of moonshine.

When the road dropped into the ocean and I found myself at the piers, I stopped the car and looked for someone to ask directions of. A bait shop was sitting at the end of a long pier next to a boat that rose and fell slowly with the breathing of the ocean. A man was sitting in a canvas chair beside the shop. His back was to me, and a fishing line dipped down from a pole between his legs, the thin line disappearing into the black water.

I walked down the pier, breathing in the salty air and fishy smell that rose from the worn wooden boards beneath my feet, until I had reached the man in the chair. "Excuse me," I said. "Can you tell me where Ballard House is?"

The man turned slowly, his hand shading his eyes so that he could see me, then set his fishing rod down and stood up. He was tall, standing over six feet, and built like a boxer. His overalls were worn and faded from what looked like endless afternoons spent sitting on the dock and fishing, as if he lived in one long, glorious hour between two and three, when the sun was bright and pure and the ocean breeze ran its thin fingers through his hair, which was lightened to a pale golden brown. His skin was likewise tanned, his green eyes looking out from a face the color of bronze with high cheekbones and a wide, square jaw.

He wore no shirt, the bib of his overalls unbuttoned so that his broad chest was bare. His nipples, dark brown and firm, stood out from the hair that brushed his skin in a dense cloud. The lines of his body, the heavy muscles of his arms, had been wrought by hard physical work. His bare feet were dusted with the red dirt upon which Louisiana sleeps. He looked like one of Tennessee Williams's rougher characters pulled from the dimly lit stage of a story and dropped onto the pier, completely unsurprised to find himself there.

He raised his hand, exposing a dark patch of hair beneath his arm. "Well," he said, his voice as slow and deep as the Mississippi, "you don't have to look any further. It's sitting right behind you."

I turned around and looked in the direction his finger was pointing. Looming across the street from the pier was a beautiful old building, its brick face dotted with big pale windows that opened onto small balconies. I felt foolish for not having noticed it myself, but consoled myself with the fact that the sign was barely visible through the drooping hair of the willow tree in front.

"You staying long?" the man asked.

"Just the summer," I said.

He smiled. "That's what a lot of people say at first. Then once this place works its magic, they decide they don't want to leave."

"We'll see what happens," I said. "Thanks for showing me the hotel." He brought his hand to his forehead in a silent gesture of answer.

I went back to my car and moved it to the hotel's parking lot. Taking my bags inside, I was swept into a parlor cooled by overhead fans and filled with shadows. An old woman thin as a bird and wrinkled as an apple too long in the sun registered my name and handed me my key. "Best view in the house," she said.

I carried my bags up the stately staircase to my room. Large and airy, it was dominated by a huge wooden bed. After examining the bathroom, which was tiled in pale green and had an ancient, claw-foot bathtub that could probably hold three drunken sailors, I checked out the view the old woman had spoken of.

Pushing open the tall glass doors, I stepped out onto the balcony. She had been right, the view was breathtaking. The window was high enough that the view cleared the tops of the trees that lined the street below. Beyond the green the sea opened up, stretching endlessly over the curve of the world.

Looking down, I noticed that I also had a perfect view of the dock, and of the man sitting on it. While he appeared as little more than a bright spot against the water, I had memorized the details of his body and could bring them to mind easily. As I watched him doing nothing but enjoying the day, I recreated his handsome face, then imagined kissing his mouth.

Stepping back into the room, I shed my clothes and stretched out on the soft bed, letting the drowsy heat of the Louisiana air cover me with its hot breath. I closed my eyes and thought about the man, about his naked body against mine. My cock began to stiffen as I imagined his hands on my back, sliding over my ass, grasping my balls. I started to jerk off slowly as the image of his prick sliding in and out of my mouth formed in my daydream until I could taste the bitter sweat on his skin and feel the light hairs on his forearms beneath my hands. I came as he asked to fuck me, his voice sinking into my head as a load of cum splashed onto my belly.

As the days wandered on and summer grew into a wild, hot beast that did as it pleased, I saw the man from the pier many times on my way to and from my class. Each time he waved silently, then went back to whatever he was doing. I never spoke to him, nor he to me, yet I was captivated by him, by his easy manner and his beautiful face. At night while the sea rustled outside and the wind blew warm through my room, I made love with him over and over, my body sliding against the sheets in slow, easy thrusts as the thought of him moved over me. In the mornings when I saw him, my face would redden with the remembrance of what I had done with him in my dreams hours earlier.

One day after class I came home just as a sudden thunderstorm was overtaking the city. Darting into the hotel lobby, I almost crashed right into the man, who was standing just inside the door. "Sorry," I said. "Just trying to outrun the rain."

"It's okay," he said, the corner of his mouth rising in a small smile. "I was doing the same thing."

We stood in the doorway as the rain pounded on the porch, watching it turn into thick sheets that swept in sensuous lines across the grass and speckled the ocean with tiny splashes. "Looks like this one's settled in for the night," he said.

I stood there awkwardly, like a high-school girl who'd just run into the football player she had a crush on. "How'd you like to come up and have a shot while you wait it out?" I asked, holding my breath.

He grinned. "Sounds like a good idea. Sure as hell beats walking home through this."

It occurred to me that I still didn't know his name, so I said, "By the way, I'm Tom."

"Luke," he said, shaking my hand.

We walked upstairs and I opened the door to my room, dropping the key twice because I was so nervous. Luke followed me in. As he looked out of the balcony doors, I poured whiskey into two glasses. Handing him one, I sipped nervously from mine, letting the warmth from the drink crawl up my insides and settle me a little. Luke downed his drink quickly, his throat moving in a single ripple, and I poured him another.

He took the drink and sat on the bed. As usual, he wasn't wearing a shirt, and I wanted badly to run my hands over his hairy chest, to reach out and feel the muscles beneath his skin.

"This reminds me of when I was a kid," he said suddenly, startling me out of my fantasy. "Whenever it stormed, my brother and I would climb into our tree house and sit there, listening to the rain on the roof. Sometimes we'd sleep the whole night there, wrapped in our sleeping bags."

I waited for him to continue, but he didn't. Instead he turned and looked at me. Putting his drink on the bedside table, he reached out and took mine, putting it beside his. I held my breath, waiting to see what he was going to do. Luke reached out and put his hand on mine. Moving it up my arm, he moved until he was between my legs, pushing me back onto the bed.

His skin was warm, as though he had just come out of the sun. As he slipped into my arms, I felt his flesh come together with mine, the hair on his torso rasping along my shirt. I was pinned beneath him, the weight of his body heavy and delicious. When he leaned to kiss me, I parted my lips and drew his tongue in. His mouth tasted of whiskey, thick and strong, and I sucked gently on his full lips.

Running my hands down his back, I let my fingers play over the bones of his spine. His muscles moved against my hands in response, pushing against them in slow waves. When I reached the soft indentation at the top of his ass, I slid my hands under the fabric of his overalls. He was naked beneath them, just as I'd hoped he would be, and almost immediately my hands were filled with the sweet mounds of his ass cheeks.

Moving around his waist, I sank my fingers deep into his crotch. His cock was half-hard, falling into my fingers heavily, followed by his fat balls. I held his prick tightly as he continued to kiss me, enjoying the heat it gave off. Reluctantly letting go, I removed my hands from his pants and undid the buttons holding them closed at the waist. I pushed them over his beautiful ass and he shucked them onto the floor. Then he helped me out of my clothes, our fingers tumbling together as we reached for the same buttons, laughing.

When I was naked, Luke knelt over me, his hands on either side of my head. His cock swung down and grazed along my stomach, swaying as he rocked slightly on the big bed. The head was fat and round, the shaft thick. His balls hung down behind his prick like a bag of gold hefted by an unseen hand. I ran my hands over his chest, through the thick hair, then leaned forward and let it brush my cheek.

Outside, the rain continued to fall quick and fierce on the stones of the street, rattling on the roof in sharp beats. The storm rolled over and around the town, playing with the town like a giant tossing a ball back and forth in its hands. Thunder grumbled low and steady, while splinters of lightning shattered cracks in the blackness of the sky. The lights flickered once and then were still, the room suddenly swallowed up.

I could feel Luke on top of me, the comforting strength of his thighs around my sides, the heaviness of his cock pressing against me. "Do you have any matches?" he asked.

"On the dresser," I said.

He got up and padded across the room. I saw his shadow move across the square of dim light that filled the doorway to the terrace and then disappear again. Then there was the scratch of a match and a blossom of flame broke from the darkness. Luke put the match to one of the candles on the dresser, then blew it out.

The light from the candle crept up his face as he held it out, turning him into a strange vision lit with gold. He carried the light toward me and brought it to the lips of several more candles until the bed was flooded with soft tongues of light that darted and played over the expanse of the white sheets and my naked body.

Luke came back to the bed and once more lay on top of me. One of his hands went behind my neck, and he started to kiss me again. As he did, he thrust himself along my stomach, the heat from his prick burning into me. Wrapping my leg around his, I pushed hard against him, feeling the muscles of his ass pumping as he moved.

My hands were tangled in his hair while we kissed, my fingers holding tightly as his tongue explored my mouth, insistent and hard. When he rolled onto his back, I came with him, so that I was lying between his spread legs. Looking down, I saw that his cock was still only half-hard.

Sliding down, I took the head between my lips. As I sucked softly at it, thick beads of sweet juice poured from the small lips. The taste of Luke's cock filled my throat as I took his whole prick into me. My face was pressed tightly against his groin as I fed on him, my tongue working the length of him, urging his cock to life.

As Luke's prick filled and swelled, I could no longer keep all of it in. While he had seemed large when soft, his growing prick was becoming even huger. The shaft was thickening until I could barely get my lips around it, the head stretching my throat. Fully hard, his dick was as straight and thick as a redwood sapling.

Unable to suck his cock to the root, I contented myself with licking the length of it. I loved the way the landscape of his tool changed as I traveled it, the softness of the head narrowing into the rock-hard shaft, the vein beneath the skin pulsing as I moved along it until my tongue felt rough hair and my lips filled with the musky hair of his crotch.

Luke wrapped a hand around his balls and pulled up on them until they were right under my nose. He rubbed the furry sac over my lips roughly, and I licked at its heavy contents. Taking one smooth ball into my mouth, I sucked gently. Luke moaned and I felt him begin to stroke his cock. He pulled his legs up so that I could have more room to move.

As he did, his hips shifted forward and his ass cheeks parted slightly beneath his balls. The area between his cock and his ass was rich with hair that trickled into his crack. Seeing it exposed like that ignited something inside me, and I pressed my mouth against it hungrily, my tongue licking eagerly. Going lower, I explored the valley between his cheeks, tasting the rich musk of his skin.

Luke's hands came between his legs and the thick fingers pulled his ass cheeks even farther apart as though he were breaking a piece of thick, warm bread. His asshole, wrinkled and surrounded by hair, lay between the meaty flesh. I dove into it, the scent of Luke's body mingling with the smell of the sea on his skin. My tongue worked across the hot skin of his hole, tracing the folds, licking up his rich sweat. The hair of his legs brushed lightly on my cheeks as I ate out his hot hole.

As I worked on Luke's ass, I could feel the rise and fall of his nuts and knew that he was jerking off. He was moaning loudly, and his hips were thrusting against my face heatedly. "I'm going to come," he said raggedly.

I looked up from between his legs just in time to see a geyser of white erupt from his prick and splatter onto the hair of his chest. His cock kept spewing gobs of jism until he was covered in it. The fingers wrapped around his piece were coated in sticky strings, and the shaft was slick with his juice. In the light from the candles, the pools of cum shone like gold.

I took his hand and began to lick the cum from his fingers, taking each one into my mouth and sucking it clean. The flesh was still hot from stroking his prick, and I could taste the combined flavors of cum and ball sweat on his skin. I moved on to his still-hard cock, washing every inch of the huge tool eagerly before licking the puddles of cum from his body. He had soaked his entire chest with his load, and it took a long time to get it all off.

As I licked up the heady smears from his torso, Luke was rubbing his cock slowly against my dangling one, pushing the big head along it until it slipped into my ass crack. That, combined with the fact that I had a belly full of his cum, was almost enough to make me shoot my own load.

"I want you to make love to me," I whispered into his ear.

Luke smiled. "Oh, I plan on it. But first I want to play with that beautiful prick of yours for a while."

Rolling me over, Luke knelt between my legs and started to pump my prick steadily. I was already worked up and was afraid I was going to burst before he got a chance to fill my ass with his big meat. But whenever I'd get close, Luke seemed to know, slowing down until my need died enough for him to resume his hand job.

Luke's lips closed over the tip of my cock and I slipped into his throat like a ship sinking into the sea. His mouth was warm, as though he held the sun beneath his tongue, and as he sucked my prick I felt acutely every movement of his mouth along my shaft. I arched my back, rising up to meet his downward strokes, fucking his handsome face. My hand on his head encouraged him to speed up his strokes, and he slid up and down my cock steadily, drawing rivers of pleasure from my near-bursting balls.

While he continued to blow me, Luke pressed a fingertip

against the opening of my ass. Rubbing in tiny circles, he loosened it up until he could slide in an inch or two. My muscles clamped greedily around his thick finger, urging him deeper, but he continued to work only on the entrance to my chute until he was fucking me in time with the path his mouth trod along my prick.

Slowly he worked his finger into me, pushing it farther every time. I thought I was going to cry out from the exquisite feelings he was coaxing from me. Finally I felt his knuckles against my cheeks and knew that he was all the way in. Luke let his hand rest for a few seconds wrapped in my warm folds before pulling out and starting all over again with two fingers.

His hands were large, and having two of his fingers in me was like being fucked by a good-sized cock. When he had three buried to the joint inside my aching hole, I felt as though my balls were going to burst from the force of the pleasure inside them. I rocked my ass back and forth on Luke's hand, moaning and begging him to fuck me. My cock was so hard I was sure it would shatter like glass if he touched it again.

Then his hand was gone. I barely had a second to catch my breath before Luke had my legs over his shoulders and his cock was pounding its way into my ass. My chute stretched to new limits as his thick shaft pushed deep inside me. I took several quick breaths, overcome by the delicious mixture of pain and pleasure that was flooding me. Every nerve in my body seemed centered on the point where his cock was burrowing into me.

My legs were flat against Luke's strong chest, rising and falling with his even breathing as he made love to me, easing his cock back and forth in steady rhythm. I closed my eyes, the sound of the storm filling my head, the song of the rain playing behind the touch of Luke's big cock.

The harder he pumped my ass, the stronger the feelings flowed through me. I started to stroke my cock in time with him until the movements of my hand became an extension of his thrusts. Luke had his hands around my ankles and held my legs apart so that he could watch his cock disappear into my welcoming hole. His face glowed with sweat in the candle flames, turning him gold and red as he gazed down at me from between my thighs.

It seemed as though he fucked me for hours, his hard prick never stopping its back and forth motions. I felt as though the whole room were filled with him, the smell of his skin, the taste of his mouth, the touch of his hands. We had built a world of warmth and light within the storm, and there we could make love forever.

Luke's thrusting was speeding up, and I saw the muscles of his neck tense as he tried to hold off the force that was clamoring for release within him. His head went back and he pumped me three more times before sinking home and letting his load roar out, filling me with sweet streams of his jism.

As he filled my ass I came in a great shivering spurt that exploded into the air and splattered my face and neck in thick rain. Three times I came, each one sending a fresh burst over my sticky body.

Luke pulled out of me and stood up. "Come on," he said, holding out his hand and pulling me to my feet.

He walked across the room to the doors that opened out onto the terrace. Pushing them apart, he stepped directly into the mouth of the storm. I followed, laughing at his foolishness or bravery, I couldn't tell which.

The rain was surprisingly warm, washing over us in wild gusts. The thunder and lightning crashed overhead, but Luke seemed not to mind. It also didn't seem to bother him that anyone might look up and see two naked men standing on a balcony in full view of the street. He ran his hands over me, wiping the cum from my skin until I was clean. Then he let the water sweep over him as well, lifting his face up to greet it.

Back inside, I grabbed some towels from the bathroom and we dried off. We lay down on the big bed, Luke's arms around me, surrounded by the flickering eyes of the candles. As I watched the storm outside, I remembered what Luke had said to me the first time I'd seen him, about not wanting to leave, and thought he might just be right.

The Men's Room

There's something unmistakably male about a men's room: the smell, the urinals, the line of guys pretending not to look at one another's dicks while they piss. There was a men's room in Boston I used to visit often on my way home because it happened to be in the subway station where I caught the train. More than once I looked down into a urinal and saw someone else's load floating in the water. This story came—as it were—from wondering who had left them.

The men's room smelled of ammonia and flowers, the strange bittersweet scent that clung to it after the cleaning person had finished washing the white tile floors and scrubbing the toilets with rubber glove–clad hands. It was after seven, and I was about to go home for the night after a long day of wrestling with contract negotiations for a television spot featuring a temperamental tennis hotshot. My bladder was aching, and I just wanted to piss and get out of the office. I walked up to the closest of the two urinals. Unzipping my pants, I reached in and pulled out my cock, feeling it hang heavily in my fingers.

The vein on the underside of my prick swelled as a stream of piss rushed out, breaking from my hole and splashing down onto the bright pink triangle of disinfectant that rested in the cupped hands of the bowl. I watched the pale yellow rainstorm tumble from my pipe, enjoying the heavy thundering sound it made when it hit the water, the way the pitch changed as the torrent became a slow stream before sputtering out.

As I shook the last drops from my dickhead, I saw that lying across the cold whiteness of the urinal's freshly cleaned rim was a single hair. Reddish brown, it curved sinuously along the surface of the porcelain like a fine vein running beneath the skin where it stretches paper thin over the bones of a hand. I stared at it, pleased by the way it cracked the otherwise seamless lip like a scar, a reminder of another man's recent presence.

Then I noticed the cum floating in the water, four small islands of sticky whiteness strung together by fragile filaments thin as cobwebs. I gazed at the sight, intimately familiar but at the same time so alien in its context, and an image began to form in my head. I pictured a man standing at the urinal, his legs slightly apart, his prick held firmly between thumb and forefinger as he pissed. He gripped himself tightly, enjoying the beating of his own cock against his fingers, stroking himself so subtly that the man next to him was completely unaware that his neighbor was getting pleasure from what appeared to him to be nothing more than another repetition of a function performed without thinking many times each day.

As I thought about the faceless man, my prick began to stiffen in my hand. The idea of him gripping his manhood, bringing himself off in the open of the men's room where anyone could walk in excited me. I imagined the look on his face as he came, the motion of his wrist as he milked the cream from his shaft, loosening the hair that lay now on the urinal. Or perhaps it had fallen from his fingers when he had been forced to tuck his sticky cock, still hard, back in his pants as the door opened and a coworker entered, nodding an oblivious greeting.

I stroked my cock as I thought about it, and soon my hard dick was sticking straight out from the dark blue folds of my suit pants, the head swollen and anxious. I started to imagine all of the men who stood in front of the urinal during a given day, each one with a different cock, individual in its shape and length, each man with a different way of holding his prick. As I beat my piece quickly, I envisioned them adding their piss to the endless stream that flowed through the urinal's open mouth and down the silver pipes of its throat, wondering how many of them knew what else went on in the bathroom.

I came in a long, furious shot that splattered against the back of the urinal. A sticky smear stained its white skin like a wet handprint across a cheek, reaching down into the water where it mingled with the other man's. I was about to flush away the remains of my hand job but decided instead to leave my load in the urinal for the next man to see. I laughed to myself as I pictured the expression on his face as he looked down and saw the sight of cum, so much like what came from his own prick when he jerked off but belonging to another man. I wondered if he, like me, would find the experience arousing. Brushing my fingers through my bush, I pulled out one black hair and laid it next to the reddish one before leaving for the night.

When I went into the bathroom the next morning, the urinal was once again sparkling clean, all traces of the cum stains wiped from its blank face. Periodically during the day I recalled the odd thrill aroused in me by seeing the man's pubic hair and jism and was overcome by the need to jerk off again. But once again I was busy untangling various work snarls, and it wasn't until long after everyone had gone home that I was able to finish up and head for my new nightly ritual. Again he had been there before me, this time landing his load on the lip of the urinal. While some had slipped into the water, most of it remained on the edge. I scooped it up in my fingers and used it to slick my own boner, sliding my hand over my cockhead until I came, thinking about the man's secret pleasure.

Every night for the next three days I found a fresh load waiting for me in the urinal. But even though I tried to keep an eye on who went in and out of the men's room, my mystery man eluded me. There are a lot of men in my office, and it could have been any number of them. I immediately ruled out all of the blond men because of the color of the hair I'd found. This eliminated five guys, but there were still more than a dozen possibilities. I decided to try the direct approach. Whenever I noticed someone I thought was a likely candidate heading for the men's room, I followed him, discreetly coming in after he was already pissing and trying to get a look at his equipment for the telltale reddish hair.

Throughout the day I observed firsthand the cocks of most of the department and was surprised at some of what I saw. Ed, an older man from accounting whose hairpiece was the focus of many a joke, sported a prick so large I couldn't believe he kept it hidden beneath his cheap, ill-fitting suit. Even soft it was impressively sized, with a silky foreskin sliding over the fat helmet. In contrast, Jim in finance hardly measured up to the stories he told every morning about the latest woman he'd brought to unknown heights of ecstasy the night before. He had glanced at my cock and left quickly, zipping his tiny dick up and leaving me alone to gloat over my discovery.

By the end of the day I was intimately acquainted with a number of cocks, some of which I wouldn't have minded being even better acquainted with. But I still hadn't figured out who my jerk-off buddy was. Discouraged, I packed up my briefcase and prepared to head home. As I was waiting for the elevator, I heard the click of a door closing. Making my way to the men's room, I listened for any sounds from inside.

I couldn't hear anything through the door, so I pushed lightly against it until a crack of light was visible. Looking in, I had a good view of the urinals. Standing there was Peter McKenna, the head of marketing. His hand was flying along a thick cock that stretched out from the fly of his suit pants. Peter's eyes were closed, and he was thrusting his prick into his fist as he pumped it. Low groans came from his throat as he squeezed his fat piece in his hand.

I couldn't believe it was Peter who had been flooding the urinal with his cream all week. A tall, handsome man, Peter was married, and his wife was the envy of every woman in the office. There was a picture of his two kids, a boy and a girl, on his desk, and he frequently spoke about family camping trips and coaching his son's Little League baseball team. Because he didn't work on my floor, it had never occurred to me that he would be the man at the center of my obsession.

I watched him jerk off for a few minutes, my own prick stiffening as I stared at his big cock. Peter was a large man, about six-three and well built. His hands were equally large, and the one wrapped around his shaft held it tightly as it moved up and down, the gold wedding band on the ring finger glinting under the harsh fluorescent light. I couldn't take having the big stud so close to me, and I walked into the bathroom. When Peter heard me come in he whirled around, his hand still grasping his rod.

"Oh, shit," he said in his husky voice. "I, um, didn't know anyone was here. I'll just go."

He started to tuck his cock back into his pants, but I walked over and put my hand on his arm. He looked at me for a few seconds with his large brown eyes, as if unsure of what to do, and then let his now half-hard prick hang free. The fat head swung in front of me, grazing against the bulge in my pants and causing my cock to jump with excitement.

I dropped to my knees, the coldness of the tile floor soaking through my thin suit pants like damp grass. Peter's cock loomed above me, the head bending down toward my waiting mouth. I licked gently at the glistening piss slit, pushing my tongue against the tiny opening to taste the juice that had crept up from Peter's nuts. He must have just finished pissing, and the bitter, masculine taste lingered on his skin. I ran my tongue under the head, into the valley formed where it joined the shaft. As I did, my lips closed around his wide tip and I sucked on his knob firmly, my cheeks pressed tightly around his shaft.

Peter's cock was warm in my mouth, and I felt it grow fatter and fatter as I sucked him back to complete hardness. Fully erect, his dick was straight and thick, the skin smooth and taut over the engorged flesh. Relaxing my jaw, I worked on the first four or five inches of his massive tool, pushing it into my throat slowly and steadily. I thought about his wife, wondering if she could take all of his massive man meat in her tiny lipsticked mouth, and slid down his prick until my nose was buried in the small patch of his musky bush exposed through his fly.

As I worked on Peter's prick, my hands were resting on his shoes. They were made of soft brown leather, and by pressing my fingers into the surface I could feel his feet beneath them. There is something about a man in a business suit that drives me wild—the way the clothes hang on his body, the way a tie encircles his wide throat or a watch the big bones of his wrist. Peter was a beautiful man, and in his suit he was a vision of power and strength. I rubbed his shoes slowly while I serviced him, the touch of the highly polished leather matching the sensuous, deliberate movements of my mouth.

Peter's cock was sunk deep in my hungry throat, my face pressed into his pants so that the zipper of his fly scraped my nose. I moved my hands from his shoes to his ankles, feeling beneath my searching fingers the silk of his dress socks and the way the muscles of his legs moved under them. Further up, the silk gave way to flesh, and I felt rough hair on my skin. Wrapping my hands around his firm calves, I massaged them in time with my sucking, my lips caressing the length of prick between them as my fingers caressed his strong legs.

Peter had his hands on my head, his fingers in my hair. He urged me to suck him more quickly, thrusting his prick into my mouth and pulling me forward urgently. I wanted to be able to touch his skin, so I reached for his belt buckle, undoing it and the button that held his pants closed. Peter's pants slipped from his waist and into my waiting hands like a sudden fall of snow. To my surprise, he was not wearing underwear. I ran my hands down his solid legs, rubbing the familiar auburn hair that blanketed his thighs and cupping the heavy sac of balls between his legs, each one the size of an egg.

Peter undid his tie and unbuttoned his white shirt, letting it hang open but not removing either one. His broad chest was covered in the same beautiful reddish hair as his legs, swirling in lazy circles over his muscular torso and trickling into the pool of his crotch. He stood in the empty men's room, looking down at me expectantly. Putting my hands on the rounded cheeks of his ass, I buried my face between his legs, sucking hungrily at his ripe balls, pressing his cock against my neck. His sac was damp with sweat, the skin salty to the taste, the smell of a man thick between his thighs. This only made me hotter for him, and I washed his balls thoroughly, every once in a while giving his cock a deep suck to remind myself of how it felt in my throat.

Peter was grinding against my face, pushing his balls into my mouth. As he did, his fingers were working on his tits, pinching them into full, ripe buds that stuck out from his chest. Rising from the floor, I moved my mouth to one of his nipples, scraping my cheek across the soft fur of his chest. As I closed my lips around his tender flesh, Peter placed his hands on my head, drawing me to him. I sucked at his tit, biting softly and teasing him with my tongue. I could feel his cock pushing up between us as he rubbed his body up and down mine.

Releasing his hold on me, Peter began to undo my shirt as I kissed his neck, my mouth moving into the sweet hollow of his throat. I helped him by undoing my pants and sliding them off. My cock was aching from being confined for so long, and now it stood up straight from my belly, electric with heat and expectation. Peter held my smooth nuts in one big hand and kneaded them as I ran my tongue over the muscles of his neck and kissed his mouth.

I slipped Peter's shirt off him and we stood completely exposed, our clothes scattered on the floor like puddles of water. I put my hands on Peter's waist and ran them along the muscles of his back. Wrapping my arms around him, I pulled him close until our pricks were snug against each other, beating hotly. His tongue pressed against my lips and entered me, hungry and demanding. He kissed me roughly, sucking the breath from my throat as he probed deeper and deeper. The hair of his belly rubbed along my smooth skin as he pulled me tight, sending tendrils of pleasure into my balls.

Moving behind me, Peter positioned me so that I was facing the wall with my hands on either side of the urinal and my cock dangling over the gurgling water. Coming up behind me, he pressed the entire length of his fuck piece against the crack of my ass, his balls hanging down against mine. He started to thrust against me, his cock sliding along between my cheeks like a steam engine. He slipped one of his big fingers into my mouth, and I sucked eagerly at it as he slowly fucked my lips, sliding over my teeth and tongue. He put two more fingers in, and I slurped at them like I was sucking his fat cock, the band that circled his finger metallic on my tongue.

He took his hand out of my mouth and started to finger my asshole. I was tight, but my spit helped him slip one finger in so he could loosen me up. Soon I was rocking back and forth over the three fingers that had been in my mouth, the warm rim of his wedding ring once again adding extra pleasure as he slipped it past my sphincter. Peter pulled his fingers out and positioned his cockhead against the opening to my chute. As he drove in, my cock sprang up and slapped against my stomach from the thrill of being invaded by him. I'd never had anything so thick up me before, and Peter filled me totally. I could feel every twitch of his prick inside my belly, and the sensation of his fat head throbbing deep inside me nearly sent me over the edge.

Peter didn't waste any time letting me get used to his size. Pulling back, he began to hammer my ass with abandon, bombarding my tender hole with his full arsenal. Grunting with every thrust, he buried his prick in me again and again until thick drops of slime were dripping from my cockhead onto the bathroom floor. My dick bounced up and down, slapping my stomach and brushing against the edge of the urinal as it thrashed around.

I imagined someone walking in on us and seeing the big stud fucking my ass in the middle of the men's room, and this made me even hornier. I pictured all of the men who had stood in that very spot, and would stand there the next day oblivious to what had happened, and imagined them all jerking off watching us. I pushed back against Peter, driving him even farther in, and he responded by increasing his speed so that his belly slapped painfully against my ass as he pumped his full length in and out of my burning hole.

Still fucking me, Peter wrapped his hand around my cock and began to beat me off in time with his thrusting. He was bent over me now, and his breath was ragged on the back of my neck.

"I'm going to shoot deep inside you," he growled in my ear. "I'm going to fucking come in your tight hole."

I was close to shooting myself, and hearing this family man talking dirty to me as he stuffed his tool up my butt filled me with a perverse joy. I wanted Peter to empty his load in me. Clamping my ass muscles around his dick, I began to ride him furiously. He started to moan, and I felt his prick swell painfully inside me just before he let out a low groan of pleasure and a thick blast plastered my shitter with his heat.

Peter came three times, each time emptying a huge load into me. The last spasm sent me over the edge. I looked down and saw a flood of jism shoot from my cock as Peter pumped it. It sprayed a sticky web all over the urinal, covering the sides and dripping from the rim to the floor in long threads. Seeing it there brought another round from my tired nuts, this time coating Peter's hand with a heavy rain that clung to the hairs of his wrist and hand.

Slipping out of my ass, Peter dressed quickly and left without another word, which was just as I wanted it. If he'd said anything else, it would have shattered the world we'd created there between the white tiled walls of the men's room. I wanted to remember him as he'd been the moment when his cock was buried in my ass, releasing his need into me.

After that night I couldn't pass Peter in the hall without my prick getting hard. But we never discussed or repeated our encounter, and there were no more reminders waiting for me in the men's room. Then, a few months later, I stopped on my way out to wash my hands. There in the water of the urinal a swirl of white broke the clear surface. And sitting on the rim was a hair, golden brown like honey. Looking at it, I felt a familiar stirring in my balls, and my hand went immediately to my zipper.

A Perfect Game

There are only two sports that I can really get into: baseball and hockey. This story came about while I was contemplating the age-old problem of partners who are devoted to different teams. In one of those life-imitating-art moments, my partner and I did in fact move to San Francisco a couple of years ago, much like the characters in the story. Although I have wholeheartedly embraced the Giants, Patrick still insists on rooting for the Anaheim Angels, and the 2002 World Series was a grim affair around here, especially for me.

"Yes!" I heard Mike yell enthusiastically from the bedroom as I opened the front door. "That's the way to throw the goddamned ball. Stop playing like a bunch of sissies and you just might pull this thing off." I had just come from the gym, where I'd been so caught up in my workout that I'd lost all track of time. When I suddenly realized that the Series had started twenty minutes earlier, I hadn't even bothered to shower before coming home, and my skin was damp and sticky with the sweat I'd worked up jogging the twelve blocks to the apartment.

I should explain that in our house, baseball is king. Mike and I both play in a weekend league made up of a bunch of guys in their thirties who should really know better but insist on dragging ourselves out to the park once a week to throw a ball around and tell tall tales about our illustrious careers on Rotary Club teams or high-school squads. While I did play second base on my college team, I enjoy running around the field catching flies and swatting the ball mainly because it's fun to be with a bunch of other guys playing a game. But Mike played several seasons for an Atlanta farm team before a groin injury (he was screwing the strength coach in the showers and slipped) took him out of big league consideration, and for him it's like being able to relive those summer days of glory all over again.

Every spring he starts getting all worked up for the season, buying tickets to opening-day games and poring over stats in the morning paper. He even keeps a chart on the refrigerator that he updates daily, tracking the progress of both leagues. I turn into the proverbial baseball widow while he gets a severe case of base-ball fever that lasts straight through September, growing worse as the end of the season draws near. Needless to say, the World Series is the highlight of his year. And this year the Braves, Mike's hometown team, were in the final sweep.

Tossing my gym bag on a chair, I went into the bedroom. Mike was lying on the bed, propped up against the pillows. He was wearing a faded pair of jeans and his Atlanta Braves T-shirt and baseball hat. All he needed was a few stripes of yellow and red war paint on his cheeks and he'd look just like the chanting fans watching the game from the stands. I told him when we moved to San Francisco that he might want to think about picking a new fa-vorite team to root for, but after growing up in the South he was as stubborn as the strong-willed Dixie women who'd met the Yankee soldiers on the road armed with nothing but their parasols and their anger.

"Who's winning?" I asked as I flopped down on the bed next to him.

He grinned, the muscles of his darkly shadowed jaw sliding into a smile. He never shaves during the Series, and after more than a week he had the beginnings of quite a nice beard coming in. "I'm not telling," he said teasingly. "If you can't show up on time, you forfeit your right to know until the next break. Besides," he added, sniffing loudly, "you really smell. You better hit the showers."

I rolled over on top of him and pinned him to the bed, strad-dling his wide chest and holding his arms down with my knees. I was blocking his view of the television, and he was struggling to see around me. "Hey," he said, "I can't see the game."

"Too bad," I said, licking his neck while he strained to pull away. "You apologize."

"No way," he laughed, trying to push me off. "Now let me up."

"If you won't apologize, then you'll have to pay the penalty," I said. I pressed my crotch forward so that the bulge in my sweats was right in front of his mouth. "Suck it."

"But it's game six," he whined. "The Braves are up three to two. If they win this one, they win the whole damn thing. Do you know how long I've waited to see the hometown boys win this thing?"

"I don't know," I told him. "You aren't being particularly good tonight. I'm not sure you should be able to watch any television." Snatching up the remote control, I clicked off the set. Mike cried out indignantly. "You bastard. Turn that back on right now."

"Not until you show a little more teamwork," I growled. Reaching into my bedside table drawer, I pulled out a couple of old ties I keep there for just such emergencies. One at a time, I wrapped the ends around Mike's wrists and secured them to the rails of the big iron bed frame. He kept trying to buck me off him, but I'm taller and outweigh him by about thirty pounds, and there was no way he was going to move me. The whole time, a steady stream of cursing came from his mouth. "You fucking shit," he bellowed. "You peckerhead. This is torture, you goddamned cocksucker. You better let me up or you'll be really sorry."

I looked down at him, his arms tied helplessly above his head. "For someone in your position you sure do have a big mouth," I said. "It's a good thing I have something in mind to fill it with. Now just lie there while Coach goes and gets ready for his boy."

I climbed off the bed and went into the bathroom, leaving Mike squirming and swearing on the bed. Tying him up had gotten me all worked up, and my prick started to harden as I mentally ran over the scene I was about to play out. In the bathroom, I quickly pulled off my sweats and T-shirt and threw them in the hamper. I really was smelling pretty strong from my workout, and the scent of my own body made me even harder. I snatched up a jock from the pile of dirty laundry and pulled it on, arranging the straps over the full moons of my ass and making a tight basket of my cock and balls. There were old cum and piss stains on the pouch, and since I'd worn it for three weeks without washing it I knew it was ripe with my ball sweat.

Also sitting on the mound of laundry waiting to be washed was the uniform I wore for weekend play. I pulled on the tight-fitting blue pants and drew the drawstring closed. The last time we'd played it had been wet, and there were a couple of really good dirt and grass stains on the legs from where I'd taken a slide into home plate. I put on the loose jersey as well, my number 33 on the back in white with Morgan written over it in block letters.

To complete the outfit I pulled my socks and sneakers back on. Then, grabbing an old batting glove from the hallway table, I went back in to attend to Mike. He had been unable to get out of the firm knots I'd made and was still tied up nice and tight. His face was red from all the exertion, and he looked like he wanted to kill me. He wouldn't even look at me as I walked to the foot of the bed and stared down at him.

"Now," I said deliberately as I fastened the batting glove around my left wrist and stretched my fingers inside it. "I think you and I have some training to do. I can't have my boys disobeying Coach's orders, can I?"

Mike glared at me. "I'm not doing it," he said. "Nothing you can do is going to make me horny, Tom. I mean it. Now turn the game back on."

I could tell that he really was mad at me, but my stubborn streak was in control at the moment, and I was determined to have him begging me to fuck him. Spreading my legs, I started to rub my crotch slowly, my fingers working on the head of my prick. "Oh, come on," I teased. "Don't you want Coach to show you his nice big cock?"

Mike grunted. He was angry, but I could tell he was having to try really hard not to look at my dick. The man is a born slave to a big cock, and he worshipped my tool whenever he could. I knew it was killing him not to watch me stroke my dick to life, especially the way it stretched underneath the confining skin of my uniform pants, pointing straight up inside the grip of the jock.

"Looks like someone's getting a little hard-on," I said, reaching over to squeeze the bulge between his legs. He twisted his lower body to one side, trying to get away from me, but not before I'd gotten a handful of his stiffening dick.

"Fuck you," he snarled.

I pulled away. "Is that any way to talk to your coach?" I bellowed. "It looks like I'll have to teach you a lesson in showing respect."

I grabbed the waist of his jeans and pulled the buttons open roughly, yanking the pants down his legs and off him. He was wearing a pair of white boxers underneath, and his prick made a nice little rise along his thigh. I especially liked the way the white line of the boxers cut across the blond-brown hair on his legs and belly, neatly severing the thick spray that rose up from his crotch to flood out across what I could see of his torso below his T-shirt.

Standing next to him, I ran my finger lightly over his skin, feeling bumps leap up under my touch and his muscles flutter as I stroked him. "Now," I said, looking into his angry gray eyes, "since you're so determined not to get hard for your coach, we're going to make a little wager. I'm going to show you just what's under this here uniform. If you manage to stay soft, you go free and get to see your game. But if this cock gets all hard for me, then I'm going to take it out on that sweet ass of yours. We're going to see what's more important to you—baseball or dick. Understood?"

Mike's face went red as he thought about what was going to happen. He knew he was going to lose, but he was going to try his damnedest not to, and that would be torture for him. "You're a sick fucking bastard," he said.

Moving back to the foot of the bed, I looked down at Mike, his wrists bound so neatly to the rails of the bed, his balls and cock covered by the thin veil of his boxers like the face of a beautiful woman. He was still wearing his Braves T-shirt and hat and looked like any jock plucked straight from the locker room of a ball club and dropped into my bedroom. The sight of him all tied up like that made my dick stretch another inch or two. Never taking my eyes off his face, I grabbed the edge of my jersey and started to lift it over my chest. Mike loves my heavily muscled chest, the dark hair covering it in soft swirls. His favorite thing is to shoot a thick load right into my fur and then lick it off again, rubbing his face from my neck to my cock.

I could tell he was trying not to think about drenching me in his spunk as I showed him inch after inch of my torso. I pulled the jersey over my head and dropped it to the floor. "You like Coach's chest, boy?" I teased as I rubbed my hand over my belly and flexed my muscles. "You thinking about how it would feel to have your balls rubbing across this fur while I eat out your ass and you suck my cock?"

Mike's dick moved beneath the skin of his boxers, the head swelling a little, and he gritted his teeth. "Up yours," he spat out.

I pinched one of my nipples between my fingers, rubbing it slowly while I lifted my other arm and showed Mike the forest of damp hair beneath it. Turning my head, I ran my tongue across the bunched muscles of my bicep and licked at the tangle of black. "Nice and sweaty," I said between licks. "Just like a coach's pit should be. All ready for some smart-ass boy to wash clean."

Mike's cock was half-hard now, jutting out across his leg while he tried to will it back down. I knew I had him, and I moved my hands to the drawstring holding my pants closed. My cock was at full attention now and was pressed painfully against my groin. Unlacing the string, I loosened the uniform pants and pushed them down my hips so that just the tip of my straining prick poked out. Mike groaned audibly as he saw his favorite toy.

"Now, now," I said. "This is only for the boys who know how to play nice. The ones who do just what Coach says." I pushed the pants down further so that Mike could see my jock.

"Go play with yourself," he snarled, throwing his head back against the pillows.

Almost immediately, he knew he'd made his fatal mistake. Removing my sneakers, I pulled the pants off completely, standing in front of Mike in nothing but a very full jockstrap and my batting glove. My dick stretched a good three inches over the edge of the jock, and Mike couldn't take his eyes off of it. His prick was almost fully hard, and there was a small stain on the white fabric where he was leaking precum.

"Be careful there," I mocked him. "You get any bigger and Coach will have to use that thing for batting practice."

Mike looked down at his rapidly extending dick and then back at me. "You haven't won yet," he said, swallowing heavily.

I started to pull the jock off, letting it slip slowly down my thick shaft and hairy thighs. The whole time I was stripping, I told Mike exactly what I was going to do with him once the jock was off. "I'm going to stick it right up your tight ass," I said huskily as I showed him more of my engorged stick. "You know you want Coach to spread your nice sweet cheeks and push his big tool inside. Want to feel him pushing deep inside your hot shitter. Want to feel him shoot his stud load in your nasty hole."

Mike's dick was hard as a rock now, tenting out his boxers where it rose up from his groin. He knew it was all over for him. Still, he was resisting, and I didn't stop teasing him. "Maybe you want to suck Coach off before he fucks you," I said as I finally slipped the jock down my thighs and let my balls swing free. My prick flopped down and hung over my smooth, heavy sac, the head swollen and red from being constricted for so long. "Slide your mouth along the shaft until you feel my bush against your face. Think you could take the whole thing in?" I gave my cock a couple of quick strokes, urging from the lips a thin stream of silvery drool that hung swinging in the air for a moment before falling to the floor.

Taking the jock off, I balled it up and went over to the bed. Gripping the waistband of Mike's boxers, I ripped them cleanly down the center. His cock sprang up from his belly, and I grabbed it, gripping the shaft painfully in the hand covered by the batting glove. "Looks like you lose," I said. Mike was silent, looking at me like he wanted to rip my heart out. I squeezed his dick again, sliding my hand up and down the shaft. "Time for a little coaching session."

The next thing I felt was Mike spitting on me, a wet spray slamming into my cheek. "Go screw yourself," he said evenly.

I put my hand to my cheek and felt the thin film of spit on skin. He hadn't really tried very hard, just enough to defy me. He knew he would pay for it later, and the thought aroused me. It also made me a little mean. Bringing my hand away from my cheek, I slapped Mike hard across the mouth. I saw his face tighten and felt his cock jump in my hand, and knew it had excited him.

"Don't you ever disobey Coach again, boy," I said menacingly. "Or it's back to the bench for good. Now, just to make sure nothing like that ever happens again, I think I'll have to find something to keep your mouth shut." Picking up the jock, I shoved the filthy thing between his lips. He gagged as he got a taste of the funky crotch, but after a minute he was sucking on the fouled pouch, tasting my piss and old cum.

"That's right," I said, jerking his cock slowly. "Chew on coach's jock. You taste that cum? That's from all the other boys I've fucked in the locker room before you. Stuck my big dick right up their asses and shot my load while they squealed for me to stop, just like I'm going to do to you later if you're a good boy. Made them suck my prick first, too. But you're not going to get any of this meat. Not after the way you behaved."

Mike's cock was throbbing in my hand as I talked to him, and I milked drop after drop of sticky lube from his piss lips. "Think about it," I told him as I jerked him off. "Imagine coach bending some nice sweet ass over the changing bench and sliding his cock right up that rosy butthole. Picture the guy's knuckles turning white as I stretch his hole out wider and wider and he grips the wood to keep steady. Think about his balls and cock slapping his stomach every time I drive home inside him."

Mike started to moan, thrusting his hips against my hand. I could tell he was close to shooting as he imagined me fucking some other man. I teased him some more. "Can't you just feel your ass-hole gripping my tool?" I whispered. "Can't you just feel yourself sliding up and down this big fucking cock, you little whore? Maybe I should let the whole team have a turn at your fucking slutty ass, let them all stick their big pieces of man meat in you while I make you lick my asshole. You'd like that, wouldn't you?"

Mike's whole body was tight with anticipation as he fucked my hand. His eyes were closed, and he was mouthing the jock wildly as I worked on his prick. He was only seconds from spraying his load all over my forearm when I stopped suddenly. His eyes flew open, begging me to bring him off. I could hear him whining for me to carry him over. Instead, I leaned down and whispered in his ear, "Sorry, but Coach has some things to do in the office. Why don't you just lie here while he takes care of them. Then, if you've learned your lesson, he just might be nice to you when he gets back."

I stood up, leaving him thrashing around on the bed. Taking two more ties from the drawer, I grabbed his legs and secured his ankles to the other end of the bed, so that he was lying helpless, his mouth filled with my dirty jock and his cock stiff and waiting between his legs with no way for him to bring himself off. He was still screaming at me through the material blocking his throat as I walked into the living room and turned on the television.

I turned up the volume on the game broadcast just enough so that he could hear it without being able to make out the words. I knew he was going nuts tied to the bed and missing the Series, and the thought made me horny as hell. I sat through two innings, thinking about him and stroking my cock to the point of exploding several times, each time stopping before I came. The batting glove I was wearing scratched my shaft deliciously, and by the time the last out was called, my balls were blue with frustration and I was ready for a good workout with Mike's ass.

When I went back into the bedroom, his cock was just as stiff as it had been when I'd left. I could tell by the way the bedclothes were messed up and by the redness of the skin around his wrists and ankles that he had tried hard to get away. I stood by his head and let my cock hang close to his mouth while I stroked it some more, a few drops of dick slime falling onto the jock. "Great game," I said. "Score's three to five, but I can't remember who's ahead. Too bad you're missing it."

Mike said something through his gag that I couldn't make out. I pulled the jock from his mouth, and he breathed in great gulps of air. "I am going to fucking kill you," he shouted. "This is really fucking cruel."

I tugged on his balls, making his cock slap against his stomach. "Big words," I said, "But this tells me you want something else." He shut up. I tossed the jock on the bedside table and climbed on top of him, straddling his waist so that I was sitting on his prick. "Now keep quiet and I won't have to gag you again."

Grabbing the neck of his T-shirt, I ripped it down the center, just as I had done to his shorts. As it fell away, I saw his beautiful chest, the small pink nipples poking up from the nest of hair that went right up to his neck. He was really beautiful, all tied up like that, and I wanted to fuck him badly. I pinched one between my fingers and felt him rise up beneath me. "Oh, you like that, do you?" I said.

Mike didn't answer, so I pinched his tit harder, making him cry out a little. "Do you like that?" I asked again.

"Yes," he moaned. "Yes, Coach, I like that."

"Much better," I said, and started massaging his tits the way I knew would drive him crazy, pinching the nipples while I pulled them out. Soon he was groaning loudly, telling me not to stop. His cock between my cheeks was beating steadily as blood pumped into it. My own prick was stretched out along the valley of his belly, pointing right up at his chest as I worked him over. The feeling of it sliding along his soft fur was maddening, like a hundred fingers jerking me off at once.

"Please," he moaned. "Please don't stop."

"Why should I do anything for you?" I asked, ceasing my tit play. "You haven't been a very good team player today."

"I'll be good," he said breathlessly. "I'll do anything for you, Coach."

"Like what?" I said.

"Suck your dick," he whined. "I'll suck your dick."

I thought for a few seconds, letting him wait. "No," I said. "Not yet. Something else."

Mike whimpered softly as he thought. "I'll eat your ass," he said quietly. "Please, Coach, let me eat your ass."

That's what I wanted to hear. Moving slowly, I turned around so that my ass was facing him, my cockhead dragging on his chest.

Pushing back, I pressed my sweaty, unwashed asshole right against his mouth. "Lick it," I ordered, "And do a good job."

Mike dove right in, his tongue making broad swirls around the thick hair of my crack. It felt great, and I ground my ass hard against him, urging him inside until his nose was tight against me. He obliged, darting his tongue into my shitter and lapping up the sweat and funk waiting for him. I let him eat out my ass for a while, enjoying the way he ran his tongue over the curves of my ass before returning to my hole and pushing his face right into it. My mouth was right over his cock, but I didn't touch it, instead breathing heavily over the flushed skin and making him crazy with desire.

"You're doing a pretty good job on that ass," I said. "Maybe I'll let you wash my cock off now. It's pretty dirty from my workout. You think you can handle that?"

"Hmmff," he said, his voice blocked by the fact that his mouth was sucking at my asshole.

I pulled away. "What did you say, boy?"

I could hear him sucking in air as he tried to catch his breath. "I said yes, Coach, I need to suck your dick."

I swung myself around and grabbed him by the back of the neck. "Good," I said, stuffing his gaping mouth with my prick. "You'd better or there will be no playing for you for a long time."

Mike gagged as I slammed my cock down his throat, but he took it all. When I had the whole thing down his pipe, I started humping his face mercilessly. His lips sucked eagerly at my shaft as I pulled my head out and teased him with it, keeping it just inside his teeth before choking him again. His tongue swirled around and around my head as he searched for the drops of pre-cum I fed him steadily.

"Can't you do any better than that?" I asked, using my hand to guide his head up and down my tool. "Suck Coach's big cock, you little pussy. Work it like a real man, not like some cheerleader whore."

Mike worked his way back down my dick until I was once more deep in his throat, drawing every bit of me into him and sucking eagerly. Putting my hands on the top rail of the headboard, I stretched out over him and pumped my hips slowly, fucking his helpless face as I watched his lips slide along the pale skin of my cock. My balls slapped against his bearded chin with each thrust, scratching the sensitive skin of my sac deliciously. He was gasping for air whenever I pulled out, and I gave him just enough time to suck in a small breath before plunging back into him. He looked so beautiful with my prick in his mouth that I wanted to shoot a load all over his face. But I was saving that for another hole, one he was going to be begging me to fill.

Pulling out of him, I held my dick in my hand and slapped his cheeks with it while he tried futilely to lick it. Soon his cheeks were covered with prick juice and his own spit, and he was begging loudly for my cock. "You want my cock?" I said contemptuously, holding it just out of reach. "Tell me why the coach should give a little pussy like you who can't even play ball my cock?"

"Because I need it," he said. "I need it now."

"What do you want Coach to do?" I said.

"Fuck me," Mike begged. "Fuck my goddamned asshole with your fat fucking cock. Shove it in there until I scream."

"Yeah," I growled. "That's right. You beg for it, baby. Beg for Coach to fuck your dirty little ass. Tell me how much you want it."

"Please," Mike sobbed, practically crying now. "I want it so fucking bad I can't stand it. I want you to rip me apart with that big fucking tool. Shove it in me, please."

Reaching behind me, I untied the bonds that held Mike's legs down. Spreading his thighs, I knelt between them and, pushing his knees back, looked down into his pucker. Running my hand over his cheeks, I slapped him hard, the batting glove making a soft thud when it connected with his flesh. He grunted, and I slapped him again. Wetting a finger in my mouth, I pierced his ass ring in one quick jab that made his whole body jump. I fingered him roughly, still rubbing his ass with the batting glove while he moaned and squirmed. I slipped another finger into him and fucked him steadily.

"I don't know," I teased. "You're pretty loose. I'm not sure your slutty ass is tight enough for Coach's dick. I need something nice and snug around my prick to make me shoot."

Mike clenched his ass around my hand, surrounding me in warm flesh. "Please, Coach," he gasped. "Fuck me. Fuck my ass."

"Are you going to give Coach any more trouble?" I asked, slapping his ass again.

"No," he cried. "No. I'll do anything Coach wants. Just fill my hole with that prick."

I pulled my hand out and spat a fat wad straight into his butt-hole, rubbing it around so that the hairs clung to the sides of his thighs. It was the most beautiful thing I'd ever seen, and I wanted him. Positioning my cockhead at the center, I drove forward in one long, breathless rush, burying my prick to the hilt inside his burning shitter. Mike let out a bone-shaking wail as I impaled him on my thick pole, crying out in joy and pain as I shredded his ass-hole. "Jesus Christ," he said between wracking sobs, "I can't take any more, Coach."

"Well, you're going to," I said, beginning to pump his hole. "You're going to take it all and love it, you damn pussy."

Mike's hole collapsed around my shaft like wet silk as I fucked him, gripping the sides and slipping along me in hot rushes every time I pushed into him. The feeling was intense, and I fucked him harder, slamming in and out until I could see his ass cheeks turn-ing bright red from the pounding I was giving him. I pushed his knees back further, until he was almost bent double and I could watch my cock slip in and out of him. It turned me on seeing his hole swallowing up inch after inch of me, and I almost lost it just watching my dickhead pop in and out of his cherry.

"Do you love it?" I asked, slowing down the speed of my thrusts so that Mike started to clench his ass around me to urge me on. "Do you really want Coach to fuck your sorry asshole, boy?"

"Yes," he said, the veins in his arms swelling as he twisted and turned against the ropes at his wrists. "Oh, Christ, do I love it. I want your cock in my ass forever, fucking me like that."

"Good boy," I said, letting myself fall forward between his legs so that I was lying on top of him and looking down into his face. "That's what Coach wants to hear." I rammed my prick in and out of him, supporting myself on my hands while I filled his ass with my piece. He was still wearing his Braves hat, and there was sweat running down his cheeks. Bending my elbows, I licked up some of the salty drops from his neck while he sucked at my fore-arms, his tongue lapping at the hair hungrily.

The smell of our sweaty bodies and the heat of our skins press-ing together overcame me. I could feel the hair on Mike's belly scraping along mine in soft rasping movements and knew I was about to lose it inside him. Pushing myself back up, I grabbed his ankles and spread his legs wide, hammering away at his welcom-ing hole while his prick bounced against his stomach and his balls slapped against my belly. "Coach is about to fill you with a big load of jock juice," I said, and grabbed his dick in my hand. "I want you to come with me."

The batting glove must have been torture on Mike's overheated cock, because he started to cry out after only a few strokes. "Oh shit," he yelled. "I'm going to fucking come all over my chest. Keep fucking my ass, Coach. Keep fucking me."

"Let me see your load, boy," I ordered seconds before I started spewing inside him. My whole body stiffened as a stream poured from my cock and slathered his insides with a sticky heat. Mike felt me coming inside him, and another stroke of my gloved hand brought him over the edge. His shaft rippled as blast after blast erupted from his tool and exploded into the air. Drops of his juice coated his chest hair from his neck to his crotch, falling onto his thighs and covering my arm in tiny white spots of warmth.

I was still shooting when I pulled my slimy cock out of his hole and pumped myself to another shattering climax, sending another blast across Mike's belly and laying two thick lines of cum down the hair of his torso. When I was finished, I looked down at him. His shirt was in tatters at his sides, and his body was sopping wet with puddles of our mingled loads. His prick, still hard, was clenched tightly in my fist, the last drops running over my gloved fingers as it throbbed with heat.

"Well," I said, leaning down to kiss his mouth. "You gave Coach quite the workout. Maybe you'll be a good team player after all."

Mike's eyes gleamed brightly beneath the shadow of his baseball cap. "You're not such a bad coach, either," he said. "Now untie me."

I got up and turned on the television. The game was just ending, and the score was not in Atlanta's favor. I turned to Mike. "Looks like there's going to be a final game tomorrow night," I said. "Maybe I'll just leave you tied up until then."

"You wouldn't," he said warily.

I walked over and climbed back on top of his sticky, cum-splattered chest, rubbing his prick along the crack of my ass and letting the head rest against my hole. "I don't know," I said as I slipped an inch of him into me. "You've proven that you're pretty good at catching. But I think your pitching needs some work."

Washing Up

*This is the very first story I ever wrote. I remember getting the
idea for it while sitting at my desk watching the window washers
go past. It's a pretty straightforward story, but it was enough to
interest a magazine in it. I think they titled it "Hi-Rise Sex."*

The computer screen in front of me stared back blankly, no expression on its empty, blue face. I'd been staring at it for
nearly thirty minutes, and I still hadn't thought of anything
worthwhile, let alone convincing, to say to the clients I'd have to
face in less than an hour. So much for getting to the office early
and whipping something up. It had seemed a reasonable enough
idea the night before while I was pumping my cock into the trick
I'd picked up at the gym instead of writing up my notes. But when
you have some squirming stud's legs over your shoulders and
your dick up his ass, anything will make sense.

As I thought back on the previous evening's activities, my
prick started to stiffen against my leg. I rubbed it through my suit
pants, picturing again the guy's face as I nailed him. His butthole
had melted under my cock, and he'd groaned like prey down for
the kill when I flooded my jism up his chute, digging his fingers
into my ass and spewing his load over his chest.

I shut my eyes, trying to clear my head. This was no time for a
jerk-off fantasy. I had to come up with a bunch of good reasons
why my clients should go with my ad campaign, or the three
months I'd spent creating ideas for selling their clothes would be
worth about as much as a pair of cum-stained shorts.

When I opened my eyes, the cursor was still blinking stupidly
back at me from the screen, flashing off and on like a demonic fire-
fly. I typed out a few lines, read them over, and then erased them.
I now had forty-five minutes left.

While I was agonizing over what to say, a shadow passed over the top of my screen. I looked across to the window at the other side of my office, expecting to see storm clouds rolling over the morning sun. A thin band of black stretched along the top of the glass, like the sea against the horizon. As it sank even lower, a pair of big scuffed work boots came into view, and I realized it was only the window washers descending from the roof of the building to do the daily cleaning.

The platform continued to come down, and the work boots turned into a pair of well-worn jeans speckled with dirt and oil. The body packed into them was large and solid, and the faded denim wrapped tightly around the curves of the muscular thighs and ass. At the crotch, the material was worn white where it ran around the contours of a near-bursting basket, outlining a hefty cock.

More of the man outside my window was revealed as inch after inch was slowly lowered into view. The jeans gave way to a white tank top stretched over a broad chest, the nipples poking up through the thin cotton like stones hidden beneath a blanket of snow. His muscular arms were tanned the rich color of dark beer, and his hands were large and strong.

Finally a handsome Italian face came into sight. Sleepy black eyes looked out from underneath a shock of thick black hair that crashed down over the forehead like a wave. Thick, sensuous lips lay beneath a straight aquiline nose, and a dusting of beard shaded the wide jaw. He looked like any one of the hundreds of blue-collar types who earned their livings working the docks or doing construction, the kind that sweated it out all day and then went home to a wife and three kids to spend the night watching the fights on television.

When the platform was level with the bottom of my window, the workman pulled a lever at his side. There was a low grinding sound, and the platform stopped its downward ride. He leaned down and pulled a wiper from a bucket at his feet. Swiping it across the top of my window, he hid himself behind a film of water, which ran down the glass in soapy rivers, weaving lines in the grime. Before the water hit the bottom of the pane, he wiped it away, pushing it to one side and leaving the glass clean and clear.

He worked the wiper across the window several more times, each time coating it with another wave of soap and then rinsing it. As he worked, I could see his mouth moving, but I couldn't see who he was talking to. Every so often he would laugh, revealing a row of even white teeth. Because I couldn't hear him, I felt like I was watching a silent movie where part of the action was taking place offscreen.

Although the window was only a few feet away, and I could see him clearly through the glass, the big stud seemed not to notice me at all. When he was finished washing, he put his wiper back into the bucket and leaned against the railing of the platform, looking out over the city below him. He was talking again, but the object of his conversation was still out of sight. I wondered how he could rest so easily on a platform that, to me, appeared to be supported only by two threadlike strands of steel thirty floors above the street.

I was turning my attention back to my now-urgent work when the big stud turned and tugged at his waist. The buttons of his fly escaped easily from the grasp of the holes, sliding open smoothly as his fingers pulled the front of his jeans apart. Reaching in, he lifted out a long, thick prick and a set of low-hanging balls nestled in a patch of black hair. He definitely had my full attention now, and all thoughts of my presentation were forgotten as I waited to see what the hell he was up to. His cock was resting on his flat palm, and he was stretching it out, as if to measure it. He was still talking, and his free hand gestured irritatedly in the air, as if he were arguing.

As he continued to talk, another man came into view. He was obviously the person the hunk had been talking to, and must have been washing the window on the other side of my office wall. He was wearing overalls with no shirt on underneath them. His close-cropped hair was blond, and his chest was covered in the same light fur. A tattoo of the Marine Corps emblem wrapped around one thick bicep. He was pointing down at the big dick in front of him and shaking his head.

The blond undid the straps to his overalls, letting the front fall down. Then, undoing the buttons at the side, he slipped them down over his waist. The hair on his chest ran down his ripped stomach in a wide swatch, ending in a tangle of golden curls between his thighs. A half-erect prick swelled out over a hairy ball-sac, the blue veins that twined around the shaft faintly visible through the pale skin.

Grasping his meat in his hand, he stood right in front of the darker man, his overalls pooled around his paint-spattered boots. They seemed to be comparing their pricks as if they were the day's catch. While the Italian's bronzed rod had a good two inches over the blond's, it wasn't nearly as thick as the other man's swelling piece.

They continued to argue as their cocks grew harder and harder. The blond was slowly stroking his dick, his hand sliding seductively up and down the hard-on that angled up from his groin. He reached out and took the other man's balls in his hand, hefting them in one big paw and kneading them roughly. The Italian responded by running his work-hardened hands over the blond's beefy chest, rubbing the hair that covered his pecs and pinching his tits between his fingers.

I was now acutely aware of a dull ache deep in my belly. While I had been watching the action outside my window, I had gotten one hell of a ramrod, and now my cock was straining painfully against the confines of my pants. Leaning back in my leather desk chair, I quickly undid my belt and yanked my pants off. Fumbling at the knot in my tie, I unbuttoned my shirt and pulled it open. My prick was lying against my stomach like a steel beam, and a trickle of cock dew stained my throbbing head.

By swinging my chair around, I could put my feet on my desk and have a front-row view of the two hunks playing with one another three hundred feet above the city. As I watched their soundless movements, I fisted my dick and let the action unfold before me. The blond was on his knees now, running his tongue along the Italian's long prick. As he washed the length of the shaft he manhandled his own balls, which swayed heavily under him with every beat of their master's hand. His head moved steadily back and forth as he slipped the other man into his mouth, shoving more and more of the glistening rod down his throat.

The Italian had stripped off his tank top and jeans and stood naked on the platform, wearing only his boots. Putting his hands behind the blond's neck, he pulled him away from his prick. Then he pushed the man's face deep into his crotch, forcing him to take his balls into his mouth. As the blond sucked eagerly, his buddy's spit-shined poker hung over his shoulder, sliding over the bunched muscles of his back as he worked his face between the suntanned legs. A thin thread of man juice slid out of the piss slit and down the curve of the blond's back.

After a few minutes of having his nuts cleaned by the blond's hungry lips, the swarthy window cleaner reached down and pulled him up. Holding their cocks together in one hand, he pumped them steadily. The dark skin of his prick stood out against the blond's whiteness, and as his hand slid up their shafts their balls pulled up and slapped together. The blond put his hand around the other man's head, pulling him in. Their lips parted, and their tongues entered each other's mouths, snaking in and out like the flames of a fire.

With both cocks still in his hand, the Italian began to explore the blond's body with his mouth, his tongue tracing the line of his jaw and running down into the hollow of his neck. He licked slowly at the thick hair on his chest, letting his mouth cover one nipple and sucking slowly. He bit gently, and the blond pushed against him and arched his back. The light-haired stud lifted his arm behind his head, revealing a forest of sweat-soaked hair, and the Italian drank eagerly, his tongue lapping up every last bit.

Following the valley of the blond's chest, the black-haired man worked his mouth down his stomach until he was on his knees, the other man's prick jutting into his face. Parting his lips, he pushed his mouth down the length of the thick tool until his nose was pressed against the hairy stomach. His cheeks moved in and out as his head slid slowly up and down, tasting every inch of the shaft buried in his throat. The blond pumped his face steadily, pulling out until the tip of his dripping piece just brushed the lips that waited eagerly to suck it back in, then burying his full length in the man's gullet until his swollen nuts nuzzled tightly against his mouth.

As I soaked in the sight of the blond bull's prick disappearing inch after inch into the Italian's beautiful face, my own hand beat steadily against my balls, rising and falling the length of my shaft in time to the thrusting of the big man's hips. Although I couldn't hear anything, the blond's face reflected what the Italian was doing to his prick. His eyes were closed, and each time his man meat slammed deep into the face of the man on his knees in front of him, the muscles in his face twitched with pleasure.

Sitting back in my air-conditioned office, with the coolness of the leather chair under my ass, I could only imagine what the men outside my window smelled like, tasted like, and felt like. It was like watching animals at the zoo, their actions visible through the thin glass but ultimately untouchable. Having to imagine their moans and whispered words made me even hotter, and I gripped my cock even tighter.

For what seemed like hours, I watched as the blond sank his crank again and again into those soft lips. Then the dark man took a final long suck and pulled away. He motioned for the blond to turn around so that he was facing me through the window. The blond put his hands on the glass and looked right into my office. I could see where his fingers pressed against the glass, as if he were trapped under ice and was trying to push through. He was staring right down at my hand flying along my dick, but his eyes looked through me as if I weren't there at all.

Dipping his hand into the metal pail at his feet, the Italian scooped out a handful of soapy water, splashing it over his cock and balls. He slid his hand up and down his prick, working the soap into a light lather. Then he slipped his hand into the blond's ass crack. With his long, circular strokes, he greased up the opening to the other man's chute, sliding his fingers in and out lazily while the stud eagerly pressed his ass against his hand.

Positioning the head of his prick against the blond's butt, he pressed forward, driving his cock home inside the workingman's ass with one thrust. The blond gritted his teeth, and I could see a momentary flash of pain cross his face as his cherry stretched around the prick inside him. A thread of fuck juice streamed from the tip of his dick and dripped down onto his hand, which was wrapped around his tool.

The Italian began to rock back and forth on the platform, slow-fucking the stud pinned against the glass. He wrapped his arms around the big man's chest, fingering his tits as he worked his ass from behind. The blond was jerking himself off as he got plowed, his tattoo pulsing as the muscle in his arm flexed. He fisted his cock quickly, slamming his balls against the glass every time the man behind him pushed further into his hole.

The length of my own strokes shortened, too, as the motion of my hand sped up. As the Italian buried his prong over and over in the blond's backside, my balls began to fill up, threatening to spill over at any moment. Watching the blond's hairy nuts swing under him with each jerk of his hand, I pulled on my own pulsing balls, rubbing them against the smooth leather of my chair.

The Italian was slamming into the blond now, gripping his

waist and shoving his prick in and out quickly and savagely. Sweat covered both of them, slicking their skin like oil. The blond's eyes were closed as he pounded his dripping dick, his cockhead red and angry where he was rubbing it in his fist. Together they moved like a living, breathing machine, their motions fluid and seamless as they rocked against one another on the narrow platform.

All of a sudden, the dark man dug his hands into the blond's sides and plunged his prick home, burying it to the hilt inside the soapy hole. At that moment, the blond's eyes flew open and looked directly into mine for the first time. Through the window I saw his mouth open in a silent roar of pain and ecstasy as the other man's load tore into him. Throwing his body back against the Italian's, he thrust his hips forward, pushing his cock toward me. His fingers were clenched around his balls and the base of his dick, and a geyser of cum erupted from his swollen head.

Instinctively, I closed my eyes, half expecting to feel a blast of hot prick spit burn across my face. When I opened them, I saw the shining drops of cum spattered against the glass. Another jet of jism exploded from his big nuts, sending thick ropes of spunk into the air and over the metal platform to the street below. Again and again he came, the cum running down his shaft and over his hand, dripping from his balls onto his work boots.

Seeing his juice on my window, I blew my own load. A flood of jism gushed from my cock and slathered my chest and the chair in rich waves of cream. I milked every drop, running my fingers up the throbbing vein under my prick, feeling my balls empty themselves onto my stomach. Sitting back in my chair, I tried to catch my breath. My nuts ached from all the pounding I had done, and there were tiny spots of cum on my blue silk tie.

Outside, the two window washers were pulling their pants back on. The glass was covered with thick smears of jism. The blond dipped his wiper into the pail and across the window, wiping away the last traces of his load. Then he reached for the control at the side of the platform. It rose up, the way it had come, and after a minute the two hunks were out of sight and I was left looking out over the city again.

I looked down at my spunk-covered body and still-hard cock, and then at the clock on my blank computer terminal. *Oh, hell*, I thought, starting to coax my prick back into action again, *I've still got fifteen minutes left.*

The Confession

This story was written as a present for a friend who complained that the porn in most gay magazines was too tame for him. This satisfied him.

When my face hit the top of the car and I felt the business end of a gun against the side of my head, my first thought was that I was being mugged. I'd dropped my gym bag when the guy had grabbed me from behind, and I hoped he would just take it and run. There wasn't much in it, anyway. I was still wearing my workout shorts and T-shirt, so all the bag held was a damp towel and my wallet, and all that had in it was my driver's license and twelve bucks. He was welcome to it. All I wanted was for him to let me go.

But he left the bag sitting there on the parking lot while he pushed up behind me, spreading my legs with his knee, and snapped something cold around my wrists. "What the fuck—" I started to say, but a strong hand grabbed me by the neck and shoved my face hard against the car. I could feel my lip split open where my teeth cut into it, and then there was the taste of blood in my mouth. Whoever the guy was, he meant to do more than rob me.

"Shut the fuck up, asshole," said a mean voice in my ear. "We've been looking for you for a long time. Now it's our game, and you play by our rules."

I was yanked back and then pushed forward again in a new direction. I tried to turn around and see who had a hold on me, but it was dark, and the parking lot lights had been knocked out long ago by kids whose idea of fun was tossing rocks at the globes. Besides, despite my being in good shape, the guy was a lot stronger than I was. He held me by the neck like a dog shaking a puppy, forcing me to walk in front of him so quickly that a couple of times I stumbled to my knees. Each time, he just hauled me back to my feet and shoved me forward again. I thought about screaming for help, but I remembered the gun and knew I'd just be in more trouble if I did, so I kept my mouth shut.

My captor led me around the corner of a warehouse that abutted the gym lot, and I saw that another man was waiting there. In the shadows, I couldn't see either of their faces, but I saw that they were wearing dark uniforms of some kind and that they towered over me.

"That him?" the second man said, his voice flat and hard edged.

"Yeah, this is the creep," the man holding me replied. "I checked his name out with the girl at the front desk. It's a match, all right."

Lucy, I thought, remembering how she had seemed a little odd when I'd left. I wondered what the guy had told her about me and what the hell was going on.

One of the men stepped forward, and the next thing I felt was a blow to my stomach as his fist exploded into me. I fell to my knees on the asphalt, unable to breathe. Through the pain I saw the second man raise a leather-booted foot, and I waited for another strike to come.

"Easy," said the first man to his friend. "We don't want him really hurt yet. Remember, Sarge said to bring him in in one piece."

"Fucking piece of crap," the second man snarled. "We should beat the shit out of him right now."

The first man laughed. "Don't worry, by the time Sarge is done with him, anything we could do would look like foreplay."

I had no idea who the men were, or why they were after me. I'd never heard of anyone called Sarge. But before I could think of what to do, someone grabbed my hair and pulled my head back. I felt something sticky on my cheek, and then my mouth was sealed shut as heavy tape circled my head, gagging me. Then a hood of some kind was pulled down over my face and tied around my neck. I panicked at first, afraid I wouldn't be able to breathe, but my nose was still free, and I sucked air in as well as I could. My ankles were held together, and I felt more tape being wrapped around them.

Once again I was hauled to my feet. This time I was dragged by the arms down an alley. From the rumbling sounds that got louder as we approached, I knew we were going to a waiting car. One of the men opened the trunk, and then I was lifted up and dropped into it, right on top of a spare tire. The trunk was slammed shut, and I was entombed in total darkness with the smell of oil and stale air. I was on my side, my legs pushed up to my chest, and my wrists were beginning to ache from the handcuffs. I was totally helpless, and the feeling made me sick to my stomach.

The car lurched forward, and I was rolled back and forth against the walls of my prison as the car sped through the streets of the city. Trapped inside the black hold of the car, my senses blurred into a frenzied rush of sound and smell as the driver made turn after turn. I had no idea where it was going or what was awaiting me when it stopped. All I could remember was a name—Sarge— and the way the men had sounded like they wanted to kill me.

Finally, the car came to a halt. The trunk flew open, and I was lifted out into the warm night air. I heard a door open, and I could tell I was being carried up a flight of steps. Then another door, and more steps, this time going down. By the echo the men's footsteps made on the stairs, I could tell we were going into a cellar of some kind. My suspicion was confirmed when I was dropped onto hard concrete. The cold was a shock on my overheated skin, and I gasped, trying to breathe through the hood.

"Leave him there," said a deep voice unlike the two I'd heard before. "And get out. I'll take it from here."

The sounds of two men going back up the stairs rattled in my head as I lay on the floor. Then I heard a door shut, and I knew I was locked in the basement with someone I couldn't see. I waited for him to speak, but there was no sound. I listened for his breathing, or for any sign that he was still there, but all I heard was the blood pounding through my veins.

I lay on the floor for what seemed like an eternity, each second spent waiting for someone to speak or for some sound to come that would let me know where I was or what was happening. I knew three men had been in the basement, and that only two had left. That meant one was still there, watching me. But he didn't make a sound. Again I started to panic, thinking that perhaps I'd been left there for good. I tried to think if I'd told anyone where I was going before I went to the gym, or if anyone would notice I was missing.

Suddenly, I felt a sharp stream of icy water blast against my chest. The sharp sting took my breath away as the thin line of pressure moved up and down my torso and legs, soaking me. As the water moved across my skin, it left behind both a burning from the intense force and a bitter cold that made me shiver. Then it was gone, as suddenly as it had come, and I was left to shake on the cement floor.

That's when I heard the first sounds. They were of feet moving across the floor toward me. Feet that belonged to someone large. I could tell he was wearing boots from the flat, dull slap that came each time he put his foot down. Then the footsteps stopped, and I knew that whoever it was was standing over me. My entire body tensed as I waited expectantly for him to kick me or dole out some other punishment.

The hood was ripped from my head, and I blinked as my eyes were flooded with the harsh glow of a naked bulb that hung in the center of the room, filling it with dirty light. Looking down at me was a big bear of a man. He had short, dark hair and a beard, and he was wearing a dark uniform like the men who had captured me had been wearing. The shirt was open, and in the opening I could see a broad chest covered in dark hair. His pants were tucked into heavy leather boots. He was holding a hose in his hand, and water fell in fat drops from the nozzle.

When he saw me looking at him, he sneered, his lip turning up in a gesture of contempt for what he saw. Without a word, he bent down, fastened a thick leather collar around my neck, and affixed a short chain to a metal ring at the back. He used this to drag me across the floor to the center of the room, where he left me in the pool of light thrown down by the bulb.

"Not such a big shit now, are you?" he said. His voice was harsh, filled with a controlled anger I knew had been sharpened like steel to a dangerous edge. Even though I'd never seen him before, and had no idea what he wanted with me, I could tell that he hated me.

He crouched down so that his head was near mine. "I bet you're wondering what the hell you're doing here, aren't you?" he said. "Well, I'll tell you. See, it seems some asshole has been taking advantage of some of the kids in the area. You know, inviting them back to his house. Showing them some homemade videos. Playing a few games that involve, shall we say, a lot of physical contact. You get the idea."

I didn't get the idea, not really. I didn't know what he was talking about or what this guy had to do with me. The man stood up. "Now, of course the force has its procedures for dealing with this kind of thing. Talk to the kids. Talk to their parents. The usual. But you know how it is. A kid won't talk. Can't remember where the house was. No solid evidence. Makes it real hard to finger the guy, right?"

He rested a booted foot on my neck and applied some pressure, so that my face was pushed against the floor. "But the Sarge here gets some leads," he said. "Calls in a few favors. Finds out the creep's name is McCaffrey."

McCaffrey? Suddenly it dawned on me what was going on. This was the Sarge the guys had spoken of when they'd kidnapped me. The man was a cop, and he thought I was some kind of child molester. I had to let him know he'd made a mistake, before he did anything else to me. I started to thrash around on the floor as much as I could, screaming through the tape on my mouth.

His boot hit me in the stomach, knocking me silent as I was rolled onto my back, the air unable to enter my lungs as I heaved. "Shut the hell up!" Sarge ordered. "I give the orders now." He knelt down and put his face very close to mine, so that I could see the rage boiling in his dark eyes. "I don't like scum like you," he said, his breath hot on my face. "But I can't do anything about you until you confess. Got it? So tonight I'm going to give you a chance to do that."

He got up and walked over to the side of the room. When he returned, he was holding a length of thick chain. Standing on a chair, he fastened one end to a clip bolted into the ceiling. Then he dragged me to my feet. Undoing the handcuffs, he moved my hands around to the front of my body and secured them with leather restraints. He attached the free end of the chain to them and then pulled the chain tight so that my hands rose above my head and I was almost standing on the tips of my toes, hung from the clip above me. Because my ankles were still tied, it was difficult to balance, and the muscles of my arms and back started to ache almost instantly.

Sarge stood in front of me, his eyes looking me up and down. He unbuttoned the cuffs of his shirt and rolled the sleeves up, revealing hairy, muscled forearms. Then he strode up to me, grabbed the front of my T-shirt, and ripped it clean down the center. A few more tugs had it off me completely. He then gave my shorts a quick yank and had them off as well. I was still wearing my jock from the gym, and he left that on. With my clothes gone, my wet skin rose in goose bumps up and down my body.

He walked around me for a minute, sizing me up as I hung, almost naked, for his inspection. He came around and stood in front of me again. "So, you like little boys?" he said.

I protested through my gag, trying to tell him he was making a mistake. But his big hand shot out and slapped me hard across the face. "I didn't want an answer, asshole!" he bellowed. "You'll tell me what I want to hear, but not yet. You got that?"

His eyes stared into mine, daring me to answer him. Instead, I lowered my eyes and nodded. I hoped that if I cooperated he'd take the tape off my mouth so I could tell him that there had been some kind of a mix-up.

"Good," he said. He turned away and took something from a workbench on one side of the room. When he came back, I saw that he was holding two small, wicked-looking clamps in his palm. Picking one up in his fingers, he opened it and brought it to my right nipple. Placing it, still open, around my tit, he looked into my face. "Now we're going to see how you like being played with. Maybe it will remind you of what it was like for those kids."

He released the clamp, and it snapped shut around my flesh. I screamed into the tape as the tiny teeth bit into me, sending hot pain through my chest. I'd never had anything like that done to my tits, and I was sure I'd pass out from the sensation. I watched, terrified, as he brought the other one to my left nipple. Sarge smiled as I tried to twist away from him, knowing even as I did it that it was no use. He forced me to be still and let the second one close. I shut my eyes as waves of pain showered over me.

Sarge stood watching as I arched my back and moved around, trying to free myself from the clamps' touch. Every time my heart beat, the blood would try to force its way past the rows of tiny metal thorns into my tits, sending new bursts of pain into my skin. My breath came in short, ragged pulses as I tried to breathe away the feeling.

"Did you like that, little boy?" Sarge teased, coming over and running the tip of one finger around my clamped left nipple, then squeezing it so that new fingers of agony gripped my heart. But behind the pain was something else. As his fingers worked my skin, I felt a jolt of pleasure course through my balls. His touch melted into the pain, becoming a mixture of both that was something I'd never experienced. I tried to let it fill my mind, to understand it. Then he let go, and it was gone.

Sarge walked back to the bench, picked up something else, and then moved behind me. I couldn't see what he had in his hand, and that made the anticipation even worse. The pain in my tits had settled into a dull ache, but the memory of their heat was still fresh in my mind. So when I felt his hand on my ass, I flinched.

He didn't say a word as he rubbed my ass cheeks, kneading the flesh with his strong hands. He ran his fingers under the straps of my jock, feeling the hard mounds of my ass. I actually started to relax as he worked my butt, and forgot for a moment that I was his victim—bound and gagged—and not his lover. I even felt my cock start to stiffen inside its pouch.

Sarge felt it, too. His hand went around me and gripped my prick, squeezing me painfully. "What the fuck is this?" he growled, taunting me. "What kind of boy are you? A bad one, from the looks of it, getting hard like that."

He released my cock, and the next thing I felt was the slap of wood against my bare ass. The force knocked me forward, and my shoulder muscles cried out in pain as the chain drew me back. The paddle came again, stinging my cheeks as Sarge landed smack after smack with fierce precision. He would let the touch of one begin to ebb and then hit me again, sending the pain back up in crashing waves that rolled over and over me in greater waves the harder he hit me.

"Bad boys need spanking," he said as he beat me. "Isn't that what you told the boys you touched?" He started to paddle me harder, moving the blows in a hot line across my burning ass.

As much as it hurt, I was ashamed to see that my cock was actually getting harder, not softer. The truth was, I thought Sarge was one of the hottest men I'd ever seen. Besides his size and his hairy chest and arms, there was something in his eyes that made me want to do anything for him. Although I'd never had anything done to me like what he was doing to me now, I found myself waiting for him to touch me again.

He finished spanking me with the paddle and began to use his hand again, slapping first one cheek and then the other, using his fingers to bring out little bursts of pain all over my ass. Every time he touched me, I'd moan into my gag as my body fell forward. When he finally stopped, I could feel the blood running just below the surface of the welts I was sure crisscrossed every inch of my skin.

Sarge came around and stood in front of me. When he saw the head of my now-stiff cock poking over the waistband of my jock, he scowled. I couldn't look him in the eyes as he ripped the jock off me and my hard-on fell forward over my balls. I knew he was angry that I'd been getting off on his punishment.

He went to his bench and returned with a length of thin leather cord. Grabbing my balls in one hand and pulling them down, he wrapped the cord tightly around my sac, drawing my nuts together painfully. Then he looped the cord around my swollen cock and pulled, cinching it so that my balls were pulled up. The rest of the cord he wrapped around the base of my cock and a few inches up the shaft. He pulled it so close that every throb of the vein running up the underside of my prick seemed to echo through my groin. The harder I got, the more it hurt.

Sarge left me like that while he pulled something from the pocket of his shirt. It was a cigar. I watched as he produced a silver lighter, flicked the flame to life, and lit the cigar, carefully rolling the end in the flame until it was glowing hotly and a rich smoke was filling the air. He took a few deep puffs and blew a cloud into my face. The thick smell filled my head and I started to choke.

Sarge took another puff, inhaling until the tip of the cigar crackled with heat. The layers of tightly rolled tobacco were translucent with orange light as he brought it close to my face. I could feel the warmth radiating out against my skin as he traced the outline of my jaw, bringing the cigar closer and closer. The smoke stung my eyes, and I could feel sweat breaking out and running down the hollow of my throat.

"Maybe I should mark you," Sarge said. "Brand you with a big *M* for molester. That way everyone will know what a fucking pervert you are."

He brought the cigar down to my chest. Holding it just above my skin, he moved it down my abdomen. Beneath its hot breath, the hair curled and burned away, leaving my skin untouched but spreading heat across my stomach and filling the air with a sharp smell. I started to tremble, waiting for him to press the searing end of the cigar against my flesh. Sensing my terror, Sarge laughed. "Now, don't shake too much," he said. "I wouldn't want you to accidentally get burned, now, would I?"

He continued to move the cigar down my stomach. When he reached my bush, he paused. Then he ran it down the length of my tied-up cock, letting the ash from the cigar flutter down onto my skin. Even though he was only a movement away from burning my prick, I stayed hard. He inhaled and blew the smoke out around my balls, surrounding them with heat. Despite my fear, I moaned.

Moving back up my belly, Sarge held the cigar close to the clamp on my right nipple. I could feel the heat begin to soak into the metal and knew it would soon pass into my chest. "Or maybe," Sarge said, "I should just burn you all over, so you remember what those kids live with every day of their lives."

Just before the heated metal began to burn me, Sarge pulled the cigar away and undid the clamp. As the blood rushed into my skin, I fell against the chain from the sudden force of torment. I thought having the clamps put on was the worst part, but this was excruciating. Every nerve in my chest hummed as blood swarmed around it, expanding the sore tissue into canals of heat and pain. When he unclamped the second one, I nearly passed out.

Sarge just stood there, quietly watching me, as though deciding what to do next. Finally, he dropped the cigar and ground it out with his heel. Then he undid the buttons on his shirt and pulled it off. As I'd expected, his broad chest was deeply furred, as was his stomach. The dark hair ran in a thicker line down the center from his navel to his groin, the hair swirling up like a dark stream. He was powerfully built, and looking at him I felt my cock stiffen inside its restraints until my balls were pulled up tight between my legs, the leather cord biting into my skin.

Keeping his eyes on my face, Sarge slowly worked open the buckle of his heavy leather belt and slipped it from its loops. He wrapped one end around his hand and doubled the rest over, forming a loop. Lifting it up, he brought it down on my aching shoulders. The leather slapped against my skin and then retreated, leaving behind a sweet kiss of pain. Then Sarge hit the other shoulder, and the leather snapped down along my back in a crack of sizzling pain.

He worked his way around me, hitting me with the belt all over my shoulders and back. Then he brought the belt down on my tender ass. It hurt like hell, but the sight of his naked torso and the thought of the belt that circled his waist being used on my body was enough to make me almost come right there. I prayed I wouldn't and had to clench my teeth as he kept me on the edge for a long time, working me over with the soft, wicked belt. As I took the pain into my body, tears rolled down my cheeks, falling from my chin to the floor.

When he stopped, my whole body ached from his beating. He laid the belt aside. Then he cut the tape from my ankles and, standing on the chair again, he released the chain holding my arms up. Instantly, I fell to the floor. My arms were so sore I could barely lift them, and I knelt there feeling my tits, cock, and ass ache while he walked around to stand above me, like some vengeful god looking down on his prey.

He put one heavy boot on my cock, pressing it against my belly. I felt the thick leather sole against the head of my dick as his toe moved slowly back and forth. I looked down at the rich dark leather. Reaching behind my head, Sarge grabbed one end of the tape and pulled quickly and smoothly. The glue ripped at my skin and lips as it came off, and I drew in a deep breath, thankful to be able to breathe freely again.

"Lick it," Sarge ordered. "And don't say a word about how you're innocent. I don't want to hear your lying shit."

I leaned forward, trying to balance myself on my bound hands. With a lot of effort, I was able to reach down and touch my tongue to his boot. The leather was cool beneath my lips and smelled of polish and sweat. Its scent filled my nose as I worked my way across the well-worn surface of Sarge's boot, covering it with eager licks. I imagined my tongue caressing the skin and bone underneath the leather, and worked over his foot slowly and hungrily. I ran my cheek over the length of leather that surrounded his calf, washing every inch.

Moving to the other foot, I dipped my tongue into the crack where the sole met the upper, running it along the stitching. Inside it I tasted oil and the ashes of his cigar. I was washing the toe when Sarge grabbed me by the hair, pulled my head back, and with no warning shoved his cock deep into my throat. I'd been so caught up in licking his boots that I hadn't even noticed him opening his pants and pulling out his prick.

His dick was half-hard, but even so it filled my mouth easily. Not even giving me a chance to breathe, he forced himself deep into me, until my lips were pressed against the dark forest of hair surrounding his shaft and his heavy balls were swinging against my chin. Even if I'd wanted to, I couldn't have told him he had the wrong guy. And I wasn't at all sure I wanted to.

His cock quickly stiffened as I worked my lips up and down the shaft, running my tongue along the underside. The big head choked me, but with all the practice I'd had breathing with the gag in, I managed to keep him down. He still had his hand in my hair, and he was fucking my mouth roughly, slamming in and out as he pleased. Sometimes he kept it in for a long while as I sucked fiercely; other times he put just the first few inches in, making me lean forward to take more of him.

All the while, he was talking to me in his deep voice. "So, you like sucking cock, do you, boy?" he said, pushing into me until his balls scraped my lips. "How's it feel to be on the other end now? You like having a real man's prick in your filthy throat? Or maybe it's too big for you. After all, I'm all grown up now, aren't I? Not like the little boys you're used to playing with."

The more he abused me, the harder I sucked his cock, working my tongue all over his thick shaft as I tried to make him come. I couldn't get enough of his big tool, and the harder he fucked my throat, the more I wanted him, and the more I wanted him to unload his cum into my mouth. I could feel precum oozing from my cockhead and down over the leather cord, but the tightness of his wrapping kept me hanging on the edge, the pain putting up a barrier that held back my approaching climax.

Sarge pulled his dick from my mouth and jerked me back to my feet. Turning me around, he slammed me against the wall of the cellar, holding me by the collar. "Now you're going to feel what every one of those kids did when you raped them," he said.

"But I didn't—" The first words I'd dared to speak were cut off as Sarge's cock entered my ass. With one shove, he drove the entire length deep into me, and all I could do was gasp as I tried to adjust to his thickness. Before I could, he pulled back and started to fuck me violently, pounding my already sore butt over and over. His hands held me by the waist as he nailed me again and again.

"I don't want you ever to forget this," he said in my ear, slamming into me and stretching my asshole wide. I leaned against the wall and closed my eyes, feeling him fill me over and over. Every thrust of his cock sent new ripples of pain through my beaten ass. My battered body gave in to his pounding, and I let the rhythm of his cock flood though my insides. A load had built up behind my balls, and despite the leather holding it back, I knew it was going to force its way out.

When Sarge came, he groaned heavily in my ear and ground his body one final time into mine, pinning me to the wall beneath him. I felt his cum explode into my ass as his cock twitched and unleashed blast after blast. His chest was pressed against my back, and I felt every inch of him along my skin. I came in a long, shuddering spasm that roared up from my balls and splattered out against the concrete wall.

When Sarge pulled out of me, I sank to my knees, exhausted and hurting. "So," he said. "You ready for that little confession now?"

I looked around, and for the first time noticed that my gym bag was sitting in the corner where the guys who snatched me had left it. I pointed to it. "Look in my wallet," I said.

Sarge picked up the bag and opened it. He took out my wallet and flipped it open. "What am I looking for?" he demanded. "You take pictures of the kids or something?"

"My license," I said.

He pulled it out and held it up to the light. "Caffrey?" he said. "That's not the name of the man I told them to pick up. Fucking morons got the wrong guy."

He turned around and looked at me. "You mean you went through all of that and never told me?"

I smiled. "Well, it's not like you gave me much of a chance."

He came over and undid the wrist restraints. He held out his hand. I took it, and he pulled me to my feet. "Shit," he said. "I don't know what to say."

I moved in and kissed him, slipping my tongue between his lips and feeling his beard against my hand. His mouth tasted of cigar smoke and heat, and as he kissed me back, I felt his cock start to stiffen once more. I pulled away and looked into his eyes. "Well," I said, "just because I'm the wrong guy this time doesn't mean I don't have any secrets. Maybe next time you'll just have to try harder to pull them out of me."

As his hand came down on my ass, I knew it was the confession he wanted.

Bachelor Party

One of the first men I ever had a crush on was one of the grooms-men at my sister's wedding. This story grew out of a conversation I had with a friend about that.

The morning Ben arrived I met him at the airport. Although the place was swarming with throngs of people rushing to and from their various planes, dragging kids and luggage behind them, I had no trouble spotting him. At well over six feet and 220 pounds, Ben is hard to miss, even in a crowd. I noticed him immediately as he exited the gate, his dark hair shaved as close as a soldier's, his bag slung over his shoulder as he bulldozed his way through the sea of bedraggled passengers. A sports announcer for a television station in Chicago, Ben has this booming voice that can carry forever, and he was shouting at me before he'd even reached the gate.

"Hey, Tom," he called out as a blond woman carrying a little white dog dodged out of his way just before he plowed into her. "What the hell's going on, buddy?"

I reached out to shake his hand, but Ben grabbed me in a big bear hug, his massive arms crushing my rib cage so that I couldn't breathe. When he finally let go, I sucked in air, trying to get some oxygen to my head. "It's good to see you, too," I said. "Now, if I haven't broken anything, let's get out of here. The guys are waiting back at the house."

"You mean they're here already?" Ben asked, picking up his duffel bag and following me out to the parking lot.

"Got in yesterday. They can't wait to see you."

The guys in question were Bill and Alan. The four of us had first met in college, where we were all on the soccer team. With his huge size, Ben had been our star fullback, intimidating opposing strikers and blocking their progress. Alan was the goalie, and Bill and I had shared halfback duties. After the first season, Ben had also been my roommate. Bill and Alan had lived down the hall from us, and the four of us quickly became good friends. Since graduation we'd all kept in contact, even though we lived in different cities. What brought us together now was my imminent wedding. Ben had flown in from Chicago to be my best man.

On the drive back to my house, Ben filled me in on what had been going on with his job. When I asked about his social life, he shrugged. "You know, same old thing. A different one every week. Who's got time?"

I laughed. Ben had never been able to keep a girlfriend for more than a month. Every time we asked him who was new in his life, it was a different name that came up. It was a running joke in our circle that the day Ben settled down would be declared a national holiday.

Back at the house, Ben met up with Alan and Bill, who had managed to get themselves up and ready after the night of drinking we'd done the night before. Alan was a quiet guy, originally from a working-class neighborhood in Chicago and now a newspaper writer. Short and muscular, he had been a standout goalie, able to stop just about any shot with his fast hands. He had intense green eyes beneath his brown hair, and he had always been the one to remind us that we needed to study instead of going out.

Blond, blue-eyed Bill was his opposite. Tall and thin, he had the body of a basketball player, and it had always surprised me how well he could control a soccer ball, considering his lankiness. He had been the practical joker of our bunch, and more than once had gotten us frighteningly close to getting expelled for some prank he talked us into. His job as an engineer for the military took him all over the world, and I was glad he could make it back for my wedding.

After everyone had caught up, we sat down to discuss what we were going to do that night. While most of our day would be taken up with the wedding rehearsal, I had already warned my fiancée that the night was reserved for the guys. I wanted one last big blowout before becoming a married man. I suggested going out, but Ben had ideas of his own. "You just leave tonight up to me," he said mysteriously. "I've got something planned that's going to knock your socks off."

I looked at Bill and Alan, but they just shrugged. Whatever

Ben had planned, it was all his doing. No matter how hard we tried, he wouldn't tell us what he had up his sleeve, saying only that it was something we'd never forget. The rest of the day went by in a blur of last-minute arrangements and minor catastrophes involving seating and flowers and so on. I barely had time to think about what I was doing, let alone what Ben had in store for me later on. I didn't even notice when he disappeared right after the run-through.

Finally it was over. I said good night to my fiancée, promised not to get too drunk, and went back to the house with Bill and Alan. On the drive back, we tried to guess what Ben was up to, but he'd been tight-lipped about his plans. When we got to the house, Ben was in the kitchen. He had made a huge dinner and was just putting the finishing touches on four giant steaks.

"I figure it's the last good meal you'll get for a while," he said, putting a plate in front of me.

The dinner was wonderful. We ate and talked about all the good times we'd had in school. Ben toasted me, and everyone made jokes about me being the first one to tie the knot. Afterward, we all went into the living room, where Ben had another surprise. Turning on the television, he popped a tape into the VCR. It started to play, and grainy images of Bill, Alan, and me running around a muddy field came into view.

"Where'd you get this stuff?" I asked him.

"I had it made down at the station," he said. "Don't you remember all of the 8 millimeter movies I used to take of you guys? I just transferred them to tape."

Back in school, Ben was always running around with his camera. It used to drive us crazy. Every time we turned around, he was there filming. I couldn't believe he actually kept all the stuff, but there it was. There was me chasing him out of the shower, my towel clutched to my crotch. There was Alan trying to slide down the hill outside our dorm on a tray from the cafeteria, ending in a collision with a tree that had resulted in four stitches to his lip.

As the tape rolled on, we relived many things we had all forgotten about. We were laughing over a scene of Bill dressed as a cheerleader for some sports day event when the doorbell rang. I started to get up to see who it was, but Ben jumped up first, beating me into the hallway. "All right," he shouted. "Now it's time for the real fun to start."

We all looked at each other. I had figured that the tape was Ben's big surprise, but there seemed to be more. He went to the door while the rest of us stayed in the living room, waiting expectantly. Then there was a shout from the other room. "Oh, shit," Ben said emphatically. "I can't believe this."

He entered the room with a frown on his face and a man behind him. The guy was a big Italian type, with large dark eyes, full lips, and a day's worth of beard. His black hair was short and gelled, and in his leather jacket and jeans, he looked like he'd just walked off a construction site for his lunch break.

"What's going on?" I asked, confused.

Ben sighed. "I ordered you a stripper," he said. "I asked for an Italian with big ones, but they seemed to have gotten it wrong."

The Italian grinned. "Well," he said. "They got part of it right. I do have a big one. But I guess it's not the kind you guys want to see. I'll just go back and tell the agency to refund your money. Sorry to have wasted your evening."

The guy was almost out the door when Ben called him back. "Wait a minute," he said. "I'd hate to see you lose your money after you came all the way out here. Why don't you at least let me pay you?"

"I couldn't do that," the man answered. "You guys didn't get what you ordered. I wouldn't feel right taking your money unless I did my bit. Thanks anyway."

Ben tried again. "Okay," he said hesitantly. "Um, why don't you just do part of it. You don't have to take it all off or anything, just enough so you can collect your pay. Besides, it might give Tom here some ideas about what to do on his wedding night."

The man laughed. "Sure," he said. "I don't mind if you guys don't."

Ben looked at me, then at Alan and Bill. I didn't really have any interest in seeing the guy's act, but Ben seemed insistent on paying him, and I didn't want to spoil his surprise any more than it already was. "What the hell," I said. "I might learn something."

The man smiled. "Great," he said. "By the way, my name's John."

Ben and John shook hands. Then John handed Ben a cassette and asked him to put it in the stereo. He took off his jacket and threw it on the couch. Underneath he was wearing a pair of very tight jeans and a white T-shirt. He had a muscular body, and every line and curve was visible through his shirt. He also had a sizable bulge in his pants, the crotch of which was worn smooth.

Ben turned off the video, put John's tape in the stereo, and then sat by me on the couch. A slow beat filled the room and John began to move his body with the sound, grinding his hips suggestively and running his hands over his chest. It felt weird watching another guy move like that, as though he was trying to turn me on. But at the same time, it kind of interested me. John had a great body, and there was something about watching him move it like that, so sensuously and gracefully, that held my attention.

I looked around to see what the other guys were doing. Bill and Alan were watching John, too, from their position on the couch. They looked a little uneasy, but they didn't say anything. Ben was reclining on the couch next to me, his arm stretched along the back. He had a strange look on his face, but I assumed he was just annoyed at not getting what he'd paid for.

The music droned on, and John kept dancing. After a few minutes, he tugged his T-shirt out of his jeans and pulled it slowly over his head, giving us the first look at his naked body. Even though I didn't consider myself an expert on male bodies, I was impressed by what I saw. His chest was perfect, the pecs molded into hard rises of flesh. His dark nipples stood at attention, brown against the tanned background of his body.

And to my surprise, his chest was covered in a short carpet of black hair. All the male strippers I'd ever seen on television or in movies had hairless bodies, and I assumed that all of them shaved. I always thought it looked odd, big macho guys with their skin bare as a baby's. But John had a full swatch of beautiful dark fur running over his washboard stomach and disappearing in a tumble into his jeans like a waterfall crashing into a pool.

John ran his hands through the hair on his chest, stroking it with his big fingers, pinching his tits so that they stood out even farther. He raised one arm behind his head and revealed a glen of the same dark hair, matted slightly with sweat. His bicep bulged out next to his neck as he flexed, the muscles of his chest expanding. He turned his head and began to lick at his arm, his long pink tongue caressing his flesh lovingly. He moved into his armpit, burying his nose in the hair, his mouth sucking hungrily at the sweat.

I was entranced, watching the big stud enjoying his own mas-

culinity. I began to imagine that it was my nose buried in that
damp pit, my tongue running through the thick fur. I thought of
what it would be like to feel his nipple between my lips and hear
him groan as I sucked on it. My cock began to swell inside my
pants, pressing uncomfortably against my fly.

I repositioned myself so that no one could see my growing excitement. I didn't know why I was getting all hot and bothered
over this guy, and I sure as hell didn't want my buddies to see me
sporting a boner over another man. But a quick glance around the
room reassured me that no one was watching me. In fact, Bill,
Alan, and Ben all seemed to be staring raptly at John.

John had finished licking his pit and was dancing again. He was
rubbing his crotch suggestively, grabbing a handful and squeezing
it tightly. Every so often he stuck his hand down the front of his
pants as though he were going to unbutton them. But each time
he pulled it away again. I thought for sure that Ben would call off
the performance at this point and pay John. But he kept quiet. Bill
and Alan too said nothing, sitting on the couch as John moved in
front of them.

John also seemed in no hurry to end the dance. Reaching down,
he began to undo the buttons of his fly, one at a time. As each one
fell away, more of the rich black hair was revealed, and I waited
breathlessly for the moment when his cock would appear. But
John turned his back to us. His back was as magnificent as his
chest, rippling with muscles as he moved. His shoulders were
wide and solid, tapering down to a narrow waist.

Slowly easing the jeans over his ass, John slid them in one
movement down his legs. Underneath he was wearing tight white
underwear, the kind that come halfway down the leg. Beneath the
field of cotton the globes of his ass swelled out round and full. His
thick legs were covered in more of the dark hair, and his calves
were rounded and well defined. John turned around and gave us
the first real glimpse of what he had in his shorts. The fly of his
shorts had two buttons holding it closed, and his cock and balls
hung heavily in the pouch, bouncing slightly as he moved his hips.
His prick stretched along the left side of his groin, the fat head
vaguely outlined.

By now my cock was at full attention, and I was filled with a
yearning I'd never felt before. I desperately wanted to take my
cock out and stroke it while I watched John. Having his big piece

just out of view yet so far out of reach was driving me crazy. I wanted to drop to the floor and rip his underwear off him so I could get to his fat hose.

John danced over to where Bill and Alan were sitting on the other couch. Standing in front of Bill, he moved his crotch invitingly, rubbing his hands over it, pulling the waistband down so that the tip of his dick was almost revealed. "Who's the one getting married?" he asked.

Everyone looked at me, and I started to protest. But before I could say anything, John had come over and grabbed my hands. I tried to pull away, but his grip was firm. Finally, I stood up, hoping my erection wasn't too obvious.

"Help me take these off," John said, turning around so that his back was to me and moving my hands down to his waist. I tried to say no, but Ben urged me on. "Oh, go on, Tom. You're going to need all the help you can get tomorrow night. You might as well practice now."

I nervously put my hands around John's waist, feeling the heat of his skin, the muscles of his torso tensing against my fingers. I'd never held another man like this, and I was suddenly overcome by a strong need to take him in my arms, to feel my hands on his chest. Instead, I took hold of his shorts, pulling them slowly down over his ass. As I did, inch after inch of honey-colored skin slipped into view. His ass cheeks were firm, swelling out like twin halves of a perfect peach. And unlike his chest, John's ass was smooth, the surface of his globes perfectly clean.

I pushed his shorts down his legs, letting my hands stroke the hard muscle and thick hair as I moved down his thighs. I could feel his cock and balls spring out as the shorts slipped over them, but I was afraid to touch them. While I was getting incredibly turned on by touching him, I didn't want the other guys to think this was anything more than a joke.

John stepped out of his underwear and kicked them out of the way. Still with his back to me, he spread his legs and bent over, so that his balls hung down between his legs and the rosy pucker of his asshole was inches from my face. The sight of his clean-shaven hole was unbearable, and I didn't care if he was a man. Without thinking, I put my hands on his beautiful ass, grabbing handfuls of his hot man flesh. Leaning forward, I licked at the smooth skin, letting my mouth move into the valley of his crack. My tongue found its way to the center and sank into the tight folds of John's hole. Inside it was musky and sweet, enveloping my probing tongue in warm folds.

John pushed against my face, driving me farther into his chute. As I ate out his ass, his smooth balls hung against my chin, rubbing seductively against my skin, and it occurred to me that this must be the one part of his anatomy he did shave. I moved under him and took one between my lips, letting the heaviness of it sit on my tongue as I sucked gently. I'd had my own nuts sucked many times, but nothing compared to the feeling I got from nuzzling John's balls, sliding my tongue around them, my lips pressed into the area behind his slick pucker.

I reached between John's legs and finally got to touch the prick that had been driving me crazy. John was only half-hard, but even so his cock was impressive. I wrapped my hands around it and stroked the shaft as I mouthed his balls, feeling it fill with heat. When it was fully hard, it stuck out from his body in a straight line. I fisted it as much as I could from behind him, enjoying the feeling of having his long, hard prick in my hand.

Turning John around, I came face to face with the object of my newfound desires. Erupting from a neatly clipped bush was a thick length of prime cock meat. The skin was the same burnished color as the rest of John, the big head slightly darker. I had never seen another man's hard prick close up before, and now I had one waiting for me to do whatever I wanted with it.

I leaned forward and ran my tongue along the length of John's shaft until I came to the head. I wasn't entirely sure what to do with it, but I opened my lips and slid as much as I could into my mouth. My jaw ached as I tried to accommodate John's thickness, but the excitement of giving my first blow job made me determined to make it a good one. I stretched my muscles and swallowed a few inches of the big Italian's tool, until I just couldn't take any more.

John began to rock in and out of my mouth slowly, letting me feel every thrust. I liked the way his skin slid so smoothly and easily over my tongue, the way the head came to rest against my lips when he was almost all the way out. Grabbing his hot ass, I pushed him into me and mouthed him heatedly, slurping at whatever I could take down my throat. John's hands rested on either side of my head, guiding my movements as he fucked my virgin mouth.

As I was deep-throating John's tool, I felt a third hand on my shoulder, and then I remembered the rest of the guys. In my excitement I had forgotten that John and I were not alone in the room. I couldn't believe I was blowing some guy I'd never seen before in front of the men who were going to be in my wedding tomorrow. I was too embarrassed to look and see who was behind me.

"Not bad for a beginner," I heard Ben say. "But maybe it's time to give someone else a turn at that mouth of yours."

Shocked, I let John's prick fall from my lips and turned around. Ben was standing there completely nude. Out of his clothes, he was stunning. His body was molded to perfection, every muscle defined, every part of him firm. And sticking out from between his legs was a cock bigger than any I'd seen outside a porn video. I couldn't do anything but stare at it as Ben rubbed the oversized head. I had seen his limp prick, in the showers and locker room, but I'd never imagined it could be so huge when it was worked up.

Ben reached down and pulled me to my feet. Then he leaned forward and kissed me, his lips closing heatedly around mine. As his tongue slammed into my waiting mouth, his big fingers quickly undid the buttons of my shirt and pulled it off of me. He ran his hands over my chest appreciatively, working his way down into my pants to squeeze my cock.

"Why don't we bring this out," he said, undoing my jeans and pushing them off along with my shorts. Free, my prick stood at attention. I still couldn't quite believe all of this was happening, and I looked around to make sure it wasn't all some kind of a dream. Over on the couch, Bill and Alan had taken their cocks out of their pants and were stroking them as they kissed. I watched as my old soccer buddies played with themselves, Bill sliding the skin of his short, fat, uncut tool over the head, Alan with his hand wrapped around a cock that, like its owner, was long and thin.

Ben led me to the couch and pushed me down on it. Then he straddled me, standing on the cushions with his hands on the wall behind me so that his big boner was aimed at my mouth. It was oozing thick drops of precum from the piss slit, and I licked them up greedily, the salty taste filling my mouth. Opening wide, I slid my lips over my best friend's prick.

While Ben slow-fucked my mouth, John knelt between my legs and started to suck my aching cock. His hot mouth slid expertly up and down my shaft, his tongue tickling the tip mercilessly. Each time I felt about to blow my load, he stopped, then began all over again, bringing me to the edge. It was the best blow job I'd ever had, and I knew that nothing any woman did would ever compare to the thrill of having a hot, masculine stud servicing my tool, unless it was the rush I was experiencing having my own mouth wrapped around Ben's massive crank.

My nuts were about to explode when John finally stopped. Ben too pulled away from me, leaving me hungry for more of his dick. John went over to where Alan and Bill were going at it on the other couch. By now they had their clothes off, and Alan was busily going down on Bill, slurping noisily at the cock in his mouth while he continued to jerk himself off. John, deciding it was time for another show, knelt behind Alan and spread his ass cheeks. Spitting into his palm, he greased his prick in long strokes while he fingered Alan's hole. Then he leaned forward and shoved his boner right up Alan's shitter, putting his hands on Alan's shoulders to pull himself in.

I watched John fuck Alan's ass, the fat cock slipping in and out. Alan continued to suck Bill's prick as John deep-ended him, moaning loudly whenever John slammed in particularly hard. Seeing my jock buddy getting rammed by the big Italian while he sucked on Bill's dong made my balls burn. I turned to Ben, who was sitting next to me, also watching the action and jerking off.

"I want you to do that to me," I said, looking at his huge piece and wondering how the hell it was going to get inside my cherry ass.

Ben looked surprised. "Are you sure?" he asked. I nodded, and he smiled. "I was hoping you'd say that."

I lay down on the couch and Ben positioned himself between my legs. Spitting into his hand, he rubbed one finger against my hole until it slipped inside. It was uncomfortable at first, but once I relaxed it was wonderful, and soon Ben was thrusting three fingers deep inside me. As I watched the action on the other couch, Ben's thick fingers worked my chute until I was squirming and begging him to fuck me.

"Put your cock in," I said.

Ben swung my legs over his shoulders and moved forward. When I felt his big head press against me, I thought about asking him to stop. But the moans of pleasure coming from across the room wiped away any hesitations I had. Ben pushed in, and I inhaled sharply as he tore into me, my hands gripping his hairy forearms tightly.

Once he was in, he waited for a minute until I could get my breath back. Then he began to fuck me, and all I could concentrate on was the incredible waves of pleasure that were moving through me as his tool slid in and out of me, stretching me wider and wider. His fat cock hammering my ass was the most amazing thing I'd ever felt. My prick jumped every time his big head hit my sensitive prostate, and pretty soon I was leaking like a stream from my swollen head.

I used my own lube to jerk off with as Ben pumped me faster and faster, grunting as he banged my hole. Alan, Bill, and John had come over to stand around the couch, watching as Ben fucked me senseless. They were all fisting their cocks, their hands flying over their meat furiously. Seeing them all beating their joints over my face turned me on even more, and I reached up and pinched Ben's big tits in my fingers, twisting them until he groaned.

Ben increased his thrusts, slamming against me quickly. He was holding my legs wide apart, his fingers clamped around my ankles so that he could hammer my butt. My balls shook every time he plowed into me, and I could feel the pressure building in them. Then he pulled almost completely out and slammed back in again, and I felt his prick tense as he shot deep inside me, his knob spitting again and again into my ass.

At the same time, John's prick shot out a thick stream of cum that hit me in the face, soaking my mouth in his rich spunk. I caught as much as I could as it slipped over my lips, sucking in the thick sweetness. Alan was next, his load splashing over my neck. Bill came last, adding his cream to the rivers that coated my body, the ropes that fell from his prick landing on my balls and covering my hand in sticky, wet heat.

Ben had continued to fuck me after he came, and now I was unable to hold off any longer. Stroking my prick one last time, I emptied my balls, spurting load after load into the air. Drops fell on my face and over my chest as I came again and again, my body shaking from the pleasure of the release.

Later that night, I lay in bed with Ben, my head on his chest. "There really wasn't any mistake, was there?" I asked him.

Ben grinned. "I couldn't think of any other way to get you into bed," he said. "John's a buddy of mine, and I asked him to do this as a favor to me."

"Now I know why all of those girlfriends of yours disappeared so quickly. But what about Bill and Alan?"

"I don't know what they're into," Ben said. "This may have been the one and only time they'll do it with another guy, although judging from the way they both took John's prick up their asses later on I'd doubt it. I didn't really think about them. I just wanted you to know how I felt about you before I didn't have another chance, that's all."

I went to sleep thinking about what had happened. I didn't know what it made me, either, but I knew that Ben had touched something inside of me that no one had reached before. The next morning the four of us were dead tired from our orgy of the night before, barely managing to get up in time for the wedding. As I stood at the altar next to my bride, radiant in her flowing white dress, I tried to keep myself from thinking about the night before. I tried to listen to the priest's words, but my mind kept returning to the image of all those men shooting their loads on me. I started to feel my cock stiffen in my tuxedo and prayed the hard-on would go away. But the harder I tried, the more the sounds and smells of fucking, sweaty bodies filled my head.

All of a sudden I heard the priest's words. "Do you take this woman as your lawful wedded wife?"

I looked over at Ben and remembered how good his prick had felt sliding in and out of my asshole. I recalled waking up in his big, strong arms with my head against his chest. He looked back at me, his dark eyes filled with longing. I turned back to the priest. I knew I was going to have a lot of explaining to do as I opened my mouth and began, "Well, actually . . ."

Conduct Unbecoming

This is nothing more than my way of working out my frustrations over the military's Don't Ask, Don't Tell policies.

Thirteen weeks of active duty running training missions for fresh-hatched leathernecks hadn't done much for my personality, and I wasn't in the mood for any shit when I drove my mud-splattered Jeep into camp at the tail end of another day mucking through the forest with a plebe squadron. Aside from nightly jerk-off sessions, I hadn't gotten laid in months, and I was getting real tired of having nothing to screw but my fist.

So when I saw the MP plates on the car parked in front of the office, I wished I'd just stayed back in the field. I've never met an MP I liked. They're all officious little pricks who aren't man enough to make it in real combat so they spend their lives hiding behind paperwork and getting off on making life miserable for us working grunts. I knew I was in for one long night.

As I got out of my Jeep and walked toward the office, I noticed the MP's car was new, without a speck of dirt anywhere on the shiny white paint. Peering through the tinted window, I could see it had air-conditioning. I looked back at my patched-up desert rat, with its cracked windshield and wired-together transmission. *Christ*, I thought, *look where a little ass kissing could have gotten you. You could be tooling around in this climate-controlled baby instead of drilling recruits in ninety-degree heat.*

I opened the screen door to the office and went in, making sure I let it slam behind me. The MP was standing in front of my desk, looking over some progress reports I'd just typed up but hadn't sent in yet. He looked to be about twenty-three or twenty-four, probably fresh out of school. His reddish hair was cut close to his head, and his skin was almost as white as the paint job on his car outside. His crisp uniform looked freshly laundered, and his black shoes gleamed like they'd just come out of the box. I looked down at my filthy pants and sweat-soaked T-shirt and decided that one of us definitely looked out of place.

Hearing the door bang shut, he turned around. He had a wide face, with deep-set blue eyes and full lips. "Sergeant Caffrey?" he asked. I nodded. "My name's John North. I'm with special projects, under Major Williams."

That explained it. Williams was an old-timer, a real pain in the ass. He hated us drillers and was always ready to knock somebody back a peg or two if he got half a chance. If this kid was part of his team, it meant trouble.

"Under Williams, eh?" I said. "So what brings you down this way? I wouldn't think there was much here to interest HQ. Just a bunch of baby marines learning how to grow up."

"That's just it, Sergeant Caffrey. Major Williams is concerned about recent problems in military morale. He's asked me to visit some of the camps and see how things are going."

"What kind of problems?" I asked. All I needed was this punk poking around my camp trying to dig up something that would satisfy Williams and win him a promotion.

North looked like he had to tell me he'd knocked up my sister. "Homosexuals, sir. You know we've been getting a lot of pressure from militant civilian groups that want us to allow homosexuals into the military. There are even some elements within the corps that are supporting the movement. We're investigating to see if the problem is as widespread as some have reported."

I stared North right in his eyes and sneered. "Queers in the marines?" I asked, frowning. "You're here because you think there are queers in my unit?"

North was startled, and he looked down at his feet, away from my gaze. "Don't take it personally, sir. This is a routine investigation. I'd just like to ask a few questions. If you don't mind."

And I have a few answers I'd like to give you, I thought. "Oh, hell. I guess if you have to you have to. Come on over to my tent and ask away."

"Thank you, Sergeant," he said. "I appreciate your time. I'm glad you understand how important it is that we do everything we can to stop this problem from destroying morale."

"Anything I can do to help," I said, slapping him on the back as we headed out the door. As we walked toward my tent, I watched North's round ass. My cock started tugging in my pants when I thought about the smooth white skin under the uniform and how I'd like to run my hands over it. *Yes, sir*, I thought. This was going to be one hell of an interview, and North was going to learn a lot more than he bargained for.

My tent sat about a hundred yards away from the office, situated by the makeshift showers. I liked the isolation. It was quieter away from the main camp, and besides, it gave me a chance to watch the men wash up. I'd blown more than a few loads watching pairs of hunky marines soaping each other up when they thought no one was looking. You'd be amazed what a few weeks in the outback will do to a guy who never dreamed he'd be sucking his buddy's spunk down his throat.

I opened the flap of my tent and ushered North in. He looked around at the sparsely furnished quarters, noting my cot, desk, and footlocker in one quick sweep. Apart from those few things, there wasn't much else to see except for the pile of dirty fatigues in the corner waiting to be washed. I pulled out my desk chair and offered North a seat. "It's not much," I said. "But it's home."

He sat down and removed a small notebook from his pocket. He opened to a clean page and made a note with his pencil.

"You don't mind if I change clothes, do you?" I asked. "These have taken quite a beating today."

"No," North answered. "Go ahead. I'm just going to ask you a few questions."

I sat on my cot and unlaced my mud-caked boots. North turned a page in his notebook. "Have you seen any evidence of homosexual activity among your men?" he asked. This guy got right to the point.

I pulled off a boot and put it under my cot. "No, sir," I replied. "Nothing like that with my boys." I pulled off my other boot. "I'd definitely notice that kind of thing."

North nodded, scribbling notes quickly. "What about any unusual behavior?"

I stood up and tugged my grimy T-shirt over my head. Even though I was ten years older than North, my body was in perfect condition. And my body wasn't the result of a few hours a week on some wimpy machines in an air-conditioned gym; it was forged from plain old hard work. The weeks of working out with my men had molded my pecs into two hard mountains, and my stomach was flat and ripped. I flexed and ran my hand over the hairy planes of my belly.

I noticed North glance up at me. When I looked back, he turned away quickly, burying himself in his notebook. "What do you mean by unusual?" I asked, rubbing my hand over my rock-hard tits.

North coughed. "Well, anything like two men spending an inordinate amount of time together. Loners not associating with the group."

I unbuttoned my fatigues and let them fall to the floor. The outline of my big marine artillery was clearly visible through my white regulation boxers, and the thin cotton clung to my sweat-drenched skin, outlining every curve in sharp detail. I strolled over and stood right in front of North, my stiffening cock inches from his face.

Lazily rubbing my nuts, I slid the leg of my shorts up until the head of my prick was exposed. Dick drool was leaking from my swelling head and clinging to the thick dark hair on my thighs. "Is this the kind of behavior you're referring to, North?" I asked.

Before he could answer, I put my hand behind his neck and pulled him roughly off the chair and to his knees. He hit the ground with a soft thud, the notebook and pencil falling out of his hand. Keeping a firm hold on the scruff of his neck, I shoved his face into my crotch, stifling anything he might have been trying to say by pushing my cock against his mouth.

At first, North struggled against me, the velvet of his shaved head working against my hand as he tried to break free. But years of hard fieldwork made me much stronger than the classroom-raised paper pusher, and the harder he fought, the harder I ground his face into my steamy forest. Realizing he couldn't break my grip, North finally relaxed. His mouth began to travel along my shaft in long strokes, his lips sucking hungrily through my boxers. When he reached the swollen head, he slid his mouth around it, lapping up the heavy dew that was streaming out in sticky trickles. His tongue was hot and soft, and I wanted to feel him sucking the length of my prick, coaxing my load into his throat. But this game was only beginning, and before he could get any more in his mouth, I pushed him back.

I let go of his neck and shucked my shorts down. Freed from its prison, my prick stood out, arcing up and then falling back down as the big head broke the curve and dragged toward earth again. North stared wide-eyed at my thick, hairy shaft, then his eyes moved to the pair of bull nuts hanging between my legs. I looked down at him, at the mixture of fear and lust on his face, and saw a bulge sticking out from his neatly pressed trousers.

North leaned forward and tried to take my dick into his mouth, but I slapped his cheek. "Not so fast," I barked. "You only get what I give you, and only when I say so." He sat looking at me, his mouth begging me to free him from his frozen position. I let him wait a minute so he could think about what it would be like to suck my meat, sliding my hand slowly along my pole, rubbing the pre-cum into my skin with my thumb. Then I pressed the greasy tip of my prick against his face, wiping a smear of cock spit across the pink blush of his clean-shaven cheek. Holding my dick loosely, my fingers around my balls, I traced the outline of his mouth, almost letting him encase my dick with his lips before moving quickly away and traveling down his neck.

I could see North was dying to suck me off, but I was enjoying teasing him. Several times I pushed my prick toward his mouth, each time changing course at the last second and leaving him hungry, his lips half-parted. Pretty soon his face and neck were coated in my precum, which he eagerly licked from around his mouth. I turned and sat on my cot, leaning back against the wall of the tent.

"I'm feeling a little sticky," I said to North. "Why don't you come over here and give me a good tongue washing."

The MP stood up and started to come toward me. "No," I commanded. "I want you to crawl."

North dropped and moved across the floor, the knees of his spotless pants picking up dirt, his hands in the dust. When he reached the cot, he knelt between my legs, looking up at me with his baby blue eyes. I put one big foot on his shoulder, smudging his white shirt with a streak of dirt.

"Start here," I ordered.

North began licking my foot slowly, caressing the sides gently. He ran his tongue in between my toes, drawing each one into his mouth and washing off the day's work. He treated each toe like a cock, eagerly rolling his tongue around it and sucking steadily. When he was finished with the first foot I slung my leg over his shoulder, resting against him and letting him run his hand over my thigh, and put my other foot against his face. He gave it the same treatment, lapping up the grime and slurping at the skin hardened from daily seven-mile hikes in unforgiving regulation boots.

When he was finished with my feet, North moved slowly up my calf, lapping at the thick muscles of my leg and rubbing his cheek against my furry thighs. As he washed me, I stroked my aching meat, tugging a stream of quicksilver up from my waiting nuts and using it to slick the shaft. His tongue was leaving burning trails behind it as he slid over my skin, and the sight of his handsome face cleaning up my dirty legs was really stoking the heat in my balls.

When North reached my crotch, he tried once more to get his mouth on my cock. But again I pushed his head away. "Not until the rest of me is nice and clean," I said harshly. I was teasing him mercilessly, but I was also tormenting myself. The thought of making North beg for my cock made me rock hard, and waiting created a delicious burn that crept slowly up my thighs and spread into my belly. Every time I held him back brought the pressure in my groin higher and higher, and I knew that when it blew I was going to shower everything in sight with my cum.

I lifted my arm and put it behind my head, flexing the muscle and exposing the forest of sticky hair. I pulled North up from his position between my legs and buried his face in my dank pit. It must have smelled like a barn in there after all the sweating I'd done, but he worked on me like it was a pool of fresh water and he'd been in the desert for three days without a drink. He sank his nose in my ripe fur and ground his face against me, his mouth working over the muscles of my shoulder and in and out of every inch of my underarm.

I let North roam free for the time being, and he proceeded to bathe the rest of me, sliding his mouth over my chest, licking up every bit of dust he could from the coarse, black hair that blanketed my skin. His lips surrounded my nipple, and he bit gently, his tongue massaging my bud into a frenzy. After exploring my other armpit, he worked his way down my stomach, licking out every valley thoroughly, like a lion washing its fur. His tongue swept into my navel, digging in and cleaning it out.

Seeing the young MP sucking up my grime was really working me up. I wanted to flip him over right there and pound the shit out of his virgin butt. Instead, I pushed his head into my groin. "Suck my nuts, boy," I growled. "I know you've been waiting for them. If you do a good job, maybe I'll let you have a taste of my cock."

North's mouth worked steadily at my hairy ballsac. One at a time, he pulled my nads in and rolled them around on his tongue, letting them slip into his throat like pieces of fresh fruit. Then he ran his tongue underneath my sac, causing me to shudder as he passed over the sensitive spot just under my nuts. I spread my legs wider, resting them on his back, and pulled my balls up with my hands to reveal the path to my asshole. North hesitated, and I pressed against his back with my feet, plunging his face headlong into my hairy ass crack and making him slurp up the funk between my meaty cheeks. I felt him probe my pucker tentatively and pushed against his face. His tongue slipped into my slimy butthole, and I groaned as he drank in my ass juice.

With long strokes, North ran his mouth from my asshole to my balls, bathing me and soaking my crack with his spit. Every so often he would swirl his tongue around my hole or tug on my balls with his lips. His brush cut was rubbing against my nuts and thighs with the movement of his head, and I felt my balls start to rise up toward the base of my cock as my excitement mounted.

Finally, I couldn't stand it any longer. Grabbing North's collar, I pulled him up to my waiting prick. His tongue washing had worked my crank up into a pounding throb, and a steady stream of dick lava was running down my pole. I pressed my cockhead against North's lips, letting him taste me. Then I slid a few inches into his mouth, feeling his lips stretch to surround my thickness like a hand grasping my shaft.

Pushing brutally on his head, I slid North's head down my full length. At first he gagged, but I quickly shoved my fat head past his gullet, and soon I was buried deep in his throat. Slowly I rode his face, pulling out and letting him take a breath before filling him up again. When my nuts were banging his chin, I leaned down and whispered in his ear. "You're a pretty good little cocksucker, North, you know that? Knew it the minute I laid eyes on that pretty face of yours. You like hosing down my big prick, boy?"

North tried to speak, but with my hard-on blocking his windpipe, all that came out was a muffled grunt. I felt the muscles in his throat vibrate against my shaft as he attempted to speak and almost lost my cargo on the spot.

I pulled out a little so North could speak. "Yes, sir," he said breathlessly. "I like sucking your cock."

I looked down at his face, into his eyes begging me for more. "Is that any way for a military man to act?" I said gruffly. "I'd say this is a clear case of conduct unbecoming, North. You better think about whether a court-martial is worth it before you do any more sucking on that dick."

North answered me by running his tongue up the underside of my shaft and wrapping his mouth around my engorged head. I slammed my rod back down his throat and started to thrust more quickly. The harder I pumped his throat, the hungrier he got, taking every inch of me as it coursed in and out of his mouth. North's spit had slicked me up, and as I fucked his face drool spilled from his lips, staining the front of his shirt. I wanted badly to let my load fly down his throat and fill his belly with my cream. But just when I was about to come, I yanked my cock out of his mouth and stood up. "Get up," I ordered him, the spunk steaming in my nuts as it screamed to be let loose.

North scrambled to his feet and stood in front of me. I grabbed the front of his shirt and ripped it down the front, scattering buttons under the cot. Exposed, North's chest was hairless. I ran my hand over it, feeling the muscles tense under the smooth skin, sensing the wild beat of his heart as he waited to see what was going to happen to him. Pinching his tits hard between my fingers, I pulled them out until they stood at attention, smiling when he winced.

Reaching between his legs with one hand, I felt his cock through his pants. It was long and thin, and there was a dark spot where he had leaked cock juice. I unbuckled his belt and pushed his pants down his legs, still massaging his left nipple. His briefs were stained with precum, and his cock strained against the wet fabric. I grabbed the waistband and yanked, the material giving way with a soft ripping sound. North's prick jutted out at an angle, a pale shaft erupting from a nest of clipped red hair. His balls were smooth and round, hanging beneath his rod like two small, pink moons.

"Turn around, soldier," I told North. He turned, and I pushed him toward the pile of dirty fatigues in the corner. He couldn't walk very well because his pants were around his ankles, and he stumbled from the force of my shove. When he was in front of the clothes, I put one hand on his shoulder and drove him to his knees. I knelt behind him, stroking my dick, letting it slap against his neck as I worked my hard-on into a white heat, the hairs on my shaft tickling his skin.

"I think it's time to show you how real men do it, North," I said.

He was on his hands and knees, his face over the mound of my sweaty shorts and T-shirts. His creamy white ass was laid out in front of me, the soft melons of his cheeks dotted with cinnamon-colored freckles. I slapped his butt hard, feeling his muscles tense under my hand. "You better relax, boy," I said. "Because in a minute that pretty ass of yours is going to be screaming for mercy. You've wanted this for a long time, and now you're going get it good and hard."

Spreading his ass, I looked into the rosy hole leading to his chute. I let a thick rope of spit fall into his crack and worked the lube into his butthole, greasing him up. As I pushed a finger roughly into him, North gasped. He was tight all right. I could tell he'd never had his butt pumped, and I couldn't wait to see what he did when my full width was plowing out his cherry.

After a minute of finger fucking, I'd had enough. Three months of jerking off had left me horny as hell, and I couldn't wait to bury my prick in the MP's tasty fuckhole. I spat another wad into my palm and greased up my tool, feeling the vein under my shaft beating wildly. I aimed my poker at the shiny lips of North's shitter, grabbed him around the waist with one arm, and drove my missile home. North stiffened against me as I ripped into him, but I pushed his head down into the pile of clothes, muffling his cries.

North's tight chute gripped my prick like a vise, rolling over the sides like hot sand around a sidewinder as I burrowed deeper into his belly. Once my balls were smack up against his butt, I stopped, letting him adjust to the battering ram inside him. Seeing my suntanned skin and thick black fur pressed against the linen whiteness of his ass made me swell even wider, and my cock twitched, bringing jolts of pleasure to my groin and gasps of pain from North's throat.

I pulled almost all the way out, feeling North's ass ring close around the head of my piece tightly, opening up again when I stormed back in. As I fucked him senseless, I buried his face in my laundry, giving him a taste of the shorts stained with dirt and my sweat and cum, letting him breathe in the scent of the man who was taking his virginity. My hands caressed his ass cheeks, kneading the skin until it was red, enjoying the smooth silkiness of it.

North moaned louder each time I hammered his prostate, his cock swinging underneath him and slapping against his belly, drops of precum flying from the dripping tip.

I was deep dicking him like a rapid-fire machine gunner blasting at an enemy target, and he was taking every hit square on. My balls beat steadily against his, sending soft fingers of delicious pain stretching up my belly to grasp fiercely at my chest. I could feel the load in my nuts reaching critical mass and fucked North for all I was worth.

Finally I couldn't hold back any longer, and the heat roared up and out of my cock, slamming into North's guts like a mortar explosion. I continued to pump him as round after round of ammo blew from my prick, slicking my dick and his hole with thick spunk that slid out of his butt and ran down my shaft, dripping from my balls and spattering the floor.

As I blasted away at his innards, North was jackhammering his cock. He leaned back, his fist sliding up and down his dick. His head flew back against my chest, and a stream of jism flew from his gasping piss slit, arcing up and falling heavily onto a pair of my dirty shorts. He tensed three more times, splashing more of his juice onto my clothes.

I pulled my cock out of North and he fell forward, his face in the cum-soaked laundry. He rolled over on his back and looked up at me. I shook the last drops of juice from my prick. Then I picked up his fallen notebook and pencil and dropped it on his chest.

"Now," I said, "do you have any more questions?"

Jesus Loves You

A friend of mine, when confronted by a pair of Mormon missionaries, responds to them with, "If you'll come back to my house and let me suck you off, I'll listen to what you have to say." It's never worked, but it's fun trying.

"For Christ's sake," I muttered as the doorbell rang, pulling me out of a sweet sleep just as I was about to shoot my load all over the rosy-cheeked face of the Irish boy who had refused to go home with me the night before. After I'd talked to him for forty-five minutes and wasted three bucks buying him a beer, he'd excused himself to go to the bathroom. I saw him an hour later, leaving with a blond with perfect pecs. I'd gone home with the blond myself once and consoled myself with the fact that the Irish boy was going to be very disappointed when he found out that despite the encouraging physique, the guy had a prick the size of my thumb.

Again the intruding buzz of the doorbell came, and I glanced at the clock. Its red face grinned back: 7:00. As I rolled reluctantly out of bed and tried to find my way to the front door in my state of half-sleep, I wondered who the hell could be coming by my apartment so early on a Saturday morning. Only two people have a key to my building—my mother and my ex—and I was in no mood for either of them, especially after having come home alone.

I opened the door and peered out into the hall. Standing there were two men. One appeared to be in his forties, with dark hair going gray on the sides. The other, a blond, looked to be about twenty years younger. From the look of their dark suits, I figured that they were with some police unit or something. I was suddenly very conscious of the fact that I was standing there in nothing but my boxer shorts.

"Good morning, Mr. Caffrey," the older of the two said. "We

were wondering if we might come in and talk to you for a few moments."

I couldn't think of any reason why two cops would be visiting
my apartment shortly after dawn on a Saturday morning, but I
figured it was a good idea to be polite.

"Yeah, sure," I said, trying to appear more awake than I felt.
"Come on in."

The two walked past me into the apartment, and I shut the
door behind them. As they walked into the living room, I tried as
best I could to comb my hair with my fingers. If the guys were
feds, I wanted to at least look innocent.

Once we were in the living room, the older man sat on the
couch and the younger one positioned himself in one of the two
armchairs directly across from it. The older man indicated that I
should sit next to him. I felt a little odd sitting there in my underwear, but I couldn't see my robe anywhere, and they didn't seem
to care. I sat down and waited for him to ask me where I'd been
the night before or something like that. I mentally ran through
the names of all my friends who could potentially be criminals,
trying to remember if I'd heard from any of them lately.

The older man smiled warmly at me. "I'm David and this is
Sam," he said, indicating the young man. "We'd like to take a few
moments to talk to you about Jesus."

I groaned. Not only was I up on a Saturday morning only hours
after coming home from striking out, I'd let two Jehovah's Witnesses
into my apartment thinking they were G-men. I was kicking myself for not asking them for identification or anything.

I looked at David and tried to smile. "Look," I said firmly. "I
think I've made a mistake here. I thought you were the police or
something. I'm not really interested in talking about God this
morning. Or any morning, for that matter."

David laughed. "But God is interested in talking to you, Mr.
Caffrey. We may not always like to hear what he has to say, but
God forgives us for that."

The direct approach was obviously not going to work. Ignoring
my protestations, David launched into his talk, telling me how
Jesus was waiting for me to welcome him into my life. Whenever
I tried to interrupt, he paused for a moment and then went right
on with his speech. Short of physically throwing the two of them

out, I didn't know how to get rid of them. I sat back and decided to wait it out.

Throughout all of this, Sam had remained silent, watching while David did all the talking. I looked over at him, and for the first time noticed that he was very attractive. His blond hair was cut short, and his eyes were a light blue the color of a cloudless morning sky. His clean-shaven skin had a healthy glow to it, and his lips were full and pink. His hands, which were folded in his lap, were wide, with long fingers. He looked as though underneath his blue suit and white shirt he would have quite a fine body.

Sam looked at me quickly and, seeing that I was staring at him, looked away again. David seemed not to notice and went on with his talk. I continued looking at the young man, waiting for him to look at me again, but he was seemingly listening attentively to what his companion was saying.

Suddenly I knew how I could get rid of my unwanted guests. Turning to face David, I brought one leg up on the couch and leaned back. This meant that he was now looking directly into my spread crotch. With one hand, I began to slowly rub the hair on my thigh, stroking it gently with my fingers as I pretended to listen to what David was saying, nodding in agreement every so often. My calf was very close to David's knee, and he glanced at it warily before going on.

"There are many things that we struggle with daily," he was saying. "Desires that prevent us from living productive lives. Jesus can help us overcome these desires so that we can more fully serve him."

I let my fingers rest on the bulge made by my prick and balls, squeezing it slightly so that David would be able to see the outline of my cock through the material of my boxer shorts. He swallowed uncomfortably, but went on. Out of the corner of my eye I noticed that Sam was moving around in his chair, so I figured my plan was working. I moved my leg so that it was resting right against David's. He flinched a little, but did not pull away. I looked over at Sam, who was watching David intently. A slight film of sweat had broken out on his lip, and he looked like he wanted to be anyplace else but where he was. I decided to go for broke.

I continued to rub my prick, slowly stroking it until it stretched across my thigh. Then I hooked my fingers under the leg of my boxers and lifted the edge so that the head of my dick slid into view. When David saw it, he stopped talking and just looked at my cock. Any second, I expected him to run screaming from the apartment with Sam behind him, leaving me in peace.

But to my surprise, he reached out and ran his trembling fingers over my exposed prick. This unexpected turn of events caught me completely off guard, and I just watched as his hand moved over my dick, squeezing the head. Before I had time to think about what was happening, David was on the floor between my legs, his mouth moving over the few inches of prick sticking out of my boxers. Then he started to suck my balls through my shorts, soaking the material as he mouthed hungrily. Ignoring Sam, I shucked off my boxers so that my cock could swing free.

David immediately sank onto my tool, shoving all of it down his pipe. I couldn't believe the man who had come to sell me salvation was giving me the best head of my life, but I had no complaints about the way his lips were milking my shaft. As his mouth massaged my crank, his fingers kneaded my balls, firmly pulling on them until I thought I'd come from the sensation. Right before I was about to shoot in his throat, I motioned for him to stop. Switching places, I got down between his legs to return his favor.

The whole time David had been sucking my crank he had remained dressed. I reached inside his suit pants and felt for his prick, finding it already hard inside his shorts. Working the fly open, I pulled out one of the biggest cocks I'd ever seen. At the end of an incredibly thick shaft the enormous head bulged out, and a thick vein ran down the underside, which was dusted lightly with hair for the first several inches.

The size of his cock adding to my excitement, I settled down to service David's stud piece. Starting at the base, I ran my tongue slowly up to the tip, savoring the musky scent of his skin and feeling his cock vein beat under the tip of my tongue. After licking it all over, I put the head and as much of the shaft as I could into my mouth, swallowing it hungrily. David placed a hand on the back of my head and kneaded the muscles of my neck as I sucked on his prick. "Oh, God," he moaned. "Please don't stop."

I had no intention of doing anything of the sort, not with the way his fat pole was filling my throat. I fumbled with his belt, undoing it with anxious fingers and then pulling both pants and briefs off. David removed his jacket and tie and unbuttoned his shirt, revealing a surprisingly well-muscled chest that rose in two hairy mounds tipped with succulent rose-colored nipples before dipping into the rippled valley of his abdomen. His arms were powerful, the forearms thickly muscled.

Hanging beneath his swollen poker was a set of meaty balls, swaying fat and heavy. I went to work on the big bull nuts, rubbing them against my lips and sucking eagerly at the soft flesh that held the juicy globes loosely in its folds. The smell of a man filled my nose as I burrowed in his crotch, stoking the passion that was quickly taking hold of me. Returning once more to his magnificent prick, I sank it deep into my mouth, trying to take in its entire thick length. While I couldn't get anywhere near the whole thing down, I worked feverishly on the inches I could as David thrust, working his knob in and out slowly.

In my excitement over sucking David's fat tool, I'd forgotten about Sam. Now I heard moaning behind me and turned to see what it was. He was sitting in the chair, his pants around his ankles. His coat was discarded on the floor, but he was still wearing his white shirt and tie. His smooth, well-developed legs were spread wide, his feet planted firmly on the floor. Between his thighs hung a golden-furred sac, which he was currently working in his big hands, the fingers fondling each ball lovingly. His cock, a weighty rod of creamy flesh tipped with the thick cowl of an uncut head, lay flat against his belly, untouched.

"Why don't you bring that over here?" I asked him.

Sam got up and walked over to the couch, his cock swinging in front of him. He sat next to David, and the older man's arm went around his shoulders, pulling him closer. They hesitated for a minute, and then their mouths met, their lips joining frenziedly. Sam's hand went to David's nipple, squeezing it into a red point.

From my vantage point on the floor, I was looking right at two of the most beautiful cocks I'd ever seen, David's big piece of meat looming up and falling across the pale skin of Sam's thigh and butting against his prick where their legs touched. I reached for Sam's crank and pulled back the foreskin to reveal the smooth whiteness of his cockhead. He pushed his prick forward, urging it into my mouth, and I was happy to oblige.

Sam's prick slid coolly into my throat until I could feel his balls against my lips and the soft fuzz of his pubic bush tickled my cheek. Moving back up to the tip, I concentrated on his sensitive

foreskin, slipping my tongue under it to taste the funky combination of sweat and precum that had oozed out. As I tongued his piss
slit, a fresh spurt of lube slid from his blowhole and I slurped it up.

Moving back to David, I began to alternate between the two
men's pricks, sucking first one and then the other while Sam and
David made out above me. Sam was biting on one of David's sensitive rosebud nipples through his shirt, and I moved up and took
the other one between my teeth. With both of his tits getting a
working over, David began to moan, his hands pushing our faces
tightly to his chest. Every so often Sam and I would take a break
from milking David's chest and kiss, our tongues exploring each
other's mouths while David's hands traveled over our backs.

Together Sam and I began to explore the older man's body. I
raised David's arm behind his head and dove into the musky pool
of his armpit. Thick with hair, his underarm tasted sweet to my
lips as I licked every inch of it in long strokes. At the same time,
Sam was kissing David's neck, his hand wrapped tightly around
David's drooling shaft.

Sam pushed me back so that I was lying on the couch. Then he
turned and knelt so that his face was over my cock and his ass was
in the air. Taking my cock in his hand, he began to inch it into his
mouth. Watching my tool disappear between his red lips made me
horny as hell, and I shoved the entire length into him, even
though I knew he wasn't ready for it. He gagged for a second,
then relaxed his throat and started sucking again.

Behind Sam, David was inspecting the exposed mounds of his
bare ass. Running his hands over them, he slapped Sam sharply,
causing him to be pushed forward on my prick, his nose slamming
into my belly. David kneaded the soft flesh in his fingers, spreading Sam's ass cheeks and exposing his tender hole. Leaning forward, he started to eat out Sam's butt, sticking his tongue deep
inside the younger man's chute. Every so often, he slapped Sam's
ass hard, the sound ringing through the room.

Pulling his face away, David wet his finger and then pushed it
into Sam's hole. I could feel the young man's throat vibrate on my
dick as he groaned with pleasure. David finger fucked Sam's shitter slowly until it was loose enough for him to push another finger
in. The harder he invaded Sam's butt, the harder Sam ground his
ass against the hand that was filling him. He started to suck me in

long slurps from the tip of my cock to the base, moaning all the while.

David reached between Sam's legs and pulled his balls back. Holding his fingers around them like a cock ring, he stretched them out while he continued to finger Sam's ass, adding two more fingers until his hand was disappearing in and out of the young man's hole, only the thumb still on the outside pressing against his delicious mound. As David pulled on his balls, Sam's cock bobbed up and down against his belly, a long string of precum swinging from the head.

Watching the young stud get fingered by his older friend was really getting me hot, and I wanted to see him get really plowed.

"Fuck him," I told David. "Stick that big piece of yours up his ass."

David spit in his hand and slicked his cock. Then he aimed his head at the opening to Sam's chute and slammed it in. It was a good thing Sam was so loose from the fingering he'd been given, because David showed no mercy. He pumped in and out of the boy's ass furiously, his balls slamming against Sam's thighs with each thrust.

On my end, I began to fuck Sam's throat in time with David's movements. The guy was getting it from both ends and loving it, sucking every inch of the prick I was feeding him while David invaded his ass again and again. Sam was still wearing his tie, and he took the end of it and wrapped the soft silk around the base of my cock, sliding it up my shaft in rhythm with his mouth.

Finally, I couldn't hold back any longer. Putting a hand on Sam's neck, I pushed him down until his face was against my stomach and pumped my load into his throat. He swallowed furiously, barely keeping up with the gusher I was sending his way. At the same time, David pulled out of Sam's ass and aimed his cock down between the younger man's legs. After a few strokes, he came with a loud moan, a stream of thick spunk exploding from his prick. His cum spattered Sam's balls, clinging to them in fat glistening drops and hanging in long ropes that dripped onto my legs.

Still sucking down my flood, Sam began to jerk his own cock, but David stopped him. "Not yet," he said. "I think Mr. Caffrey here deserves a turn at that fine ass of yours. After all, we are here to share the message, aren't we?"

Sam reversed his position so that he was lying on his back with
his head underneath David's cock. I lifted his legs and placed them
over my shoulder, and this time it was my cock pointed at his hole,
now wet and dripping from the fuck job it had received at the
hands of the older evangelist. At first I didn't think I'd be able to
get hard again so fast, but I was surprised at how quickly my
equipment jumped to life when I thought about burrowing into
that tasty chute.

Scooping up some of David's cum from Sam's balls, I used it to
lube my prick, sliding the thick jism along the length of my rod.
When I slipped my cock into Sam's hole, I was surprised to find it
still very tight. I was sure that with the fucking David's massive
prong had given him he'd be loose, but that wasn't the case. My
dick felt like it was sinking into velvet.

While I was busy attending to Sam's ass, David was having
more fun of his own at the other end. He was rubbing his slimy
prick all over Sam's face, teasing him with it. Just as Sam would
open his mouth to suck off the cum and ass juice that covered
David's pole, he'd pull it away again. Sam was whimpering, begging David for a taste of the prick that had so recently pleasured
him.

Instead, David let him suck on his big fingers. Sam took them
eagerly, sucking two of them into his mouth like they were the
cock he so desperately wanted. David played with him, thrusting
his fingers in and out of the boy's mouth slowly, fucking his lips
like they were another asshole. Every so often he wiped off some
of the scum from his dick and let Sam have a taste of what he was
missing.

David moved his hips over Sam's face so that his ass was right
over his mouth. Then, wrapping the young man's tie around his
hand, he pulled his face right up into his ass crack. Forced to lick
David's hole, Sam went to work, his mouth sucking noisily at the
older man's furry butthole and sucking at his low hangers. He
moaned as he thoroughly washed David's hole, gasping for breath
as he was pulled tighter and tighter into the man's pucker, his
head held in place by the sticky length of silk in David's fingers.

Finally, David let him have what he wanted, and Sam eagerly
licked every filthy inch of the big piece that slapped his face.
Watching him lick David's tool, I began thrusting harder against
him, pulling all of the way out and then ramming back in. David

seemed willing to take whatever I could give him, and I banged his butt for all I was worth, leaning back and watching my cock slide in and out of that pink hole until I couldn't hold off anymore.

"I'm going to come," I said to David.

He nodded and pulled out of Sam's throat. We knelt at either end of the horny boy, both of us wanking our meat. Suddenly, David tensed, and his load burst across Sam's handsome face, coating his mouth and lips in dripping lines of cum. I shot right after him, three long spurts that drenched Sam's neck and chest, staining his tie and shirt with sticky splotches.

I slid my still-hard cock back into Sam's asshole and resumed fucking him while David knelt over him and sucked on his, stoking him toward his climax. It didn't take long for the pent-up load in him to reach a boiling point. He threw his head back, and a wad of cream flew from his tired cock. Over and over he came, his jism exploding in white splashes that streaked the hair on David's chest.

When the last drop had been drained from Sam's balls, he lay back exhausted, our cum drying on his shirt. We let him rest while David showed me just how big his cock really was by shoving it up my chute, but it wasn't long before he was ready for more. We had another round of sucking and fucking, with both David and I riding Sam's hooded pony until it was time for them to go.

As Sam and David left my apartment, David turned and handed me a brochure with his name and phone number written on it. After both of them had kissed me good-bye, Sam turned around at the head of the stairs. "Don't forget," he said, smiling, "Jesus loves you."

The Memories of Boys

This is a true story. It's funny how the people we most despise can also be the ones we most desire.

Gym class. Eighth grade. Forget the horror of facing thrice-weekly rounds of bombardment. Forget picking the ball up on the soccer field thinking it's out-of-bounds and hearing the jeers of teammates. Forget even the anxiety produced while waiting to be chosen last for basketball teams. Or for any teams.

No, the real horror came after the final merciful bell rang and those things were already-fading memories. It came in the locker room, while rushing to get dressed and safely away before an army of naked boys could appear, their skins a rosy pink as they emerged from the scrim of steam produced by the communal showers, their hair wet and glistening like the fur of seals.

That was the dangerous time, the time when the placement of eyes was of utmost importance. The time when one too-long look at an exposed crotch or a passing pale ass could mean the difference between just another horrible adolescent memory and something much worse. And it was gotten through by holding the breath and praying until the suffocating heat of hot water and adolescent need was replaced by the cool safety of the hallway and the comforting sound of footsteps echoing along the corridor as I hurried away, willing my eyes to forget.

These are the moments I remember most from those years—the times spent in escape, in running not from others so much as from myself. The stings of "queer," spat like acid as it was so often, have faded to dull throbs. The days of not belonging have faded into one vague stretch of gray. But even now I remember the running.

The one who carried the most danger for me was John Dobbins, wearing it like a second skin that fit him more comfortably than his own. Tall, with the muscles of the farm boy he was, he was closer to manhood than the rest of us, as though at birth he'd been dealt a right to take up more space and had ignored even that generous offering. Adopted—I don't know how I knew this—he was a mystery, his dark hair and blue eyes so dissimilar to those of the red-haired, fair-skinned family that chose him, like the most rambunctious puppy, from the rest of the litter.

What I remember now, in addition to the blueness of his eyes, are his teeth, crooked and sharp in his mouth. And, of course, the cock, for that is what made John famous in the locker room of Cold Falls Central School. The cock was huge, hanging thickly between John's legs like a full-grown man's before he'd even reached the age of thirteen. Besides its size, John's dick was, for some reason, uncut. Ostensibly, this is why the other boys felt they could remark upon it without fear of crossing the line into queerdom. Difference was a safe topic of conversation; size was certainly not, although that didn't stop some imaginative redneck from nicknaming John "Horse."

It was John's cock that I feared, and not so much John himself, although he and I had a history of animosity since once, in fifth grade, he had threatened to kill me for calling him an asshole on the playground. It says something about the both of us that I waited for the next six years for him to carry out this promise, and that he never did.

But in fifth grade I had not yet seen John's cock. When I did, it changed something between us, even though I'm sure he could never recall the exact moment it happened as I still can even twenty years later. I have only to think back and see vividly the gray skins of the lockers, reserved for the high-school boys and seemingly sacred, and feel the smoothness of the tile floor as though I'd just walked through the door of that room. I remember, too, the wooden bench, and John bent over it, his balls hanging down between his legs. He turns, and I see his cock, the wrinkled skin folded over the head, the black hair around it still wet from the shower.

The actual event was hardly momentous, a fleeting glimpse of his prick as he turned to say something to a friend and I darted out the door to the safety of English class, where I could move

words around the page as skillfully as John moved the ball around
the basketball court, not that it saved me from the curse of being
the school fag. Afterward, though, there was a subtle shift in the
way John made his way through my world. Where before I
avoided him in the halls out of general fear, now I did so for far different
reasons. I feared what he made me feel, despite my hatred
of him and him of me. I hated that sometimes at night, my cock
hard from thoughts that came seemingly out of nowhere, I recalled
the sight of his dick as I stroked myself into a wadded-up
tissue. When one day I was kneeling on the gym floor tying my
shoe and John, passing by, said, "Hey, faggot, while you're down
there why don't you give me a blow job?" the words hung before
me, ripe with hatred. But despite their bitterness, I wanted nothing
more than to swallow them down.

I never saw John's cock again. And after a hurried departure
from high school three years later, I never saw John himself again.
Yet sometimes I see a similar face, or perhaps a similar hatred reflected
in the eyes of a man on the street or on the subway, and I
am reminded of him. And still sometimes I close my eyes and
imagine sucking a cock, long and thick. Its owner's hands hold my
head, not in love but in hate, as he fucks my mouth. It is an act of
need, pure and simple. And inevitably, when I open my eyes and
look up, I am in a junior-high locker room, and it is John's cold blue
eyes looking down as he releases his load into my throat and, happily,
I swallow.

The Night Before Christmas

It all started with the singing elves and way too much eggnog.

I'd been working as a security guard at the James Madison Mall for almost eight months, ever since leaving the corps. Actually, since they'd asked me to leave after discovering me in the shower with my sergeant's cock up my ass and a big load streaming from my prick. Because his daddy was someone important in Washington, he came out of the whole thing with no trouble and even managed to make it so I wasn't given a dishonorable. Early retirement they called it, except there was no good-bye party or big gold watch. Still, it was worth all the trouble to have his thick tool in my shitter, even if it was just that once. I was practically still coming when the MPs slapped the cuffs on me, my ass aching from the banging he'd given it.

I had some money saved up, so I'd taken the job at James Madison mainly for something to do. Most of the time, patrolling the mall was a cakewalk. During the day it was filled mainly with older couples with nothing better to do than totter around for a couple of hours buying candles in the shapes of cats and dragging their grandkids to Sears to have their pictures taken. Every so often gaggles of teenage girls training to be world-class shoppers would get caught trying to lift clothes from The Gap and I'd have to give them a scare. But usually things ran smoothly, and I spent most of my time walking around cruising the guys whose girlfriends or wives dragged them along to look at silk panties and new toaster ovens.

But the holiday season was another matter altogether. Starting the day after Halloween, every shop in the place was crammed

with Christmas displays, half-price sales, and anything else that
might bring customers in and make them part with their cash.
The whole place was covered in endless yards of red and green
tissue paper, like some demented gift wrapper from Macy's customer service department had done the whole thing up as her contribution to the big celestial grab bag.

For eight weeks I was trapped in Christmas hell. From the
minute I unlocked the doors in the morning until the last person
was shooed away when the mall closed at ten, the place was packed
wall to wall with people carrying bags and boxes, kids screaming
and crying, and the sounds of mall workers with painted-on smiles
spritzing everyone with perfume samples and announcing impromptu sales on such indispensable items as cheese logs, four-in-
one tools, and ceramic gnomes that doubled as toilet-scrubber
holders.

The center of the holiday madness maelstrom was the mall's
main court, a big empty space surrounded by food vendors that
was used for special occasions like auto shows, cooking demonstrations, and other assorted galas. For many years, local reli-
gious groups had staged a traditional manger scene there, with
Mary and Joseph and the whole bit, right down to the lambs made
out of cotton balls and shepherds dressed in someone's old
bathrobes. Then, a few years back, there had been a big fight between the church people and those who said religion had no place
in a public space. Things came to a head when someone managed
to snatch the baby Jesus when no one was looking, so that when
you got close enough you realized that Mary was smiling down an-
gelically at a smoked ham with pineapple rings where a face
should be.

After that, the church people had completely given up, and
every year since then the court had been transformed for eight
weeks into this weird Christmas Land where kids could have
their pictures taken with Santa. Mounds of fake snow were scattered around with giant plastic candy canes sprouting up like impossible red-and-white trees and the whole place was hung with
flashing colored lights. The centerpiece of the whole thing was a
couple of garish gingerbread-inspired houses that were supposed
to be Santa's house and workshop.

To make the spirit of magical holiday joy complete, there were
mechanical reindeer and a chorus of singing elves equipped with a

tape of various Christmas songs. Normally the elves were harm-
less enough, running through their endlessly looping repertoire of
"We Wish You a Merry Christmas," "Frosty the Snowman," and
the like, their robot mouths and eyes opening and closing in ran-
dom order like actors in a badly dubbed Japanese monster film. But
for some implausible reason, the tape also included the "Hallelujah
Chorus," and about once an hour the elves would launch into this
shrieking rendition of Handel's classic piece, sounding like a bunch
of drunken drag queens performing at a *Messiah* sing-along, all of
them fighting for the soprano parts. But people loved it, and it
made piles of money, so it went up year after year.

Every day starting at noon the court was thronged with kids
piled in long lines to see Santa. They'd stand for two hours or
more waiting for the chance to sit on some strange fat guy's lap
and tell him what they wanted for Christmas. By the time they finally got to the front of the line, they were so hyper that most of
them forgot their names, let alone what they wanted. A couple of
them simply threw up from the excitement. If they did make it
that far, they were rewarded with a few hearty chuckles from
Santa and a promise to bring them exactly what they wanted,
which when the sought-after gift didn't materialize Christmas
morning would inevitably result in gales of tears. When time was
up, a grinning elf (usually a graduate student from the university
who needed the money badly enough to wear pointed shoes and
fake latex ears) would drag them off, sending them away with a
candy cane and a picture to hang on the refrigerator.

The whole Santa thing bothered me, and I made it a point to
stay as far away from the scene as possible. It was bad enough
doing battle with the legions of big-haired women clicking madly
through the halls in their high heels and clouds of sickly sweet
perfume without having to contend with unhappy parents whose
kids were about to explode from all the Christmas buildup and
who wanted to know why the elves couldn't move the line just a
little bit faster. As far as I was concerned, Santa was on his own,
and good luck to him. The sooner Christmas was over, the better
in my book. I gritted my teeth and counted down the days until
life could return to normal.

Finally it was Christmas Eve. On that night the mall turned its
back on the pleading face of commercialism and was only open
until seven. At a few minutes before the hour, there were still peo-

ple dashing around snatching up anything that was left on the shelves. Even as shop workers were pulling down their gates and preparing to go home, people would try to run in to get something they'd forgotten. I wrestled the last of them, a disheveled woman shrieking that she just had to get one more gift for her sister-in-law or what would everyone say at the party, out the doors into the snow. Turning the lock on the door, I congratulated myself that Christmas was now over. With everyone gone and the lights off, the mall was eerily silent and still. All I had to do was make one last walk around the whole place and make sure that no one was still inside. Once that was done, I could go home and settle in for my much-needed long winter's nap.

After checking all of the stores, I went to take a quick look around the main court. The elves were silent for once, and the mechanical reindeer were throwing long shadows over the floor as the moon shone through the big skylight that covered most of the ceiling. Satisfied that everything was in order, I was just about to leave when I heard someone moving around inside one of the wooden houses. I crept quietly along the wall of the nearest gingerbread house until I was at the door. Jumping into the house, I shone my flashlight around. As I did, a figure in the room whirled around, and I found myself face to face with Santa Claus.

"Holy shit," he said in a startled voice. "You scared the hell out of me."

I stood in the doorway, not sure of what to say. I'd expected a thief, not some guy in a Santa suit. "What are you doing here?"

"Packing my sleigh," he said seriously.

I walked over and stood in front of him, looking up and down his body from his shiny black boots to his stocking cap. "Aren't you the guy who sits here all day talking to the kids?"

"The very same," he said. Then, much to my surprise, he put his black-gloved hand on my crotch, squeezing it. "And just what is it you want for Christmas this year, little boy?"

I couldn't believe it; I was getting felt up by Santa. I still wasn't convinced the guy wasn't a thief, but his hand was moving up and down my cock which, to my embarrassment, was growing rapidly. All I could do was stare at the shiny buttons on his red suit as he stroked my hard-on.

"Someone has a big toy," Santa said, chuckling.

He dropped to his knees, unzipped my pants, and reached inside to pull my prick out. Then he leaned forward and sank his rosy mouth onto my knob. My tool sank easily into his lips as he teased the head with his tongue, flickering it over the tender slit and along the ridges of my fat knob. As he sucked me, I completely forgot that he was still dressed as Santa and put my hand on his head, wrapping my fingers in the white curls that peeked out from beneath his red felt hat.

After working the first few inches of my cock for a couple of minutes, he suddenly pushed the whole length of my dick into his throat until his nose was buried deep in my bush. His head moved forward, and I was left holding a handful of hair, the stocking cap it was attached to dangling from my hand. He looked up from between my feet, and I saw that his head was covered in short black hair.

"Now you've discovered my secret," he said. "Promise you won't ruin the surprise for the other children?"

I laughed. "Not if you keep doing what you're doing, I won't."

He nodded. "Deal."

With that, he went back to sucking my prick, his lips gliding sensuously up and down my shaft in slow strokes. He was still wearing the long white beard of his costume, and as he blew me the soft white hairs tickled my cock, sticking to my skin where his lips had passed over it. I pumped his face slowly, moving several inches of my meat in and out of his mouth. He was an expert cocksucker, and before long I felt a tensing in my groin.

He must have felt it too, because he started to move his mouth in faster strokes, his lips pulling at my head. His hand moved up to my cock and began to stroke it as he concentrated on sucking just the tip, the leather of his glove wrapping around my prick and holding it tightly. The load in my balls was released in a single blast that blew from my cock and slammed into his mouth. His cheeks filled with my cum as I poured more and more of it into his hot throat, and he gulped several times trying to get it all down. Even then, some of it trickled from his lips, streaking the beard and the front of his red jacket with sticky clumps.

He licked his lips and smiled. "That's a hell of a lot better than the glass of milk they usually leave for old Santa," he said.

I reached down and pulled him to his feet. "Well, that's just the beginning. You haven't even started on the plate of cookies yet."

Tugging on the beard, I pulled it off him, revealing a handsome face with a wide jaw covered in dark stubble. My hands moved down the soft red jacket to the wide plastic belt at his waist. Taking it off, I unbuttoned the jacket and slipped it over his shoulders. There was a thick layer of padding attached to the suit, and now that it was gone I saw that underneath he had a lean, hard body. The hills of his chest were covered in thick hair clipped into a short carpet that swirled down the ripples of his abdomen, and his shoulders were broad and muscled.

"You've got a great body for a man hundreds of years old," I said.

He started to take off my uniform, his fingers slipping the buttons of my shirt from their moorings. "It's from lifting all those toys," he said, pinching my left nipple forcefully and running his tongue along my neck before slipping it into my mouth. I kissed him back, tasting my cum on his lips and plunging deep into his mouth. I could feel his prick pressing against me as I held him, my hands against his strong back.

We fumbled with one another's pants at the same time, anxious to get to the goodies inside like greedy children sticking their hands into Christmas stockings. Without taking our mouths off one another, we undid buttons and zippers until our pants fell to the floor, followed by hurriedly discarded underwear. Once they were off and we were naked, our hands roamed over legs and asses. His butt was smooth and round, firm and muscular beneath my hands as I cupped his cheeks and ground my cock against his.

As for his prick, it was one of the sweetest treats I'd ever seen. The huge shaft lifted up from a set of wonderfully hairy sweetmeats that hung between his strong thighs like ornaments on a tree. Straight and smooth, his cock was crowned with a round sugarplum of a head that just begged for sucking. I held it in my hand, feeling the beating of the vein that ran along it and thinking about it throbbing in my throat. But before I could start feasting on it, he pulled away.

He flicked a switch behind the door of the gingerbread house, and the courtyard bloomed with thousands of tiny lights. After a minute, they began to twinkle, as if all the stars in the sky had been replaced with blue, green, and red lights. Tucked beneath the clouds of cotton snow, they glimmered like jewels, appearing and disappearing as they winked their bright eyes. At the same time, the elf chorus took up in the middle of "Winter Wonderland," their reedy voices echoing strangely through the empty mall.

I looked to see where my mysterious visitor was and saw that he was lying in a big fluffy bank of snow, his naked body sprawled out as though he were in the middle of his own bed. His cock was stretching up across his belly, and he was jerking off slowly as he watched me. Going over to him, I sank down into the snow, the cotton soft against my skin. Straddling his chest, I pushed my ass into his face. My balls pressed against his hungry mouth, and he began to suck on them eagerly.

My face hovered above his cock as I lay against his stomach, feeling the hair on his body rubbing over my skin and his mouth massaging my nuts one at a time, moving from one to the other. Leaning down, I ran my tongue down the length of his tool, from the tip of the fat head to the soft, hairy place where his balls tumbled into the space between his legs. His thighs were hairy, and my cheeks brushed against them as I rooted in his crotch, savoring the rich taste of sweat and maleness of his skin.

Moving back up, I took the tip between my lips and sucked at it. I was rewarded with a stream of sticky precum that coated my tongue and slipped down my throat, coating it with the thick taste of his jism. Urged on by this delicious beginning, I slid as much of his cock as I could into my throat, groaning as his thickness swelled inside me, his shaft expanding as his excitement mounted. At the same time, he moved his mouth from my balls to my ass, slipping his tongue into my crack and finding my sensitive asshole. My prick jumped against his chest as he found his way inside my chute, his tongue forcing its way past my hole as his hands gripped my ass painfully.

As I loosened up, he started to thrust his tongue more deeply into me. I began to match his movements in my ass with those of my mouth on his prick, sliding inch after inch into my anxious throat as he reamed me from behind. After a while, his tongue slipped out of my ass and was replaced by a finger that slid in and out of my slicked opening in time with the dick penetrating my mouth. Soon it was joined by a second, then another and another until four fingers were grinding into my butt, stretching it wide.

Having my ass fucked as I sucked his big cock was an amazing feeling, as if we were connected by a line that ran through the middle of my body. I ground myself fiercely against his hand, sliding my cock against his chest while I tried to push every last inch of his prick into me, loving the way the hair on his body tortured my sensitive cockhead and the way his dick choked me with its size. I imagined how his fingers would look sliding in and out of my hole, what my heated walls must feel like against his skin, and became even more turned on.

I wanted to taste his ass as well, so I let his cock fall from my lips and lie against my neck as I put my hands beneath his knees and pulled his legs back toward his waist. As I leaned my weight on his thighs his beautiful ass spread out before me, the cheeks parting to reveal his fur-rimmed hole with a pink pucker at its center. Diving in, I licked and kissed his hole until the spit-soaked hair swirled in delicate circles around the opening like a wreath. He tasted wonderful, thick and heady, and I wanted to lick him forever. My mouth traveled over the mounds of his beautiful ass, biting at the skin as his balls rolled against my throat and the sounds of the elves singing "Silver Bells" swirled through my head.

His cock was pressing insistently against my throat, and I was overcome by the need to have it inside me. Letting his legs fall back down, I turned myself around so that I was sitting on his chest facing him. His face was bathed in a changing wash of blue, green, and red as the lights around us twinkled. I leaned forward and guided the head of his prick into my waiting hole. As I pushed back, he lifted his hips and drove his tool deep into my willing ass until I was sitting against his balls, my cock pressed flat against my belly it was so hard.

"A nice tight fit," he said. "Just like going down a well-built chimney."

I couldn't respond, my mind reeling from the size of the dick filling me. It was a good thing he'd loosened me up with his hand first. I felt his head twitch somewhere in my belly and groaned, my ass clamping tightly around his shaft. He put his hands on my chest and once more gripped my nipples tightly, twisting them as I began to ride him in long strokes. When I reached the tip of his cock, he fucked the opening of my chute in short thrusts, sending flutters of pleasure through me as if snowflakes had tumbled onto my bare skin.

Sinking back down the length of him, I was once again filled with his solidity and his heat. My ass swallowed him greedily, feasting on every inch. My cock began to ache as I rode him, and beneath me he started to breathe heavily, working my tits even harder the more I pumped him. The fire inside me reached the point where it threatened to burst into my chest, and I felt my balls tense with the need to release. I started to pump his rod more quickly, anticipating the delicious spread of pleasure I knew would accompany my explosion.

"Don't come," he whispered, just as I was about to blow my load. "I want you to fuck me."

It took everything I had not to spray my spunk across his chest, especially as he gave one final push and I felt him swell inside me and gush streams of heat into my bowels. As I concentrated on holding back the torrent that roiled restlessly in my nuts, his mouth opened in a silent cry as he reached the edge, his tool scattering drops of seed throughout my insides. I felt them plaster my chute in thick waves and held my cock tightly in my hand to prevent myself from shooting.

Pulling out of me, he rolled me off him and knelt on his hands and knees with his head down on his hands. His cock, still hard and slick with his own cum, hung down, fat drops sliding into the cotton snow. All worked up from my own need to come and from feeling him explode inside me, I wasted no time moving behind him and slamming my prick into his delicious ass. My stomach slapped against his butt as I drove my cock to the root with one thrust, my hands tightly clamped on his waist. I thought I might pass out from the sensation that enveloped my overworked tool, and began to fuck him as hard as I could before I couldn't hold out any longer.

As I worked toward my climax, my head swam with a mixture of heat and the sounds of the manic elves, who had now reached the "Hallelujah Chorus" segment of their repertoire. My cock was sliding in and out of him fiercely as I pumped his beautiful hole, and I wanted it to last forever. Lifting his head, he began to beat his cock in time with me. His ass coaxed my prick to new heights of joy, and I pounded him furiously as the voices of the elves rose up dizzyingly through the chorus of hallelujahs that signaled the song's end.

As they reached the shattering climax, their tinny voices hanging on the last note sharp as an icicle, he and I came together. My prick exploded in rejoicing, showering his ass with a snowstorm of cum that roared through him with a wild howl. At the same time, his head flew back and a stream shot from his cock and spattered against the wall of the gingerbread house, where it trickled down like slowly melting snow.

Exhausted, I collapsed in the snow, pulling him down on top of me. The elves, finished with their concert, were quiet as the tape rewound itself somewhere inside them. The lights twinkled merrily around us, sparkles of color spinning over our sweaty bodies as we tried to catch our breath. Through the skylight, I could see that it was snowing heavily, swirls of white scattering across the glass in frosty eddies. We lay there silently, his softening cock against my leg.

"Looks like it's getting stormy out there," he said. "I should probably be on my way."

He got up and began to dress, pulling on the red suit as I put my uniform back on. When he was fully costumed, the white beard back in place and the cap on his head, he reached into his pocket. Pulling out a candy cane, he handed it to me. "Merry Christmas," he said, as he walked out of sight, "Merry Christmas to all, and to all a good night."

Remembering

I wrote this story at the request of an editor who wanted "something about leather." However, I was told the story could not contain any references to S-M, rough sex, or anything even remotely resembling force. Uh-huh. This is what I came up with. You may be interested to know that the dream I describe in the opening was one I really did have as a kid.

When I was a child, I had a recurring dream in which a man was staying at our house for the night. I didn't know his name or why he was there. I didn't know anything about him except that for some reason he excited me in a way no one else ever had. Hearing his voice would make me tremble, and when he touched my arm to say good night, the warmth he left behind was deeper than that of any fire.

In this dream, I fell asleep feeling the man's presence in the house, as though despite the walls that separated us he was holding me in his arms. In the morning, he would be gone, leaving behind a well-worn T-shirt on his bed. I would pull the shirt over my head and be immediately surrounded by the smell and heat of him. It was intoxicating. My head would swim as I breathed in his scent and felt the shirt, which had fit so tightly on his large body, float around my smaller one. Inevitably, I would wake from the dream to sticky sheets and a breathlessness born of unnamed desire.

No man ever left me his shirt in those days, but many have since. I have a drawer filled with them, a drawer I never open. I like to know that it's there, that inside are collected, like the discarded skins of wild animals, the shirts of men whose bodies I have felt sliding against mine as their cocks entered my ass, men whose mouths have closed over mine as they spilled their loads deep inside me and whose fingers have gripped my wrists above my head as they led me once again into those adolescent dreams.

The shirts are stained—with sweat and cum and sometimes

the faint scent of soap—and each holds the smell of its owner tightly in its arms. I do not take them out, because there is memory in objects, and I do not want the memories to fade. I prefer to keep them, neatly folded, in their drawer. Sometimes as I pass the dresser I feel their presence, and sometimes on summer nights I can smell their fragrance rising from the drawer like the breath of the flowers comes from the garden below my window. On those nights I wake, as I did when I was twelve, with my cock hard in my hand and my mind swimming with the memories of men.

There is one thing I do allow myself to touch. It is a jacket, made of black leather and much like any other motorcycle jacket seen on any number of men. But it is also unlike all other jackets, in that it belonged to one man not like any other man I have ever known. A man I wanted more than I have ever wanted anything.

The jacket hangs in my bedroom closet, toward the back, hidden behind rows of neatly pressed dress shirts. I do not look at it often, fearing that overuse will cause the memories to fade. I cannot risk forgetting. Knowing it is there is usually enough. But sometimes, especially when the air begins to change from the warm breezes of summer to the crisp breath of fall, just knowing is no longer enough. That's when I reach inside and, feeling the smooth leather beneath my fingers, it all comes back. . . .

I saw Gabriel for the first time on an October night. I had been working late at the bookstore, and it was after midnight when I finally finished and locked up. It was one of the first cold nights of the season, and I remember very clearly the way the wind felt as it played around my face. The moon overhead was almost full, and as I walked toward home, everything seemed to be glazed with a covering of soft, bewitching gold.

Dunstable is a small college town, the kind found scattered all throughout New England like rice at a wedding. It began life as a small fishing port, which over the years changed personas several times as fishing died and the people were forced to find different ways of life. Unlike other towns in the Northeast, it did not have the advantage of being either the scene of a witchcraft panic or the site of a historic uprising, so it had to make do with what it had, which was its quiet and its beauty. When Farley University set up house and the people began to come, first with their big ideas and later with their Volvos and their PhD's, the town found its true calling and embraced this new way of life as it had all the others before it.

Since then, the town had grown to surround the university. A new world of coffeehouses, meditation centers, and bookstores was built alongside the fish markets and auto shops, and within a decade no one would ever remember that once it had been different. The town had settled into a cycle of seasons that easily became familiar to anyone who stayed there for more than a year. I noticed Gabriel precisely because he did not fit into Dunstable's normal pattern of life. He appeared in my vision as something out of place, perhaps even out of time, breaking the ordinariness of my nightly walk home. Where usually I would see nothing but the smooth brick face of the wall next to the Black Sheep Pub, I saw instead a man leaning against the stone in a waterfall of electric light, watching me.

It surprises me now that I sensed no fear. If anyone told me a story that began with their chancing upon a stranger after midnight, I would immediately suspect some sinister motive behind it all. But it wasn't like that. Maybe it was the spell of the first autumn night, or perhaps just that after almost a decade in Dunstable I was incapable of thinking in terms of imminent danger. Whatever the cause, I simply nodded and said, "Hello."

Gabriel, although of course I didn't yet know his name, responded with a nod of his own, but he remained silent, watching me as I walked past him. While I didn't stare at him, I did glance long enough to take in his appearance. Tall and broad, he was wearing jeans and black boots. His upper body was wrapped in a leather jacket. He looked, in fact, like a lot of the boys who attended Farley, many of whom tried to adopt an aura of what I guessed they assumed was hypermasculine sexiness simply by putting on a motorcycle jacket plucked off the rack at James Dean's Closet.

Sometimes I would go to these young men, waiting in bathroom stalls or under the trees in the park, and suck their dicks. As I moved over the lengths of their cocks, I let my hands play over their jackets, only to find the surfaces stiff with newness, the zippers stubborn with disuse. Then I would bring them off quickly, with no desire or pretense of need, and leave before they'd even finished coming. Their posing disgusted me, their attempts at taking on what they would never earn leaving me cold.

Only Gabriel was no pretender. He looked like he'd been born in his boots and jacket. I could tell by the way he stood that he wore them with the confidence of someone whose body demanded them, that every crease and fold had been put there by experience. And I knew instinctively that he wouldn't look quite right in anything else. On his body, anything besides jeans and that jacket would always appear the wrong size, no matter how carefully it was tailored. It was he who made the leather come alive, and not the other way around. That, and not his strangeness, is what made him dangerous to me.

I hurried past him and made my way down the street. I knew he was watching me, and that he knew I was thinking about him. It was as though there was nothing else I could be doing, even if I wanted to. I tried to think of anything else—the night's receipts, the author arriving for a signing the next day, the leftover roast beef in the refrigerator. But his presence filled up all of the empty air around me until, halfway down the block, I was forced to turn around.

He was waiting for me. Still leaning against the wall, he had hunted me down with his eyes as I'd tried to escape. Now, even in the dark, I knew they were focused on me. I moved slowly, as if in water, retracing my path until I was only a few feet from where he stood. As I approached, he smiled. "Come on," he said, and I followed.

He led me to the alley that ran between the Black Sheep and my store. Stepping into it, he was swallowed by the darkness, and for a moment I thought about just running away, back to the safety of my well-lit home and the security of rooms filled with familiar things. But then I remembered the way his jacket moved around him, and I slipped into the night behind him.

The alley was narrow, flanked on either side by the high brick walls of the buildings. The moon overhead shone down between them, creating a thin river of golden light that ran between the brick banks. It was in this river that Gabriel and I moved. He turned to me and pressed me against the wall. I felt the coldness of the bricks against my hands and the weight of his body against my chest.

"Tell me what you want," he said.

I looked into his dark eyes. His face, I saw now, was almost boyish, with pale skin and full lips. But he was no boy. The strength in the hands that pinned me was that of a man, a man who knew what he was doing.

"I want to taste you," I said at last.

Gabriel smiled. "That's what I thought," he said, and kissed me. His tongue slammed against mine, pushing its way inside. His hands were in my hair, pulling my head back as he ground against my body. I felt his knee move between my legs and press up into my groin.

My hands freed, I reached out and touched the skin of his jacket. The leather was cool with night and as soft as Gabriel's kisses were rough. My hands moved over his arms and back slowly, searching out every curve of the body beneath the second skin. They traced the edge of his collar, treading the line between flesh and leather, between the warmth of blood and the smoothness of the jacket.

I moved my mouth away from Gabriel's and down his throat, my tongue running over unshaven skin until it reached the top of his jacket. When I tasted the rich sensation of leather, I put my hands on his waist and began to lick the edges of the zipper holding the jacket closed. The metal scraped lightly on my teeth as I moved down, sinking until I was on my knees, looking up at Gabriel. My hands rested on his boots.

"Please," I said.

Gabriel looked down at me, then reached for his zipper. He pulled it down, opening his jacket. Underneath he wore just a plain white T-shirt. I reached up and undid the buckle of his wide leather belt, then pulled at the buttons holding his jeans closed. They slid open easily, sliding down his muscular legs to his knees. He was wearing a jockstrap. The thin bands crossed the mounds of his ass, stretched tightly. The pouch hung down, weighted with his cock and balls.

Leaning forward, I ran my hands up under his T-shirt, feeling a thick cover of hair on his belly. My mouth worked on his pouch, sucking at the hidden prick. I could smell him in the material and breathed deeply. It was the smell of a man, heavy and rich, and it filled my nose as I licked hungrily at his balls.

Moving my hands around to Gabriel's back, I slid the jockstrap down, feeling his ass fill my hands. Tugging it down in front, I freed his cock, which sprang up half-hard over a pair of juicy balls.

I took it into my mouth, slipping the tip inside my lips and sucking softly. I could feel the blood beating in his shaft as his dick filled with heat and swelled to its full length.

Gabriel pushed against me, sliding deep into my throat. The heat of his skin, so different from the coolness of the air around us, surrounded me as I took him in. My lips moved over his shaft, sucking at his hard flesh while his swollen head filled my throat. His hands gripped my shoulders steadily as he pumped himself in and out of my mouth.

I sucked Gabriel for what seemed like an eternity, savoring the taste of his skin, the smell of him when I buried my nose in his thick bush. From time to time I ran my hands over his boots, sucking harder when I had the leather under my hands, as though drawing my need from it.

Then Gabriel pulled out. "Stand up," he said, and I obeyed. "Now strip."

Oblivious to the cold, I pulled my clothes off, dropping them to the ground. In a minute I was standing naked in front of Gabriel, the wind raising a chill up and down my exposed skin as I waited.

Gabriel stepped forward and grabbed my cock in his hand. He squeezed hard, making me gasp. Until that moment, I hadn't even realized how hard I was. Gabriel's fingers on my prick almost made me shoot. Even more beautiful was the feeling of his jacket against my naked skin.

"Turn around."

I turned, and Gabriel pushed me forward so that I was leaning against the wall. He moved in behind me, putting his arms around my chest. I could feel his cock pressed against my ass. I bent my head forward and felt leather beneath my cheek. Gabriel began to thrust, rubbing his dick up and down the crack of my ass. The small metal teeth of his zipper scraped against my sides as he moved, drawing forth tiny fingers of pleasure.

I ran my tongue over the sleeve of his jacket. His hands held me tightly, and the touch of leather pressed against my naked skin made me want him more than I'd ever wanted anything. The fact that he was teasing me with his cock was almost too much.

"Please," I whispered. "Please fuck me."

But he didn't. He just pushed against me ever harder, until I was almost shaking from his touch. I was sucking at the sleeve of his jacket, licking the surface, biting at the small snaps at the cuffs. Behind me, the head of his dick taunted me with every push.

Then he was inside me. Pulling back, he found the opening of my hole and drove home. My head flew back as he entered, and I felt his arm around my throat, blocking my cries. I bit the sleeve of his jacket where it pressed against my mouth.

Then he began to fuck me, in long, slow strokes. As his rhythm filled my body, I began to shake. The pressure of his cock as it slid in and out of my ass brought everything into sharper focus. I felt the coldness of the air and the softness of his jacket. I drew the night air into my lungs and smelled mixed within it the scent of leather and desire.

I pushed back against Gabriel, asking him to ride me harder. He answered by building to a fierce rhythm, slapping against my ass roughly. His arms remained around my chest, pulling me back against his thrusts and driving him deep inside me. When he came, he tightened his grip on my chest, pushing up into me in short jabs as his load spurted into me.

When he was done, he pulled out and turned me around. "Come on me," he ordered. He stood close to me, his hand on my shoulder, his booted foot pressed against my leg.

For the first time, I touched my own cock. Looking into Gabriel's face and feeling the leather against me, I didn't take long to bring myself off. With a few tugs on my dick, I watched as a heavy load splattered over the surface of Gabriel's jacket and dripped onto his boots. The cum lay pale and white against the darkness of the leather. Gabriel ran his finger through the stains, rubbing my cum into the leather. He was smiling.

I saw Gabriel many other nights after that one, until I knew the feeling of his body against mine as well as I did that of a familiar shirt. Even now the smell of him lingers in the jacket, left on my bed the morning he had to leave for good. I take it from the closet and pull it over my bare skin. My cock stiffens, and as my hand begins to slide up and down my shaft, I remember everything.

Danger: Fast-Rising Water

This was the second story I ever wrote. I remember sitting at my desk thinking, "The way to do this is to come up with a place for the characters to have sex that no one has done yet." Apart from the setting, this is really just a basic jerk-off story. But sometimes that's good enough.

Standing on the riverbank looking down into the black rushing water, I started to think that maybe a daylong rafting trip wasn't as good an idea as it had seemed when I was reading the Whitewater Adventures brochure I'd picked up at the station while planning what to do on my weekend off. In the pictures, smiling people had bobbed along down a peaceful river without so much as a drop of water on them. It seemed like the perfect way to relax and forget the pressures of having to whip thirty new recruits into shape.

But the pictures in the brochure were nothing like what I was looking at now. Although I got a lot of swimming practice in the police academy, these rapids looked rougher than anything I had experienced, crashing in white sheets over the stones that rose out of the river like the mossy teeth of some underwater monster.

I was about to turn around and head straight back to my Jeep and the safety of the crime-riddled city when my guide showed up. About thirty, he stood over six feet tall. He was wearing a white tank top and had the lean, well-muscled body of a man who spends most of his time out of doors. His dark hair was cut short, as if it had been shaved close at the beginning of the summer and was just starting to grow back in, and he had a day's growth of beard shading his wide jaw.

But what I noticed most was the bulge hanging between his legs. He had on blue nylon running shorts, and although they hung loosely around his legs, there was no hiding the equipment stashed beneath the soft ocean of material. I decided maybe the water might not be so rough after all, at least not if I could look at this guy all day.

"Hey," he said pleasantly, walking over and extending his hand. "You must be Tom. I'm Brad." His grip was firm and confident, and he smiled easily. "Looks like we're going to have a good day for rafting."

"I hope it isn't too rough," I said, trying to keep my eyes on his face. "I don't have much experience with white water."

"Don't worry," Brad reassured me. "I've been down this river a hundred times, and I haven't lost a customer yet." He laughed. "Besides, the action's always best when it's a little rough."

As I was thinking of what to reply to that, and trying not to stare at Brad's bulging shorts, another man came down the path to the river. Shorter and stockier than Brad, he looked to be in his early twenties. He was wearing shorts, too, but was shirtless. His beefy chest was covered with thick fur a shade darker than his light brown hair, and his skin was tanned golden. He looked like a jock, and I guessed he was one of the many college kids that spent their summers earning tuition money before heading back to play ball for another semester.

"Tom, this is Craig," Brad said, introducing the newcomer. "Craig plays lacrosse for Hanover," he continued, confirming what I had suspected about Craig's academic leanings. "He's helping me out this summer."

"Yeah," Craig said, "Brad here's showing me the ropes. I figure in another week I'll be leading trips downriver by myself." He had a low, smoky voice, and winked at me as he spoke, including me in his joke.

Brad slapped Craig on the back. "Don't get too cocky, buddy. You've still got a lot to learn before you can go solo."

Introductions over, the two of them set about preparing the raft for our trip, checking the knots that secured the nylon guy ropes and making sure there were no leaks in the yellow rubber raft. They worked with the easy grace of men who depended on one another, each doing his job quickly and smoothly, never getting in the other's way. As a police officer, I appreciated good teamwork and enjoyed watching them go about their jobs. The fact that they were half-naked didn't hurt, either, and I thought of a lot of other things I'd like to see them do together.

When Brad was satisfied that everything was in order, it was time to shove off. He handed me an orange life vest and showed me how to secure it around my chest and waist. When he put his arms around me, I could feel his cock pressing against my ass and had to work hard not to pop my own bone right on the spot. All I needed was for him to toss me overboard for getting too friendly.

"All right," he said once I was strapped into my vest. "You set for the ride of your life?" I smiled weakly, looking at the water, which I was convinced was now rushing twice as quickly as it had been ten minutes before. "I guess so," I said, trying to sound more excited than I felt, hoping he wouldn't hear the apprehension in my voice.

He and Craig also put on life vests. Craig told me to climb onto the raft, which I did none too gracefully. It was an odd sensation feeling the water rising and falling beneath me, and it took me a minute to get the hang of letting my body move with the motion of the water instead of against it. Once I had it pretty much under control and could keep my balance, Brad handed me a paddle. Then he and Craig waded into the river up to their knees, guiding the raft out toward the faster water.

Craig heaved himself into the raft in front of me, taking up the lookout position. Then, after giving a final push from behind, Brad jumped in behind me. "Don't use your paddle too much in the rapids," he said. "Just let the water take us where it wants to go."

I didn't have to be told twice. I was more concerned about staying in the raft than I was about showing off my paddling technique. As the raft moved out into the center of the river, the current grabbed hold, pulling us right into the rushing water. Pretty soon we were shooting in and out between the massive stones, riding the water like a leaf. Although I knew Brad wouldn't intentionally put us in any danger, I still kept my eyes glued to Craig's back, watching as he carefully used his paddle to push us away from the biggest stones.

After a few minutes, I actually started to enjoy the experience. Sandwiched in between two hunky studs, I was feeling the thrill of just letting go and letting the river take control. From behind me I occasionally heard Brad's voice as he shouted instructions to me about when to use my paddle or which way to lean into a rapid. As we dipped into one wave and rode up the other side, spray splashed over into the raft. Soon all three of us were soaked through, our clothes clinging wetly against our skin. I especially noticed how Craig's shorts wrapped tightly around his muscular ass, showing off the smooth curve of his cheeks as he knelt in front of me. A couple of times I almost lost my balance because I was deep in fantasy, thinking about giving his butt a good tongue washing.

Finally, the raft shot past the last rock, and we were out of the rapids. The river lay stretched out before us like glass, flowing smoothly and easily. "Well," Craig asked, turning to look at me. "How'd you like that?"

"It was great," I said, noticing for the first time how blue his eyes were. "I really felt like part of the water back there."

"It is something else," Brad said. "Now we have a good hour of smooth sailing ahead. It'll give us a chance to rest up some. You can even swim if you want to. The current here is pretty calm."

"I think I'll just sit for a while and enjoy the scenery," I said, eyeing the outline of Brad's cock where the water had soaked his shorts.

"Suit yourself," Brad answered. "I'm going in."

He shed his life vest and peeled off his tank top, revealing powerful, smooth pecs and a rippling stomach. Then he sat back and slipped off his shorts. His dick hung down between his legs, curving gently over a set of juicy hairless balls. Much sooner than I would have liked, Brad had slipped over the edge of the raft and was swimming away. His strong, even strokes carried him out into the river, where he turned and floated on his back, his beautiful prick resting on his stomach.

"Might as well enjoy the sun," Craig said. "It's not too hot this time of day, so you don't have to worry about getting burned."

He had also removed his shorts and was sitting with his back against the side of the raft, his legs spread. His head was thrown back, and his eyes were closed. One hand was between his legs, and he was rubbing his hairy ballsac, rolling his nuts between his fingers and tugging on them. His cock was stretched over one big thigh. Even half-erect, it was longer than most men are hard, the bulky shaft ending in a smooth, round head. He had no tan line, and like the rest of him, his cock was the color of honey.

The sight of the big college jock spread out in front of me like that was all I needed. I quickly removed my clothes, freeing my own stiffening prick. Feeling the raft move, Craig opened his eyes and looked appreciatively at my piece of prime lawman meat and smiled. "Looks like the sun's making everything grow today," he said.

I moved forward in the raft until I was kneeling in front of him. Running my hands over his wide chest, I felt the warmth of the sun where it had soaked into his skin. His nipples had stiffened in the slight breeze. Pinching them between my thumb and forefinger, I kneaded them until they were throbbing like tiny hearts in my hand, coaxing little moans from Craig's throat.

Craig lay back, putting his arms on either side of the raft and letting his hands drag in the water. Still massaging his tits, I bent down and took the tip of his cock in my mouth. My lips slid easily over the swelling head and down the shaft until I could feel the rough hair at the base tickling my tongue and my nose was engulfed in his bush. His crotch had a rich, musky smell to it that reminded me of a locker room. I pictured him in the locker room with his team after a game, and it made me horny as hell.

As I worked my mouth up and down Craig's rod, it grew harder and harder, swelling under the pressure from my tongue. Soon he was filling every bit of my throat, and there was no way I could keep his full length down my pipe. What I couldn't suck in I pumped steadily with my hand, wrapping my fingers around his shaft so hard I could feel the vein that ran under his cock pulsing against my palm. With his hand on the back of my head, Craig gently thrust his hips against my face, slowly fucking my mouth. Each time he pulled almost out, I wrapped my lips around his cockhead and sucked eagerly, milking drops of sweet precum from his slippery slit.

After a few minutes of working my throat, Craig pulled my head away. He shifted forward so that he was lying flat on his back and swung me around so that I was straddled over him, my cock hanging in his face. Wrapping his big arms around my waist, he pulled my hips down against his chest, slamming my prick into his throat. I was amazed at how easily he swallowed my dick without so much as taking a breath. This kid was one goddamn fine cocksucker, and I almost lost it as his throat muscles rippled along the length of my cock.

As Craig sucked me, I rubbed my body against his hairy chest, grazing his nipples with my stomach, feeling the roughness of his beard on my balls where they slid over his chin. Looking down at his quivering prick, I found myself staring at his nuts. I'd wanted a taste of Craig's huge balls ever since I saw him pulling on them, and now they were right in front of me, ripe for the picking. Letting my face sink down between his thighs, I pulled his horse nuts into my mouth and sucked them slowly, enjoying the feel of their roundness on my tongue. As I did, Craig fisted his meat under me, jerking roughly on his beautiful piece as I gorged myself on his hairy ball fruit.

Sliding my tongue underneath his balls, I ran it lightly along the sensitive ridge that led to his asshole. Craig's body jumped, and I felt the moan in his throat echo along my shaft where it was buried in him. He pulled his legs back, putting his hands behind his knees and pulling them apart so that I could look right into his crack. Like the rest of him, his ass was covered with fur. I buried my nose in the jungle between his cheeks, drawing the thick man scent that lay there into my lungs.

Spreading his ass with my fingers, I ran my tongue down his valley, slurping at the hairy sides. Licking slowly, I worked my way into the delicious center of his jock butt. His hole was slick with sweat and my spit, and I slid inside him effortlessly, his ass ring closing around my tongue like I was sinking into warm water. He locked his muscular legs around my neck and pulled me even deeper, the hair on his legs brushing my face as I ate out his tasty hole. I slurped eagerly at his pink pucker, flickering my tongue in and out of him until he was pushing as hard as he could against me and moaning.

I was really getting into feeling Craig squirm from the ass work I was giving him when a voice came from behind me. "I can't leave you two alone for a minute, now, can I?" Brad was leaning on the edge of the raft, watching the proceedings with an amused smile on his face.

He pulled himself up and into the raft in one quick motion. As he did, I noticed that his cock was hard as a rock, swinging up from between his legs and pointing toward his chest. Judging from the line of precum that drooled down the side of his tool, I guessed he must have been watching us for quite a while. Drops of water dripped from his balls, plopping heavily onto the rubber floor of the raft. "I think it's time to show you just how rough this water can get," he said, slipping into place behind me.

Brad knelt, his legs on either side of Craig's head. Taking his prick in his hand, he ran the still-wet head over my back, tracing a path over the skin just above my crack. Then, with one strong hand gripping my cheeks, he spread my ass and slipped a finger into my waiting hole. As his finger slipped through my butt door and slid into my burning chute, he pulled roughly on my balls, tugging them away from Craig's hungry mouth and holding them in his fist. My sphincter tensed around his finger, and it took all I had to keep from filling Craig's throat with a load of jism.

Once Brad had me loosened up, he pressed the head of his prick against my hole. I'd seen the size of his throbbing knob, and I knew it was going to be a real tight fit, but I wasn't prepared for the fire that ripped into my ass as Brad shoved his thick piece all the way into me. It was a good thing Craig's cock was buried in my throat, or I would have screamed for sure.

Brad lay against me for a minute, his arms locked under my stomach. His skin was still wet from his swim, and the water that dripped from his hair felt cool against my baking back. I tried to relax my ass muscles, letting my butt adjust to his thickness. Brad pumped against me in small, short thrusts, stretching my hole until the pain subsided and he could slide back and forth without tearing me to shreds. I could feel every movement his prick made inside me, like a piston sliding home inside a well-oiled machine.

As Brad gunned his cock in and out of my shitter, I slicked the length of Craig's pole with my spit, greasing him up until he flowed into my mouth like butter. The feeling of being filled by Brad's dong from behind and Craig's heavy artillery from the front was fantastic. Craig was still licking at my aching prick, and now he also had Brad's bull balls hanging in his face. Whenever Brad would slam up against me, Craig would slurp at his balls for an instant before Brad pulled them away again, dragging his nuts across Craig's face.

I'd almost forgotten we were on the water, but Brad's fucking reminded me, sending ripples underneath the smooth rubber skin of the raft like the muscles of a large animal tensing. The rocking of the waves also put Craig's and my bodies into motion. As Brad pumped me harder and harder, the raft rose and fell, sending our cocks sliding in and out of each other's throats with every thrust.

As the raft rocked back and forth in the water, we became like one big wave, rolling and swelling inside and against each other like swirling water, filling mouths and assholes with inch after inch of white-hot heat. Each time Brad's dick pressed into me, my own prick swelled inside Craig's throat as the fucking filled my balls with a churning load. I knew it wouldn't be long until I came, and I began to pump harder at Craig's face. As my shaft slid against his lips, I felt Brad's poker stiffen inside me. His hands clamped on my shoulders, and he pushed himself as far as possible into my churning butthole, his belly slapping against me like a hand across the face.

Having Brad's cock up my tight ass and Craig's in my mouth made me lose all track of where we were, and I didn't notice that the river had sped up. Suddenly I realized that we were moving along more quickly now, rolling over gentle swells. Behind me, Brad was groaning softly as he deep-dicked my aching hole. His motions matched those of the raft; he slammed every inch of his prick home as the raft slid over another wave, then pulled out as we rode the crest back up.

Just then, the raft slid into a narrow gully between a row of stones and shot quickly down the rapids like a bullet. Water splashed off the rocks and over the front of the raft onto our fucking bodies. The sudden rush shoved Brad against me, and with a loud grunt he began to fill my butt with load after load of cum, his cock spurting wildly, stretching my ass walls. At the same time, he pushed me deep into Craig's mouth. I felt his face against my stomach, and his lips clamped around the base of my cock. The combination of his warm mouth, Brad's spewing prick, and the motion of the raft was too much. I felt a comet of spunk roar up from my balls and explode into Craig's throat.

As my juice flooded his mouth, Craig began to pump his rock-hard jock meat furiously. His fist flew up and down the shaft, his cock beating heavily against my cheek. Suddenly he pulled up hard, gripping his swollen head tightly, and let out a loud moan. Through the spray from the river I saw his balls pull up, and then my face was bathed in waves of sticky cum. Craig continued to jack his piece, sending more whitewash over my chest and neck until it dripped down onto his stomach like rain.

As the raft exited from the end of the rapids, Brad slipped his still-hard prick out of my ass and sat back. He looked at Craig and me, exhausted and covered in each other's juice, and grinned. "Not a bad ride, boys," he said, stroking his cock. "And by my calculations we have about another hour until the next run of white water."

The Eye of the Beholder

This story began with the image of a man eating an orange. It developed into a story about finding beauty in unexpected places. I think I was really tired of only seeing stories about young, perfect men.

When I finally met Lorenzo Maschelli, he was eating oranges while a man with black hair and full lips sucked his cock. This took place in the back garden of Lorenzo's house in Rome on a summer afternoon shimmering with pale golden light. Lorenzo was sitting in a wooden chair in the shade of an ancient birch tree surrounded by the bright bobbing heads of scarlet and pink poppies. He was naked, and the man, also naked, knelt between his legs with several inches of Lorenzo's prick in his throat.

Lorenzo was patiently separating the slices of an orange he had taken from a large blue bowl that sat on the table next to his chair, peeling the fiery curves one from another and slowly placing them between his lips. Holding the orange in his long, thick fingers, he looked like a giant pulling apart the various pieces of a small world and devouring them. His eyes were closed, and as he sucked the juice from each segment, the lines of his face registered his pleasure at the sweetness of the fruit.

Not wanting to disturb him, I said nothing. The man looked up at me briefly when I first entered the garden, his dark eyes heavy with lust, and then went back to his work. Lorenzo himself took no notice of my presence, and I leaned against the trunk of the tree to wait. Despite the shade, enough light fell through the birch's leaves to make me sweat through the thin white cotton shirt I had put on that morning. It was beginning to cling to my skin, and I was thinking wistfully about nightfall, when the city would be washed in the cool of evening.

I had come to Rome to see Lorenzo and speak with him about

art. A friend had shown me Lorenzo's drawings, delicate pencils of men going about various activities in the nude, the previous spring. I had been enchanted by the strength and beauty of the figures and found myself drawn to them again and again. His subjects were the men of everyday life—a carpenter lifting a hammer to strike a nail, a farmer bending to check the soil, a priest about to settle a crucifix around his shoulders. Except for their nakedness, they appeared just as they would in life.

But the most intriguing thing about Lorenzo's men was that they themselves were not beautiful. Many were well into middle age, their bodies long since past the time when they would have been the objects of attention because of their youthful grace. Others simply had features that normally would have rendered them ordinary, eyes set too far apart, hands scarred by work, a nose slightly off center. They were the men that lifted nets of fish from the holds of ships wrapped in the mists of early morning, handed drinks to partygoers who never looked at their faces, polished the windows of buildings hanging on thin threads of steel above the heads of oblivious passersby. In a world of the young and beautiful, they went about their business unnoticed.

Yet Lorenzo had managed to catch his subjects at points where the movements of their bodies were at their most natural and, as a result, the most beautiful, filled with an unconscious masculine strength that had the power to rouse the most sensual and unexpected responses from the viewer. The farmer, the head of his cock nearly touching the ground as he squatted in the familiar crouch of a man who works the earth, was even more connected to his element by the fact that he wore no clothes. The priest, his cross hanging against a bare chest, drew even closer to the God he served by virtue of coming before Him naked.

Not everyone was pleased by Lorenzo's work, and there were several outcries when public exhibitions were mounted. Still, his works elicited a fury of attention as word of their beauty spread throughout the art world like fire through brittle autumn leaves. His sketches quickly became the stuff of dreams as collectors tried to buy them up, only to find that they were not for sale. Lorenzo, who seemingly supported himself from what was assumed to be a family fortune, would not offer his work for money, refusing all requests for purchase.

Satisfying my interest in his work by buying the several books that contained his drawings, I studied Lorenzo's style feverishly, hoping to capture the essence of his figures and discover what connection he had to them that enabled him to render them with such exquisite effect. I attempted to copy what he had done, but my efforts resulted in lines that failed to leap off the paper in flesh and blood, and shading that suggested sallowness rather than the flush of muscle rising over bone.

Finally, convinced that he held some secret that I had not been granted knowledge of, I set about finding him. After much searching, I was able to locate someone, a friend of a colleague's sister, who knew Lorenzo, and had thus acquired his address in Rome. I wrote to him, telling him of my desire to learn from him, and he had responded with surprising generosity.

Over the next months, we exchanged letters regularly, becoming as good friends as is possible when acquainted only by mail. But although asked several times what his method was, Lorenzo neatly avoided answering me time after time, instead writing vague comments about knowing his subjects and suggesting that his technique was not one that could be explained. I took his reluctance as an unwillingness to share his secret and stopped pressing him for information.

Then, in the spring, Lorenzo suggested that I come to visit him in Rome and see his studio firsthand. I responded enthusiastically, convinced that if I hesitated even for a moment he would retract his offer, and we had arranged for my visit. After landing in Switzerland, where I had business with an art dealer who wanted to show some of my work in his gallery, I boarded a train for Rome, my excitement at finally meeting Lorenzo mounting steadily the closer I came to Italy. As the mountains slipped away outside my window and faded into the flat golden expanses of wheat fields, I created an image of him in my mind, erasing it several times and starting over as I decided upon new details.

But any images I might have had of Lorenzo vanished when I entered the garden and found him with the black-haired man. I was surprised, certainly, to see him as he was. But something about the naturalness of his posture, the ease with which he and the young man made love, prevented me from leaving in embarrassment or training my eyes elsewhere. I felt as though I had his unspoken permission to watch, and studied him carefully.

I guessed that he was almost fifty. His hair was rinsed through with silver, and his skin was tanned the color of stained wood. Tall and trim, his body was neither heavy nor muscular, settling about him comfortably like a familiar coat. His skin was brushed with thick hair that swirled over his chest and abdomen, and his cock, long and thin, stood up proudly between his legs as the man ran his tongue over its considerable length. The man himself was very large and muscular, with the body of a laborer. The smooth mounds of his ass cheeks rested on his heels as he rocked back and forth. He also had a good-sized erection, which he was stroking slowly as he sucked, his balls swinging with the motion of his hand.

Lorenzo continued to eat the orange, every so often reaching down to rub the man's neck and push him farther onto the flesh that slid in and out of his mouth. He pulled gently on his hair, and the man moved his mouth to Lorenzo's heavy balls, mouthing them softly as Lorenzo jerked himself to climax. A splatter of white spewed from his cock like a net cast out by a fisherman, landing on his chest and on the man's wide face. Several more strands of heavy cream streaked over the hair of Lorenzo's belly, falling in thick lines across his torso as his hand pumped the last drops from his balls.

The man looked up, a smear of Lorenzo's cum on his cheek, and Lorenzo motioned for him to rise. Standing between Lorenzo's legs, he fisted his cock while Lorenzo rubbed his balls and the tender spot just below his asshole. When he came, it was in a series of short spurts that rained down on Lorenzo's chest and stomach. Picking up an orange slice, Lorenzo wiped it along his stomach, coating it with the man's cum before lifting it to his mouth. A string of pearly white hung from his lips as he swallowed the fruit. He did the same with a second segment and fed it to the man, who eagerly accepted it.

Having finished, the man walked away, disappearing into a doorway at the rear of the garden. Lorenzo turned and looked at me, his cum-stained hand shading his eyes from the sun. "Hello," he said. "You've come a little early. I would shake hands, but as you can see, that might not be a good idea at the moment."

"I see that," I said. "I hope I didn't interrupt."

Lorenzo laughed. "No," he said. "As a matter of fact, Antonio seems to perform better when there is an audience. Why didn't you join us?"

"It seemed more appropriate to watch," I answered. "Not that I didn't enjoy it."

"Ever the artist," Lorenzo said, standing up and leading me into the house. Showing me to my room, on the top floor looking out over the garden, he said, "Why don't we both wash up, and then we can have a drink."

Leaving me alone, Lorenzo retreated to his room at the other end of the hall. I washed in the small bathroom off my room and put on another shirt. By the time I was done, Lorenzo was waiting for me. Leaving the house, we walked into town and settled into chairs in the piazza. Before long, a waiter arrived bearing two glasses of iced tea, which I decided must be Lorenzo's regular drink.

Almost immediately, Lorenzo turned to me and said, "You would like to know the secret of my men, correct?"

I looked at him and saw that he was smiling, not angry. "Well," I began, "it is something that fascinates me. I have never seen drawings with such life in them before. Your subjects are ordinary men, yet they hit me here," I said, indicating my stomach, "as though they were the most beautiful young men. I don't fully understand why."

Lorenzo laughed lightly. "I will tell you the secret," he said. "But it will take something more than my saying it for you to understand." He leaned forward, and I waited breathlessly for his words.

When all he said was, "It is because I am in love with them," I felt disappointment flood my insides.

"That is easy when the men are beautiful," I said. "But your men are not so beautiful. How do you fall in love with them?"

Lorenzo laughed. "Every man has something about him that invites desire, one trait which, when brought forward, causes the person looking on him to want to look forever. The puzzle is in finding what that thing is. It could be the way his hands hold an apple as he eats it, the way his mouth turns up to show his teeth when he smiles at a private joke of his own, the way the hair on his forearms lies against his skin as he sits reading with his shirt sleeves rolled up."

Lorenzo took a drink from his glass and returned it to the table. He looked around the piazza and pointed to a portly waiter busily removing dishes from the table of a young couple. "Take

that man, for example. When you look at that scene, your first inclination is to notice the young man sitting down. He is very handsome, and it is easy to become aroused by thinking about making
love to him, about what his body would look like without clothes.
The waiter you would not think twice about. He is overweight.
His face is not beautiful. But look again at him carefully, and what
do you see? Observe the way his apron is tied around his waist.
Look at the way he moves so confidently about the table, knowing
where everything is without looking. Notice how he is in command of what he does."

I watched the waiter picking up dishes and putting new ones in
their place. There was something about the way he performed
these ordinary tasks that was mesmerizing. As he sliced a cheese-
cake and put it before the diners, he knew just how to hold the
knife to get a perfect edge, just how to place the slices on the
plates. Although I wasn't fully convinced, I began to see what
Lorenzo meant about finding the beauty in him.

"He is very confident," I said.

Lorenzo nodded. "Now, imagine making love with him. Think
of him taking the same time with lovemaking that he is taking
with his service. Imagine his hands stroking you as deliberately."

I thought about this, and was surprised at how easily the
image came to me of the waiter in my arms, and even more surprised at how the thought of it excited me. I imagined his prick,
short and pink and thick, in my hand, the heat of it beating against
my palm. I pictured myself fucking him, the round curves of his
ass beneath my fingers as I pumped, the sound he would make
when he came and the way his mouth would soften as he shot his
load over his belly.

"You are thinking about it," Lorenzo said, knocking me out of
my trance. When I looked at him, he was grinning. "You see," he
said, "it is, as the saying goes, all in the eye of the beholder."

We remained in the piazza for several hours, until the sky
began to fade in upon itself and dusk came creeping over the
stones of the square. Lorenzo paid and we returned to the house,
which was lit with the warm cinnamon light of outdoor lanterns
and scented with the sweetness of oranges from the trees in the
garden. I was fully prepared to sit and continue our conversation,
but Lorenzo led me instead through the garden and up a flight of
steps to his studio.

The small space was cluttered with pencils and paints, discarded cloths stained with multicolored bruises and papers with half-completed drawings scattered over the large wooden table that was the centerpiece of the room. The roughly plastered white walls were covered with rough sketches, some of which I recognized as the earliest incarnations of finished works I'd seen in books. Smells of turpentine and pipe smoke lingered like the perfume of a woman who had just walked through moments before.

"I thought that you might enjoy seeing the process firsthand," Lorenzo said, clearing a space on the table and setting out a handful of pencils and a clean pad.

"I would very much like that," I said. "But who will be the model?"

"I have asked a man from town to come over tonight," he answered. "A blacksmith by the name of Marcello Antovicci. He is due here in a few moments."

The idea of watching Lorenzo work was more than I'd hoped for from my visit, and I couldn't wait to begin. A few moments after Lorenzo finished, there was a knock at the studio door. Lorenzo opened it, and Marcello Antovicci came in. In his mid-forties, he was of average height. He was dressed in his work clothes, heavy pants and shirt and thick leather boots. His dark hair was cut short, and his wide, open face was clean shaven. In one hand, he carried a heavy leather bag that I supposed held his tools.

Lorenzo greeted the man warmly, as though they knew each other well, kissing him on both cheeks. He introduced Marcello to me and then clapped his hands together. "Shall we begin?" he asked. "Marcello, you may undress and then stand over there," he said, pointing to a spot in front of the table.

Marcello put his bag down and began to unbutton his shirt, his big fingers fumbling with the buttons. As he took it off, he revealed a broad chest, heavily muscled and covered in thick dark hair. His arms were likewise developed, his shoulders rounded from hours upon hours of lifting his blacksmith's hammer. After removing his boots, he lowered his pants and stepped out of them, folding them neatly before laying them with the shirt on a chair. Like the rest of him, his legs were thick and strong, the thighs heavy and the calves rounded.

Turning toward Lorenzo, he asked how he should stand. Lorenzo positioned him beside a small table and, opening the bag

Marcello had brought, removed a hammer. He handed it to him and asked him to raise it as though he were striking an iron freshly drawn from the fire. Marcello did so, holding his arm halfway between his shoulder and the imaginary piece of iron. When Lorenzo was pleased with his position, he told him to hold it.

Coming back to the table, Lorenzo took up a pencil and began to make a hurried outline of Marcello on the paper. I was amazed at how quickly the lines came together and the shape of the man emerged. After only a few moments, a rough image of Marcello had begun to form beneath Lorenzo's skilled fingers.

"His body is exquisite," Lorenzo whispered to me. "Look at how smoothly the lines flow together in his arms, at how the muscles at his waist stand out. It's as if he is at his forge right now, a piece of iron before him waiting to be struck."

I looked at Marcello, standing silently in the warm amber light of the studio lights, and pictured him in his shop, surrounded by the smoke from the fires, translucent lines of heat rising in swirls around his sunburned face. I imagined a thin bead of sweat running down his cheek and slipping along the muscles of his neck until it reached the hollow of his throat. I saw the muscles of his legs tensing and releasing as his hammer rang out on the glowing iron, sending showers of sparks into the air.

"Go to him," Lorenzo said quietly. "Discover what it is that draws you to him."

Lorenzo gave me a push in Marcello's direction, and I moved toward him. As I came closer, he never moved, holding his position as I moved forward and placed my hands on his back. The muscles lay in thick layers across his shoulders, and my hands moved over them lightly, feeling their power, picturing them moving rhythmically like waves as Marcello worked. I slid down to his waist and ran my hands over the full curve of his meaty ass, letting my fingers slip between them to feel the rough hair, then moving on to cup his large balls. His cock was thick and warm, and I wrapped my hand around it from behind, pulling it downward in a slow stroke.

Only then did he release himself from his pose, putting down the hammer and turning to face me. His dark eyes looked into mine, and his callused hands cupped my face. Then he reached for my shirt and undid the buttons, pulling it off quickly and dropping it to the floor. I placed my hands on his chest and felt the rough hair on it as I slid to my knees and took his swelling prick between my lips. The head was smooth and round, and my tongue moved around it in lazy circles, tasting the sweat of Marcello's skin, drinking in the rich smell of him.

His cock hardened quickly to its full length, the thick shaft straight and covered with dark hair several inches up the underside. I soon had the entire length buried in my throat, my lips pressed against the musky hair of Marcello's crotch. As I sucked him, letting his delicious prick slide along my tongue, I once more thought of him at work, his cock covered by his heavy pants, his hands twisting and bending the steel. I wanted him to hold me the same way, to take me with the same force.

Standing up, I dropped my pants. My cock swung up from between my legs, the head stained with beads of precum. I saw Marcello look down at it, saw his eyes cloud over. He came forward and pressed against me so that I was forced to lean against the edge of the table, which pressed uncomfortably into the small of my back. Positioning himself between my welcoming legs, he began to rub his body against mine, his cock sliding against my stomach, our balls slapping together.

Putting his rough hands under my ass, he lifted me so that I was sitting on the table, then pushed me back so that I was lying on my back looking up at him, my legs around his waist. His face was not that of a beautiful man, but I was enchanted by his power, wanted to feel him in me desperately, wanted him to fuck me. I raised my feet and put them on his shoulders, exposing my hole to him.

Marcello positioned his cockhead at the opening of my chute and pressed forward, pushing into me in one quick motion that brought with it a rush of pain that took my breath away. His big prick was stretching me wide open, and the feeling was amazing. I closed my eyes and lost myself in it as he started pumping my ass in short thrusts, the thick head rubbing over my sensitive opening every time he pulled out to the edge.

Marcello fucked me for a long time, adjusting his movements as he sensed that I was close to coming. He knew exactly what he was doing, and I felt as though I were made of glass and that if he touched me for one moment more I would shatter in his hands. My entire body was trembling as he made love to me, his hands as skilled at working me as they were at working a piece of raw metal.

When I finally came, Marcello stroking my chute with his prick in short thrusts that coaxed the swelling load from my balls, ropes of wetness flew from my swollen head and covered me in sticky smears from my throat to my waist. Marcello continued to pump me after I came, then pulled out and jerked himself off, his thick fingers holding his piece tightly as they moved up and down, his balls slapping against them fiercely. His first burst slammed into my face, a spray of hot jism that coated my lips and dripped from my chin. His next few landed on my balls and still-hard cock, fat drops that drenched me in Marcello's heat.

Marcello came several more times, each new spasm washing another load over my skin. Finally he stopped, letting his cock fall from his fingers and looking down at my cum-splashed body with a satisfied smile on his lips.

"It seems you've learned something from what we talked about, Mr. Caffrey," I heard Lorenzo say, his voice breaking the silence like a stone dropped onto the surface of still water from a great height.

The next morning, as I was leaving, Lorenzo handed me a package wrapped in brown paper. "This is for you to open on the train," he said. "It is something for you to remember your visit by." He kissed me good-bye, and then I was walking to the station.

Later, as the train moved slowly through the mountains taking me back to Switzerland, I carefully opened the package. Inside was the drawing of Marcello, his arm raised and holding the hammer. A spray of hair was visible beneath his arm, and Lorenzo had drawn the lines of his cock and balls perfectly. He must have stayed up all night finishing it. As I looked at it, I smelled once more the sweat of Marcello's skin and felt his hands on my body, and my prick began to swell within my pants.

Pass Completed

Playing touch football in the fall brings out something in a man. . . .

"You throw like a little old lady," Paul yelled from down the field as he trotted after the ball I'd just tossed to him. Falling short of reaching him by a good fifteen feet, it had bounced off into the trees. It was the fourth incomplete pass I'd thrown that morning, and this time it was really off the mark. As I watched him run after it, I thought once more that for a man who'd just had his thirty-seventh birthday, he had one fine ass.

Paul and I had played together on a weekend football league for about a year. Every Sunday when the weather was decent a bunch of us would get together at the park and toss a ball around for an hour or two. Strictly weekend athletes, most of us were well past the age for showing off our passing and receiving skills, happy just to get a break from the everyday routine of our jobs as teachers, doctors, or policemen. More often than not, we'd play for a while and then head off for breakfast at the diner, where we could brag about our minor triumphs while we loaded up on pancakes and coffee.

While I'd been attracted to Paul almost immediately, I'd been disappointed to discover that he played on the wrong team. For a long time after he'd first joined the group, he'd talked about little else but his divorce, which had recently become final. He and his ex-wife had met in college, where Paul had been studying to be an architect and she was the daughter of one of his professors. After graduation, they'd gotten married and Paul took a job in a small firm. Things had gone along as planned for a number of years until the day he came home to find her with her legs in the air and the FedEx man banging away.

Paul had moved to our small New England town shortly after, thinking that a change of scenery would do him good. He'd joined the football league a few weeks after he arrived, when he'd seen us playing while he was taking a run through the park. It turned out he'd played some ball in high school, and we welcomed him as someone who could add some skill to our amateur game. Watching his enthusiasm as he played, I'd quickly developed a big crush on him that made me feel embarrassingly like a schoolboy at the age of thirty-three. I hadn't had a relationship since breaking up with my lover and moving to the coast to work on my writing, and now the one guy I was really hot for turned out to be off limits.

On this particular day, the park was largely deserted. The first killing frost had arrived the week before, and all of the grass had rapidly turned brown under its icy touch. The trees had burst into color almost immediately at the first stirrings of winter, and now the ground was scattered with their leaves, as though someone had papered the field with patches of red and yellow. The air had taken on a palpable crispness, and the evening came earlier each day, driving people inside to sit in front of their fireplaces to wait for the first snow. A couple of the other guys had been playing when I first showed up, but the late October chill had sent them home after half an hour, and only Paul and I had stayed. Now, as I waited for Paul to come back with the ball, I rubbed my hands together to keep warm.

"Getting pretty cold," he said as he ran up holding the ball. "Feel like coming over for some coffee?"

Although he'd stopped talking about his wife so much lately, I wasn't sure I wanted to spend a whole afternoon alone with Paul knowing I could never have him. Especially with the way he looked. He was wearing dark gray sweatpants and a white T-shirt covered by an unbuttoned blue-checked flannel shirt. Tufts of dark hair were visible along the neckline of his T-shirt, and despite the baggy clothes I could see the curves of his body, especially the heavy bulge at his crotch. His brown hair was still uncombed, as though he'd just woken up, and the way he looked at me with his big brown eyes made him look like a little boy asking if his best friend could come out and play. Except this little boy was six feet tall and built like a logger.

"Sure," I said, watching his face break into a smile.

Paul actually lived a little ways out of town, in a big old house he was using his architectural talents to fix up. I hadn't seen it yet, but I'd heard all about it from him at our Sunday morning breakfasts. As we drove over there in his truck, he told me all about the new roof he'd recently put down. I kept myself occupied by looking at the trees slipping by us and the way the cold autumn sun glinted off the waters of the reservoir Paul lived near. Turning into his long driveway, we pulled up in front of the house. A grinning jack-o'-lantern was sitting on the steps leading up to the side door, and I imagined Paul carefully scooping out handfuls of seeds and cutting out the face alone in his kitchen.

As we walked toward the house, Paul was passing the football from one hand to the other. When we reached the long sloping yard that ran up to his door, he hefted it in one hand. "Go out for a long one," he said, pointing toward the house. "I'll show you how it's done."

I dutifully took off, running up the leaf-strewn yard as he pulled his arm back and threw a long, solid pass. The ball arced up, spinning, and then fell back down toward me. I put my hands together and it landed awkwardly in the nest made by my fingers, sliding sideways and threatening to tumble to the ground. As I brought my hands to my chest in a desperate attempt to keep the ball from falling out of them, I looked up and saw Paul running straight at me.

Before I could dodge him, Paul's arms went around me and I fell to the ground, pulling him down with me. I landed hard in a patch of leaves, the football still cradled in my arms as I stared up into the clear, blue sky. Paul had fallen right on top of me, pinning me beneath him, and I was very conscious of the weight of him bearing down on me. Then I felt something else, something hard pressing against my stomach. It took me a second to realize that it was Paul's cock, and that he had a hard-on. I could feel his breath on my neck where his mouth was next to my head and the way his arms were holding me loosely. His prick was getting thicker, stretching along my belly.

Then Paul suddenly pushed against me and stood up. Leaning down, he held out his hand. "Sorry about that," he said, grinning. "Guess I took you down a little too hard. Even winded myself there for a minute."

I took his hand and he pulled me up. Paul said nothing as he walked up to the side door of the house and unlocked it. I followed him into a large, bright kitchen. He threw the football onto the big wooden table and gestured around. "This is it."

"It's great," I said, looking around at his handiwork. I knew he had done everything himself, right down to building the cabinets, and again I felt sorry for him living alone and having no one to share it all with.

"Come on, I'll give you the whole tour," he said, leading me through a doorway into the rest of the house. Walking room to room, he showed me everything he'd done to the place. He had really done a great job, carefully stripping the old wallpaper and repainting, plastering the ceilings, rehanging windows. While he didn't have much in the way of furniture, the house was very comfortable. Paul was like a kid showing off his new toy, and I made sure he knew how impressed I was, asking questions about everything he showed me.

"The best part is upstairs," he said, opening a door in a hallway to reveal a staircase. "Wait until you see the view from up here."

The stairs went up for a ways, turned sharply left, and then opened out into a large, open space that Paul had turned into a bedroom. Nestled at the top of the house, it had two big dormer windows that looked out over the backyard and the pine forest that rambled behind the house. The narrow boards of the wooden floor had been carefully stripped down and refinished, and the walls were painted a soft green. He had furnished it very simply, focusing the room on a large wooden bed covered in a soft white goose-down comforter.

As I was looking out the window admiring the view, Paul came up behind me. His hand brushed the back of my sweatshirt, and I jumped. "Sorry," he said, pulling his hand away quickly. "You had some grass on it from when I tackled you."

"I'm not surprised," I said. "You really knocked me over."

Paul sat down on the edge of the bed and removed his sneakers, pulling them off and tossing them aside. "You just have to learn how to catch the ball without looking down," he said. "Come here, I'll show you what I mean."

I walked over and stood in front of him. Still sitting, he took my hands in his. "Look," he said, putting his big hands over mine, "you need to hold them closer together. Like this."

He held my hands loosely, his fingers brushing the backs of my hands. Having him touch me that way was making me a little too excited for my own comfort, and I hoped I wouldn't appear too nervous. I tried to concentrate on what he was saying, nodding but not really hearing anything as the pressure of his fingers on my skin increased. Then his grip tightened and he pulled me down, leaning back on the bed so that I was on top of him. He was still holding my hands, and I was looking down into his face.

"See what happens when you look down," he said.

His voice was strangely soft, as though he was afraid of something. But he made no move to let me go, his dark eyes looking into mine expectantly. I looked at his handsome face, his jaw shadowed with dark stubble, the small scar on his chin. His lips were slightly parted, and I felt his heart beating heavily against my chest. Without thinking, I leaned down and kissed him gently on the lips. When I pulled my face away, I saw that he was smiling.

He let go of my hands, and I ran them over the worn, soft flannel of his shirt, feeling the muscles of his shoulders and moving down his sides. I reached inside and ran my hand underneath the bottom of his T-shirt, touching his warm skin and feeling the hair of his belly rasp against my palm. Sliding my hands up his stomach, I pushed his T-shirt up, exposing more and more of his torso.

I stopped when I had reached halfway up his chest, letting my hands rest on either side of his rib cage and enjoying the warmth and solidness of him in my arms. His navel was surrounded by a splash of short hair, and I bent down and ran my tongue in circles around it, dipping into the center and kissing him. Moving my mouth slowly upward, I followed the line of hair that ran from his belly to his chest, lightly licking his skin. He tasted slightly of the sweat he'd worked up playing ball, and the sweet muskiness of it on my tongue combined with the rough touch of his hair against my lips in an overpowering way.

Throughout all of this, Paul hadn't once moved, just watching my every movement on his body. It was as though he were under some kind of spell, holding his breath until something woke him. When I reached the line his T-shirt formed across his body, I told him to sit up and slipped his flannel shirt off and pulled the T-shirt over his head. His chest was broad and solid, his pecs firm. The hair I had seen over his collar dusted his chest, and his nipples formed small rosy peaks against the lightness of his skin.

Standing up, I shed my own clothes quickly. Paul's eyes remained fixed on me as I removed my shirt and slipped my sweats off. His gaze traveled from my well-developed chest to my cock, which hung half-hard between my legs and was rapidly filling out. Climbing back onto the bed, I lowered myself onto him, once more kissing his mouth. His hands went onto my back and rested there, tentatively feeling the muscles of my shoulders and then moving down to my ass, where his fingers gripped me tightly. The feel of his sweatpants on my bare skin was a sharp contrast to the warmth of his naked torso, and I rubbed myself against him as we kissed, enjoying the way the rough material scraped against my cock and balls below while above I was pressed closely to his flesh.

Paul began to moan softly as I kissed his throat and tickled him by rasping my unshaven cheek against his skin. My tongue slid behind his ear and then into it as I worked slowly along his jaw and down his neck, exploring his body with my mouth. Taking hold of his thick wrist and raising it behind his head, I slipped into the dark forest beneath his arm, my lips sinking into thick hair wet with sweat. I nuzzled deep in his damp patch, breathing in his masculine scent and licking him clean.

I could feel Paul's cock pressing against me through his sweatpants, growing harder and harder. As I had suspected from the size of his bulge, it was long and hard. My own prick had stiffened as well, and the two of them lay alongside one another like great sleeping beasts. Moving down between Paul's legs, I pulled the waistband of his sweats down until the tip of his cock was sticking out. Wide and tapered to a heavy, blunt point, it was leaking a sticky stream that had matted the hair on his belly. Taking the tip into my mouth, I closed my lips around it and sucked gently, washing away the heady fluid. I could feel the blood pounding beneath his skin as I worked my tongue along the ridge and into his hole, drinking up his juice.

Sliding Paul's pants farther down and off, I got my first glimpse of his massive prick. The shaft was thick between his thighs, his balls heavy and round in their smooth sac. I hefted the big tool in my hand, sliding my fingers up and down it slowly while I milked more juice from the lips of his swollen head. It ran in a steady line down the underside of his cock before I wiped it away, sliding my tongue in long strokes up Paul's shaft.

Paul sat up, watching me lick his prick. "Come up here," he said nervously. "I want to suck you, too."

Positioning myself alongside him so that our faces were between one another's legs, I went to work on his balls, taking one into my mouth. Paul put his hand on my ass and pushed me toward him as he took my cock into his mouth. I was surprised at how easily he took the whole thing in, his lips eagerly moving up and down my shaft. His mouth was hot and soft, surrounding me like a warm blanket as he worked every inch. Looking down, I watched as my prick slid in and out of his face, his cheeks swelling and releasing as he blew me.

Turning back to his cock, I lazily ran my tongue all over the big piece, darting into the spot behind his balls and then licking his shaft while his prick slid against my cheek. I could hardly believe I was finally getting a chance to service the big stud I'd jerked off thinking about for the last year, and I still didn't quite believe I wouldn't wake up and find it was all a dream. But the cock in my hand felt very real, as did the mouth slurping up and down my crank.

Going down on Paul, I pushed as much of him as I could into my throat. He helped by pushing himself forward and driving the last few inches into my mouth. Wanting to feel as much of him as I could in my throat, I turned onto my back, pulling Paul on top of me so that he was straddling my face. That way, he could pump his prick into my mouth while he sucked me, his balls sliding against my face as he moved in and out, driving his fat head into me. Running my finger down his crack, I felt for his asshole. Pushing just the tip of my finger in, I massaged his tender opening, rubbing it while our cocks slammed in and out of one another's mouths.

We came at the same time, each of us unleashing torrents of cum that gushed down the other's throat. My mouth filled with Paul's hot cream as his cock pulsed again and again and I struggled to swallow it all, not wanting to lose even one drop of his milk. I in turn exploded repeatedly, and Paul drank in every bit of it. When he rolled off me, I could see that some of my cum was on his chin. Sitting up, I licked it from his skin and then kissed him.

We kissed for several minutes, our tongues slipping in and out of one another's mouths as we stroked each other back to hardness. Then Paul turned over so that he was on his stomach, his head resting on his hands and one leg pulled up so that I could see his cock and balls laid out against the whiteness of the bed in the space between his legs. His hair had recently been cut, and the back had been shaved so that his hairline ended in a clean, soft line that curved across his neck before giving way to the pale skin of his shoulders, which were speckled with light brown freckles.

Bending down, I kissed the space where the bones of his back pressed up against his skin in a succession of small hills, stretching my body along the length of his so that my weight rested on my arms and my cock was pressed into the hollow of his back just above his ass. Rubbing slowly against him, I ran my prick over the curves of his mounds. Paul spread his legs farther apart, and the head of my dick slipped into the narrow valley between them. I could feel the wrinkled mouth of his hole against my head and pushed against it. An inch or two of my cock slid inside, and I heard Paul gasp. But he made no move to stop me, so I continued to push in until my head had passed the tight ring of muscle and I felt the walls of his chute caressing my shaft.

Once I felt the rise of Paul's ass touching my stomach, I stopped. My whole prick was buried in his hole, my balls lying against his. For a minute I just lay against him, feeling the heat of his skin soaking into my chest as I stretched my arms along his and held his hands in mine. Then, slowly, I began to move in and out of him in short thrusts. He grunted softly as I loosened his tight butt, and I could feel the muscles in his legs soften as he gave in to the feeling of having me inside him.

I started to pump him in longer, faster strokes, pulling almost all of the way out and then sliding back in until I was completely inside him. Paul began to thrust back against me, his ass closing around my cock as I pulled out, his shoulders bunching beneath me as he forced his ass up to meet me. His fingers were entwined with mine, and he pulled me farther into him with every entry. I felt my prick begin to swell in anticipation of coming, and I increased my movements so that my stomach was sliding over his back in smooth, fluid movements, the bed rocking rhythmically under our weight.

When I came, I felt as though I had fallen into a deep pool of warm water that was fast closing over my head. My whole body shook as I flooded Paul's ass with my load. He seemed to swallow me up as I poured stream after stream into his eager hole, coaxing every last drop from my willing balls. When I had finished, I pulled out of him and he turned over. Lifting his legs, I slid once more into his welcoming chute.

Paul worked his cock steadily while I pumped him in short strokes, teasing the first few sensitive inches of his tunnel. Before long, he groaned loudly and threw his head back. A flash of white erupted from his tightly held dick and landed with a wet smack on his neck. Three more blasts covered the rest of his chest in thick drops as he cried out and squeezed his spurting tool. The sight of him blowing his load brought me off again, and I pulled out of him just as I came, covering his balls and prick with a fresh coat of jism before I collapsed next to him, completely drained.

After we washed up, Paul and I lay in his bed watching the sky outside the windows melt from gray to black as the stars came out and the moon appeared full and round above the trees. It was going to be a very cold night, and the wind was already beginning to moan around the house. But there in Paul's room it was warm, and as I ran my fingers through his still-damp hair, I felt as though I wanted the winter to last forever so we would never have to leave.

"There's something I want to tell you," he said. He was fidgeting with the sheets, his fingers rubbing the material together nervously.

"Not more surprises?" I was waiting for him to tell me he had just done this because he was horny, and that now it was time for me to leave.

Paul took a deep breath. "You know that story about my wife and the FedEx guy? Well, it was kind of the other way around."

"You mean . . ."

"I was the one getting the banging," he said. "I couldn't help it. Once I got a look at his legs in those blue shorts, I asked him in. One thing led to another, and before I knew it we were in bed and his cock was slamming into my ass. My wife came home just as I was shooting my load. She took one look and packed her bags."

I was speechless. "What happened to the FedEx guy?" It was the only thing I could think of to ask.

Paul laughed. "I don't know. I never saw him again. I was too busy telling myself it was just a one-time thing, that I didn't really like men. At least that's what I told my wife. But she must have known better. She asked for a divorce and I came here to try to get on with my life."

"And it worked?"

"Well, it did until I met you. At first I thought it was just because I was lonely, you know. Then I started having dreams about you and wondering what you were doing during the day. But I wasn't sure you were into guys, so I didn't want to ruin it by doing anything stupid."

"Until today," I said, ruffling his hair and rolling on top of him so that I was looking down into his face.

"Yeah, until today. It just seemed time to do something."

I leaned down and kissed his mouth. "I'm glad you did."

"Me too," he said as he pulled me close in his arms. I could feel his cock pressing against mine, beginning to swell again. "And you know what, it's the first pass you completed all season."

The Boxer

A friend of mine was putting together a collection of stories about sports and asked me to write about an archetype. I had a framed magazine cover featuring boxer Rocky Graziano on my office wall at the time, so I decided to write about a fighter. The story is like I imagine an encounter with such a man would be like—short, rough, and no-holds-barred.

The man I want is a fighter. Dark and brooding, he spends his nights in the sweat-soaked air of a downtown gym surrounded by other muscular, half-naked men, all of them working out their aggressions on punching bags and each other. No air-conditioned health club could ever hold my man; he prefers the run-down cement walls and musky air of a real boxing hall, where old men stand and smoke cigars in the corner while they search for the next great brawler.

When I arrive, he is in the corner, his fists beating the soft sides of the heavy bag that hangs from the ceiling by a thick chain. His big hands are wrapped tightly with tape that twists around his wrists and forms a ribbon of white across the thick hair of his forearms. He is wearing white shorts as well, and his chest is bare. He is a big man, well over six feet tall, and his body has been hardened by years of hard physical labor. He is a man of the streets, untamed and fearless, and watching him work out makes me want him more than ever.

I stand in the shadows of the doorway and watch him moving around the bag, pummeling it while his trainer shouts instructions at him. His face is set, his dark eyes intense. He has been working out for some time, and his muscled body is dripping in sweat. His short black hair falls over his eyes in wet strands, and his unshaven jaw is shadowed with the stubble of a beard. The thick swirls of hair on his chest are wet with the streams of sweat that run down his sides, and the trail of hair on his belly shines with tiny drops.

I have wanted him for a long time but have been afraid to even speak to him. Whenever we pass in the hallway, I hold my breath as his skin brushes against mine, feeling the heat of him pulse though me where our bodies have touched. I have longed to see him naked, but I fear that he will sense my lust at seeing his unclothed body and be angered by it. Whenever I see him come into the showers, his thick cock swinging between his legs, I leave quickly and go home to jerk off thinking about servicing him.

But tonight is different. It is summer and very hot. The air is thick with the threat of rain, and I need to feel another man's hands on my body, his lips against mine. After too many nights spent lying in my bed and fantasizing about him, I have come to the gym to meet my fighter, to tell him what I need from him, to give him what he will take from me. I know I am taking a chance, but I can't wait any longer.

He finishes with the bag and does a quick series of push-ups on the dirty gym floor, the heavy muscles in his arms bunching and releasing as he presses his body down and up again. When he is done, his trainer laces a pair of gloves onto his hands. Then he places a mouth guard between the big man's lips and sends him into the ring to face his sparring partner, a large black man in red-and-blue trunks.

They knock their gloves together to signal the start of the fight and then begin to circle one another. My man has his head down and his fists at the ready, waiting for a break in his opponent's guard. The black man throws several jabs at his chest, but my lover easily dodges them, leaving the man's fist to poke at the empty air. He moves like a great dark animal circling its prey, and he is beautiful to watch.

Then his break comes, and he lands a quick right to the other's jaw, sending him reeling back in several unsure steps. The black man pauses for a moment, shaking his head. He is angry, and he rushes like a bull at the man I am waiting for. They come together, their fists landing randomly against one another's bodies in a hail of punches that ends with them wrapped in each other's arms. They stay entwined for a moment, breathing heavily, until the trainer pulls them apart. I watch them and think about holding him that way until my cock is so hard I think it will shatter if I touch it.

They fight for several more rounds until they are both ex-

hausted and the sweat pours off their bodies, every punch that
connects with flesh sending a shower of wetness across the canvas
of the ring. My lover's trunks are soaked, clinging to his thick
hairy thighs. I want to pull them from him and suck the wetness
from his prick, to taste his bitterness on my tongue while his fingers entwine themselves in my hair.

The battle ends when the dark man goes down, the casualty of
my fighter's instincts. He has landed a solid blow to the other
man's face, and there is blood on the floor of the ring, blood that
runs from the fallen man's nose and across his open lips. My lover
stands over his prostrate body triumphantly, his gloved hands at
the ready in case he should somehow rise again. When he realizes
that it is over, he returns to his corner, where his trainer gives him
a drink of water and unlaces his gloves.

I wait inside the locker room for him, watching him come closer
to me as he walks across the gym floor. I am wearing nothing but
a towel around my waist, as though I am just about to enter the
showers, and I know that my hardened cock is visible. My heart
beats harder and harder inside my chest as he nears, and several
times I think about running away. But my desire for him is too
strong now, and I can't go back. When he enters the room, I keep
my eyes on his face. When he looks back at me, then down at my
prick, I force myself not to turn my eyes away. He moves across
the room toward me, and I feel my body start to tremble as he
nears.

Before I can think, it has begun, just as it does in my dreams.
Without a word his hands, still taped, come up and slip behind my
neck, pulling me into his body. I feel his strong fingers gripping
me tightly as his mouth covers mine. His tongue pushes roughly
between my lips and he is kissing me. I put my hands on his broad
back and feel the mingled sweat and heat on his skin as I run my
fingers over the tight muscles of his shoulders and down his spine
to the space just above his ass.

The smell of him fills my head and makes me dizzy with lust. I
want to melt into his body, to be consumed by him here in this
place that is so much a part of him, so filled with his presence. I
run my tongue along the muscles of his neck, licking up his sweat
and feeling the roughness of his beard on my lips. The rasping of
the hair on his torso against my body is electric. His hands go
down to my towel and strip it from me, leaving me naked in his

arms. My hard-on presses against the wet silk of his boxing shorts, and I can feel that his cock is stiffening as well.

His hands go to my shoulders and push me down to my knees. I kneel before him, looking up at his handsome face from between his legs. His dark eyes bore into me and command me to do what he wills. Reaching up, I grab the waistband of his shorts and pull them down his legs. He lifts his feet and I pull the trunks off completely. The material is soft and wet in my hands, and I bury my face in it, breathing in his scent and licking at the sweat-soaked cloth.

He is wearing a jockstrap, and his swollen cock pushes against the pouch. Leaning forward, I cover the barely covered tip with my mouth, sucking on it through the mesh. My hands wrap around his thick calves and slide up his legs to feel the full mounds of his hairy ass while I run my mouth over the length of his big tool, soaking the jock with my spit. When I can't wait another second, I slip my fingers under the narrow straps that cross his ass cheeks and pull the jock down, freeing his engorged piece.

Fully hard, he is even bigger than I imagined. Long and rigid as steel, the shaft is smooth and straight, the cut head round and perfectly halved down the center. His ballsac is heavy and covered in hair, the twin eggs hanging down between his thighs while his cock points out at me waiting for my lips. I lean forward and slide him into my throat, so hungry for him I take his whole length in one smooth movement until his thick bush is pressed against my lips.

My fighter wastes no time. He fucks my mouth in long, fierce strokes, his balls banging against my chin while he delivers blow after blow. My lips slide along his thick shaft lovingly as he shoves in and out of my mouth, and I lick up the drops of precum that ooze from his burning piss slit like they are water that will cool my burning throat. But nothing quenches my need for this man. I want more and more of him and could suck his cock forever. I savor every inch of his stud pole as he thrusts in and out of me.

I can tell my lover is going to come by the way his fingers clench in my hair and move my head more quickly along his shaft. I want to taste him roaring down my throat, to feel his cum pour into me. But he pulls out suddenly and uses his hand to bring himself off. After only a few jerks from his big paw, the first blast rockets from his prick and slams into my face, covering my mouth with a sticky smear of heat. More follow, coating my cheeks and nose in his spunk, and I lick it up greedily. I open my mouth and he shoots inside it, covering my tongue with his juice.

The taste of him fills me with new desire. I want to be taken by him, invaded by him. When I see that his cock is still hard, I know that he wants it, too. I lie back on the floor and spread my legs for him. He kneels, spreading me with his hands as he pushes between my thighs. My legs slip over his shoulders, and I feel him pressed against my ass. My cock is hard against my belly, and he grips it in his fist. The tape that is wrapped around his fingers scratches against my sensitive head as he milks a stream of pre-cum from it, but the feeling only heightens my yearning.

He takes his fingers and finds my waiting asshole. Using my own precum, he slicks my tight opening and pushes a finger inside me, making my prick jump and drawing soft moans from my lips. He fingers me slowly, opening the way for his dick. When he feels that I am loosened, he removes his hand and replaces it with the tip of his big piece. He leans forward and drives himself into my ass.

I cry out as he fills me, the thickness of his tool stretching me out cruelly. I love the way he feels, the way his head plunges into my depths and opens me up. He is being driven solely by his need to empty himself in me, and he thrusts quickly and savagely, the way he fights his opponents in the ring. His hands grip my legs tightly as he fucks my willing ass, and his eyes look at me teasingly. He knows that I would do anything for him, and that makes him fuck me even harder.

While he plows me, I jerk my cock, which has become sore and aching from holding back my load for so long. My movements match his, and soon we are moving in perfect rhythm with one another, my hand stroking up as he enters me and pressing down into my balls as he leaves. It's not long before we're both ready to come.

I wait for him to begin shooting inside my hole before I permit myself release. When I feel the first blast of him splatter my walls, I let go, my whole body shaking as stream after stream spurts from my overworked dick and covers my chest in ropes of heavy cream. We come together in long, agonizing shudders until we are both spent.

After he pulls out, we go into the showers, where we wash one another under the hot water, using soapy hands to bring our cocks back to life. Then my bruiser needs another round in my ring before he's satisfied.

Revelation

I am deeply interested in religion, particularly in how people respond to crises of faith. Many people have asked me whether the man in this story is an angel or a demon. I don't think it matters, so I leave that question for you to answer for yourself.

Father John Maguire was not having a good day. Morning Mass had been sparsely attended, with only a handful of the homeless looking for somewhere warmer than the subway grates to rest for a few moments facing him from his perch in the pulpit. Oddly, some of them seemed to know the complicated ritual of sitting and standing as well as, if not better than, his usual parishioners. They had listened attentively to his message about the Crucifixion, their unwashed faces staring up childlike and wondering, then left to resume their hunt for discarded cans and leftover sandwiches.

The afternoon had not fared much better, spent in the tight confines of the confessional listening to the weekly laundry list of petty misdemeanors of a young woman by the name of Rose Mahoney. A thin, lipless girl who whispered her transgressions from behind the screen as if she were passing on the secrets of life and death, Rose normally came for her weekly absolution with little of interest to tell him. This week's admitted sins included the imbibing of several glasses of cooking sherry, the occasional taking of the Lord's name in vain and, rather unexpectedly, a fleeting lustful thought and temptation to masturbate, for which Maguire rewarded her with three Hail Marys, impressed by her progress.

Once the girl had gone, Maguire had sat thinking in the airless cell for several hours, ignoring the calls of his assistant. He had remained there until the bells began to ring for vespers, and only then reluctantly dragged himself wearily from the comforting darkness. Rain was pouring down Amsterdam Avenue, and the candles scattered throughout the sanctuary did little to drive out the shadows of the November dusk. The few people who scuttled in beneath their umbrellas greeted him cursorily and headed to their seats, wrapped in unhappiness and damp coats.

When the final bell pealed, Maguire plodded the length of the sanctuary and climbed once more behind the pulpit. As he looked out at the scattered figures waiting for him to begin, the church suddenly seemed too large, the stone walls rising up and disappearing into the eaves. The stained-glass windows, with their colorful depictions of the saints and apostles, frowned down upon him with disapproving eyes. The altar boys moved about the sides of his vision like moths flapping around a flame. His head began to pound horribly, and he thought for a moment that he might faint.

As he was trying to clear the ache in his temple, one of the big wooden doors at the end of the sanctuary opened with a crash and a man entered, bringing the wind and the rain with him. From behind the pulpit, a crack appeared in the gloom that had enshrouded Maguire, and everything else faded into shadow as he looked up and his eyes were drawn to the stranger standing at the back of the church. While he could not see the man's face, he could see that he was tall and muscular, with the powerful body of someone accustomed to hard work. His short black hair was slick with rain, clinging to his head like wet leaves, and he wore dirty jeans and a battered black leather jacket.

He shut the door behind him with a shove of one black boot, then ran a hand through his hair, scattering rain and leaving it slightly tousled, a stray shock falling across his forehead. He walked slowly up the aisle and took a seat in the last row. Leaning back, he placed his boots on the back of the pew in front of him and put his hands along the back of his own seat. Besides Maguire, no one seemed to take the least notice of either him or his unorthodox behavior, even though one big boot was perilously close to the head of one of the more elderly members of the congregation and one arm hung loosely about the shoulders of George Pederson, the head deacon and a local banker of no small wealth.

Pulling his gaze from the man's face, Maguire continued with the service. Whoever the man was, his apparent invisibility to everyone else was not something the priest wanted to think about. He concentrated instead on the notes in front of him, which he had hastily scribbled a few minutes before the last person had sat down. The theme of his sermon was faith, something he now had very little of, and he was trying his best to muster up some semblance of sincerity. He had had it once, in abundance. As a student at St. Anselm's Seminary he had believed wholeheartedly that the world was a good place that only needed a little of his help to become a wonderful one.

But ten years of patient serving had worn him down. Things had only gotten worse, and the clear, bright joy that he had once conjured up so easily had faded into a heavy stone in the center of his chest. As he watched the parishioners of St. Mary's grow older and increasingly more unhappy despite his weekly attempts to show them that faith could wake them out of a spiritual stupor, he had become more and more bitter and doubtful. Now the ritual of proclaiming a belief in something he couldn't see was beginning to appear to him as the act of a madman talking to spirits.

He managed to finish his sermon without faltering, feeling the whole time the man's gaze on him like a shadow. The service over, he gave the call for Communion, and a line began to form as people shuffled slowly into the aisles and came forward to kneel at the mahogany rail in front of the altar. Maguire dutifully approached the first celebrant, attempting to avoid looking into her face. It was when he saw the faces that he was the most saddened, seeing in the eyes and the nervous set of the jaw as they opened their sticky mouths to receive the wine and the host that they were drawn forward more by guilt than by joy. Often he had to fight back an overwhelming urge to smack them forcefully across the cheeks, instead whispering "the blood of Christ, shed for you," playing his part in their weekly pantomime.

He moved swiftly through the row of partakers, administering first the wine and then the wafers, like a spiritual vending machine doling out candy for the soul. They came in waves, falling onto the worn velvet cushions before the rail and retreating again once they were fed, like seabirds scavenging the beach for picnic scraps. When he came to the end of the last row, he saw the hands clasped on the rail and knew instantly that they belonged to the man from the last pew. The fingers were long and thick, the pale moons of the nails clipped neatly and evenly. Black hairs sprinkled the knuckles, and he could see that the same hair began again at the solid wrists. There was a thin, pale scar running over the back of the left hand, disappearing into the cleft between the middle and ring fingers.

Maguire studied the hands for a moment, wondering what had made the scar and marveling that such work-hardened hands could be so clean; he had expected to see a fine coating of oil or paint on them. Then he remembered the cup in his hands and stirred back to life. Moving his gaze up, he saw that the man wore a dark blue shirt, the first two buttons undone to reveal a patch of dark hair at the throat. Looking further, he saw that the man was looking back at him intensely, and that he had large, dark eyes that glinted faintly with gold, like stones streaked with precious metal. His nose was straight and perfectly rounded at the end, and his wide jaw narrowed into a stubble-dusted chin with a small cleft just below full lips.

The man looked at Maguire expectantly, as if he were waiting for the priest to answer a question he already knew the response to. Fighting a strong urge to run, Maguire brought the cup to the man's mouth, noticing suddenly how heavy the chalice felt against his palm, which was trembling. As he tipped the cup forward, he watched the sensuous lips part, allowing the dark wine to flow over them. A drop slipped and began to run down the man's chin, and Maguire wiped it away quickly with the cloth. He did not, as was his usual custom, wipe the edge of the chalice where the man had drunk from it.

Returning the cup to his acolyte, he took a wafer from the pile on the plate, wondering at the thinness of it as he held it lightly between his fingers. He waited for the man to hold out his hands to take the bread, as most of them did, but he simply raised his head and opened his mouth to be fed. Maguire held out the wafer, placing it on the outstretched tongue and reciting, "The body of Christ, broken for you." As he received the host, the man opened his mouth slightly wider, taking in not only the sacrament but Maguire's finger as well. The priest felt the warmth of his lips as the man closed his mouth, then sucked softly, his tongue enfolding Maguire's finger. The rest of his hand was holding the man's chin and he felt the unshaven beard pressing against his palm.

It was over in a matter of seconds, and then Maguire felt the smoothness of the man's teeth as he pulled his hand away. He saw that the man was still looking into his face, only now a slight smile teased at the corners of his mouth. Maguire turned back to the altar quickly, trying to get the sensation of the man's tongue against his skin out of his head. He wrapped the remaining hosts in their cloth and then raised the cup, intending to drain the last dregs of wine. He could still see the faint impression left by the man's lips, the fine lines of his flesh in sharp relief against the cold silver. He paused, then placed the cup at the foot of the cross that stood on the altar. Later he would drink the remaining wine, as the service demanded.

When he turned back to the pulpit, the man was once again seated in the last pew. The choir swept through the final hymn and settled into the threefold amen. Maguire, barely hearing the last note die away, tore his gaze painfully away from the man in the last row and stood for the benediction.

The sanctuary emptied quickly after that, as people rushed home to dinners and evening plans, their consciences cleansed for another week. Maguire busied himself with the ceremony of extinguishing the candles and folding the white linen cloth. As he went about the work of cleaning up, he avoided touching the chalice or looking at the wine. He did not know why, but he could not bring himself to taste what had passed the lips of the stranger in the last row. He had not watched to see where the man went after the service, or whether anyone else had seen him go. The whole incident had disturbed him, and he preferred not to think about it.

A voice behind him broke the stillness of the air. "You feed your flock well, Father."

Maguire whirled around and saw the man leaning against the communion railing.

"Can I help you?" the priest stammered, suddenly very much aware that he was alone in the church.

The man opened the small gate that gave access to the altar area and walked slowly toward him, his boots tapping a steady rhythm on the floor. He moved with liquid strides, his weight shifting from side to side like an animal content with the knowledge that it is in complete control of a situation. He stopped several feet from Maguire. "Faith, Father," he said. "I'd like to talk to you about faith."

Maguire cleared his throat. "What exactly did you want to talk about?"

The man smiled, revealing the whiteness of his teeth. Maguire's hand burned in recognition, and he put it behind him, pressing it tightly into the small of his back.

"It's hard, isn't it, Father? To believe, I mean."

Maguire ran his free hand through his hair. He couldn't look the man in the eyes. "It is," he said slowly. "Very hard sometimes."

The man came closer. He ran his hand along the railing as he moved, trailing his fingers along it lightly as he moved.

"Sometimes, you feel as if it isn't worth doing anymore," he said. "As if there really isn't any reason to go on doing anything, any of this. You give and give but don't seem to get anything in return."

He stopped in front of the priest. Maguire stared at his boots, fascinated by their shiny blackness, by the way he could move so quietly in such large shoes. The man reached out and ran his hand up Maguire's chest, pushing his chin up so that he was staring right into the black-and-gold eyes. Maguire realized that the man was a good six inches taller than he. "Am I right, Father?"

Maguire nodded. The man's smile widened. He moved his hand up along Maguire's cheek to his hair, entwining his fingers in it. Bringing his hand toward his chest, he pulled Maguire forward, forcing the priest's mouth against his own. Maguire felt the soft lips press heavily against him, the roughness of the man's unshaven skin scraping his face. He tried to keep his teeth clenched and not let the man in, but in the end he couldn't. He gave way, parting his lips and letting the stranger kiss him deeply, his tongue filling his mouth with wet heat. He tasted the sweetness of the man's mouth, was drawn into the warmth of him by the force of his breath and the pressure of the rough hand on his neck.

The man released him, and Maguire stumbled back, catching himself on the corner of the altar. He steadied himself and caught his breath. His neck ached from where the strong fingers had grasped it, and his mouth burned. The man had bitten his lip, and the earthy taste of blood teased at his tongue.

The man was watching Maguire intently, and the priest felt as if he were looking deeply into the center of a pool of dark water, trying to catch a glimpse of something that lived at the bottom and kept scuttling in and out of view. He stared transfixed as the man removed his jacket and began to unbutton his shirt, watching numbly as the fingers slid the buttons from their closings, the fabric slipping apart to reveal a broad chest thick with dark hair. The man pulled the shirttail from the waist of his jeans and undid the remaining buttons until the front of his shirt hung open.

Hair covered his well-muscled torso in fernlike sprays, running down his abdomen in a wide swatch before disappearing into his jeans. His nipples stood out cinnamon colored against his skin, and a small gold circle pierced the right one cleanly like a halo. He ran a broad hand over the planes of his belly and up to the ring, twisting it silently between his fingertips.

The man reached forward and took Maguire's hand, placing it on his chest. The hair felt rough beneath his fingers, and the skin radiated a warmth that seared his flesh and sent shivers through him. He moved his hand down tentatively, feeling the curves and valleys formed by the man's bone and muscle, covering the expanse of his wide torso with trembling fingers. He put his other hand on the ringless nipple, feeling it press into his palm like a small tongue.

He ran his hands down, stopping when he reached the border marked by the man's waistband. He didn't know what would happen next, but he knew to wait until he was told.

"Sometimes, Father," the man said softly, "faith needs to be restored."

He put his hand on Maguire's shoulder and pushed him down to his knees. From his position on the floor, Maguire was looking directly into the well-worn crotch of the man's jeans. He saw the whiteness of the creases where they slid around the man's heavy cock and full balls, the cloth worn thin and smooth from constant contact with his body. There was a threadbare spot where the fat cockhead swelled out and threatened to break through, and the priest could see a glimpse of flesh through the straining threads. Suddenly he needed desperately to know what was beneath the faded denim.

But the man had other ideas. He lifted one booted foot and placed it on the priest's shoulder, rubbing it against his cheek. Maguire smelled the wetness of the leather, felt the heaviness of the boot against the bones of his shoulder.

"Worship is such an individual experience, don't you think, Father?" the man said. "We all need something different from our God."

Maguire nodded as the man ran the boot across his face and over his lips. The leather was old and worn soft and smooth from repeated rubbing and exposure to the wind and water. The priest licked tentatively with his tongue, tasting the faintly musty scent of the cow skin and the man's scent mingled with the more recent addition of rain. The stipples of the hide teased his lips, and his mind was filled with the image of the man walking in the boots over city streets and faraway roads, the miles of wear impressing themselves into the leather like an imprint of his travels, the bones of the man's foot softening the resistant leather with each step.

He ran his mouth over the black skin as if kissing the foot that lay beneath it, trying to reach through the tough leather to caress the toes and the skin made rough by miles of walking. He felt the curve of the boot over the toe and then the valley where it joined the sole. Soon he was eagerly washing, slurping at the leather, grinding his mouth against it. He ran his lips along the thick stitching on the sides, caressing the seam with his tongue. As he did it, snatches of thoughts, half-formed, swirled through his mind mixed with the peculiar ecstasy he was experiencing from worshiping the man's feet. Was sex perhaps just another kind of religion, just as visceral and heart-stopping as the celebration of the Eucharist? Was he in some way drawing closer to his own soul, becoming more alive? He felt that somehow this was true, but the answer danced just out of reach.

His hands were holding the boot tenderly as the man leaned against the altar, staring down at Maguire and pinching his tits, twisting the gold ring slowly. The leather was warming under the priest's searching fingers, and he marveled at how alive it felt. He was also aware that his prick was straining against the pants he wore under his robes. It pressed along his belly painfully, and he wanted very much to touch it. But attending to the man's boots called him, and he knew that stopping now to free his cock would break the spell that held him tightly in its grip.

He noticed, too, that the man had a hard-on. It stretched down his left leg, the fabric bulging out like a pale blue vein beneath the skin of the jeans. Maguire reached forward hesitantly, expecting the man to push him away. But when he looked up, the man simply nodded and he continued, his fingers fumbling uneasily with the buttons. Finally, he managed to get the first one undone. After that, the others came easily, sliding open like the locks of a hidden door. He saw that the dark hair formed a thick patch, and pulled at the sides of the man's pants to better see what grew in the strange garden.

As they slid over his legs, his cock came into view. As thick as Maguire's wrist, its head arced downward, pushed forward by a set of large hairless balls that swung like ripe fruit beneath it, the ballsac stretching under their weight. The oversized head was round and tapered to a blunt point, halved on its underside by a valley that led to a dark piss slit surrounded by tiny pink lips.

Maguire stared at the big prick in front of him, watching the balls rise and fall with the man's breathing. He reached up and cupped the sac in his hand, feeling it roll over the sides of his palm, sensing the life within it. He ran his fingers along the thick shaft, tracing the hairs that covered the first several inches before giving way to smooth warm flesh.

He leaned forward and kissed the heavy knob at the end, his lips parting and his tongue sliding into the mouth of the piss hole, tracing the smooth curve of the head as it ran down and then back up and over the shaft in an arc. He put his mouth carefully around the tip, letting his lips close over it and tasting the thick scent that filled his head.

The man's hand fell on his neck, urging him forward. The head slipped into Maguire's throat, blocking his breathing and forcing him to take in air through his nose. Still the man didn't stop. He pushed several more inches into the priest's gullet. Then he began to work himself slowly in and out, pulling the head along Maguire's tongue until it reached his lips, then drilling back in, each time forcing another inch in. Maguire soon learned to adjust to the thickness and sucked eagerly at the big tool working his mouth.

The man leaned forward, shoving his entire prick into Maguire's face. The priest shuddered, gagging on the meat that poured past his lips, the hair that scratched at his lips and tongue. Then his nose was pressed against the man's stomach, his chin nestled in the warm ballsac between his legs. The man's full length snaked into him, the vein under his dick beating fiercely against Maguire's tongue and filling his throat with heat.

Again the man worked his way out, and Maguire was able to suck more easily, slurping hungrily at the head as it exited his mouth. The man didn't move, so Maguire continued to bathe the head, rolling his tongue around and around the big crown while kneading the balls in his fingers. He slid his tongue along the veiny shaft, tracing the hardness to its root in the man's crotch. When he felt the prick melt into the softness of the man's ballsac, he began to lick in wide strokes, washing the pouch eagerly. Holding the beating cock in one hand, he burrowed deeper into the musky jungle between the man's legs, sucking at the hair on his thighs, rubbing the precious contents of his sac against his lips.

Maguire slipped one of the fat round balls into his mouth, sucking gently and letting his tongue feel the weight of it. It felt to him like eating the egg of a strange bird, and he thought of the sweet syrup he knew lay at its center. Letting the nut slip out of his mouth, he slid back up the man's prick, licking every inch until he reached the pinnacle once more. A thick stream of cock juice was flowing from the man's hole, and Maguire lapped at it eagerly. He slid his lips around the tip, milking it slowly and steadily. With his hand he pumped the shaft, matching the motions so that the man's dick became a part of a machine made of flesh and blood and bone, a piston that worked its way in and out of the channel of Maguire's throat.

The man moaned above him, a deep growl that rang in the priest's ears. He was using Maguire's mouth for his pleasure, thrusting quickly and savagely, his big hand pressing the priest's face against his groin until his balls slapped dully against his lips. This excited Maguire, and he felt something in himself open up as the big cock burrowed in his throat. This was something he could feel, something he could grasp on to and believe in with all of his heart. He sucked eagerly and needfully, taking from the man what he so desperately needed.

Suddenly the man pulled out of Maguire's mouth, leaving him gasping for breath, a string of cock slime dangling from his lips like a broken spiderweb. He stood back, smiling, and picked up the chalice from its place at the foot of the cross. Holding it in one hand, he continued to jack his tool, his big hand wrapped so tightly around his shaft, wet with Maguire's spit, that the head blazed a deep purple. His balls rose and fell like clockwork with the motion of his fist, and the priest stared at them, awed by their raw beauty.

Watching the man jack off reminded Maguire of the pictures of martyrs he used to look at in the seminary library, their bodies pierced and torn but their faces masks of ecstasy, as if the purity of pain were also the perfect joy. The man was wholly caught up in the rapture of his own prick, his face reflecting every pull and tug of his hand, lines of pain and pleasure crossing his lips as he groaned to the machinations of his prick and balls. He stretched his dick out in front of him, his hand pulling it down and out to its full length, the head pointing into the cup he held below it. Drops of precum slid from his gasping slit and fell fat and wet into the remains of the sacred blood of Christ. Maguire was dimly aware that he should be outraged at this, but instead he was overcome by the purity of the act.

As the priest stared, the man tensed, his hand grasping his balls tightly around the base. The engorged cockhead grew even larger as blood roared into it and a flash of white spilled from its lips, falling in long ropes into the chalice. The man continued to come, his seed streaming out in spurt after spurt, his fingers pumping his balls for the last drops. When he had finished coming, he put one long finger into the cup and stirred slowly, mixing his spunk with the wine. He lifted his hand, drawing out a thin strand of wine-colored cum, then slowly licked the liquid off, sucking his finger deep into his mouth.

Setting the chalice down, he carefully removed his boots and pants, folding them and setting them aside. Completely naked, he shone with a pale gleam of sweat that looked to Maguire's eyes almost like moonlight. His thick legs were covered in the same hair that spread over the rest of his body, and he somehow seemed more complete without clothes than with them, as if the jeans and jacket had been a disguise to hide what he really was.

He picked up the chalice and stepped toward Maguire, his bare feet making no sound on the stone. Leaning down, he offered the cup to the priest, holding it against his lips as if he were now the one administering Communion.

"Faith, Father," he said, "comes only to those who partake."

Maguire shut his eyes and drank. The mixture of cum and wine filled his mouth and he gulped, tasting the mingled flavors of the juice and the man's scent. His hands trembled as he tried to hold the man's hand back, to stop the flow that filled his mouth. But the stream came thick and steady, and he nearly choked getting it down.

When he had drained the cup almost to the bottom, the man pulled it away. Maguire opened his eyes and saw that the man was smiling at him and holding out his hands. The priest took the offered hands and was pulled to his feet. The man came forward and lifted the robe from around his head, leaving him wearing the black pants and shirt that were under it.

The man's cock was hard again, jutting out from his body and

up toward his belly. He undid Maguire's shirt, pulling the buttons
open roughly. He pulled it off and tossed it on the floor. Then he
undid the priest's pants, shoving them down his legs. Maguire
stepped out of them, standing before the man wearing only the
silver cross around his neck. The man reached forward and pulled
on Maguire's cross, snapping the chain easily. He held it up in
front of him, watching it turn in the air slowly like a bird on a
string unable to fly away.

"Symbols, Father," he said, "are so important. They help us believe in what we can't see."

Maguire winced as the man grasped his balls tightly and pulled
them down and away from his body. Holding the cold metal of the
cross tightly against the tender area below the priest's asshole,
the man wrapped the chain around his balls and cock, pulling it
taut until the metal bit into Maguire's skin. The tie beam of the
cross pressed painfully between his balls, one falling on either
side of it. His prick, engorged with blood, stuck stiffly out, the
chain encircling it and binding it to the crucifix.

The man turned Maguire and came up behind him. Dipping his
hand into the chalice, he took the remaining wine and stroked it
onto his dick. His thick fingers slid between Maguire's ass cheeks,
coating his crack with wine and cum.

"Do you believe in miracles, Father?" he asked, his voice low in
Maguire's ear.

The priest shook his head. "I don't know," he said slowly. "I've
always thought that miracles belonged only to those who talked to
angels."

The man laughed. The head of his cock was tickling Maguire's
hole, rubbing teasingly against the tight opening.

"Angels come in many forms, Father," he said, and slid his
prick deep into the priest's ass.

Maguire's mouth flew open as a searing pain tore through his
body, threatening to shatter his bones. But no sound came out,
only a short burst of air. He leaned forward across the altar, his
head resting at the foot of the cross, his lips open in an unspoken
prayer. The man's cock throbbed deep inside his belly, pulsing
with heat, each spasm sending new tremors throughout the
priest's burning bowels.

The man pulled back, his cockhead ripping through Maguire's
guts like hot lead. Then he roared back in, slamming against the

priest's ass and pushing the cross lashed to the priest's cock against his nuts. He grasped Maguire around the waist and began pumping steadily at his aching hole, each thrust slapping painfully against his bound balls.

Maguire lay under the man's body like a sacrifice, the pain clawing at his insides. His hands held tightly to the sides of the altar, his heart beating ferociously in his chest like an animal in a trap. He fought to keep the pain from overcoming him, tried to ignore the grasp of the chain around his balls and the cock in his ass.

Then, almost as quickly as it had come, the pain began to fade. It became a part of him. As the big prick beat against him, he let each thrust travel through him, welcomed the pain as pleasure, the fucking as a holy act. He let himself open to what was happening. The man's thrusts became quicker, his cock ramming in and sliding out on the wine and cum. His fingers gripped the priest's ass cheeks tightly, bruising the soft skin.

Having his ass plowed by this strange angel became for Maguire an awakening from the sleep that had plagued him for so long. He felt his own prick, stiff and hungry beneath him, rubbing against the altar as the man's weight bore down on him again and again, the trinity of his cock and balls touching his soul.

"Do you feel it, Father?" the man gasped. "Do you believe now?"

Maguire nodded, feeling the flesh inside him stiffen and swell, and he knew it was almost time. The man, sensing it also, plunged into the hungry chute, pushing his head deep into the priest's welcoming hole. Maguire's balls ached as they strained against their constraint. He felt a storm break loose in him, a wave of pleasure wash up and over his mind as he came in long spurts, coating his belly with sticky jism. At the same time, the man let out a roar that echoed through the sanctuary and shot in his bowels, a thick load that streamed out in a rush and flooded his insides with heat. The giant piece swelled and pulsed, and each time Maguire's aching muscles clamped around it, sucking the last drops.

The man pulled out, leaving Maguire's hole satisfied and renewed, and began to put on his clothes without a word. The priest lay spent on the altar, the man's cum slipping down his leg, his own cock half-hard and a dull ache in his balls. He did not turn to look at the man, but as he listened to him leave he knew that the next time he needed it faith would come very quickly to him.

The Perfect Man

I was trying to capture the experience of a couple making love to each other while each is thinking about someone else, in this case the same man.

They saw the man at the same time, but since neither one openly acknowledged it, each thought that he was the only one to have noticed. He was buying a newspaper at the magazine stand on the corner of Twelfth and Broadway, his black-and-white dog sitting patiently, waiting to continue their walk. He was not remarkably attractive or even particularly well built. In the world of bars and dance clubs in which they moved, he would never have stood out as one of the sought-after ones.

In fact, he looked like any number of men who had exchanged their weekday suits for jeans, a blue work shirt, and sneakers. His dark hair was graying at the temples, and he wore round, gold-framed glasses. They passed by him quickly, and anyone watching would not have even been aware that anything had passed between them. Certainly the man himself was unaware that he had been the object of their notice.

Perhaps it was his ordinariness. Or perhaps it was the dog. Whatever it was, he remained in the backs of their minds for the rest of the walk home like a secret waiting to make itself known when the moment was right. As they made the necessary rounds of the grocers and dry cleaners, their conversations were about the price of beef and the friends they would see the next day. But the man moved in the shadows behind their words, growing in size until it was time to be born.

The time came for both of them that afternoon. As Patrick showered, he suddenly thought about kissing the man's mouth and was surprised to find that the idea excited him. He ran a soapy hand over his balls, and his cock responded by swelling quickly, filling his fingers with wet heat. As he stroked it idly, he imagined running his tongue along the man's neck, then slipping it between his lips and feeling the hardness of his teeth. He came into his hand as the man's lips closed on his collarbone.

In the bedroom, Scott lay on the bed trying to focus on the book in his hands. His eyes scanned the page, reading and rereading the same sentences as his concentration wavered like heat lines from sun-baked pavement. The hard-on that pressed uncomfortably against the buttons of his jeans forced him to think not of the characters in his book, who were in the middle of solving a mystery he could no longer remember, but about the man at the newsstand. He felt a sudden need to jerk off and rubbed the head of his prick between his fingers through the rough denim, enjoying the feeling of the scratchy cloth on the sensitive skin of his cock.

In his daydream, he had met the man late at night while walking home from some unspecified activity. After a confirming nod and brief conversation, he had gone with the man to his apartment. The man was now standing behind Scott with his arms around him, unbuttoning his shirt and slipping his hand inside and along the smooth curves of Scott's chest. His breath came warm against the back of Scott's neck as he tugged at his nipple, whispering in his ear exactly what it was he was going to do to him.

Patrick emerged from the bathroom in a cloud of steam. He had a white towel wrapped around his waist and his skin was flushed from the shower. He looked at Scott lying on the bed, the hard-on obvious through his pants, and saw in his mind the man lying there smiling at him. His cock began to stretch with new life, pushing slightly against the towel as he walked over and sat on the edge of the bed and placed his hand on Scott's crotch.

Scott, irritated that his daydream had been interrupted, but feeling also a little bit guilty about his secret pleasure, touched Patrick's forearm, feeling the hardened muscles beneath the skin. He wondered if the man was hairy, and decided that he was. He liked the feel of hair on a man's body, the way it was both soft and rough against his skin. He liked the way it slid against his own smooth flesh when he lay against another man, their legs entwined and their cocks pressing against one another's stomachs.

He felt his fingers traveling up the man's arm, stroking the thick fur of his forearms and slipping into the forest of his chest. The man's chest hair was short and dark, spreading in a soft splash across his pectorals and shading his torso, where it formed a whirlpool around his navel.

As his hands swept over Patrick's well-developed chest, Scott's vision of the man became clearer. His body was wide and solid, his muscles firm but not sculpted into the too-perfect lines of the gym rats Scott was tired of seeing in all the magazines and infesting the bars like some kind of human vermin. His stomach had the slight softness of a man who did not think twice about indulging himself, a reassuring weightiness that Scott found intensely comforting.

Scott's touch on his arm was stirring Patrick's prick to attention. He took his lover's hand and moved it down to where the towel formed a boundary across his waist. He undid the buttons of Scott's fly, feeling beneath it the cock aching to be free. Scott lifted his feet up, his weight resting on the small of his back, and Patrick pulled his jeans down and off, depositing them on the floor. Scott pulled off his T-shirt, throwing it unceremoniously on a chair by the bed.

Now Scott's cock lay hard and straight against his groin, a streamlined wand pointing up from naturally smooth balls that nestled snugly in the valley between his legs. He pictured himself in the man's bedroom. In his mind he furnished it with a large wooden bed covered in white sheets, across which his nude body now stretched while he looked up at the man as he undressed slowly, carefully folding each garment as he removed it and placed it carefully in a pile on his dresser.

He watched as the man removed his shirt, unbuttoning the cuffs one at a time and then letting the shirt fall down his back. His pants came next, each button on the well-worn fly released by the thick fingers of the man's broad hands. Once they were off, revealing the long, straight legs, the man was left in his boxer shorts. Turning his back to Scott, he slid them over his ass, the firm moons of his cheeks emerging from the ocean of white cotton. Scott waited for him to turn, holding his breath as he tried to imagine what the man's cock would look like.

After seven years together, Patrick had memorized every line of Scott's body, knew even in the dark where to place his fingers and what it would feel like. He knew that if he wrapped his hand around Scott's tool that he would relax and push himself against Patrick's fingers, knew well the low groan that would come from Scott's throat if he were to take his cockhead between his lips.

He wondered if the man would moan also when touched, and thought as Scott sucked him about what his body looked and felt like. Unlike Scott, Patrick did not worry about matters of the how and the why. He and the man were alone together, that's all that he needed or wanted to know. The only detail he allowed himself was that it was on neutral territory—the steamy room of a bathhouse, perhaps, where names meant nothing and what occurred there had no bearing on what came before or after.

The man was once again kissing him, his lips searching Patrick's face and neck before resting on his mouth. He was already naked, his cock rising hard and insistent from his loins. Patrick's hands moved over his back easily. For him the man was smaller than he was for Scott, his shoulders narrower, his height slightly less than Patrick's. The skin of his chest was smooth and silky, the nipples well formed. Patrick slid his hands down the taut stomach and grabbed the waiting prick tightly.

When the man finally turned toward Scott, holding the shorts in his hand, his cock swung easily between his legs. He paused a moment, letting Scott soak in the sight of him shadowed by the moonlight from the window, before moving softly toward the bed. When he was standing beside the bed, Scott rolled over and took his prick into his mouth. As he sucked it, it grew harder and longer, filling Scott's mouth easily. When it would no longer fit completely in his mouth, Scott concentrated on the head, sucking on the smooth surface of it as his hand played with the man's hairy ballsac.

The man put his hand gently but insistently on Scott's neck, directing him with subtle movements of his fingers how best to give him pleasure. When Scott sucked too eagerly, the man slowed him with pressure from his palm, urging him to take time with the sensitive head, letting his tongue explore the tiny piss slit and the valley that merged into the shaft. Scott wet his lips with his tongue and let several inches of the man slide into his throat, where he let it rest while he soaked up the taste of his musk.

Patrick too was indulging in the man's prick, but which of them was getting pleasure from the experience it did not occur to him to ask. When Patrick did bend down to put Scott's cockhead into his mouth, it was the man's prick that slipped between his lips. Thinner than Scott's, it fit comfortably in his mouth like a hand slipping into a glove. The head was not much larger than the shaft, tapered to a blunt point and uncut. The thin foreskin slid smoothly over the warm flesh as he moved farther down the shaft.

As Patrick sucked the stranger's cock, the man groaned, urging him to take more of it into his mouth. He spread his legs wider and rocked his hips back and forth, fucking Patrick's mouth in short, gentle thrusts as he lapped slowly at the head, drawing drops of sticky juice from its manhole. Patrick fingered the man's balls while he sucked, tugging them a little roughly to bring deeper groans from his throat.

While Patrick blew him, Scott explored beneath his lover's towel, finding the throbbing prick that waited for him. Patrick's dick was drooling precum, and Scott used it to slick the veiny length of flesh, running his palm over the thick inches of man meat between Patrick's thighs. He pulled the towel from Patrick's waist and pulled him onto the bed.

Although it was his lover's body that moved against him, it was the man who lay beside Scott now, his hot mouth sucking on Scott's cock gently, taking his time. Scott ran his hand along the man's back, sliding into the valley between his buttocks, feeling there the dense hair he loved, so different from Patrick's smooth body. Bringing the man's legs over his chest, he was positioned directly beneath his balls, which hung enticingly down inches from Scott's mouth. The man's cockhead rested on his chest.

Scott leaned forward and licked the area behind the man's balls, feeling his body tense at the sensation. He ran his tongue lazily across the fat nuts. Then, putting his hands on the man's ass, he buried his face between his cheeks, something Patrick would never allow, finding it distasteful. The man's ass crack smelled of sweat and heat. At its center lay the puckered opening to his chute, and Scott dove in hungrily. Barely able to breathe, he kissed deeply, his tongue pushing into the man's ass, feeling the muscle close around it, tasting the sweet flesh.

The man responded by grinding his butt harder against Scott's mouth, at the same time taking Scott's cock deep into his throat. As Scott fucked him with his tongue, the man rocked back and forth, driving Scott's tool into his mouth, then reversing direction and letting his hole brush against Scott's lips. Together, they rolled like a paper boat on the ocean, rising and falling against one another's motions in an endless flow that would be broken only when one of them broke away.

Patrick stopped sucking Scott's cock and rolled onto his back. He stroked his prick as Scott knelt between his legs and began to lick at his balls. In the steam room, the man was on his knees in front of Patrick, hungrily deep-throating the cock, bigger than his own, that hung before him. While the motion of Scott's mouth on his cock was slow and steady, the man's was heated. Patrick enjoyed watching the man suck his prick, enjoyed the lust that seemed to drive him into pushing inch after inch into his throat.

He held the man's head in his hands, fucking the soft lips with long strokes that brought the head of his cock to just inside the warm mouth before going in again. The man's hair was rough beneath his fingers, the muscles of his jaw moving beneath the skin as he slurped on Patrick's tool. Patrick pulled his prick out of the man's mouth and shoved his balls forward, urging him to wash them. The man sucked first one and then the other of Patrick's orbs into his hungry mouth while Patrick continued to stroke his shaft.

Scott and the man were now intertwined in a tangle of arms and legs. The man had his hands on Scott's ass, with Scott's legs crossed around the man's neck. His mouth was busily working on Scott's prick while his own cock was enjoying the attentions of Scott's lips. Scott was pressing himself up, his arms locked around the man's hairy thighs and his stomach rubbing against the man's chest.

They broke apart, and Scott began to explore the man's body with his tongue, beginning at the feet. His tongue darted hungrily into the places between the man's toes before he took one of them into his mouth, the rough skin sliding against his lips. Releasing it, he ran his mouth over the top of the foot and up the leg. It felt wonderful to be tasting every inch of the man's body, every curve of muscle and rise and fall of flesh.

The man stretched, lying back on the pillows of the bed as Scott bathed him. Scott traced the inside of the man's thigh, letting his tongue flicker momentarily over his exposed cock and balls before sinking into the soft fur of his groin. The man's flesh gave way under his mouth, and Scott pressed his face into the warm skin, moving up until he reached the man's nipple. Covering it with his lips, he bit gently, just enough to make the man groan softly. The man's hands were behind his head, and Scott licked at the thick fur of his armpits, feeling beneath the skin the muscles of the man's shoulders.

Patrick, aroused by the vision he was having of the man servicing him, pulled out of Scott's mouth and urged his lover to lie down on his stomach. Moving behind him, he positioned himself so that his cock was resting between Scott's cheeks. He started to rub his body over Scott's, his prick sliding against the smooth skin of his ass.

But for Scott it was the man who was now grinding against him, the hair on his chest scraping pleasantly along Scott's back as he covered him with the broad expanse of his chest, his arms stretching over Scott's, his strong fingers holding Scott's wrists. The man's breath was hot and ragged on the back of his neck once more as he groaned with the desire that Scott's tonguing had roused in him. Scott waited, holding his breath, for the moment when the big cock that teased his asshole would enter it, filling him completely.

In Patrick's steam room, the man was bent over the table that was the centerpiece of the room. His legs were spread, and Patrick was concentrating on rubbing lube into the tight pucker of his asshole. Pink and clean, it was nestled between the round globes of the man's smooth buttocks like a small flower waiting for him to discover it.

His finger slipped into the man's opening, gliding in up to the knuckle. Patrick could feel the muscles of the man's sphincter contract around his hand, hugging him tightly. He turned his finger, loosening the man slightly, and began to thrust. The man rocked back, meeting his hand as it entered him from behind, his balls swinging between his legs as his cock bobbed untouched with the motion of his body.

Patrick removed his finger and pushed himself up against the man's backside, his cock snug in the valley of his ass. He reached around and pinched the man's tits in his fingers. As he did, his cock slipped down and into the waiting hole. Holding the man around the chest, he slid swiftly into him.

Patrick's cock entered Scott's ass, but it was the man's prick that he felt filling him. With one deft movement he was inside Scott's hungry tunnel, stretching it around his thick width. As the big head plowed past his prostate, Scott felt a stream of juice dribble from his dickhead. He reached down and smeared it into his palm, working his hand up and down his cock.

Scott pulled his legs forward so that he was on his knees, giving the man more room to move. The man pulled back, his dick leaving behind a pleasant sort of pain that reminded Scott of the man's size and made him anxious for its return. Using the first few inches of his prick, he teased the opening of Scott's ass, massaging the sensitive walls expertly until Scott was squirming and rubbing his face in the pillow.

Patrick was busy in his own world, his cock hammering the man's asshole mercilessly. The harder he fucked him, the more the man cried out for more, until Patrick was pounding his prick in quicker and quicker thrusts, each one bringing his balls into painful contact with the man's butt. He wasn't sure how much longer he could hold off the tide that was threatening to break inside him.

The man, sensing that Scott was nearing the edge, began to fuck him in long strokes, giving him every inch of his big tool. At the same time, Scott was jerking his cock in time with the man's movements, his hand gliding over the layer of sticky ooze that slid from his dickhead.

As Patrick shot the first volley of his load into Scott's ass, he grabbed the man around the waist and drove his prick home, filling the man's shitter with cream. The man shot his own stream of cum in short bursts that coated the top of the table in fat drops, his balls pumping out round after round until they were empty, his voice crying out to God.

Scott came, too, the spunk streaming out over his hand as he pumped himself dry. Behind him, the man was moaning as his load emptied into Scott's chute in a shuddering orgasm. His thick piece tensed and released, twitching inside Scott's aching hole.

When it was over, Scott and Patrick lay exhausted and drained in each other's arms, each telling the other how good it had been. Then, rolling apart, each went to sleep dreaming about the perfect man.

The Ways of the Father

I did have a college roommate named Adam, but I never saw him naked and never met his father. Pity.

I could tell by the off-key singing and the thin mist of steam coming from beneath the bathroom door that Adam was taking a shower. I knew he was in a good mood because he was really letting loose, belting out the words in his deep voice as the water spattered against the plastic curtain. He always forgot to close it completely, and there was probably going to be a huge puddle on the floor by the time he was done. His clothes were scattered around the room, and the biology textbook on his desk was still opened to the same page it had been on when I left for my ancient history class an hour before.

Adam had transferred to Evans from another university at the beginning of the year, after being recruited by the baseball coach. We played on the team together, he in right field and I at second base, and we ended up living together when my original roommate dropped out after the first month. When Adam asked if he could move in, I was quick to say yes, since by then I had a major crush on him. But I also knew it was a big mistake.

The first time I'd seen Adam naked in the locker room I'd fallen for him. Closing in on six feet tall, he was the kind of guy you'd expect to see working shirtless in a cornfield somewhere in the Midwest, his skin tanned by days under the sun and his muscles tight from hard work. His light brown hair set off his startlingly blue-green eyes, and he had a slow, relaxed way of talking that made me wonder what it would be like to kiss his full lips and feel his hands running over my back. It didn't help any that he had a beautiful cock to go with the rest of him. Long and cut, it swung between his legs as he walked, the head hanging a couple of inches below his heavy, hairless balls. His ass was just as delicious, and it was all I could do not to reach out and touch the round curves of his cheeks every time he walked by me.

As I listened to the sounds of Adam showering, I began to picture how he would look doing it. I imagined the water running over his smooth, muscled chest and down his strong legs, the soap slipping around his cock and balls and falling in soft clouds as he lathered himself up. I saw his wet hair plastered to his forehead and knew just how it would smell if I nuzzled him behind the ear, what it would feel like to lick his neck. I wondered if he was playing with himself, his prick stiffening in his hand as he stroked it slowly, the water beating on his skin like fingers as he rubbed his balls. I could see the thick head of his dick swell as he pumped it full of heat, his hand gliding along the long shaft on a skin of soap.

As the picture in my mind grew more intense, my cock began to harden in my jeans. I rubbed it through my pants as I thought about Adam jerking off in the next room, pleasuring himself while he thought he was alone. I wanted to see him bring himself off, arching his back under the water as the long thread of warm, creamy cum I knew would shoot from his dick smacked against the tiles. Better yet, I wanted him to come on my face, his load covering my lips and neck with sweet jism that I could lick off and taste on my tongue.

The idea of it was too much. Checking to make sure the bathroom door was tightly closed, I quickly unbuttoned my jeans and slid them off. My prick strained against the cotton of my boxers, and there was a thick smear of cock juice staining the thin material where the head of my tool was leaking in anticipation. Removing my shirt, I lay down on my bed and spread my legs. My dick lay straight along my furry belly, the whiteness of its skin pale against the dark hair that surrounded it. My balls had pulled up against my body, and I worked them in one hand while I started to stroke my tool, urging a stream of silvery drool from the little pink lips of my bullet-shaped head. As I pumped my shaft I envisioned hot soapy water sliding down the crack of Adam's bare ass and how the heat would make his skin flush as the blood surged to the surface. I wanted to be standing behind him, rubbing the head of my dick along his crack, sliding it beneath his balls as I fucked him slowly between the legs.

I pictured Adam bending over in the shower, his golden ass cheeks parting to reveal his rosy pucker as he braced himself against the wall so that I could enter him. I could practically feel the warmth of him as I soaped my cock up and slipped it into his tight hole, sliding my prick up his chute in one long rush. I would put my arms around him to pull him tightly against me, and I knew how his nipples would feel in my fingers when I pinched them gently as I fucked him from behind, my hairy stomach slipping along his smooth back. It was so real that I started to groan as I got closer and closer to spilling over.

My fantasy seemed so real that I didn't hear Adam turn off the water. Just as I was about to come, I saw a shadow move as the bathroom door began to open. Quickly, I flipped over onto my stomach at the same moment that Adam walked in wearing nothing but a towel wrapped around his waist. His prick made a sizable bulge under the white cloth, and I knew that only minutes before it had been hard and was still half-stiff from the workout he'd given it. My own cock, swollen and overheated, was pressed painfully against my groin as I pretended to be resting casually on the bed. I was still close to coming, and my balls were aching from the need to release their load.

Adam walked past me and slapped me roughly on the ass, just as if we were in the locker room after a practice. The touch of his hand on my butt sent me over the edge, and I blew my load in three giant spurts. I could feel warm cum squirting all over my belly and ground my face into my pillow as I tried not to moan out loud from the intense feeling crashing through me. I came so hard that my asshole was tensing and releasing as my balls emptied beneath me.

"So, what's going on?" Adam asked as he dropped his towel and pulled some underwear and jeans out of his dresser drawer.

I was still riding the wave of my orgasm and had to swallow a few times before I could answer him. "Not much," I finally said, feeling the hot load beneath me soaking into the sheets and sticking to my hair. Adam didn't seem to notice that anything was out of the ordinary, and I wondered how the hell I was going to get up without him seeing the mess on my belly and dick. To make things worse, he came and stood right beside me while he pulled on his shorts, his big cock bouncing only inches from my face as he tucked it away.

"Hey, what are you doing this weekend?" he asked.

I cleared my head and tried to sound normal. "Nothing, I guess. Why?"

Adam sat on my bed and pulled on his socks, his ass only inches from where my prick was still burning from the force of my shots. I could feel the warmth of his skin and started to get hard again. "My dad has a vacation house on a lake about two hours from here," he said. "I'm going up there, and he said I could bring someone along if I wanted to. Feel like coming along?"

While I'd certainly thought about it enough times, I'd never tried anything with Adam. There had been many nights when I'd lain only feet away from him with a raging hard-on, thinking about lifting the sheets and giving him the blow job of his life. And more than once I'd seen him in the showers after practice and had to leave before my stiffening cock betrayed what I was thinking about doing to his sweet ass. But I'd always been too scared to actually approach him, and now with summer closing in on the school year, my chances were running out. A weekend in a house with him seemed like a perfect opportunity, even if his mother and father would be there.

"Sure, I'd like to meet your parents," I said.

"Oh, it'll just be my dad," Adam said. "My folks divorced when I was seven."

Great, I thought. *It's going to be a father-and-son weekend and I'll be spending it trying to get into Junior's pants.* I could just see it, meeting Adam's father and saying, "It's really nice of you to invite me up, sir. Do you mind if I suck off your son in your house later on?" Fortunately, Adam got up then and sat down to study some more and I was able to get up and into the bathroom before he could see the cum stain on my stomach. A quick shower of my own and another round of beating off, and he never knew anything had happened.

Friday afternoon we cut our last two classes and drove the three hours up to the house. The whole time we were on the road, I kept thinking of ways to get my hands on Adam's body. I pictured doing him in the woods near the lake or on the living-room floor while his father slept. I even fantasized that maybe we'd have to share a bed. A couple of times my hard-on poked against my jeans and I had to think about something else to keep from giving myself away.

When we got to the house, Adam pulled in and honked his horn in greeting. A man came out from behind the house and waved. "That's Dad," Adam said as he pulled to a stop. "Don't worry if he seems a little surprised at seeing you. I think he thought I was bringing a girlfriend with me or something."

"Oh, thanks," I said, punching him in the arm. "I'll just tell him that we're special friends. That should really make him happy." Adam just grinned wickedly and opened the door. "Come on," he said. "It won't be so bad." I got out and followed him, wondering for the first time why it was Adam hadn't brought a girl with him. There certainly were enough who would have come in a second if he'd asked. My spirits rose as I let myself think that maybe he was interested in me after all.

But first I had to get past his father. In his early forties, Jake Hendricks was simply an older version of his son. He was a little taller and a little broader in the shoulders, but he had the same blue-green eyes and the same light brown hair, although his was cut shorter than Adam's and was beginning to gray at the sides. Adam had once told me his father owned a construction company, and it was easy to picture him walking around a building site barking out instructions. When Adam introduced us he grasped my hand in a firm grip and smiled as he shook it, his lip curled up in the same way Adam's did. I could easily picture Adam looking just like him in twenty years.

"Good to meet you, Tom," he said evenly. "I wondered who Adam would bring with him."

"Thanks, Mr. Hendricks," I said, hoping he wasn't going to ask what his son was doing bringing another guy home. "It's nice to be here."

We went inside, and my first fantasy crumbled to dust as Adam took his bag into one bedroom and pointed down the hall to where I would sleep. Not only were we not going to share a bed, we weren't even going to share a room. Dejected, I walked down what seemed an endless hallway and into my room. Large and airy, it had a big bed and a window that opened out on a view of the lake. I sat on the bed and was thankful that it didn't squeak. Since it seemed the only action I was going to get all weekend was going to be with my fist, it was nice to know the whole house wouldn't hear me beating off alone.

While I was having a great time, it became clear very quickly that my plans for a sex-filled weekend were not going to happen. I tried several times over the next two days to be alone with Adam, but it seemed doomed. Sunday night came much too quickly. That night, Mr. Hendricks cooked steaks outside and we sat on the big screened-in porch eating while the sun settled into the lake, turning it into a pool of copper fire. Jake treated us like two best friends, and it was relaxing to just sit drinking beer with two other guys so far from anyone else. The beer even made me a little bold, and I decided that after dinner I was going to try to get Adam alone.

When we were done eating, I stood up and stretched. "That was really great, Jake," I said cheerfully. "I think I'm going to take a walk and work a little of it off. You want to come, Adam?"

Adam shook his head. "No. I think I'm going to head up to bed. We have to leave pretty early tomorrow if we're going to make our first class, and I'm really tired."

I saw my last chance go up in smoke. After a long dejected walk by the lake, where I must have thrown half of the stones on the shore back into the water, I wandered back to the house. It was dark, and I figured Adam and Jake were both in bed. Pausing outside Adam's door, I heard his rhythmic breathing. I listened for a minute before finally going into my own room alone. Undressing, I went and stood at the window, looking out at the streaks of silver moonshine slipping over the black waves.

Just as I was about to turn around and go to bed, I felt someone come up behind me. Arms went around my waist and I was pulled back against a hard, rippled stomach. Warm breath tickled my neck, and then there was a tongue running along my skin. The hands caressing my body slipped between my legs and started playing with my cock and balls.

"I thought I heard you come back in," a voice whispered low in my ear. "I've been waiting for you."

I couldn't believe it. After all this time, my fantasy about Adam was coming true. My cock hardened quickly as his strong fingers stroked it in long, slow movements and his mouth worked its way over my neck, kissing me gently. I could feel the soft hairs on his

arms rasp against my skin as he held me. He was naked, and as he
slid his body up and down my ass, I felt his prick swelling against
me, thick and warm. It was just like I'd imagined, only now it was
real, hot flesh that touched my skin. I wanted him in my mouth.

Turning around, I dropped to my knees in the darkness, anxious to taste Adam's big dick. I reached for his stiff pole and
wrapped my hand around it. It was a lot larger than I had imagined it being, and it was a stretch even to get my fingers all the
way around the rock-hard shaft. I held him in my hand for a moment, feeling his hardness, then leaned forward and kissed the soft
skin of his balls, breathing in his scent as I started to lick his cock
from the root up the shaft. When I reached the head I sucked it gently, running my tongue around the ridge. "I've been waiting a long
time for this," I said, looking up at him from my position at his feet.

But it wasn't Adam's face I was looking into. It was Jake's.
Between the shadows in the room and the surprise of what was
happening, I hadn't even noticed that it was Adam's father and
not Adam who was making love to me. Now I knelt with his stiff
cock in my hand and my mouth on fire from having kissed his
warm dick flesh. I could still taste him on my tongue and wanted
more. So many feelings raced through my head that I couldn't
even think straight. I just sat there feeling the blood beat through
Jake's prick as I looked into his eyes.

I stopped thinking when Jake's hand gripped the back of my
head and urged me forward. The touch of his strong fingers
seemed to break the spell, and I opened my mouth to receive him.
His cockhead slipped between my lips easily, and several inches of
dick poured into my throat as the taste of him flooded me. Jake
continued to push me onto his tool, and I let myself give in to his
insistent hands.

When he'd gotten as much of his cock into me as he possibly
could, Jake started to pump my mouth slowly, letting me feel
every inch of him as his shaft passed over my tongue and lips. As
I sucked him, I reached up and played with his balls, rubbing one
and then the other. Jake responded by increasing his thrusts,
drawing the head of his dick out and sliding back in so I could
feast on him. He was making me so hot I didn't care that he was
my roommate's father. In fact, knowing that the cock and balls I
was sucking had produced the guy I'd been lusting after made it

even hotter. All I wanted was to feel him inside me, to service him until he rewarded me with his cum.

"You look so hot with my cock in your mouth," he whispered. "Why don't you come over here so I can work on yours."

I stood up and moved to the bed, where Jake motioned for me to lie down. When I was settled back against the pillows, he knelt between my legs and gripped both of our cocks in one hand. Jerking slowly, he pumped the lengths of our shafts while holding them together. I could feel his prick beating along with mine and his balls slapping softly against my own as they rose and fell with the movement of his hand. With his other hand, Jake rubbed the muscles of my chest, letting his fingers pull at the thick hair.

"I'd love to see that nice hairy chest covered in some fresh cum," he said, pulling up hard on my cockhead.

"Just keep it up," I gasped, "and you won't have to wait long."

Jake leaned back and gripped our pricks so that they were both sticking straight up, held in his firm grasp. He increased the speed of his movements, and I felt my load boiling to the surface. "Oh, Christ," I moaned. "I'm going to shoot all over the place."

"That's exactly what I want to see," Jake said, and squeezed his cock against mine as the first volley exploded from my dick. A thick string of jism, pale as milk, splashed into the air and onto my chest, landing in a long line from my throat to my balls. A second and third sent even more sticky drops onto my stomach and across Jake's hand. He continued to pump both of us, and I watched as his dickhead swelled and then released a mammoth load straight up in the air. The pearls of man juice scattered over his chest and fell back onto my balls, soaking me as he came repeatedly. I felt his prick jerking wildly as he shot again and again, unloading more cum than I'd ever seen.

By the time we had both finished, my whole torso was spattered with spunk and Jake's hand was dripping with it. Jake brought his hand to his mouth and licked some of the cum from his fingers. "Tastes great," he said as he swallowed our mingled loads.

"Yeah, well, there's sure enough of it," I said as I fingered the sticky swirls on my chest.

Jake laughed, low and pleasant just like Adam, and leaned down. Taking my cock in his mouth, he sucked it clean of every drop of leftover cum. Then he moved up my body, licking up the smears of white as he worked his way toward my chest. His tongue darted into my navel and roamed through the line of fur on my stomach, sucking eagerly. When he reached one of my nipples, he bit it slightly, and a shiver ran down my spine. He sensed it and began to suck, gently at first and then more forcefully, until I was writhing on the bed. I put my hands on his head and pressed him to me, feeling my cock harden again as he worked me over with his tongue.

I was arched against Jake, my cock sliding between his legs as his mouth tortured my nipple, when he finally released my aching tit and moved his mouth up to my lips. He was hovering over me, resting his hands on either side of me as he bent and kissed me for the first time, the head of his cock resting on my stomach. My mouth welcomed his, and his tongue slipped inside. I reached up and pulled him down on top of me. The heaviness of him crushed me pleasantly as I let him cover my body with his, my arms going around his back.

Feeling Jake's hardness between my legs, I couldn't wait to have him inside my ass. I lifted my legs up a little on either side of him, and his cock slipped naturally under my balls and into the crack of my ass. I felt his bush press against my balls and pushed myself against him in return. "I want you to fuck me," I said in his ear. "I want you to fuck me as hard as you can."

Jake didn't have to be told twice. Sitting up, he pushed my knees back so that my asshole was exposed. He ran his hand across my hairy ass cheeks and massaged them roughly before plunging one thick finger into my waiting hole. I cried out a little as he penetrated me, but it felt great to have him inside. I hadn't been fucked in a long time, and my body welcomed the pressure inside my ass eagerly. When after a minute Jake pulled out and I felt the tip of his cock pressing against me, I held my breath.

Jake pushed forward and slid deep into my ass, my legs sliding over his broad shoulders. I clenched my teeth as pain ripped through me, and I felt tears coming to my eyes as my hole stretched to its limits. Then, just as suddenly, he was in, and I could relax and enjoy the way he filled me up, the way his hands gripped my thighs. I could feel his dick twitching as he waited to start his thrusting, and I clamped my ass muscles around him.

At first he fucked me gently, slowly sliding the length of his tool in and out of my aching pucker, teasing me with the tip before popping back in. As he did, I stroked my cock in time with him. It felt so good to have him inside me that I was glad it was him and not Adam. Jake probably knew a lot more than his son about how to really fuck a man, and I was enjoying every one of his tricks. He had me begging for more, and I was loving it.

Once I was worked up, Jake really began to pound me. Putting my hands on his ass, I could feel the thick muscles dimpling and releasing as he slapped against my thighs. My balls smacked heavily against his stomach as he plowed me, and my hole started to burn from the friction of his pistoning cock. Jake pushed my legs back until my knees were almost against my shoulders, giving him even more room to fuck me senseless. Again and again he pulled his prick out to the very end, letting my hole close over the tip before ripping me open again. I came close to losing my load several times, but each time I forced myself to wait, not wanting it to be over.

Jake began to groan, and I felt him start to come deep inside me, his cock swelling even wider as the load tore into my shitter. Feeling Jake's man load stream into me, I couldn't stand it anymore. "I'm going to shoot," I moaned.

Jake slipped out of my ass and bent down. Grabbing my balls, he held them tightly as he slid my piece into his mouth. My dick began firing off round after round of jism as his lips closed around it. It felt like I was being split in two as my body shook over and over and I came inside Jake's throat, pushing myself as far as I could into him. He slurped down every shot that blasted from my cock, his throat rippling as he drank it and his fingers pushing the last drops up my spent crank.

When he'd swallowed the last of my cum, he let my dick fall from his lips and once more lay on top of me. I felt his heart beating as we lay in the darkness, and I ran my hands over his back. My asshole was warm with his load, and I could feel the ache where his prick had been.

"Does it bother you that it wasn't Adam?" he asked. "I kind of got the feeling that you were interested in him. But you looked so hot standing there naked that I couldn't hold back any longer. I've been thinking about that ass of yours ever since you got here."

I laughed. "Yeah, well, I know what that's like. But no, it's okay. Besides, maybe that old saying is true. You know, like father, like son."

Jake kissed me. "Well, I don't know about Adam. But if that's the case, then I'd sure love to meet your dad."

The next morning, as Adam and I were getting ready to leave, Jake came over to the car to say good-bye. "It was good having you, Tom," he said, his eyes shining. "Be sure and come again."

"Thanks, I'm sure I will," I said. Then, leaning close so that only he could hear, I added, "I'm just not sure whether it will be with you or with Adam."

Three Wishes

This was my contribution to an anthology I edited of gay erotic fairy tales. Personally, I'd wish for Giants season tickets, a gig writing for Oz, and a pony.

Three wishes.

That's what the lucky ones always get in the fairy tales—three wishes, right? Only they always fuck it up, asking for shit like hair more golden than the sun, or to be as beautiful as the day. And more than likely, whatever freaky fairy it is that gives them the wishes in the first place decides it would be a real laugh to make it all backfire, so they end up with golden hair all right, but it's on their backs, or the day they're as beautiful as is a gray, rainy Thursday in November, or some other crazy shit. It never works out right. Never.

So we all read these things and we think about how fucking smart we'd be if *we* were the ones doing the wishes. Remember as kids, sitting around talking about how bad-ass we'd be if some crazy bitch in a ball gown appeared and said, "Okay, go to it"? Saying how we'd wish for all the money in the world first, all the chocolate in the world second, and then always use the last wish to wish for three more wishes so it could go on forever. We thought we were so damn smart, smarter than any enchanted frog or genie or whatever the hell it is that dishes the wishes out. Yeah, well, we thought watching *Little House on the Prairie* was cool, too, and look how far that got us.

Flash ahead about twenty-five years. Picture those same little kids (well, not all of the same ones, but all about the same age, anyway) that were sitting around acting so smart, but now they're all grown up. This time they're sitting around in a bar. Or, to be more precise, they're standing around in a bar. And this bar happens to cater to the type of men who sometimes find themselves in the position of granting wishes, although none of them are what you'd call fairies, at least not to their faces, and the wishes aren't exactly the kind you think of when you think of Cinderella and her pals.

I'm one of those men. That little boy who grew up sitting on the couch in *Star Wars* pajamas watching half-pint Laura Ingalls scamper all over the Wisconsin countryside grew into a damn fine top man. Six-three. Two-ten. Hung big. I won't bore you with the details. Suffice it to say I could take on Almanzo and Pa together in the old hayloft and have them walking out sideways begging for more. I've learned a thing or two since those Thursday nights in front of the tube waiting for Nellie Oleson to get hers in a pile of mud.

So the place is a bar on a fairly typical Sunday night. Not your usual setting for a fairy tale, but enchanted castles and cottages made of candy are hard to come by these days, the real-estate market being what it is. And wandering through the woods has never been my thing. The men are in the corners, watching but not watching, listening to John Michael Montgomery blare out of the speakers. You know how it is. They stand around seething sex but pretending they get it so often it doesn't matter if anyone notices or not. They aren't important anyway; they're just there for background.

The boys, on the other hand, are lined up at the bar, waiting, hoping one of the men seemingly not looking at anything is in fact looking right at their asses and sizing them up. Consider it a casting call for the role of the ingenue in the tale that's about to unfold. Someone's got to play Little Red or Snow White, right? Fairy tales don't go so well when there's no one to root for.

I'm standing where I always stand, against the wall nearest to the bathroom. That's where I do my best work, in there where the air tastes of sweat and heat and the floor is pooled with piss. I like the way hungry boys lick the drops of other mens' water off my boots, the way they look when they're kneeling on that floor and their faces are turned up to me just before I shove my dick down their throats. What can I say, if you've ever been there, you know what I mean.

That's when I start thinking about this wish thing. I don't know why. It just comes to me out of the blue while I'm looking at this boy's ass and wondering if he could take me dry. I say boy, but you know what I mean. He's twenty-five if he's a day, but he's a boy as far as I'm concerned. So boy he is. And this boy looks like he needs someone to teach him a thing or two. That's how the story starts. No once upon a time or any of that shit. Just one guy wondering what it would be like to fuck another one's ass. It's the same thing.

I take a swallow of my whiskey, and there it is. The characters are chosen, the story begins. The boy does have a nice ass. The kind you—or I, anyway—would like to see humped over a urinal while I slap it good and pink. The kind with big, firm mounds that beg to be pushed aside to reveal the tight little ring inside. It's packed into faded jeans, and the denim is worn soft.

He turns around, and I get a good look at him. The rest of him is standard-issue boy: white T-shirt, military-short dark hair, cute face, work boots. He looks as though he just got off work at the factory, but he's probably an accountant. He probably drives a Saab and drinks flavored water. He probably reads *Architectural Digest. Mr. Benson* may have been great for business, but it's not reality. Just another kind of fairy tale.

But there is that ass. And tonight I'm feeling generous. I walk over to the bar and stop in front of him. "Bathroom," I say. "Now." I turn and walk away.

Yeah, I know, in most of the old stories the hero has to go through all of these trials before you get to the good part. Well, dragons went on the endangered species list years ago, and I'm all out of magic beans, tricky foxes dressed up as giggling girls, and impossible riddles. I figure what he's going to get if he's still behind me will more than make up for the lack of two-headed giants, bewitched forests, and troll-infested bridges.

Of course he follows me. There wouldn't be a story if he didn't. And they always do anyway. It's why Jack climbed the beanstalk. It's why the hero always opens the door he's told not to. It's why they always pick the one rose that's off limits. That's why they're boys.

The bathroom hasn't been cleaned in a while. It being Sunday night and all, the help has the day off. There's piss on the floor, and the smell is strong. Some guy is taking a leak in one of the urinals. He turns around when I come in, his dick half-hard in his hand.

The boy is behind me when I turn. He is looking at the floor, not saying anything. So far, so good. I walk over and rip his T-shirt from throat to waist. His chest is smooth, well developed in a lean way. Both nipples are pierced through with thick hoops. There is a black tattoo around his right bicep, some typical boy thing that does nothing for me.

I yank his jeans open and down. He's not wearing underwear, and he's shaved. He has a long, fat dick and heavy balls, and his cock is half-hard. There is another thick ring through the head of his prick. *Boys are all starting to look the same,* I think. Why do queers think assimilation is alternative? Again, it's his ass that saves him. Naked it's even prettier than it was wrapped up in jeans. *Snow White, indeed,* I think as I admire his pale skin.

I pull his head back by the hair, which is just long enough for me to be able to get my fingers into. His white throat is exposed as I look down into his eyes, which are dark and expectant.

"Three wishes, boy," I say. "Tonight you get three wishes. And I suggest you use them wisely, because if you don't, this ball is over way before midnight."

I push the boy to his knees. He hits the floor hard, his knees splashing in a pool of rank piss. He looks up at me, his sweet face a mirror of confusion. *He doesn't understand what I have given him,* I think. *He's probably never even read "The Fisherman and His Wife."*

I slap the boy's face fiercely, partly because he is slow to answer me and partly because there's no excuse for not knowing at least the basic tenets of fairy law. My hand leaves a dark red print on his cheek.

"Wish one, boy."

The boy pauses a moment, then spits out his first thought. "I wish to suck your cock, sir."

Good boy, I think. I open my jeans and pull my dick out. The boy's mouth opens, and I shove myself inside, feeling his warmth surround me as he begins to suck. My dick quickly hardens as his tongue sweeps up and down my length, and soon he is riding my full width. I grip the back of his neck and show him how I like it. I wonder if Jack and the giant did it like this. I imagine the singing harp belting out "I Will Survive" as Jack rushes away with her.

The man at the urinal is still there. He's jerking on his prick as he watches us, his balls slapping with the rhythm of his hand. I let him stay because I enjoy showing off, and because I know the boy will work harder with an audience. Every good story needs someone to hear it, right?

I have to admit this boy is good. His lips pull at my head while his tongue runs along my shaft, coaxing a load up from my balls. His head moves smoothly and efficiently as he sucks. Between his legs, his cock has stiffened, the ring filling with his engorged head. He does not touch it.

I pull my cock out of his mouth and come, spattering his boy face with a nice load. It hits him first just beneath his left eye, the stain spreading down his cheek. The next burst slathers across his lips. His tongue snakes out, and he licks my spunk from his skin, swallowing with his eyes shut. I slash a final ribbon of sticky heat across his neck, where it lies for a moment like a translucent vein before dripping, ice-creamlike, down the hollow of his throat.

After the boy has washed the last traces of cum from my cockhead, he looks up into my face. The drying remnants of my need crackle on his skin as the movement of his muscles breaks the thin layers of white into tiny lines. He has made no motion to wipe away these stains on his flesh. He still has not touched his cock, which rears up hard and insistent, the tip drooling a thin string of precum that just touches the pool of piss in which he is kneeling.

"Wish two, boy," I say.

This time there is no hesitation. "I wish to be fucked by you, sir." His voice is soft, but clear.

Again, he has wished well. I grab his arm and pull him to his feet. His feet are still bound by his jeans, and he stumbles as I push him toward the urinals, but he does not fall. He puts his hands on either side of the urinal and leans forward. His face is over the bowl, breathing in the ripe scent of piss left there by dozens of men. His ass is facing me, waiting. The man who has been watching us has moved over. He leans against the wall, as though waiting for a bus, while he strokes his shaft.

I part the boy's ass cheeks with my hands. His hole is smooth, pink, and tight as I slip my cock inside. It is rough going without any spit, but he takes me easily, moaning as I invade him. When I am fully inside, I pause for a moment. This is the part I relish most, the feeling of being surrounded by the hungry throat of a boy's ass. The length of my cock beats with his heat as I begin to fuck him.

How come the characters in fairy tales never have sex? We all know that's what they're about, but no one actually ever fucks anyone else. Like Rapunzel was inviting the prince up to have a fucking tea party or something. And Beauty lived with Beast as a prisoner and no good S-M scenes ever went on? You know he had her ass in a sling first chance he got, and she liked it, too. I figure all the old guys who wrote these things down sat in their studies scribbling out stories and jerking their cranks at the same time.

The boy pushes back against me, impaling himself on my cock. I fuck him harder, smacking into his ass with enough force that his face comes dangerously close to hitting the wall each time I enter him. His hands are gripping the rim of the urinal, keeping him steady. I look at the tips of his fingers submerged in the yellow water, as if the blue ball of disinfectant that sits half-eroded in the center is some magical talisman he's reaching for so he can return it to some weeping princess in exchange for her gold ring. The sight makes me want to come.

The boy's cock, which has been swinging between his legs as I fuck him, suddenly begins to shoot. Fat drops of his cum scatter over the floor as he empties himself, helpless, beneath me. Thick strings hang from the steel halo of his dickhead as his hole releases what seems to be an endless amount of jism. His cream mixes with the piss on the floor.

I hear the man against the wall cry out as he, too, comes. I glance over to see him, eyes fixed on me and the boy, with his fist wrapped tightly around his spurting prick. He seems oblivious to the fact that his blasts are covering his work shirt in thick smears. His other hand holds his balls tightly, pulling them downward as he unloads onto his chest. Apparently, he has enjoyed the story.

I figure it's time for the happily ever after. I have used this boy's hole enough. With a final thrust, I empty myself into him. I pause, holding for as long as possible the delicious moment between feeling my orgasm begin as a small tremble deep in my belly and releasing myself into his ass. This is the payoff, the treasure, right? This is what the hero gets for being a good boy and never straying from the path. Or maybe it's the opposite—what he gets for straying from it. I'm never sure.

I pull out and wipe my dick on the boy's ass, leaving a smear of cum and shit on his milky skin. In the fairy tale, everything would be neat and clean and surrounded by the scent of roses. But this is real life, where people stink and shit and piss on a regular basis, where sex is about what's left on your dick when you're done.

I button myself up and begin to leave the bathroom. Then I remember he has one more wish. The story can't end yet. This is the part where he asks for something ridiculous, like my phone number or a kiss from the prince of his dreams or some other shit, and ruins the whole story. It's where the whole thing collapses. I turn around. The boy is standing, looking at me. He has not pulled his pants up. His cock, still hard, juts out at an angle.

"So, boy, what will it be?" I say. "What's your third wish?" I wait for him to wish incorrectly, so I can tell him he's fucked up and has to go back to being content with one of the ugly stepsisters waiting outside the door for their turn.

He smiles. "Three more wishes," he says.

Okay, so maybe sometimes they don't fuck it all up. Smart-ass boy.

Downtown Train

Believe it or not, this story was written one afternoon while I was listening to Mary Chapin Carpenter's version of the classic Tom Waits song "Downtown Train." Sometimes you just can't help yourself.

Because of the rain that had been pouring steadily since late afternoon, the rush-hour crowd was more anxious than usual to get home and out of the wet weather that had suddenly gripped New York in the middle of July. Added to the soaring temperatures, the rain had turned the whole city into a steaming jungle, leaving everything and everybody in it sticky, hot, and irritable. It was still raining when I left the office, and because I'd left my umbrella at home I was soaked through when I finally made it to the Fifty-first Street subway station.

The platform was crowded with people waiting for the number 6 downtown, so when I saw the headlights of an approaching train I decided to wait for the next one. Being packed into a hot subway car is bad enough; being packed in with wet, unhappy people for forty blocks is sheer hell. I stayed in back and watched as people poured into the doors, scrambling to pull purses and umbrellas inside before they clanged shut. Finally, after the doors had banged open and closed several times as last-minute riders attempted to squeeze into overcrowded cars, the train left.

A handful of other people had decided to wait for the next train as well and stood on the platform craning their necks out to watch for the telltale yellow dots on the horizon that signaled the next train. Fortunately, one came along only a few minutes later and, since there hadn't been time for another crowd to gather, it was mostly empty. When the doors whooshed open, I stepped inside and dropped into the first open seat to wait for my stop at Astor Place.

If you live in New York for any length of time and ride the subway regularly, you develop the habit of scanning the cars to see who you're riding with. There were about a dozen other people in the car besides myself, including a couple of schoolgirls dressed in the usual plaid skirts and white blouses of the city's Catholic institutions, but with the forbidden after-school additions of lipstick, chewing gum, and cigarettes in the front pocket. Apart from a scattering of business types, the only other occupants were an elderly couple carrying net bags bulging with apples and paper-wrapped parcels that smelled suspiciously like fresh fish.

When the train pulled in to the Forty-second Street station, most of the riders got off to connect with trains at Grand Central that would take them out of the city. Several more people got on, including a transit cop, who stood in the doorway looking over the car. He surveyed the riders in the car and, satisfied that everything was in order, relaxed and leaned against the doorway as the train began its rattling voyage through the tunnels beneath the city.

Since the cop was facing me, I found myself looking at him. He appeared to be in his early thirties, with an open, handsome face shaded by a day's worth of stubble and deep brown eyes that were looking out from beneath his hat at the graffiti-scrawled walls flashing by the windows. He had his arms crossed in front of him, and his blue uniform was stretched tightly over his large, muscular body. Because of the heat, his shirt was open, and a line of black hair peered over the edge of his white T-shirt where it crossed his thick neck. Best of all, he had muscular forearms covered in soft black hair and thick wrists that ended in huge hands.

Pretending that I was looking at an ad for laser hemorrhoid removal on the wall above his head, I tried to make out his name tag. Because of the way he was standing, all I could make out were the letters *nni* at the end. The rest was hidden from view. *An Italian boy*, I thought briefly. *It figures.* Italian men, especially big hunky ones like this cop was, have always been one of my biggest weaknesses. I kept stealing glances at him until finally he leaned to one side and the rest of the name came into view. Giovanni. I'd been right about the Italian part.

Moving my eyes back down his body, I passed over the thick leather belt holding his revolver and nightstick and my eyes froze on the bulge between his legs. Even in the cheap-looking uniform

I could tell that he was packing a big piece. There was a thick line running down the left side of his pants, and when he shifted his weight I saw his cock move with him. I could only imagine the beautiful pair of balls that must have been waiting behind the zipper of his pants. When he moved one hand to his crotch and squeezed slightly, it was all I could do not to drop to me knees and start sucking him off.

Looking up, I saw that he was staring right at me, his dark eyes boring into mine. *Oh shit,* I thought, *he caught me looking.* I tried to pretend I was looking at someone next to him, but I knew he'd seen me. I hoped my face wasn't as red as it felt and wished I at least had a newspaper I could pretend to be reading. When he reached in his back pocket and pulled out his notebook, I waited for him to come over and give me a ticket. For what, I didn't know—lewd staring or obvious perversion or fantasizing in a public place about a New York City transit cop with a beautiful big prick or something.

To my surprise, he just turned his back on me. When I looked up, all I saw were the firm round globes of his meaty ass. While I would have liked to look at them for a little longer, I decided not to push my luck. I busied myself with looking in my briefcase for something until the next stop. Then, when the doors opened, the cop walked off the train and I breathed a sigh of relief. As the train pulled out of the station, I looked out the window and saw him strolling along the platform with another cop, laughing at some private joke. *Probably telling his buddy about the queer who was checking him out,* I thought as I got up and went to stand at the door to wait for my upcoming stop.

As the train ground to a halt at Astor Place, I noticed that there was something on the seat where the cop had been standing. At first I thought it was just the usual ad for word-processing services or Madame Woo's Fortune Palace, but it was too shiny. I picked it up and saw that it was a Polaroid snapshot. Flipping it over, I couldn't believe my eyes. It was a picture of the cop. Only he was naked, wearing just his uniform hat as he lay on a bed. And he was sporting one of the biggest hard-ons I'd ever seen. His fist was wrapped around a massive cock, and his balls hung down like two overripe peaches between his hairy thighs. He was looking right into the camera, and I could see every line of his masculine face.

I was so surprised by my find that I didn't notice that the train had come to a stop until someone poked me in the back and said, "Let's go, buddy, you're blocking the door." I quickly pocketed the picture and exited the subway, walking briskly through the turnstile and up the stairs to the street. Once I was in the daylight I was tempted to pull the picture out again and make sure it really was the cop I saw and not someone else. But it was still pouring, and the sidewalk was crowded with people, so I walked the few remaining blocks to my apartment as quickly as I could, the image of the big man stroking his prick burning in my mind as I fingered the photo in my pocket.

The instant my door was shut and locked, I pulled the picture out of my pocket again and stared at it. There was no doubt about it, the man in the picture was the same cop I'd been staring at. All I could do was take in his wide chest, his big nipples, and most of all his beautiful dick. The big head was held tightly in his fist, and I could see drops of silvery precum slipping from the hole. My cock was starting to swell the longer I looked at the image in my hand and was pressing uncomfortably against my soaking pants.

Going into the bedroom, I reluctantly laid the picture on my bedside table. Hurriedly pulling at my wet clothes, I tossed them on the floor and dried off with a towel. Naked, I climbed onto my bed and lay back against the pillows, the picture in my hand. As I tried to memorize every detail of the photo, I began to stroke my dick. It didn't take long before it had stretched out to its full length and was lying flat against my stomach.

I tried to imagine the circumstances surrounding the photo. Who had taken it? I figured it was his girlfriend who had snapped it, probably right before he'd pushed her over the side of the bed and fucked her lucky pussy with his big pole. She'd most likely given him head first, until his stalk was nice and stiff, and then they'd taken pictures of each other before getting down to fucking. I envisioned him coming up behind her after she'd put the camera down and sliding the tip of his prong into her from behind, his hands on her waist as he pushed the entire length into her box. I pictured her cunt lips spreading open as his manhood invaded her, imagined her whining as his thickness stretched her open.

The idea of the big hunk using his cock on a willing hole was making me horny as hell. Reaching into the drawer of my bedside table, I pulled out a dildo and a bottle of lube. Propping the photo

up on the table where I could look at it, I arranged the pillows behind me so that I could lean against them. Squirting some lube
into my hand, I rubbed it into my anxious pucker, wetting the lips
and slipping two fingers inside to stretch it a little. Then I slicked
up the length of the dildo, a thick monster I could only get into my
ass when I was really horny and needed a good hard fuck. Pulling
my knees up toward my chest, I spread my legs and positioned
the fat head at the entrance to my waiting chute. It hurt like hell
as the tip invaded my asshole, but I kept my eyes on the cop's face
as I pushed inch after inch inside me.

After a few minutes of pushing and relaxing, I felt the base of
the dildo touch my ass cheeks. My entire shitter was filled with
man meat, and my prick had responded by slopping out a load of
precum onto my belly. With my free hand I scooped up some of the
scum and used it to grease up my rod, which I pumped steadily
while I got used to the size of the dildo. My butthole was twitching
as it stretched to accommodate the girth, and I could feel the head
pressing deep inside me. It felt great, especially when I imagined
that it was Officer Giovanni's tool in there.

After a minute I tugged on the dildo's base and slipped it out a
couple of inches. As I did, I shut my eyes and pictured taking the
cop's fat prong up my ass. I could almost feel his hands on my
chest as I imagined him penetrating me, his big fingers tugging at
my tits as he worked my hole into a frenzy. I pulled the dildo out
another few inches and then pushed it back in, groaning as it filled
me again.

I imagined him growling commands in my ear, his rough cheek
scratching against my face as he lay on top of me. "Take my cock,"
he'd order. "Take every fucking inch of it in that tight ass of
yours." I pulled the dildo out until just the tip rested inside my
gasping sphincter, then rammed it home as I pictured his big nuts
slapping against my butt cheeks. I could feel his warm breath
against my neck as I fisted the dildo in and out, tearing at my
chute until it was raw and sore. The whole time, the image of him
fucking me played out across my mind.

I could feel the load of cum ready to blast from my aching nuts
and began to pump my dick faster, my fist sliding along on the skin
of sticky precum that had been leaking steadily from my swollen
head. Matching my strokes, I pulled up on my cock every time the
dildo slid home in my butt, creating a smooth rhythm that quickly

brought me to the edge. Just as I came, I opened my eyes and looked at the picture sitting on the nightstand. The first shot splashed onto my chest as I stared at the cop's stiff tool and imagined it swelling with his load. As I pictured his chest drenched in cum, my balls responded by spewing out rope after rope of jism until I was covered in the stuff and it ran down my sides onto the bed. When the last spray had blasted from my overworked pipes I fell back against the pillows exhausted, my ass ring still clamped tightly around the dildo and the cop staring back at me, his cock still stiff and ready in his hand.

Every time I looked at the picture that night I got hard immediately. I jerked off three more times, putting away the blueprints I was supposed to be working on for a client meeting the next morning and wanking off thinking about the stud cop. I still couldn't figure out how he'd dropped the picture, or even why he had it in the first place. It must have been tucked inside the notebook he had in his pocket and fallen out when he opened it. I was just glad I'd found it. I was having better sex with the guy's picture than I'd had with most real men.

The next day I looked for Officer Giovanni on the train, but he was nowhere to be seen. The same was true for the next week; every day I'd wait to see him get on, to see his face looking in the subway door at me, only to go home disappointed. I had to content myself with going home and beating off to his picture every night. It wasn't like I even had anything to say to him if I did see him, but I still checked every time the train pulled into Forty-second Street.

Then, about two weeks after I'd found the picture, I saw him again. I had worked late at the office on a rush project, finishing up the final construction details on a house. At a little after midnight I had written in the last instructions and stumbled bleary-eyed into the station to catch the subway home. When the train came, I settled into my seat and waited for my stop, thinking about the treat that awaited me on my bedside table. I had almost fallen asleep when I felt a hand shaking me awake. "Hey, buddy, wake up," a deep voice was saying. "I need you to come with me."

Startled, I looked up right into the face I'd just been thinking about. The cop was looking down at me, and his hand was still on my shoulder. I glanced at the name tag to make sure it was him. Sure enough, it was Giovanni. "What's wrong?" I asked, confused.

"You've got to come with me," he said again. "Let's go." Grabbing my upper arm, he pulled me to my feet and ushered me toward the door. The few other passengers in the car barely looked twice at us as he pushed me out onto the deserted platform. I didn't even know which stop we were at.

"I think you've made a mistake," I said. "I don't know what—" "Save it," he interrupted as he pulled his handcuffs from his belt and snapped them around my wrists. "You and I have some unfinished business to attend to." He didn't say another word, pushing me in front of him as we moved along the empty platform toward the subway stairs. As I walked ahead of him, his hand gripping my arm, I tried to figure out what he wanted from me. He couldn't know I was the one who'd found his picture. And even if he did, why did he have me in handcuffs?

I started to get really nervous when, at the top of the stairs, he took a key from his belt and used it to unlock a door behind the token sellers' booth. Neither of the two women sitting behind the glass looked twice as he pushed me through the doorway, and for the first time I found myself wishing that people in the city paid a little bit more attention to what was going on around them. When I heard a lock snap into place behind me, I knew I was in trouble. "Look," I said, "If there's some kind of problem here I'd like to know—" "I said shut up," he barked, and I decided that I'd better listen to him.

The cop led me down a narrow, dark hallway to another door, which he pushed open with his shoulder. He made a soft grunting sound as he opened it, and I felt warm breath hit my cheek. Shoving me through the doorway, he came right behind me. We were in a room lined with gray metal lockers. A couple of wooden benches were bolted to the floor, and along one wall heavy blue coats and empty equipment belts hung from wooden pegs. Tall black boots were arranged in ordered rows beneath them, the leather shining dully. It smelled faintly of sweat and heat, and I noticed that the air was moist, as though someone had recently taken a shower. It seemed to be some kind of police changing room.

Giovanni pushed me into the center of the room and then moved around and stood in front of me, his dark eyes looking me up and down. I wanted badly to look at his face, to see if he was as handsome as I remembered, but I was afraid to. Instead, I looked down at his heavy shoes and waited for him to speak. As he walked around me slowly, his shoes making soft thuds on the cement floor, I could feel his gaze traveling over my body, as if his eyes were seeing right through me and he could tell what I had done with his picture.

I should never have thought back to the photograph, because even though I was handcuffed and waiting for the big cop to beat the crap out of me, all I could think about was his massive cock and hairy balls. And the more I thought about them, the harder my dick got, until it was pushing out the front of my pants. I knew that Giovanni had to be able to see the bulge, and when I felt him move up to stand behind me, I closed my eyes and waited to feel his fist in my kidney. "You been having a good time with my picture?" he asked from behind me.

I wasn't sure how to answer him. If I said yes, then he'd know for sure I had it. If I said no, he'd probably know I was lying. Either way I was in serious trouble. "Yes," I said finally. He moved closer so that I could feel his chest pressing against my back. "I saw you looking at me that day on the train," he growled. "You looked like one hungry little cocksucker staring at my dick. Looked like you wanted to drop to your knees right there and have me shove my prick down your throat." Since that was exactly what I had been thinking, I didn't argue.

His deep, masculine voice was doing wonders for my aching hard-on, and the more he talked the hornier I got. "I see a lot of guys like you," he continued. "They like to stare at me on the train, check out what I've got in my pants. Most of them don't amount to shit, wouldn't know what to do with a real man if they ever got their hands on one." He was leaning into me now, as though telling me a secret, and the warmth of him was electric. "But I got the feeling you'd know what to do," he continued, "so I left you my little calling card. I hope you put it to good use."

My jaw must have dropped open from surprise when I heard him say that. He'd actually left the picture there on purpose for me to find. He brought his mouth closer to my ear, so close I could smell the mix of aftershave and sweat on his skin, and whispered, "You get off seeing my big cop dick? Did you like that?" One of his hands slipped around my neck as he pressed against me from behind, the big fingers stroking my throat, and I almost shot my load when I felt his hardness against me. "Did you come thinking about my cock up your ass?" he said. I couldn't help but moan as I answered him, "Yes."

Still standing behind me, Giovanni pulled at the knot of my tie, his big fingers tugging the tangled silk open easily. Then he worked open the buttons on my shirt, popping each one free as he moved down my chest. When it was hanging wide, he slipped his hand inside and began to rub my pecs. "Nice and hard," he murmured, his fingers massaging the smooth flesh I worked on a couple of times a week at the gym. He gripped one of my sensitive tits and pinched, making me shiver. When he saw my reaction, he brought his other hand up and began to work on both nipples, turning them in his fingers as he rubbed against my ass. Leaning back against him, I let him support my body as I gave in to his caresses. "Oh, yeah," he said slowly as his mouth covered my neck with hot kisses, "I think you'll know just what to do with a man like me."

His hands quickly ripped open my belt and yanked my zipper down, and it wasn't long before my pants were on the floor. I slipped off my shoes and Giovanni kicked everything out of the way. Then he ripped my shirt off my body, tearing the thin cotton easily to get around the handcuffs and tossing the shreds aside. My underwear soon joined my other clothes in a pile on the floor as he pushed them down and off, and I was left standing naked, my hands shackled behind me.

Giovanni walked around me, his fingers lightly touching me as they traveled up my stomach, over my shoulders, down my back, and across my ass. Finally he came back around in front of me and his hand encircled my stiff prick and tugged at my balls. "Nice cock you have here," Giovanni said as he stroked my shaft slowly. "Almost as nice as mine." He slid one fat finger between my lips and ran it across my teeth as if it were his prick. I sucked at it gently, feeling it play over my tongue and licking the soft hairs on his knuckle. I ached to touch his wrist and guide him in and out of my mouth but had to be content with slurping on his hand.

He was rubbing his own dick through his pants, and I could see the outline of the fat head where it swelled out halfway down his thigh. "How would you like to see it in the flesh?" he asked. "Maybe if you ask nicely I'll show it to you." He pumped more blood into his cock and the thick tube grew another inch underneath the blue material. "Yes, please," I gasped as he squeezed my sac tightly and pulled down on my balls, causing a glob of cock spit to dribble from my hole. "I want to see it."

To my considerable disappointment, he walked away and sat down on one of the wooden benches facing me, leaving me alone with a dripping tool and no way to satisfy it. Keeping his eyes on me, he began to unbutton his shirt slowly. It seemed to take forever as he carefully pushed each button through its eye and pulled the material apart, and his striptease was making me crazy. He had a white T-shirt on underneath his uniform, and a wide sliver of white came into view as more and more of his shirt opened up. When the last button was undone, he pulled the shirttail from his pants and shrugged the whole thing off completely.

The ridges of his massive chest were visible through the T-shirt, and his body was even more beautiful than I'd remembered. I held my breath as he reached down and grasped the edges of the shirt. Lifting his arms across his chest, he peeled the shirt off slowly, his sexy torso coming into view inch by inch as he pulled it over his head. He paused for a moment when it reached his neck, the muscles of his arms swelled out and the dark forests of his armpits revealed below the scrim of white as he yanked the last bit over his head.

Leaning back on the bench, he let me take in the length of his hairy, muscled body as he ran his hands from his tits down to his groin, stopping at the belt of his uniform pants. He knew he was teasing me, and a playful smile tugged at the corners of his mouth as he waited for an excruciatingly long moment before unhooking his belt and beginning to pull the zipper down, parting the metal teeth slowly and deliberately. When it was open he sat up and, bending over, began to take off his shoes, giving me a glimpse of his furry groin and leaving the rest a secret while he took his time.

I thought I was going to shoot all over the floor just from watching the big stud undress. I loved seeing the way his hands moved over his body pulling buttons from their clasps and peeling away the blueness of the uniform to reveal his flesh and bone. I desperately wanted to play with my cock, but the handcuffs kept my hands behind me, and all I could do was wait for him to continue. It seemed like he took forever pulling off his shoes and socks, but then he stood up and hiked his pants over his hips. My eyes followed them as they slipped down his legs and I finally saw what I had been waiting for.

Giovanni was wearing white boxer shorts, and the clean lines of the material cut across the darkness of his tanned skin beautifully, his hairy thighs encased in their softness and the waistband breaking the line of fur on his belly. His balls were cupped between his legs in a heavy pouch, and his cock bulged down one side like a thick vein beneath pale skin. He was the hottest thing I'd ever seen, and I wanted him more than I'd ever wanted a man in my life.

Turning around, he bent over the bench, his hands resting on the wide board as he spread his legs. His boxers tightened over his ass cheeks as he did, showing off the big rounded mounds and the long, rippled muscles of his back. A patch of hair shaded the small of his back just above the waist of his shorts, and his rounded calves swelled out as he bent his knees. Hooking his thumbs in the waistband, he pulled the boxers off slowly, revealing more and more of his furry ass. When he had them off, he bent over again and spread his cheeks with his hands, giving me a glimpse of the hairy hole at the center. His balls dangled down between his spread legs, and I could see the shadow of his cock bobbing in front of him.

The stud cop was putting on a real show for me, and I was loving every minute of it. The more he pawed at his meaty ass, the harder my balls beat with excitement as I thought about how it would feel to bury my tongue in his juicy hole and feel his balls sweep against my chin as I licked every inch of his hot butt. When he finally turned around and I saw his prick, it was all I could do not to spill my nuts. His dick was even bigger than I'd imagined, the head stretching well past the fist that encircled it.

Sitting on the bench, Giovanni started to play with himself, jerking on his engorged prong in long, deliberate strokes that slid sensuously up and down his beautiful cock. The sight of his thick fingers wrapped around the shaft and of his hairy, muscular forearm as it moved up and down held me captivated, and I felt like I could watch him jerk off forever. Just seeing his balls rise and fall with the motion of his arm was almost enough to make me come.

He knew how hot he looked working himself, and he sat there pumping his dick for what seemed like hours while I got more and more frustrated from being unable to do anything. Several times I could tell by the way his face tensed that he was close to coming, and I waited to see his big cop load spew out over the floor. But each time he wrapped his finger tightly around the root of his crank and paused a moment until he cooled down enough to continue. Then he would start all over again, smoothly caressing his shaft with his big hand, his other hand sometimes rubbing his hairy chest and playing with his tits, sometimes moving down under his balls to finger his hole.

Finally, just when I didn't think I could stand another second of watching him work his meat, he stopped. "Come over here," he ordered. I moved over to the bench and knelt between his legs, looking at the throbbing tool he held so close to my face. The shaft was covered with a scattering of dark hair that rose up from his balls for several inches before giving way to smooth, hard flesh, and the tip was wide and flushed with blood. A drop of precum was sliding down the valley of his cockhead, and my mouth watered just thinking about how good it would taste. But I waited for him to tell me what he wanted.

"Suck it," he said. "Do what you dreamed of doing when you looked at my picture." Inching forward until I was right between his legs, I leaned down and slipped the crown of his prick into my mouth, closing my lips around it greedily. The cop's dick felt so hot in my mouth and I was so horny that I immediately sank down on it until I felt his bush against my face. My throat ached with the size of him, but he tasted so fucking good I didn't care. I slurped on his crank like it was the best thing I'd ever had in my mouth, and it was. I could feel the blood coursing beneath his skin as I sucked him, and tasted his delicious precum as it began to flow from his hole.

I looked up into Giovanni's dark eyes as I blew him, watching pleasure flood his face as I moved up and down his tool servicing him. His mouth twitched whenever I reached his sensitive knob and drew my teeth across it, and I could see a small scar on his stubble-shaded chin ripple whenever he clenched his jaw. He was so fucking sexy I would have done anything to please him. When he put one hand on the side of my neck, I rubbed my face against the soft hair of his arm as I worked on his cock, taking in every inch of him until my throat roared with pain. I loved the feeling of his fingers pressing on my skin and the way his arm muscles tensed along my jaw while his dick played in and out of my mouth. He was everything I'd ever wanted, and I could have blown him all night long if he'd let me.

But he had other ideas. Pulling his cock out of my mouth, he lay back on the bench, his prick stretching out over his belly and his balls hanging over the edge of the wooden slab. "Get up here," he said, his voice deep and lust filled. I could tell he was ready to use his big piece for something other than show, and I couldn't wait to see what the man could do to my asshole with his cock.

Standing up, I straddled him, sitting on his stomach. My legs stretched over his waist and his hands gripped my ass cheeks as I leaned down to suck on his nipples. He groaned as I bit one softly, and I felt his dick jump beneath my ass. While licking his tit I slid myself along his hairy body, enjoying the sensation of him against my smooth skin, the way the hair tickled my balls and the head of my prick. I could feel his cock slipping along my ass crack and lifted myself up so that the big tip pressed against my hole.

Giovanni was more than ready for me, and he pushed into me urgently as I lowered myself down onto his fat prong until I could feel his wrinkled ballsac brush the fingertips of my bound hands. The walls of my chute swelled as his flesh filled me tightly, and I knew I was going to be sore as hell later. Still, I pressed down until I was sitting on his stomach again, his whole piece lodged inside me. "I knew you'd have one sweet ass," he said breathlessly. "But this is even better than I expected."

That was all I needed to get going. Rising up, I slid up Giovanni's fuck stick until just his knob was inside me, then went back down again. His hands cupped my ass as I rode him, and after a few minutes he began to lift his hips up to meet my asshole. Soon he was pounding in and out of my chute mercilessly, my balls slapping his stomach as his ass rose off the bench repeatedly, coming back down with muffled slaps.

I'd never been fucked so hard before and never enjoyed having a cock up my ass so much. When he took my dick in one hand and began to jerk me off, I knew it would all be over soon. Giovanni began to moan loudly, and I could tell from the way his cock became even harder that he was near the edge. "Shoot your load in my butt," I said. "Fill it with your hot cum." His eyes clouded over. "I'm going to blow in your ass," he gasped, and held my waist as he pulled me down onto his weapon.

My chute filled with sticky warmth as he released torrent after torrent of cop jism deep in my bowels, each blast exploding inside me like a gunshot. I came with him and watched as my dick splattered his chest and the floor with load after load. He kept pumping me with his hand as I came, and soon his fingers were thick with my juice.

After we both finished blowing our loads, I collapsed against his chest. He was still hard, and I felt his cum slipping down the walls of my ass as he pulled out of me and sat up. "I guess I can take these off now," he said, grinning as he held up the small silver key that unlocked the handcuffs. "Somehow I don't think you'll be running away any time soon."

"Oh, please don't, Officer Giovanni," I said jokingly, rubbing my freed wrists. "I kind of liked them." He laughed. "Just call me Mike," he said, using what was left of my shirt to wipe the cum from his belly and then starting to get dressed. "It's really Michelangelo, but only my mother still calls me that." He picked up his sweat-stained T-shirt and tossed it to me. "Here," he said. "Wear this. I'm afraid yours is out of commission." I pressed the shirt to my face and inhaled the musky smell of him, then pulled it over my head. Because he was bigger than I, it settled around my body loosely, and it made me horny just knowing that he had worn it.

Mike must have noticed the smile on my face, because he came over, put his arms around me, and gave me a long, deep kiss, his tongue sliding between my lips. When he finally pulled away, he picked up his gun belt and fastened it around his waist. "Time to get back to work," he said. "But how about I come over when my shift ends? I've got a feeling you and I have just started to get to know one another."

"Sounds fine by me," I said, straightening his hat. "But maybe you should ride with me to my stop. After all, you never know what kind of people are riding the trains this time of night."

Paying the Tax Man

Do I really need to explain the inspiration for this one? Rather than locate all my receipts one April 14, I wrote this instead. It must have been bad karma, because ten years later I was audited. Sadly, they demanded a check.

Even before I opened the ominous blue envelope lurking in my mailbox like some deadly creature waiting for its dinner, I was overcome by an intense feeling of imminent eternal damnation. There were no clues to its contents on the envelope, just the fateful words Official Business printed in tidy letters in the right-hand corner. Not even a return address. I tried to tell myself it was just another sweepstakes notice, or another one of the endless stream of feminine-hygiene-product circulars I seemed to always be getting that told me how I could feel fresh and smell like a field of daisies. At the worst, I allowed myself to think that it might be a jury-duty notice, and was oddly comforted by this idea.

But once I opened it, my worst fears became instant reality. There it was in black and white, a letter requesting the honor of my presence at a meeting with the jolly tax men. I was supposed to appear at the local IRS office in three weeks with all of my "pertinent receipts and forms," ready to discuss "a possible error in the computation of your 1991 return."

1991? I couldn't even find the receipts for groceries I bought that morning; how the hell was I supposed to find a bunch of ancient documents from before the dawn of man? I spent the afternoon rummaging frantically through my hopelessly unordered file cabinet. All that was left in my optimistically created tax file were four taxi fare slips, assorted receipts for things I didn't even remember buying, and a check stub from a restaurant that had some guy named Sean's phone number on it.

"That's really too bad," said my friend Mark helpfully that afternoon when I called him to bemoan my fate. After a dozen moves, Mark still has every receipt for everything he's ever bought in his entire life, alphabetized in labeled storage boxes in his closet. If he needed to, he could produce an item-by-item list documenting everything from the first bicycle he bought when he was twelve to the dildo he picked up on a trip to Amsterdam. He, of course, has never been audited.

"Let me borrow your receipts for the day," I suggested hopefully. "I promise I'll bring them back safe and sound."

"Not on your life," he said. "You're a writer. Why don't you just make them up? I think Ellen did that once. You could ask her how she did it."

In my moment of need, this actually sounded like a very good idea. I hung up and went right to work. Racing to the office supply store, I snatched up an adding machine that printed receipts. Then I found ink cartridges in assorted colors, thinking that I could cleverly use them to make it look like the receipts all came from different places. At the checkout counter, I carefully pocketed the receipt so that I could write everything off next year as a business expense. I returned to my apartment triumphant.

Four and a half hours later, I called Mark back. "You are an evil bitch," I said venomously, trying to wipe four different colors of ink from my hands and in the process sending all of the thousands of bits of paper on my desk fluttering onto the floor. "Have you ever tried making up receipts for your entire life? Not only do you have to go by the assumption that you actually do something that would warrant deductions, but you have to make all of the pieces of paper match the totals you put on your forms. Do you have any idea just how many reams of paper you have to buy to equal nine hundred and fifty-two dollars?"

"It's not your entire life," he said defensively. "It's just a year. Besides, I told you Ellen did it."

"I called Ellen," I said evenly, smudging my face with green ink as I yanked a cartridge out of the adding machine. "She said that not only did they grill her for six hours about her deductions until she started to cry, she ended up paying two thousand dollars in fines on a six-hundred-dollar bill. She said it was only last week that she could ask for a receipt from a cab driver without bursting into tears, and that's after eight months of nondeductible therapy."

"You're hysterical," said Mark. "I think you need to lie down."

"I think you need to bite me really hard," I shrieked. "You'd better give me those receipts of yours, you little creep. Besides, you owe me. Remember when you gave Jim crabs and you told him you got them at the gym? And I told him I had them, too, just so he wouldn't know about your little fling with that delivery boy from the bodega. Pablo, or Paco, or whatever it was."

"It was Pedro, and Jim and I broke up weeks ago," said Mark sullenly. "If you called more, you'd know that."

"When I get a hold of you," I started, but Mark hung up, making weird humming noises and saying that someone was buzzing his apartment. "Maybe you'll meet someone nice in jail," he said right before the line clicked off.

That night I lay in my bed staring at the ceiling and thought about the worst that could happen to me. Would I actually have to go to prison? I had no idea. In my mind I conjured up a vision of a cell, small and airless with bunk beds and a single dirty sink. I created a cellmate named Hank. A big brute of a man, he was in for armed robbery and shooting a cop. I gave him a thick cock and fat, hairy balls that he liked to play with while he jerked off in the bunk above me, the springs creaking rhythmically.

Surprisingly, my prick responded to my little fantasy and stiffened almost immediately. As I stroked it I let the scenario become even more wild. I pictured Hank ripping my orange prison uniform off me and fucking me senseless on the stained floor of the cell while I begged him for mercy. His prick slid in and out of my burning ass as he plowed me in full view of the other inmates. They in turn all jerked off watching us, their hands pumping fat rods until they gushed thick loads all over the concrete floors of the jail.

By the time I came I couldn't care less about my audit. As I shot my load all over my stomach I was ready and willing for them to take me away to Hank and his big cock. I could almost feel him emptying a gusher deep in my shitter. In my delirium I actually believed that everything would work out all right. But then the moment was over and I came to my senses. As cold cum slid down my sides onto the sheets I realized I was screwed but good, and it was the IRS and not Hank who would do the screwing.

* * *

For the next three weeks, I had a recurring dream where I was tied to a chair while a group of faceless men in badly fitting suits and wide ties shone bright lights in my face and tried to get me to tell the truth about my finances. "Where are all of your receipts?" they screamed in unison. I'd try to give them an explanation, but every time I said anything, a big red light over my head flashed and a robotic voice cried out, "Lying. Lying. Lying." I woke up every morning drenched in sweat with my pillow over my face.

The morning of my audit, I scraped together my meager pile of tattered receipts and put them into my briefcase. I was still clinging desperately to the vain hope that maybe all of this was a big mistake and they would just let me go home. I thought about wearing a suit, then remembered that I didn't own one. I decided jeans and a T-shirt would make me look more at ease anyway. I did, however, decide to walk to the IRS office. I didn't want to look too wealthy by showing up in a cab. I told myself I wasn't being paranoid. Somehow, I just knew they would know all of these things.

The building itself was rather unimpressive. I had been expecting big marble halls and long corridors lined with doors and stony-faced guards in black uniforms. Instead, it was a fairly ordinary-looking office building, with windows that didn't open and blue carpeting the color of antifreeze. The receptionist was a large, middle-aged woman with too much make-up and a bad dye job that made her hair an odd shade of purple. It took me a minute to realize that she looked faintly like Barney. As I checked in, I hummed the purple dinosaur's moronic "I love you, you love me" song and wondered how years of watching people come to their executions had affected her mentally.

"Just wait over there," she said flatly after looking long and hard at my signature and then staring at me with her eyes all squinted up. "Someone will be out to get you shortly."

"Aren't they already out to get me?" I said jokingly. She didn't smile, and I retreated quickly.

I sat down and looked at the other people waiting. Most of them had thick files of papers, nicely ordered records of their expenses. Unlike me, they all looked calm and collected, as though they would be perfectly able to explain their four-hundred-dollar deductions for office supplies without breaking down and confessing that it was actually a trip to Provincetown with a hunky construction worker they'd picked up outside their apartment building. I remembered my handful of receipts and wanted to die. I thought about running out or faking a cardiac event, but a voice interrupted my daydreams.

"Mr. Caffrey?"

I looked up. Standing in the hall was a man holding a file. He was looking around expectantly, like a lion searching for the one antelope in the herd with a gimp leg.

"Here," I said, feeling like I was once more in Mrs. McGuffey's second-grade class.

"Come with me, please," the man said. He held out his hand as I stood up. "I'm Mr. Mitchell. I'll be performing your audit today."

I tried to detect any trace of glee in his speech, but he gave no indications of his attitude toward my impending torture as he shook my hand. His grip was firm, and I hoped my palm wasn't too sweaty. As we walked down the hall to his office, I tried to get a sense of what Mitchell was like. He seemed to be in his late thirties. Several inches shorter than my six feet, he was built compactly. His face was handsome, kind of like the models you see in department-store circulars every year around Father's Day posing in knit polo shirts and khaki shorts. He was wearing suit pants, but the sleeves of his white shirt were rolled back, revealing forearms covered in thick dark hair. At least I'd have something good to look at while I died a slow, agonizing death.

When we reached his office, Mitchell ushered me in and closed the door behind him. The office was small and a little airless, but there was a window that let in some sun. Mitchell's large wooden desk was covered in papers and stacks of files in precipitous piles that seemed on the verge of collapsing. He gestured to a chair across from his paper-cluttered desk and I sat down, gripping my briefcase tightly. He settled into his chair and opened my file.

"Well then," he said, "I guess we should get started. The sooner we begin, the sooner you can get out of here. As the letter you received states, we have some questions about your 1991 return."

I tried to smile, managing what could only have looked like a death grimace. "Ask away."

Mitchell pulled something from my file and looked it over. "It says here that you're a writer."

"That's right," I said.

"What do you write?"

I hesitated. Lately I'd been making most of my money writing porn. I wasn't sure telling Mitchell that was going to help me out any. "I write a lot of different things," I said vaguely. "Books. Magazine pieces. Whatever comes along." I smiled reassuringly. "Church bulletins," I added impulsively.

He looked at me strangely and nodded. "Well, you know, the deductions professional writers can take can be kind of tricky. I'd like to go over some of your deductions and just make sure everything is okay. As long as you have receipts for everything, though, there shouldn't be a problem."

For the next hour and a half, Mitchell went over every deduction I'd claimed. One by one, he asked to see receipts for my taxi fares, business dinners, postage costs, and miscellaneous items. When he found out time and again that I didn't have any receipts, he just shook his head. By the time we'd reached my six-hundred-dollar deduction for computer equipment, I was about to cry.

Mitchell put down my file and looked at me. "Do you mean to tell me you don't have receipts for any of these things, Mr. Caffrey?"

"Well, you know, my apartment isn't very large," I started. "And there isn't much closet space."

Mitchell's face was blank. "All right," I said. "I give up. Why don't you just figure out how much I owe and we can call it a day."

"Well, there are a few other things I think we need to clear up, Mr. Caffrey. For instance, this $79.97 for magazine subscriptions in May. What exactly is that?"

I couldn't bring myself to tell Mitchell that those were for my subscriptions to *Advocate Men* and *Freshmen*. He already had me by the balls, and I didn't want to give him any ammunition. I briefly considered telling him they were for *Good Housekeeping* and *Field and Stream*, but I figured I was already in enough trouble.

"Those are research materials," I said weakly, hoping he'd buy my bluff and not ask any more questions.

"Research materials?" he said grimly. "What kind of research materials?"

"I write for those magazines," I said.

"Can you prove that?"

He had me up against a wall. Opening my briefcase, I pulled out a recent issue of a magazine with one of my stories in it. It had a big muscle stud on the cover along with a headline about outdoor sex. As I reluctantly handed it to Mitchell, I was thinking about the nasty letter I was going to write my editor as soon as I got home. He was going to owe me big for this.

Mitchell leaned back in his chair, opened the magazine, and began thumbing through the pages. Every so often he stopped and looked at something. I watched the expression on his face, waiting for him to toss the magazine at me and tell me to get out of his office.

After a few minutes, he looked up. "You're Tom Caffrey?"

"Um, yeah," I said, taken aback. "Doesn't it say that on my file?"

He shook his head. "I just didn't put the two together until I saw this. I love your stuff. Had more than a few good jerk-off sessions with it."

I couldn't believe what he'd just said. "Well, thanks. I'm glad you like it."

"Sure do," Mitchell said. "Helps me get to sleep on those restless nights. I always wondered if any of this stuff actually really happened to you."

I considered the position I was in. Mitchell was good looking. And I couldn't really get in any deeper. "You want to find out?" I asked, holding my breath while I waited for him to respond.

Mitchell looked at me. After a second, a smile broke out on his face. "Sure," he said.

He didn't seem to know what to do next, so I helped him out. Getting up, I checked the door to make sure it was locked. The pane was frosted glass, so there was no chance of anyone seeing in. If they did look, all they'd see is shadows and they'd probably think I had gone nuts and was trying to kill Mitchell.

Turning back to Mitchell, I walked over to where he sat in his chair. "Stand up," I said, adopting my butchest voice.

He stood up. I moved closer to him until my face was right in front of his. He was breathing heavily and was obviously nervous. I put my hand on his chest, and he flinched. I pushed him back until he was backed up against the desk, then began to unbutton his shirt. Swirls of dark hair appeared as more and more of his shirt opened beneath my fingers. While he wasn't overly muscular, he had the body of a man who managed to get to the gym a couple of nights a week.

When his shirt was fully undone, I pulled it off him and threw it on the floor. Sweat had formed on his face, and a bead of it was running down his neck toward the hollow of his throat. I ran my finger over his skin and stopped the drop just as it was about to roll over his collarbone. Mitchell watched intently as I brought my finger to my lips and licked his sweat off it. I stared deeply into his dark eyes as I moved my finger over my lips, wetting it. Then, never taking my eyes from his, I brought my hand to his nipple and squeezed. His eyes fluttered shut and he pushed against the desk.

I had started to get hard the minute I saw his beautiful hairy chest, and my cock was rapidly swelling against my jeans. Moving in toward him, I put my hands on the desk on either side of him and leaned in to kiss him, pressing my growing hard-on against his stomach. As I did, Mitchell put his hands on my chest, as though he were trying to push me away. I felt like the boss putting the moves on a pretty secretary in an old 1940s movie, and half expected Mitchell to slap me across the face and tell me he wasn't that kind of a girl.

Instead, his hands moved down my body and around to my back, pulling me tighter. His mouth opened, and his tongue entered me, warm and wet as it slipped past my lips. One of his hands went up my back to my neck as he kissed me deeply. I felt the whiskers on his cheeks scrape against my skin as he pulled away and moved his mouth to my neck, sucking forcefully. I was going to have one hell of a bruise there, but it felt great.

Soon his fingers were pulling at my T-shirt, urging it out of my jeans. I helped him out, fumbling at the buttons on my pants until they finally fell open and my shirt came free. Mitchell quickly pulled it over my head and dropped it to the floor. Without a word, his mouth dropped onto my nipple and began sucking, his tongue working in small circles around it. At the same time, his hands went right to my crotch, slipping into my jeans and grabbing my prick. His fingers slipped under my balls and held them tightly as he licked at the hair on my chest.

"I'm glad to see that it's just as big as you say in your stories," he said in my ear, running his hand the length of my shaft.

Now I was the one getting all worked up. Urging Mitchell up, I undid his belt and pushed his pants down. His prick was rock hard and stuck straight out from his body. It was topped by a thick head that rounded to a perfect point, just right for fucking. His balls, fat low hangers, dangled between his legs waiting to be sucked dry of their load. I ran my hand under his nutsac, feeling the thick hair that lined the path to his asshole and letting his balls rest in my hand as I rubbed them.

Once more I pushed Mitchell back onto the desk, this time until he was actually sitting on it, his ass resting on top of some files. His full sac hung down between his spread legs and slid over the edge of the desk. Sitting in his chair, I pulled it up until I was right between his legs. He leaned back, pushing his cock toward my face. Close up, his prick was quite a sight. Perfectly straight, it rose up in a neat line, one thick vein running up the side of it. The crown split neatly in half, as if a sharp knife had been plunged into the very heart of a soft, ripe peach.

The dark fur that covered Mitchell's chest exploded at his crotch in a dark cloud that surrounded his prick like fog around a tower before spreading out again over his thighs. Even his balls were hairy, covered in soft tendrils that stuck to his skin with his sweat. I put my hands on his legs, running them up his calves and onto his knees. Pushing them farther apart, I leaned forward and ran my tongue over the soft folds of his pouch. Carefully, I took one round nut between my lips, sucking on it softly. Mitchell's hand came down on my head and began to rub my hair as I did this, his long fingers kneading my skin.

"That feels so fucking good," he said.

Remembering that my financial future might depend on just how good Mitchell felt in the next half-hour or so, I went to work on his cock. Starting at the base, I ran my tongue lightly up the shaft until I reached the top. Pausing just long enough to make Mitchell uncomfortable with anticipation, I went down on him until I felt his bush beneath my lips. His prick slid into my throat smoothly and easily, and soon I was moving up and down his big tool, slurping at the sides and teasing him by running my tongue around the tip before deep-throating him again.

His prick tasted wonderful in my throat, and pretty soon I forgot that this was an IRS agent I was blowing. While I sucked his big dick, I played with my own cock, which by now was hard as a rock. The friction of my hand on my meat was too much. I stood up and put Mitchell's legs over my shoulders, pulling up on them so that he was forced to lie back on top of the papers that covered the top of his desk and knocking a few piles onto the floor. Spitting into my hand, I rubbed it into his ass crack, roughly fingering his tight hole.

Positioning the head of my dick against his pucker, I entered him slowly, letting him feel every thick inch of my piece as it slipped past his hairy lips. The sight of my cock disappearing between his cheeks almost made me shoot my load, especially when I saw his prick twitch against his belly and ooze a stream of pre-cum as I filled him up. When I was all the way in, I started to pump him, watching his face as I screwed his nice tight butt. Mitchell began to moan as I moved more quickly. He wrapped his hand around his cock and jerked it in long strokes. The harder I fucked him, the harder he beat his tool.

When he came, I felt his ass tighten around my prick. A stream of cum blew from his hole and streaked the hair on his forearms with thick pale lines. More of it streamed out and coated his chest. I pulled out and used some of Mitchell's still-warm juice to whack myself off. It didn't take long before I shot a volley that peppered him with a fresh round of stickiness that rained down from his neck to his balls, drenching him in my spunk. When I finished, I looked down at him sprawled across his desk, our combined loads making wet swirls in his hair.

I leaned down and rubbed my chest over Mitchell's sticky torso, feeling our cum slide over my skin like a warm mouth. Lying on top of him, I could feel that his cock was still hard between us. Kissing him on the lips, I whispered, "How was it?"

"It was great," he said, running his tongue over my ear. "Now I want to see if you can take as good as you give."

Now, I can't say getting fucked is my favorite thing. But if it got me out of paying some taxes, I was all for it. And besides, Mitchell looked so damn hot covered in cum, I would have done anything for him. Mitchell got up and I bent over his desk, giving him a nice view of my round ass and dangling balls. He came up behind me, and the next thing I knew, he was sliding his cock deep into my shitter.

My hands gripped the sides of the desk tightly as I took every inch of his thick poker without a sound, that fat round head of his plunging into me like a bullet. Once he was in, Mitchell wasted no time in pumping me hard. Fucking me so forcefully his stomach slapped against my ass, he rammed his fuck pole into me over and over until I thought my ass was on fire.

And he was getting more vocal. "Nice tight ass," he growled. "I'm going to shoot one hell of a load up this hot hole of yours."

I have to admit, he was one damn fine ass rider. After a minute, the feeling of his big head splitting my cherry wide open started to feel pretty good. My cock was slapping against the desk, and my nuts started getting all worked up as he banged me. I started to jerk my aching rod, and soon enough I was ready to spill a load. I reached the edge when I felt Mitchell start shooting deep in my hole. I could feel his warm spew filling me up as he came again and again, continuing to pump me the whole time.

"Oh, Christ Jesus," he moaned behind me, his hands gripping my shoulders as he fired away. "My balls are going to explode."

Mitchell pumped one more shot into my overloaded ass and I came. Four blasts of jism ripped from my pipe and slathered the papers on his desk in thick cream. The biggest rocket splattered all over my file, staining the brown folder with a spiderweb of white. I collapsed on top of the desk, my body still reverberating from the force of Mitchell's fucking, as his cock slipped from my asshole and he fell back into his chair, exhausted. His body was soaked with sweat and covered in drying cum, and his skin was flushed.

After I caught my breath, I picked up my spunk-spattered file and waved it at Mitchell. "Shall we go over the rest of my deductions?"

"Don't worry about this," he said, taking it out of my hand and ripping it in half. "I'll just put it in the computer that everything checked out."

I picked my pants off the floor and started to pull them on. "Thanks. Now, can you do anything about my overdue library books?"

Mitchell looked at me seriously. "Don't push it," he said, grinning. "I'm still suspicious about that seven-hundred-dollar claim for postage."

He leaned down and picked something up off the floor by his feet. "By the way," he said, waving the magazine with my story in it, "do you mind if I keep this?"

I laughed. "Be my guest. Who knows, someday you might just even see yourself in there."

Hitting Home

The title story from my first collection. Of course, the baseball theme is self-explanatory. But really this story is about what can happen when you run into someone you've fantasized about for a long time. If you're lucky.

T he old wooden bleachers had been replaced by concrete-and-steel ones and there was a new electronic scoreboard, but otherwise the field looked just like it did when I played second base. White chalk lines stretched out across the green, bases crowning the corners where the lines intersected. In the center of the diamond, the pitcher's mound rose as if some giant were pushing a hand up through the earth.

It had been ten years since I had played ball with the Booneville Central Wildcats. I could hardly believe it when I opened my mail and saw the invitation to the reunion. Ten years, a whole decade. It seemed like only a few months since we had thrown our hats into the air at graduation.

I wasn't really looking forward to going back to my old high school. I've always thought reunions were kind of silly—a bunch of men who should know better trying to impress each other with their pretty wives and BMWs and aging prom queens bragging about their kids and their Amway commissions. Besides, I didn't really feel like fielding questions about my social life, which had been about as exciting as a scoreless inning lately anyway.

That night while I was getting ready for bed, I looked at myself in the mirror. There was a little bit of gray in my black hair, but my eyes were as blue as ever. I ran my hands over the smooth muscles of my chest. Not too bad after ten years. I might not be able to fit into my old uniform, but regular workouts kept my body in shape.

What the hell, I thought, I might as well show everyone that I still have it. I also have to admit that I wanted to show off a little. Ten years ago, I was barely passing my English classes. Now I was writing for a major sports magazine. It would be great to show up everyone who thought I was just a dumb jock.

Now here I was, back at the old ball field. The reunion wasn't scheduled to start for another couple hours, but I wanted a chance to look around by myself before facing my old schoolmates.

No one was around, so I indulged myself and relived a few of the old glory days. Standing at home plate, I looked out over the field and thought back to the warm spring days spent out there with the Wildcats. I was never the best ballplayer, but I had a few proud moments, even hit a homer or two. Even ten years later I could still remember the tight feeling I got in my stomach every time I faced the pitcher, the mixture of excitement and fear knowing that whatever happened in the next few seconds would determine whether I was running the bases or walking back to the bench in disgrace.

Just for fun, I ran the bases, jogging slowly around the diamond. As I crossed home plate I raised my hands in victory. I imagined the crowd cheering for me and tipped my baseball cap in appreciation.

I heard clapping coming from behind me, and a voice said, "Not bad for an old man."

I spun around, embarrassed that someone had caught me in the middle of my little fantasy. Sitting in the front row of the bleachers was Jack Carpenter, the pitcher from my old baseball team. He had a big grin on his face.

"Looks like we both had the same idea," I said, hoping my face wasn't as red as it felt.

Jack stood up and came over to where I was standing. As he walked toward me, I felt like I was seventeen again. In high school I had been in awe of Jack, and now I remembered why. He was a huge man, well over six feet tall with a well-developed body made hard by the work he did on his family's dairy farm. Many nights after games I had lain in bed, stroking my cock and thinking about watching him in the showers after a game.

Jack's hand on my shoulder brought me out of my daydream.

"It's good to see you again, Tom," he said.

I managed to mutter something in return. Jack didn't seem to notice that he had turned me into a stuttering idiot. He stood and looked out over the field, his hands in the pockets of his faded jeans. He was wearing the same old letterman jacket he had in high school.

"Jeez, it looks just like it did when we were kids." He laughed. "Remember all those times Coach Roberts made us run laps around the outfield? What a bastard he was. And that stupid motto he had. 'Don't think. It hurts the team.'"

"If I remember," I said, "he was usually yelling that at you about five times a game."

Jack laughed again. "Yeah, I never was the by-the-book type. But as long as we won, he couldn't really do anything about it. He just used to storm around the locker room afterward, trying not to let on that he was pissed at me."

Jack stepped up to home plate. He easily slipped into the old stance he had when he was batting, knees bent and head up. He swung at an imaginary ball and watched it sail up over the scoreboard. "It's outta here," he said proudly. Then he turned and looked at me. "Let's go check out the old locker room. See if it all looks the same."

We walked up the small hill behind the field and over to the gym. As we walked Jack talked about our high-school days. We had never talked much in high school, and I guessed we didn't have much in common now either, so I just listened to him talk, nodding every now and again so he'd think I was paying attention.

The door to the locker room was open, and we just went right in. There was some new equipment, but it all looked pretty much as it had ten years ago. Rows of gray lockers and wooden benches filled most of the room. On the bulletin board there were notices about soccer and wrestling tryouts and schedules for upcoming games. There must have been a game earlier in the day. Puddles of water spotted the floor, and there was the smell of sweat in the air. Someone had thrown one of the familiar white towels on a bench.

Just the thought of a locker room filled with men sweaty from playing ball is enough to make me hard, and I felt my prick start to swell against my jeans. I hoped Jack wouldn't notice. I'd spent enough time in high school trying to hide the hard-ons that always seemed to come at the wrong time, like while watching Jack strip after a game.

While I was trying to get my uncooperative prick to cool down,

Jack came up behind me. He put one of his hands on my crotch and massaged my cock through my jeans. "Looks like we're both having the same idea again," he said and pressed himself against my ass so I could feel his bulge. "Ten years is a long time to wait to see that cock of yours hard. Why not take it out."

I turned around and faced Jack. His dark eyes locked onto mine, and I waited for him to tell me he was just fooling around, that this was all a big joke. Instead, he leaned forward and kissed me, his tongue entering my mouth slowly and deliberately, his hand on my neck pulling me into him. I put my arms around him, feeling the soft wool of his jacket under my hands.

Jack was still rubbing my prick, his fingers wrapped around the shaft through my jeans. I was still too surprised to say anything and could only watch as he unbuttoned my pants and let them fall to the floor. He continued to stroke me, the heat from his hand burning through my underwear as he worked my cock. His other hand ran over my stomach and up my shirt. Gently, he pinched my nipple, and I moaned. Then his tongue was back in my mouth, probing and hot.

Jack's kiss brought me out of my trance, and I ran my hands through his short dark hair, pulling him away from me. "How about getting out of those clothes?" I said. As I removed my shirt and shoes and stepped out of my jeans, he took off his jacket and dropped it to the floor. I unbuttoned his shirt, exposing a chest covered with thick dark hair. Ten years later, his body was, if anything, more beautiful than I had remembered. I ran my hands over his wide shoulders, feeling the muscles tense beneath my hands.

Kneeling in front of Jack, I ran my tongue over the bulge in his jeans. I could feel his cock under my tongue straining to get out and began to work at the buttons on his fly. Soon his pants were off, and he stood in front of me wearing nothing but white boxer shorts. The pale cotton stood out against his tanned skin, and his prick stretched lazily down the side of his leg.

Jack sat on a bench and leaned back against the lockers, spreading his legs invitingly. Hungrily, I knelt between his thighs. My mouth went to work on his tight stomach, my tongue tracing the hard ripples of his abdomen, my hands running up and down his muscular legs.

Jack put his hands behind his head, watching as I licked the hair on his thighs and stomach. When I sucked his nipple, he let out a low growl like that of a big animal and the muscles of his chest tensed. Burying my face in his crotch, I could feel his balls and sensed his cock pulsing against my neck. I ran my mouth over it through his shorts, letting my tongue slide over the cockhead that peeked out through the edge of his shorts. Jack moaned softly above me and shifted his hips, pushing himself against my face.

Reaching into his boxers, I pulled his cock out through the fly. I had never seen Jack hard before. I had always been quick to get out of the shower when he came in, afraid my own raging hard-on would give me away. Now I was holding his hard tool in my hand. I ran my tongue slowly over the head, sucking gently and enjoying the feel of his hot skin in my mouth.

Jack reached down and put a hand on my head, pushing me down on his prick. His cock slid easily into my mouth, my tongue caressing its smoothness and licking up the sweet precum that dripped from his hole. Jack moved his weight forward, and several inches of hot manhood slipped into my throat. His balls were still covered by the shorts, so I rubbed them from the outside, feeling their heaviness roll around in my fingers.

Jack groaned. "That's right, baby," he whispered softly. "Suck me off." His hand pressed against the back of my neck, and I felt the hair of his legs against my face as the entire length of his dick went in and out of my mouth. Still massaging his balls, I let my tongue travel the length of his cock, tasting the salt of his skin, feeling his thick pubic hair against my face when I sank all of him into my throat. I couldn't wait for him to shoot his load so I could taste the hot cum I knew was boiling in his balls.

Just as I thought he was about to come, Jack pulled out of my mouth. I looked up, wondering what was wrong. Jack just smiled. "Come on," he said. "Time to hit the showers."

We both stood up, and Jack slipped his boxers off. Seeing him completely naked, I almost came on the spot. His cock stood straight out from his body, his juicy balls hanging heavily below it. I followed him into the shower room, my eyes fixed on his beautiful round ass as he walked in front of me.

In the showers, Jack turned on one of the showerheads, adjusting the water until it was warm enough.

"Here," he said. "Stand under this."

The water hit my back, rhythmically massaging my muscles and wetting my hair. Jack was on his knees in front of me, the water from my body splashing over him. Taking my cock in his hand, he rubbed his cheek over it, the stubble of his beard sending bursts of pleasure up my groin. He slipped my wet prick into his mouth, taking it all in until his nose was pushed up against me, his tongue moving crazily all over my dick. He started to move his head back and forth slowly and deliberately, my cock sliding in and out of his mouth, his lips sucking eagerly at the tip each time I entered him.

As I fucked Jack's mouth, the water streamed over us, dripping off his face and running over my cock whenever it left his mouth. As he sucked me, Jack was slowly stroking his own cock, and I could see the water dripping from his balls as his fingers worked them. The sight of this big stud blowing me got me really hot, and I wrapped my fingers in his wet hair, pushing myself as far into him as I could.

After sucking my cock for what seemed like forever, and bringing me to the edge several times, Jack stood up. Standing in front of me, he put our cocks together and began stroking them both with one hand, his long fingers easily encircling our pricks. Our balls slapped together as he beat faster and faster. With his other hand, he caressed my ass, working my cheeks steadily to the rhythm as he brought us closer and closer to coming.

"You know what I'd like now," Jack said, just as I thought for sure I couldn't take any more of his hand job. "I'd like to taste that beautiful ass of yours."

He turned me around so that I was facing the wall of the shower, the water running down my back and over my ass. He knelt behind me and, his strong hands pulling my cheeks apart, began tonguing my tight hole. He pushed his face against my ass, his probing tongue working its way slowly into me. Every so often he would pull my balls back and suck on one or both of them, letting them slip in and out of his mouth with the water.

Once he had loosened me up with his tongue, I felt him enter me with one finger. *Christ*, I thought, *his finger is bigger than most guys' cocks*. What the hell was his dick going to feel like? Jack was back on his feet, leaning against me so I could feel his chest hair against my back and his huge dick against my ass. "My God," I said. "I haven't felt anything that big since batting practice."

Jack laughed. "That's right. And I'm about to make a home run." He reached over to the soap dispenser mounted on the wall and pumped out a handful, rubbing it into my asshole. Then he slipped the tip of his dick into me and pushed gently. I groaned and pressed against him, feeling the rest of his cock slide up my ass with one smooth motion. He didn't stop until his groin was pressed against me, all of him buried deep inside me.

Luckily, the water and the soap made Jack's dick slippery. His wet prick slid in and out easily. Jack thrust, moaning softly in my ear and tonguing my neck as he worked his throbbing piece in and out of my hungry ass, pulling almost all the way out and then ramming back in as far as he could go.

Now his hips were pounding against me, his dick pushing at my hole, his balls slapping at my legs. With a final moan, he put his hands around my waist and thrust his cock straight up my waiting ass, pulling me back onto his prick. I felt his dick swell and his load shoot into me. His cock throbbed several times, each time sending another wave of thick cream into my ass.

Jack lay heavily against me, his face on my shoulder. His cock was still hard inside me, and I could feel his heart beating wildly against my skin. Finally, he slipped out of me and turned me around to face him.

Kneeling in front of me again, his mouth went to work on my balls, sucking and licking them. His big tongue ran the length of my meat, and I was inside his mouth once more. I was so worked up from the fucking he gave me that it took only a minute of sucking before I was ready to come. Jack let my dick fall from his mouth and finished me off with a few strokes of his hand. I came with a cry, my load covering Jack's neck and chest with rope after rope of cum. When I was done, he licked the last drops of cum off the end of my cock and stood up. "Christ," he said, looking at his chest. "If you had handled balls like that back in high school, you might have had a better batting average."

We washed off under the shower, just like we used to do after a game. Only this time, I let Jack know just how hot I thought he was. Then we went and joined the rest of our classmates, knowing that at the end of the night we'd have another chance to practice our ball playing.